KING OF THE RED ▮▮▮▮
The *Spider* heard the ▮▮▮▮ ▮▮ ▮▮▮
councils of the Underworld. A keen-witted, ambitious
criminal leader named El Gaucho—backed by a powerful army of brutal killers—was pillaging the West.
Looting, ravaging, slaughtering wantonly, the master-
mind of crime was ruthlessly following a plan which
would make him King of America! Richard Wentworth—the debonair aristocrat who is in truth the
deadly *Spider*, protector of the oppressed—knew that
he must strike quickly, or die! For Wentworth, ever
running a double risk, forced now to sacrifice a brave,
dear friend to ghastly torture, faced a grim, new danger
in the bounty-hunters who wanted to collect El Gaucho's reward—its own weight of the purest gold for
The *Spider's* head!

GREEN GLOBES OF DEATH
Richard Wentworth attended that gala masquerade ball
in his own secret identity—as The *Spider*, nemesis of
the Underworld, the lone-wolf anti-crime crusader who
battles always in the cross-fire between Law and law-
less. For grim necessity summoned The *Spider* to his
duty this night. His shrewdest, most valiant foeman—
the Fly—had risen from the dead to reorganize his ruthless slaughter syndicate. Armed with a deadly green
vapor, the Fly's hired butchers were spreading ruin,
dishonor and wanton death. And The *Spider*, lone-
handed, his darling Nita working tirelessly for the
enemy, must battle both the murdering hordes and the
girl he loves!

Also available from Carroll & Graf:

THE **MASTER OF MEN!** ™ #7
SPIDER

Grant Stockbridge

Carroll & Graf Publishers, Inc.
New York

First Carroll & Graf edition 1993

Carroll & Graf Publishers, Inc.
260 Fifth Avenue
New York, NY 10001

ISBN: 0-7867-0039-4

Manufactured in the United States of America

This volume is dedicated to
the first issue of
THE SPIDER Magazine,
dated October 1933,
and its novel,
THE SPIDER STRIKES!

King of the Red Killers

Looting, maiming, slaughtering, El Gaucho launched his colossal plot to unite the Underworld—to make himself King of America! No torture was too cruel for him to employ; no deed too bloody; no life too precious, except his own. Richard Wentworth—the SPIDER, who exacts justice when the Law fails—realized he alone could save America from wanton butchery, in spite of the grim reward posted for his head—its own weight of the purest gold!

CHAPTER ONE

The *Spider's* Warning

The elevator operator's cap was dragged down over his right eyebrow. He leaned against the gate with a cigarette dangling from his lips. "Listen, babe," he said flatly, "you ain't goin' up to de boss wit' no phony stories about de *Spider* comin' here. De boss . . ."

The man's voice choked off as the girl's hand flew from her waist and presented the point of a slim, long knife to his belly.

"Up, fool," she ordered softly.

The cigarette dropped from the man's lips. He went backwards into the elevator before the pressure of the knife and the door slammed shut. When it had began its upward moan, the shadows moved in the stairway just to the right of the shaft. From the blackness a man stepped forward on alert, silent feet. His shoulders were twisted as if by the painful giant hands of disease so that he walked hunched far forward. A black, slouch hat was on his head and he wore a long black cape that accentuated, rather than masked, his affliction.

Standing before the elevator door, the man stopped. Light slanting under the wide brim of his hat showed a mouth that was a straight, lipless line.

"So," he chuckled softly, "he thinks the presence of the *Spider* a phony story?"

The mouth twisted into a slow, tight smile that was strangely sinister. No one seeing this man could have mistaken his identity. And if that one had guilt upon his conscience—the blood of a fellow being, the rifling of a poor man's till—he would have fled in screaming terror. For the *Spider* was known throughout the length and breadth of the land as the avenger of the innocent, a lone wolf of justice who struck down the guilty without mercy!

The hunchback turned toward the stairway and once more it was as if the shadows moved. There was no sound as he swiftly mounted the steps. That was well for the *Spider*. If the criminals gathered here tonight to plot robbery and murder believed him present, they would hunt him down ruthlessly with machine guns. And the Underworlds of the universe would shriek for joy at his death!

But the *Spider's* progress was noiseless, unfaltering, though the smile faded from his lips. A week ago, he had dared to hope that organized crime was smashed! Now there was bitterness in the gray-blue eyes beneath the hat brim. He had been prosecuting a vigorous war against minor Underworld leaders and killers and they had been fleeing from him with a shrill terror, like frightened rats. No new evil genius had arisen to lead them. Yes, he and Nita van Sloan, the one woman who held his trust and his love, had dared to hope that at last they might claim the happiness they had battled to afford to others. And then this. . . .

In the West, a man calling himself El Gaucho—a queer, mocking name since it meant merely one of the wild-riding cowboys of the South American *pampas*—this butcher of humans had pillaged three towns within three days; the small army of desperados he had gathered about him had swept clean the banks and richer stores, burning homes, and killing wantonly.

In the first raid on Morgantown, Arizona, five men and three women had been shot down on the streets, mercilessly, without other reason than that they had seen the masked faces of the raiders. In Hawleyville, twelve had crumpled before the ruthless guns of the bandits. And in Carson . . . The *Spider* felt a cold rage grow within him at the memory of those pitiful reports of last night . . . a machine gun had sprayed a school yard full of playing children. Twenty-one dead there besides five adults slain in the streets, and the wounded. . . .

It was such insensate criminals as this one who called himself El Gaucho that the *Spider* had vowed to track down and kill. It mattered not that the man had gathered all the renegades from both sides of the Mexican border and schooled them in his murderous assaults. Even though they rallied about him two hundred strong, the *Spider* would break through to exact the vengeance which the law, somehow, so often failed to get. He had been prepared to fly westward to join battle when he heard a news whisper that struck terror to his heart. Not personal terror. Fear was a thing that the *Spider* did not know for himself. But terror for the new millions that were threatened.

He had heard that the Underworld, demoralized by the *Spider's* coldly efficient warfare, was uniting to invite El Gaucho eastward to command them! A united Underworld, working voluntarily under a leader who slaughtered like a Turk! No wonder the *Spider* had come here tonight! Here it was that the intimidated leaders of the city's robbers, killers, blackmailers and thieves would assemble under the powerful domination of Oscar Piltsdown, whom the liquor racket had known of old. Or so at least the *Spider's* information hinted. It had been confirmed now by the arrival of the girl to warn Piltsdown. He knew her, too, as it was the business of the *Spider* to know all the Underworld of importance. She was Yvonne Musette, Piltsdown's latest love.

The *Spider* was climbing toward the third floor now, hearing the dim murmur of voices from above. Ah, then Yvonne had not yet given the alarm! He had made haste to reach the upper levels before she cried that the

Spider was on his way. He must prevent their sending an envoy to El Gaucho. That was the oddest part about the entire menacing business.

A young man named Tom Barker had come to New York with tales of having seen El Gaucho loot a town, with the boast that he could reach the man again at any time he wished. Police had been seeking Barker to find if he told the truth and the *Spider* had sought him, too. Tonight he had learned that the Underworld had found Barker first. He had come into the power of Oscar Piltsdown, one of the few remaining leaders of the Underworld whom the *Spider* had been unable to locate. Unable, that is, until tonight, when he had trailed one of Piltsdown's men to this building which, by daylight, was the gymnasium of an athletic club.

And now Piltsdown's current sweetheart, Yvonne Musette, had rushed here to give warning of information obtained, God alone knew where, that the *Spider* was on his way to call on Piltsdown. The *Spider* frowned as he circled the elevator shaft and slipped on toward the third floor. He heard voices there. . . .

How had Yvonne learned the *Spider's* plans? No one but Nita had known his secret and death itself could not have wrested it from her. Still, Yvonne had learned, and the men said to be gathered here with Piltsdown to invite El Gaucho east through the agency of Tom Barker would be warned of the *Spider's* impending visit. . . .

Once more the grim, hard smile crossed the *Spider's* lips. Well, even that warning should not save them. He was determined that El Gaucho should not come eastward with an already united Underworld to welcome him. There would be no limit to the man's power, no end to his atrocities if once such an alliance were formed.

Peering from the darkness of the stairway into the hallway of the third floor, the *Spider* shut speculation from his mind. He could see the girl beside the elevator door, see the elevator operator arguing vehemently with three men who lounged against the wide door opposite.

They were careless seeming, those three, but when they moved, their hands were quick and flexible. Their eyes held a flat, cold gleam. Killers all! If they should see the *Spider*!

"Cheez," the elevator man was saying, "I'm telling you I couldn't keep her down. She pulls a shive on me and says she'll gut me if I even open my trap. She did. And damn it to hell, *she meant it!"*

In the darkness, the *Spider* smiled faintly. He thought it very likely Yvonne Musette had meant precisely that. In the Montmartre, whence she came, the *Apache* girls had been known to kill on even less provocation. And there was a certain cold poise about Yvonne. . . .

The girl's small red mouth smiled prettily. "Of cours'," she agreed, a faint accent clipping her words. "You are one ignoran' peeg. *Attendez, foux!* Listen, fools. I tell you thees *Spider* is already 'ere. Eeef you do not let me see Oscaire, there will be 'ell to pay!"

The men stirred uneasily, looking at one another. The girl stood straight and still, graceful as a cat with her long, taut body firm beneath the close embrace of her russet-brown dress. The silk caught shimmering highlights from the dim bulb that illuminated the hall. Her face beneath the cloche that pressed down her dark curls was still gently smiling.

One of the men shifted his feet uncertainly. "Listen, Yvonne," he muttered. "The *Spider* couldn't possibly know about this."

Yvonne shrugged her right shoulder, pursing her red lips. The *Spider* glanced quickly over the hall and saw that there were only the four men and the girl. Should he allow the girl to get through with her warning, or should he stop her here? If she gave the message, they would be watchful—might even search for him. But also, they would become apprehensive, so that his warning to forget El Gaucho, when he gave it, would carry more force. Furthermore, it was unlikely he could

conquer all of them without an alarm being given . . .
Even as he made up his mind, Yvonne acted. She
turned as if to enter the waiting elevator, then she
darted between the men. Before they could intervene,
she had rapped on the door.

The *Spider* heard her cry: "Oscaire! Oscaire! The
Spider comes. . . ."

Then the door slammed shut.

The *Spider* sprang into instantaneous action. These
four men in the hall must be eliminated now, while
they were disconcerted by Yvonne's break—while they
stared at each other and tried to decide what to do was
the best time to strike. As the *Spider* bolted from the
darkness of the stairways, his right hand flashed out
and his stiffened fingers jabbed at the elevator operator's throat, struck nerve centers which rendered him
instantly unconscious.

There was no pause in the *Spider's* swift movement.
His guns flew to his hands and the two forty-five caliber
automatics which he carried in clip holsters beneath his
arms struck simultaneously, butt-first, against the napes
of two of the guards. Thus far, there had been no sound
save the thud of his blows—and the falling operator
had not yet reached the floor!

The third guard whirled, with his hand clawing for
his gun. Once more the *Spider's* automatic slashed out,
caught the temple. The man collapsed to the floor with
a choked cry rising in his throat.

The *Spider* stood rock-still, guns in hand, before
the door through which Yvonne had vanished.
Within, he heard the excited gabble of voices and he
nodded to himself, smiling thinly. Their own shouting would have drowned the sounds of the swift battle
in the hall.

The *Spider* moved rapidly then, loading the four unconscious men into the elevator cage. He hooked the
operator's belt over the handle of the control so that
his unconscious weight would start the cage downward
as soon as the closing of the door released the safety
stop, then slid the gate shut. He turned again toward

14

the door of the room where Piltsdown and Yvonne, and the others who would join with him in the invitation to El Gaucho, were in conference. His lips drew back thinly from his teeth. But the expression was not a smile. . . .

CHAPTER TWO

Disaster Threatens

As Yvonne Musette dashed into the room where Piltsdown held conference with twelve other criminals, the men whirled to face her. The room was the main gymnasium of the athletic club and the men had taken careful pains that light should not escape to the street. A long table had been set in the middle of the vast room and the only light came from seven candles in a single, many-branched stick. The shadows in the corners seemed enormous.

"Oscaire! Oscaire!" the girl cried again. "The *Spider* comes!"

There were thirteen men about the table. They leaped to their feet as one person, and the massive, square-built man who had stood at its head came forward on quick, solid feet to meet the girl. Yvonne seized his arms, pressed close against him.

"For the sake of *le bon Dieu*," she cried, urgently. "You must leave here at once."

The man patted her shoulder with a thick, short-fingered hand. "Come, come, Yvonne," he rumbled, "the *Spider* cannot hurt us now."

He turned back toward the head of the table, leading the girl. The other twelve men watched them come, cast apprehensive glances into the dark, looming shadows. The candlelight reached only feebly into the gloom. It gleamed on dangling acrobatic apparatus, on the stanchions of the running track that circled the hall like a balcony, but did not disperse the darkness.

"Listen, Piltsdown," one of the men broke out nervously. "What's this about the *Spider*? How do you know he can't hurt us? God! He's killed twenty men in the last month!"

Oscar Piltsdown said nothing until he had regained his seat at the head of the table and pulled the girl down on the arm of his chair. "Pah! It is nothing," he scoffed amiably, blinking mildly at his confrères from behind horn-rimmed spectacles. "Have we not joost plan' how to rid ourselves of this fool insect, the *Spider*? Barker is already started for Newark. Soon he will be flying to see El Gaucho . . . *Nein*, he cannot harm us. Yvonne joost want to be with her Oscar!"

Yvonne's hands clutched at Piltsdown's shoulder. "No, no!" she said, quickly. "It is true, what I say. I was comin' here to see you, yes. But from my taxi I see a man in a black cape sneak into the alley behin' here. He has the hunch-back an' . . . an' jus' lookin' at heem make me so frighten'!"

Oscar Piltsdown looked up at the girl's dark, comely face with shrewd, blue eyes. The men about the table stirred restively.

"Listen, Piltsdown." It was the same man who had spoken before, a slenderly built, smooth-haired Latin. "If Yvonne saw the *Spider* . . ."

"I did not have a gun," the girl mourned.

". . . If Yvonne saw the *Spider*, we'd better turn on the lights and get the other men. . . ."

Piltsdown grunted. "Pah! We turn on the lights and the police come to see why we are all lighted up at night. They know nothing is supposed to be here. Also we make the *Spider's* work easier for him. We give him targets . . . *Pah!* Yvonne is mistake'. And if she is not, then . . . we *kill* the *Spider*!"

"Don't be a fool, Piltsdown!"

"I am no fool, *nein*," Piltsdown shook his heavy head. "This *Spider* is a man like other men. He can be killed. Meantime, we go on with our plans. Come, my friends, if you work with me, we shall own the city. Yes. Joost that!" He put both his big hands on the table, leaned forward confidentially. His voice lowered: "This Gaucho robs whole cities and nobody can stop him. If someone gets in his way . . . Poof! He is dead. If Gaucho wish, this *Spider* is dead, too. Look what Gaucho did tonight."

Piltsdown shook a newspaper at the others about the table. Heavy black headlines across the front pages were smeary with ink.

"Two million dollars!" Piltsdown shouted. "Two million dollars he took tonight. Two policemen get in his way. He runs over them! Think. Think what it mean to have this man on our side, leading us, killing our enemies. The *Spider*!" Piltsdown tilted back his head and bellowed out guttural laughter. "The *Spider*, why Gaucho joost step on him!"

Piltsdown's voice choked off in his throat. Every man there was suddenly a frozen statue of fear.

But Yvonne got softly to her feet and lifted her pert dark face toward the black shadows above. Then they heard the laughter, mocking, hard laughter that bit into their ears like the tocsin of death. When the laughter was finished, words came and the words held the same menace:

"Fools!" it said softly, "do you think to escape the *Spider*?"

Yvonne's eyes quested back and forth along the running-track balcony, but the voice seemed to come from everywhere. It was not loud, yet it carried to the trembling men below. Piltsdown was the first to recover from the paralysis of fear that seized them. He heaved to his feet, deliberately plucked an automatic from his coat pocket. It seemed tiny in the largeness of his hand.

"Pah!" he exploded. "Show yourself, *Spider,* if you are not afraid!"

"Certainly," came the *Spider's* voice. "Where would you like me to show myself?"

He was as courteous as in a drawing room, solicitude in his every word, but still behind it was that mocking hardness.

"Here," said Yvonne clearly. "Here!" She pointed toward the running-track directly opposite the table, not more than thirty feet from where the twelve men were bunched.

"Just a moment," the *Spider* agreed.

Complete silence fell upon the great hall. Yvonne held her knife in her hand now and Piltsdown's automatic was ready at his hip. Other men's hands were stealing toward their weapons now.

"Before I show myself," called the *Spider,* "I have a warning to give you. To any man who allies himself with El Gaucho, I bring certain death! I will not speak again except with bullets. Take heed!"

With his final word, a tiny spot of light from an electric torch glowed into being from the rail of the balcony. It illuminated a man's face beneath the brim of a black hat, a face with a strong, hawk's nose and grim, straight lips; eyes that were black pits. . . .

That spot of light signaled a broadside of gun-fire. Thirteen automatics and revolvers blazed lead at that face so deliberately exposed. Their weapons seemed to be hysterical, blasting, hiccoughing leaden death in a frenzy of haste. But Yvonne did not hurl her knife. She held it at her side in a white, clenched fist and her teeth gleamed between drawn-back lips. She did not look long at that illuminated face which a half-hundred leaden slugs were battering. As the guns went empty, she suddenly screamed a warning and jumped toward Piltsdown, striking him violently on the shoulder with both hands to hurl him aside.

Even as she screamed, the laughter of the *Spider* rang through the hall. The illuminated face on the balcony swayed and spun from side to side as if the *Spider* had

19

hanged himself there for the bullets of the criminals to strike. Men turned to flee from this hall where a man targeted by scores of bullets still laughed at them tauntingly. Then a shadow swept out of the darkness. A caped figure, with a gun in its right hand, leaped downward in an arc from the edge of the balcony and flung itself directly toward the spot where Oscar Piltsdown tottered on his feet, his massive inertia fighting against the thrust of Yvonne's frantic hands. While the two still struggled there, the *Spider* swept past them, cape snapping behind him with the wind of his passage. His gun reached out.

There was a crunching thud as his gun-butt slapped against the back of Piltsdown's skull. The blow accomplished what all Yvonne's pushing had failed to do. It toppled the man off his feet, spilled him headlong across the long table from which all the others had fled. Yvonne was whirled off balance and spun half across the room. She fell to her hands and knees and crouched there like some wild animal, poised to spring.

The *Spider* sailed on, the whole length of the table, clasping a length of fine, silken line by which he had swung down from the balcony. At the extreme end of his pendulum swing, he released the line, landed lightly on his feet against the wall. He was firing deliberately into the fleeing press at the door and a reloaded weapon was beginning to answer from the fleeing criminals. The darkness which had shielded the *Spider* before now protected his enemies and Yvonne, recovering herself, lunged toward the table and sent the candles crashing to the floor.

With the darkness, courage seemed to return to the criminals. Their limping fire redoubled and the *Spider's* gun ceased to answer them. Yvonne's voice rose shrilly.

"He has killed my Oscaire!" she cried. "Kill the *Spider*! Kill him!"

Her voice broke into a moan, then became sharp again, more determined.

"He must die. The *Spider* must die," she shrieked. "You let one man rob you of riches! Kill! Kill!"

Lights blazed suddenly as one of the men found the switch. For an instant, guns ceased and there was utter silence, utter blankness in the gymnasium. *The Spider had disappeared!*

CHAPTER THREE

Death at the Wheel

The *Spider* heard the thwarted shout that went up from the gymnasium when the men discovered that he had escaped them during the period of darkness. It had been very simple. He had merely climbed back up the silken line by which he had swept down from the balcony to attack and kill Piltsdown. He was stooping to pick up the steel mask which he sometimes wore to conceal his own features in assuming the identity of the *Spider,* and which he had offered to the men below as a target to draw their bullets.

He heard Yvonne's shriek, "The balcony! You fools, the balcony! He climbed up a rope. . . ."

The *Spider's* eyes were narrowed as he fled from the balcony. The woman was a shrewd opponent. The fear of the *Spider* did not affect her, perhaps because she thought her sex exempted her from his vengeance. At any rate, her mind worked clearly in an emergency. He paused a moment in the doorway of the balcony, gun in his hand. The *Spider* had never slain a woman, but he would not hesitate if his duty demanded that he should—if he deemed it necessary for his defense of humanity. Yvonne drew herself erect above the body of her slain lover, her swelling breasts turned toward the *Spider's* gun. It was almost as if she saw him there, knew that he stood with weapon tentatively raised.

22

"Send men to the airport," she cried. "He'll be after Barker now. Hurry, fools!"

The *Spider* leveled his automatic, then cursed raggedly, whirled and raced down the hall. He would probably curse himself many times for not killing the woman, but he could not believe that she would be a serious menace. Men would not listen to her, however shrewd she might be. She was only the sweetheart of a dead criminal. . . . But she was right about one thing. He was after this young fool, Barker, who was about to fly westward with the word that would plunge New York into a maelstrom of murder and crime. And he must be fast. Already, he had delayed too long in punishing these minor pawns in the battle. It was some satisfaction to have killed Piltsdown, but first of all now, he must prevent Barker from flying to summon El Gaucho.

The *Spider* ran silently, on sure feet, an automatic in his right hand, his cape drawn in about him with his left, to prevent it from flapping out a warning of his passage. The *Spider* had not entered the building without a sure knowledge of its layout and he raced now toward the fire-escape which zigzagged across the back of the building, down into a black, unlighted alleyway. Already he could hear the beat of men's feet behind him, racing up to the balcony, scudding up the stairway about the shaft. His pace quickened.

The hallway along which he hastened was straight, lighted by a single red globe at its far end which marked the exit to the fire-escape. To his right, three doors at widely spaced intervals gave on the balcony. To his left, there was a series of small dressing rooms lined with lockers. A frown grew on the *Spider's* forehead as he ran. It became increasingly evident that he would not be able to reach that fire-escape exit before one of his pursuers got sight of him. Damn that girl. If it had not been for her shout. . . .

But there was no time for speculation. He must act— and quickly. Should he risk their seeing him, and defy the accuracy of hostile guns? Or should he duck from sight and attempt an escape later? So far he had not been sighted. There was only the girl's warning cry to set men on his trail. . . . But, damn it, there was no time to wait. He must escape this building at once and stop Barker, who was already on his way to the airport.

With a grim setting of his lips, Wentworth spun, began to run backward, traveling almost as swiftly as he had with his quiet lope—a heavyweight champion of the prize ring had taught him that trick—and now his gun was ready for the first of his pursuers to show himself. His stratagem was performed just in time. Even as he whirled, two men sprang from a balcony door within twenty feet of him.

The double roar of the *Spider's* shots sounded almost as a single blast, but the leading man stared at him with a shocked pain in his face, then doubled forward on his face. The second spun sideways, clawed the wall as he slapped down. There was a bloody tear in the back of his coat where it pinched in across the loins. The slapping thunder of the forty-five was still crashing through the building when the *Spider* reached the exit door and ducked out on the fire-escape. There was no time to affix his tiny mocking death seal to his victims' forehead. Capturing Barker was far more important than hurling that minor mockery into the faces of his enemies.

Caution was cast aside now. The *Spider* went down the fire-escape steps with great, leaping strides, his heels making the iron ring and ring again. He heard the door above him fling open again, heard a gun crash, but he did not even look upward. The iron slats were closely interlaced above him. They formed an adequate shield. The danger would come later, when he left the protection of the fire-escape and raced along the alley toward his car, which would be waiting at the alley's end.

As the *Spider* whirled along the second floor platform, he drew back his lips and whistled shrilly between his teeth. His Hindu servant, Ram Singh, who was in the car, undoubtedly would have drawn close on hearing the shots. The whistle would summon him to battle. . . . But he would have to act swiftly if he were to help. The *Spider* paused a moment at the end of the second story platform, leaned out over the rail and slanted three quick bullets upward. They would not wound, but they might frighten. . . . On the heels of his last shot, he gripped the railing of the fire-escape, somersaulted neatly over it and dropped to the ground, diving instantly to the protection of the platform again. He whirled to dart for the street, then shrank back against the wall, smiling.

A low-slung sedan was backing rapidly into the alleyway, its engine roaring between the narrow walls. Ram Singh had indeed caught the signal and was answering as his keen fighting mind directed. The door of the tonneau stopped within inches of the *Spider's* hand and he jerked it open, swung in and rapped the glass between him and the Hindu in the same movement. The car lurched forward, hurled the *Spider* deep into the cushions and rocked into the street on squealing tires.

Even before he righted himself, the *Spider* snatched the speaking tube. "Newark airport! Fast!" he shouted. "That was well done, O Ram Singh!"

The *Spider*, disposing himself more comfortably on the cushions, saw the lift of the Hindu's turbaned head, the proud bracing of the shoulders as if to say, "Does not Ram Singh always serve his master well?"

With a slow smile, the *Spider* drew out his platinum cigarette-case, extracted one of his privately blended smokes and lighted up with a deep inhalation of satisfaction. He began to reload his guns . . . The sedan was rocketing through the city, working its way southward across the lights at terrific speed, but with only a low hissing of power from the motor.

The *Spider's* body was at ease, but his mind raced ahead to the battle that soon must be fought. Although gangster pursuit had not yet developed, he was positive that they would reach Newark airport, where Barker was going, almost as quickly as he. He could forestall them, of course, by phoning police and demanding Barker's arrest at the field, but that would not serve. Even if he was compelled to pursue by plane, the *Spider* must capture Barker himself. The man had information which the *Spider* must possess if he were to destroy the criminal alliance in the city and defeat El Gaucho. No, he would take the chance himself, alone. He smiled slightly. Well, the *Spider* was accustomed to single-handed battle against incredible odds. Deliberately, he picked up the speaking tube again.

"Find me a taxi, Ram Singh," he ordered, "then carry this word to the *missie sahib*."

Wentworth outlined then all that he knew about El Gaucho and Tom Barker and the gangsters and knew that Ram Singh would deliver the information perfectly to Nita van Sloan. If anything happened to the *Spider* in the battle to come, at least his work thus far would not have been in vain. *If anything happened . . . !* Yes, there was always that possibility for the *Spider*. He had one defense. When the disguise was removed almost no one knew what manner of man he became. There was Nita and Ram Singh and Jackson, who had been his sergeant during the war and who served him variously now; Jenkyns, his ancient butler. There had been another, Professor Brownlee, mentor of his college days and assistant in scientific matters in later, grimmer days. But one of the master criminals the *Spider* fought had caused Brownlee's death. The grief was still in the *Spider's* soul, though he had exacted hundred-fold vengeance. . . .

Should he now assume his real identity? The *Spider* considered while Ram Singh bored southward. His hand dropped to the cushions to his left. A touch on a hidden button there would reveal a secret wardrobe, and disguise equipment in the seat's back, the means of becoming again that dilettante clubman and sportsman which was his real self—that of Richard Wentworth, scion of a wealthy old family of which he was now the sole living member. Slowly, he shook his head. No, that would not do. He must still battle, and it must be as the *Spider* that he struck.

The sedan ground to a halt beside a taxi and the *Spider* alighted without a word. His cape hung over his arm now as a coat and his shoulders were straightened to their natural, easy confidence of carriage. His black slouch hat sat more jauntily on his head. But the gaunt, strong-nosed face of the *Spider* remained. He kept it masked in shadow as he ordered the taxi to speed.

"Newark airport!" he said sharply. "Fifty dollars if you make it in fifteen minutes!"

The cab jumped forward, its motor bellowing, the driver bent forward over the wheel. Wentworth saw his sedan whirl a corner and vanish and knew that within minutes Nita would be receiving Ram Singh's report. His hands strayed to his holstered, reloaded automatics. He would need them soon. Even as his practiced fingers touched the butts, he heard the staccato blast of guns behind and whirled in his seat. No car was roaring in his wake, no stabs of flame heralded an attack. He frowned at the empty street, then faced front again, grim-mouthed.

He knew now what those shots meant. Ram Singh had been attacked in the car the gangsters had trailed. Wentworth's eyes were cold, the set of his lips bitter. He could not return to the faithful Hindu's assistance. The car was bullet-proof, strong as a fort and the *Spider* must hasten with his task. His lips tightened even more. It was his code that he followed throughout the wars which racked his heart and soul. Never self, or loved ones; always the service of humanity came first.

The taxi seemed to crawl, though its speedometer wavered always near fifty. It was well after midnight and there was scant traffic, all going very fast. There was a heart-breaking delay when they got a ticket for the Holland tunnel that burrowed under the Hudson River. Two policemen there were talking about El Gaucho. One of them shook a newspaper at the other.

"Look at it!" he said hoarsely. "Two million.

Twelve people killed, five of them cops! Suppose that bozo takes it into his head to come here!"

Wentworth bought the paper from the officer for a dollar and read it with scowling eyes while the taxi droned through the tunnel at the required thirty miles an hour.

GAUCHO LOOTS TWO CITIES

So screamed the headlines, and the news explained that a second town forty miles from Jackson City which had been robbed first, had been struck two hours after the first depredation. Destruction of telephone wires all around had prevented the news from leaking out earlier. The toll in the second town, Harvester, was twenty-two dead. A school bus had got in the way of the escape.

Wentworth read the story with eyes that burned. His jaw clenched until it ached and he felt the hard angry throb of his blood in the knife scar that laid its tracery across his right temple. Soon now he would fly to strike back at El Gaucho.

The cab was speeding now along the elevated motor highway, which bridges the congested cities of northern New Jersey, out to the airport that lay on the southern outskirts of Newark. Minutes dragged past, but finally the field came in sight. They had made incredibly good time. Wentworth was sure Barker could not yet have taken wing.

Thus, the *Spider* reassured himself as he draped the cape again about his shoulders and twisted them into those of the hunch-back whom all the world knew. He dragged the hat down over his brows and the taxi swept around the great traffic circle that marked the turn-off to the field.

Even as the cab circled, Wentworth saw a bunched group of men start out from a hangar toward a place that was warming up on the field. He rapped sharply on the glass.

"Stop!" he ordered, and thrust his gun against the taxi driver's nape.

The man twisted his white frightened face about, dragged on his brakes. Wentworth thrust a hundred-dollar bill into his hand, sprang to the wheel himself, sent the taxi surging forward under its full power. He made no effort to make the long circle that would take him by the regular road to a place behind the hangars, but headed straight for the white, wooden fence that formed the airport's outer boundary. He struck it at forty-five miles an hour, smashed through and roared with increasing speed straight for the plane that the group of men was approaching now. . . .

Seemingly the *Spider* was driving blindly to attack an anonymous group of men, but he was wise in the way of gangster tactics. He recognized the fighting wedge which they formed with their bodies about a man they protected—knew at first glance that this must be the guard which had been sent to see Barker safely aboard the plane. Within moments, his suspicion was confirmed. An instant after the taxi had crashed through the fence and bounded to the attack, the first bullet sped toward him. It was wild, uncalculated, merely a messenger of defiance. But it was enough to confirm Wentworth's suspicions.

With a hard laugh, the *Spider* bent over the wheel, spurred the car to its maximum speed. He held the wheel with his left hand, his right clutched his automatic. Deliberately he reached forward, rapped the windshield from its frame, brought splintering glass back into his lap. Better that he knock it out, than that bullets spear it into his face at a crucial moment.

Even after that, the *Spider* did not open fire. Some of these men he would kill, but there was one he must spare. One of them could help him in his pending battle with El Gaucho, of which this was merely an opening skirmish. Nevertheless, men died as surely in skirmishes as in the most wide-flung battleline. On the *Spider* charged, and now bullets were flying more thickly. The close group of men had resolved itself into a moving firing-line, four men spread out thinly, behind which another man ran headlong for the waiting plane. Lead pinged off the empty windshield strut and a second thudded into the upholstery near Wentworth's shoulder.

Once more harsh laughter issued from his lips. He deliberately opened fire. He could distinguish now between the men he wished to kill and the one he would spare. That was sufficient for the *Spider*. His bullets sped where he willed them to go. At his first shot, one of the four gunmen was straightened out of his crouch, spun about and dropped dead to the ground. Wentworth leveled his automatic again, but abruptly he twisted his head about, held his fire. A new element had entered the battle. . . .

From beside the hangars, a motorcycle engine blasted into action and the machine instantly rolled forward, saddle and side car occupied by men in the uniform of State police. Wentworth cursed. He did not battle with the police, regardless of what action they took against him, but they never showed him mercy. If they recognized him, they would discard all effort to apprehend the armed gunmen there who were plotting the nation's destruction and concentrate all their efforts on killing him. The laughter that came from the *Spider's* lips was bitter now. This was the penalty he paid for his impatience with cumbersome legal machinery. In the eyes of police, he was a murderer, not an executioner of his own swift justice. The price on his head was fifty thousand dollars. . . .

With his eyes grimly set, the *Spider* fired, once, twice, a third time and the three remaining gangsters went down, like clay pigeons in a shooting gallery. The fifth man, who must be Barker, raced on toward the plane—was almost at the doorway now.

Wentworth held his fire. He did not wish to kill the man, nor to wound him unless it was absolutely necessary. Nor did he wish to disable the plane. It had become, suddenly, his sole hope of escape from this predicament into which his service of mankind had thrown him. The policeman in the side-car was firing now and with his third shot, a front tire of the taxi flattened with a hissing blast. The two tons of cab went wild, wrenching at the steering gear, lurching in a mad yawning swerve to the left. Wentworth stood up beneath the wheel, fought it with both locked hands, the automatic neglected on the seat beside him. The policeman continued his closely spaced shots.

The *Spider*, with the desperation of necessity, manhandled the lurching cab into a reasonably straight course for the plane, now only fifty feet away. Barker was already scrambling into the doorway, and the instant he ducked inside, the plane began to turn its nose into the wind. It would move slowly at first, and would have to run at least two hundred feet on the ground before it lifted. That was the *Spider's* only hope.

Wentworth whirled the steering wheel desperately, put the steady, spaced firing of police behind him. Now the back of the cab was turned toward the bullets, offering some shelter. The flat tire was pounding, and with a moaning crescendo it ripped loose from the rim and went wobbling off to one side. The cab rode more smoothly now, though the *Spider* was hard put to hold it to a straight course as he plummeted after the plane. If he could only reach the doorway and hurl himself through it, the pull of the flattened tire on the left front wheel would whirl the taxi away from the plane. . . .

Frantically, Wentworth ground the accelerator to the floor, fighting the clanging pull of the tireless wheel. He was oblivious to the cracking of guns behind him, to the hammer of lead against the car. Only one thing was important—that he catch the plane. Fortunately, in leaping into the ship, Barker had neglected to unhook the door that was fastened open against the side of the plane. But the powerful slip-stream of the racing propellers was battling to tear it loose. The door jerked at his fastenings.

Wentworth's shoulders ached with the wrenching

strain of the wheel, but his eyes remained calm and clear. He saw exactly what he must do and estimated his chances narrowly. He was even with the tail of the ship now, but it was rapidly gaining headway. Even as Wentworth drew abreast, the tail lifted. Another hundred feet and the plane's wheels would lift from the earth and moments later, it would pull upward. Then there would be no chance left for the *Spider* at all.

Before this deathly chase had begun, he had hopes of pursuing by plane if he were too late to intercept Barker, but that was ruined now. If he failed to catch the ship, not only would he have no chance at all to catch the man, but no hope even of living! For the taxi's steering-gear would not stand up much longer under the fearful punishment of high speed and crippled wheels; the motorcycle was rapidly overhauling him. Soon the police guns could not miss. And he could not fire on agents of the law, even if it meant his own death. . . .

These thoughts flashed through Wentworth's mind as he gave the last of his ability and strength to the task of overtaking the ship. He crawled ahead steadily, but slowly—oh, slowly! Once the plane left earth. . . . He was still ten feet behind the doorway when he saw the tires lift slightly for the first bound. He was straining forward, as if with his own weight he would lend the taxi additional speed. A bullet whined past his ear. He was no longer laughing, but there was a smile on his mouth, a tight-lipped smile that matched the hard, cold gleam of his eyes. He must make it, *he must*!

Only seven feet to gain, now only five. Wentworth jerked the hand throttle of the taxi to the last notch, caught the wheel with his left hand and eased out from under it. He had to strain frantically to hold the cab one-handed while he got into a position to spring. The plane's wheels were lifting again, even more lightly. Three feet now before he would be opposite the doorway; three feet that might well be his doom. He stooped cautiously, caught up his automatic and pocketed it. Even in his extremity, he did not forget that. He had dozens of automatics, perfectly matched for balance and barrel, all registered in different identities, but the particular pair he carried now were in his own name. No, these must not fall into the hands of the police. The wheels of the plane lifted finally from the earth, just skimming it, but clear, none the less. Within seconds, it would be battling its way toward the skies. Now, at last there was only a scant foot of difference in the doorways of taxi and plane. Wentworth could wait no longer. He braced himself, released the cab's wheel at the same instant that he vaulted high into the air and sprang straight away for the open door of the plane.

In the split second of time while he hung suspended there in the air, empty hands outstretched toward the sides of the ship, he saw two things. The door was tearing loose from its fastenings and swinging violently down-wind, as if evilly inspired, as if to slam in Wentworth's face or strike him from the precarious hold which he sought. He saw, too, that Barker, his face desperately white, stood braced in the doorway, his hands balled in fists, to knock him loose if he should gain a momentary grip on the door frame. And either one would mean the *Spider's* death. Taxi and plane were both making sixty miles an hour. A plunge to the hard earth at that terrific speed would smash every bone in his body. And if he survived that, there were the police . . . !

CHAPTER FOUR

Battle in the Sky

If there had been time, in that brief moment when he flew through the air, Wentworth would have screamed defiance, would have laughed aloud. His courage was indomitable, his will supreme. He drew his feet forward, doubled his legs under his body and catapulted into the narrow open space of the doorway at the same instant the slip stream of the propellers slammed the door shut. The door caught him on his back and its impetus pitched him against the man who stood with clenched fists to hammer him back to his death. Together they rolled across the narrow width of the cabin. Wentworth felt the plane yaw beneath him, stagger with the weight of his leap. Its wheels banged against the earth. Then the whole ship shuddered its way upward to steadiness again.

The *Spider* was more than half-stunned by the violence of his entrance, but with the trained reflexes of his remarkable body, he was on his feet almost instantly, battling against Barker's attack, while his mind reeled from shock. His guns stayed in their holsters. He had not struggled this far to keep this man alive only to kill him at the end of the chase. He knew at least that there would be no help for Barker from the pilot, even if the man were armed. His hands would be busy getting the ship aloft after that narrow escape close to the earth.

Gradually as he fought, clinching, warding off blows, his head cleared and from behind his lifted arms, he looked into the face of the man he battled. The whiteness of fear was gone from Tom Barker's cheeks and there was something almost merry in the twinkling of his brown eyes that was strangely familiar to Wentworth. The man was young, not more than twenty-three, and had a remarkably high and well-developed forehead. His face was round, almost chubby, and his mouth, smiling now, had the determination, the strength of an older man for all its young cheerfulness. Touseled brown hair lay in curly clusters close to his head.

Wentworth's remarkable stamina had pulled him completely out of his daze now, but before the hard hammer of the younger man's fists, he feigned hurt, wobbling even more on his feet, retreating stumblingly until he got the position he wanted. Barker's young enthusiasm misled him. He bored in for the knockout and Wentworth's left lanced out to the face, pulling Barker up short, straightening him for the knockout right that came whistling in at exactly the right heartbeat of time. Barker arched backward, stumbled and thumped down supine in the aisle, eyes closed, out cold. . . .

The *Spider* stooped slowly, picked up his hat, set it on his head. His chest was heaving with his exertions, his heart pumping hard and swiftly in his throat, but he did not delay. He made his way forward, opened the door behind the pilot and met the man's frightened stare as he pulled his chin about on his shoulder.

"This ship has been re-chartered," Wentworth told him dryly. "There's a small landing field at Bedford, New York. Head for it."

A trembling jerked at the pilot's shoulders; his face was drawn, and words gurgled in his throat.

"The *Spider*!" he gasped. "The *Spider*!"

35

Wentworth nodded gravely. "Quite so. You have my instructions?"

"Yes, sir. Yes, sir!"

Wentworth nodded again, found that the pilot was unarmed, and shut the door on the cockpit as he turned back to Barker. The man was stirring on the floor of the cabin. The *Spider* dropped into a seat near him, gravely lighted a cigarette while he waited for Barker to recover consciousness entirely. There was a quiet satisfaction in Wentworth's movements. He was rapidly throwing off the exhaustion of the pursuit, his gray-blue eyes were hawklike and keen beneath the black brim of his hat. He removed the hat slowly, laid it on the seat opposite him and revealed the smooth, high reach of his forehead which even the sinister disguise of the *Spider* could not conceal.

There was a kindliness in his eyes now that seemed strange in a man of so savage a reputation. The men he had killed were numbered somewhere in the police files of a hundred cities in half the nations of the world. Somewhere, too, in secret archives, Nita had kept account of them. They ran into high hundreds, and each had died for some evil deed, for some fierce crime against humanity or against some innocent individual. But Wentworth's eyes were not those of a killer. They were keenly intelligent, warmly human. In his natural face, in repose, there was a touch of sadness, of the universal grieving for mankind which no language can express so well as the German *Weltschmerz*. But now, there was a gentle humor in his face, too.

He had come after Barker, prepared to find him a brutal criminal, such a man as might well represent so great a killer, so murderous a robber as this El Gaucho. Instead, he had found a youngster whose eager fighting smile might well match the *Spider's* own. There was something clean about the boy, clean and healthy. The *Spider* was suddenly glad that he had not killed him.

Barker stirred again on the floor, lifted a hand to his jaw and breathed out a sound that was almost a moan.

He sat up abruptly, looked at Wentworth. His eyes widened at sight of the sinister garb and face; then their eyes met and, slowly, uncertainly, Barker smiled.

"Man!" he said. "You sure pack a wallop!"

Wentworth did not smile. When he smiled in his disguise, it did sinister things to his face as it was meant to, but his eyes remained kindly.

"It's necessary sometimes," he replied briefly. "How did you get yourself involved with that band of criminals. I almost killed you."

Barker was silent for a dozen heartbeats, staring up into Wentworth's face. His cheeks drained of color and an involuntary shudder touched his shoulders. Then he smiled sheepishly. "I'm not a coward," he said, "but . . . the way you say that! I can almost . . . *feel* death. Who are you?"

Wentworth looked down at his captive speculatively. When he questioned men, he frequently terrified them with a sight of the red seal which he so often placed upon the dead foreheads of the victims of his swift justice, but there was a clear intelligence in the eyes of this man that struck a sudden chord of sympathy in Wentworth's heart. He leaned forward a little, elbows on his knees.

"The *Spider*," he answered simply.

Barker caught his breath, but there was no terror in his eyes, and Wentworth was glad of his decision— pleased again that he had not shot him. His lack of fear was the surest proof of his complete honesty. Wentworth was suddenly sure that Barker had had no criminal part in the negotiations between the New York criminals and El Gaucho.

Wentworth said calmly, "I can see that you have no fear of me, and you are right. The *Spider* never harms an innocent man. However, you have certainly placed yourself in an incriminating position. I think you would do well to explain in detail just what happened to you that you got mixed up with that crowd."

Barker pushed himself to his feet, dropped into a seat facing Wentworth. "You're right. I want to thank you for getting me out of a damned bad jam.'' He leaned forward, elbows on his knees. "I'll come clean, but it's a crazy story. It will be hard for you to believe.''

Wentworth offered his cigarette-case and, after they had both lighted up, asked gravely, "Why not try me?''

Barker nodded eagerly, his brown eyes serious and intent. "My father and mother are dead,'' he began. "A few months ago, my grandfather was killed by some crooks here in New York. I was in C. C. C. camp at the time and as soon as I could, I came east. Hitch-hiked. I thought I'd give some other guy a chance in the camp and maybe granddad would have left me enough to live on. I found a guy named Wentworth was executor, but I couldn't reach . . .''

Wentworth could not prevent the start that jerked at his muscles, but his face betrayed nothing at all. He stared at Barker and forced himself to calmness, made his voice slow.

"This grandfather of yours who was killed—who was he?''

There was a choking in Wentworth's throat. He looked again at the man's brown, alert eyes, his high, intelligent forehead, and was sure in advance that he knew what the answer would be. An old grief rose up to overwhelm him and there was a dryness in his eyes that made them sting.

Barker looked up, a little surprised at the interruption. "Why,'' he said slowly, "his name was Brownlee, a professor he was, and . . .''

Wentworth came to his feet. "Professor Brownlee!''

He had been right then! The certainty that he had hesitated to phrase in his own mind overwhelmed him. This man was the grandson of Professor Brownlee, the cheerful old man who had been his closest associate through the years of his battling against the Underworld, the man who had been a father to him in his parentless days, who had died fighting the *Spider's* battle. No wonder he had taken so instantly to this youngster who had so many brave features of the old professor. It was rarely that any happening could pierce the hard composure that had many times been Wentworth's sole protection against his enemies, but this sudden discovery of Professor Brownlee's grandson . . . Wentworth remembered now that Professor Brownlee had had a daughter who had died a while after the *Spider* had been born. . . . He found himself gripping Barker's hand hard, looking into brown, slightly puzzled eyes.

"He was a great—a brave—man, that grandfather of yours," Wentworth said, pushing down his emotion. "I am proud to know his grandson."

Tom Barker smiled. They both sat down again. Wentworth became preoccupied with lighting a cigarette. Barker said eagerly, "Then you knew him?"

Wentworth shook his head. "Wentworth and I frequently fight the same battles," he said quietly. "There have been times when we helped one another. Professor Brownlee was one of Wentworth's most intimate associates, helped him out in his fights. That's how he was killed. A great man."

While Barker went on with his story then, Wentworth watched him covertly, seeing anew resemblances to his old friend. That certain quick way of moving his hands in a gesture, that occasional uplooking cheerful glance, the merriness that lurked in his eyes. Yes, there could be no mistake. It was remarkable that he had himself not noticed the resemblance. . . .

Barker's story was simple enough. He had been hitchhiking his way to New York and had happened to be in a city that El Gaucho raided. When he arrived in New York, he had been unable to get in touch with Wentworth—the *Spider* had been busy in the Underworld and Wentworth had been "away on a trip"— and he had managed to sell his story of El Gaucho to a newspaper as a means of supporting himself until Wentworth returned. Afterward, the police had come for him and he had run away in fright. Yvonne Musette had found him and taken him to see Piltsdown. . . .

"I had to repeat my brag then, sir," he said, looking

up at Wentworth, "or it would have gone hard with me. My brag, I mean, that I could find El Gaucho any time I wanted to. . . ."

"Can you, Tom?"

Barker grinned. "Of course not. But Piltsdown believed I could, chiefly because he wanted to. He surrounded me with his gunmen and I had no choice but to do what they wanted. I didn't want to die yet awhile, especially . . ." His voice died, his cheeks reddened a little. Wentworth waited patiently, but he did not continue. He went on with another line of talk. The *Spider* felt a sharp disappointment at learning that Barker's story of being able to find El Gaucho was false, but his curiosity was aroused by his awkward lapse into silence, his flush. Finally, he penetrated Barker's reserve.

"Well, sir," Barker said slowly, "it's like this. I'm kind of ashamed of anything so kiddish, but there it is and I can't change it. When El Gaucho raided this town, I saw a girl with him, and . . . and, damn it, sir, I won't be happy until I see her again!"

Wentworth frowned down at his hands. A memory came back to him, a memory that stretched across years. In those days, the *Spider* was a new terror across the red skies of the Underworld, an angel of sudden death. One night, bowing suavely in a friend's home, above a white hand among so many white hands, Wentworth had looked up into eyes that were violet and warmly deep. . . . *Damn it, sir, I won't be happy until I see her again.* . . . Strange that he should feel so close to this boy, this man.

Wentworth said dryly, "You'll probably be better off if you never see her again. Now, you must talk fast. We'll land in a few minutes. I want to know how El Gaucho works, and what Piltsdown and his crowd are planning. . . ."

Barker harked back to the girl.

"You'll think it awfully funny, sir, about the girl, when I tell you what this Gaucho does. Why, I saw him push his gun up against on old man's throat and blow a hole through it. He almost tore his head off, sir, and here I am thinking about a girl that was with him.''

Wentworth's jaw hardened beneath its firm skin and his lips parted in a smile that was not pleasant to see.

"Tell me more of this Gaucho," he said softly.

Barker looked at the *Spider's* face and a shudder touched his shoulders. "I'd like to be with you, sir, when you kill him," he said simply. He sat silent for a full minute, staring down at his brown, calloused hands, began abruptly to talk.

"Gaucho's men all dress in yellow slickers and they cover their heads with red hoods so nobody can see their faces. They wear a band of scarlet and purple around their left arms.

"They have all kinds of guns. They shoot everybody they see on sight. I think the girl saved my life. I was in a doorway staring at them and a man looked my way and the girl rode her horse in front of me. I think she saved my life."

"El Gaucho, Barker," the *Spider* prompted softly.

"Yes, sir. Well, I saw a man fire a shotgun at him from fifteen feet away and it didn't hurt him. He killed the man and kept on shooting him after he was on the ground. One of the men threw a girl across his horse, a kid that couldn't any more than have finished high school. I chased him, but he shot at me, got clean away. They set the town on fire before they left."

Wentworth's eyes were gray-blue flame. His voice still came softly, but there was an edge like surgical steel in his words.

"Now, tell me about Piltsdown."

The anger still flamed in Wentworth's face when Barker had finished, but there was a frown on his forehead and an impatience in his every gesture. He was on fire to battle this Gaucho, but he knew that the fight might well be long, and Barker's story of Piltsdown and his plans had made it plain that the *Spider's* first duty was to the city. The alliance that was planned reached to the last rat-hole of the Underworld and would weld all its sly, poisonous strength into a machine that would throttle mankind within a few months. They would truly, as Piltsdown had said, "own the city" within weeks.

No, it was plain that he must strike first here in New York City, destroy this festering terror before the leaders could bring this super-bandit here for the Underworld to acclaim emperor. Once more, he must delay his trip westward. With that decision, a new grimness settled upon the *Spider*. How could one man hope to cope with so widespread and powerful an organization? Lop off the head? He smiled bitterly. That sanguinary activity would probably entail first battling his way through the entire army of El Gaucho!

Wentworth leaned to the window and saw that the field toward which the pilot slanted the plane was empty in the gray light of early dawn. He turned back to Barker, took out a blank card and swiftly scribbled a note and an address upon it, signed it with the *Spider's* seal.

"This lady is a friend of Wentworth," he said. "You will be cared for until he returns. By all means, keep clear of Yvonne Musette and her crowd."

Barker smiled wryly. "You can count on that, sir, if I see them first!"

Wentworth nodded slowly. The plane set down lightly on the field, taxied to one of the two small hangars on the edge of the narrow macadam road that led past, killed the motor. Wentworth left the plane, taking Barker with him in an automobile they rented from a caretaker on the field. On the edge of the city, they parted. Wentworth clasped Barker's hand.

"Go to that address," he said, "and I can assure you your troubles will be over."

Barker seemed reluctant to release his hand. "But you, sir? When will I see you again? Where are you going?"

The *Spider* smiled and his eyes were no longer

friendly to lighten its sinister aspect. "I am paying a call on these erstwhile friends of yours."

"But not alone?"

Wentworth laughed. He thrust Barker from the car, made it roar down the street, leaving the man standing there on the curb. He laughed again, softly, as he raced southward toward the rendezvous that had been arranged for Tom Barker, bearing the answer of El Gaucho. The *Spider* would keep that appointment . . . bearing death!

CHAPTER FIVE

Rendezvous of Death

The place of rendezvous was another—though much smaller—athletic club. Wentworth wondered grimly if Piltsdown had control over every such place in New York City. He realized at once, however, the advantages for Piltsdown of such an establishment. Men of all sorts could go to the clubs without question and that would afford facility of contact with the underlings which he must have.

The criminals would be present, all right. According to Barker's information, there was always a large force there and tonight the leaders would be panicky over the *Spider's* successes. They would keep together for strength and courage. Was it mad for one man to plan such an invasion single-handed? Perhaps, but Wentworth had gone many times into such traps and come out alive and triumphant. True, this time he would have no rear guard, no second line of defense, such as Ram Singh, lurking in the background to catch his signal, or attempt rescue if something went wrong. . . .

Speeding the slatternly touring car, Wentworth felt an abrupt reversal of his feeling of self-confidence. It was as if some inner warning had been sounded, as if Death had blown its fetid breath in his face, laughing as it held out bony hands of welcome. Wentworth tried to shrug the feeling aside, but it persisted. He repeated to himself steadily that he had conquered against much greater odds and when the reiteration brought no relief from gloom, he thrust the whole aside, relegated it to the back of his mind. It did not matter that apprehension bestrode his shoulders. . . . One concession he made to his dread. He stopped at an all-night drug store and, carrying his cape, cocking his hat, went into a phone booth to call Nita van Sloan. He knew she would be awake. When the *Spider* roved abroad, she did not sleep until he had come, as he invariably did, to her studio apartment high above the Hudson on Riverside Drive.

When her quiet contralto sang to him over the wire, Wentworth closed his eyes for a long moment, but when he spoke, his voice was vigorous and confident as he knew so well how to make it.

"Nita, darling," he whispered.

Nita cried, "Dick, you rascal, why didn't you call me sooner?"

They laughed together then and there was more talk, but Wentworth stopped that soon and told Nita rapidly what had transpired since Ram Singh had left him. His faithful Hindu, he learned, had eluded the attack after giving the pursuing gangsters a brief battle.

"I'm sending Barker to you," Wentworth told Nita briskly. "He should be there in an hour or so. I imagine he'll be dubious about coming before eight o'clock anyway. I'm on my way now, Nita, my sweet. Yes, of course I'll be careful. . . . See you soon. . . ."

Wentworth hung up the receiver and stood for a long moment with his head hanging, his eyes closed. That *See you soon* had cost him a pang. He could say that when the presentiment of disaster was cold within him, but he could not deceive himself. Abruptly, his head came up. Was this the *Spider* who could talk and think such things? Nonsense. The *Spider* had always won. Always would. There could be no defeat for him. At least, there should be no thought of defeat. . . .

He reentered the car, sped on southward, presently braked to a halt a block from the building of the rendezvous and sat silently studying it. About him, the early traffic of New York was beginning to rumble, a few street cars were rattling, clanging past; motorists hurrying home from all-night tasks or speeding to early work; bums awaking from their doorway beds and shuffling along with sagging shoulders and sleep-fuddled heads. The last, dreary, street-washing truck was lumbering home with its spray nozzles dribbling water. And the streets were still dirty with the litter of last night's crowds. This was Broadway after sunrise, with its glittering signs extinguished by the dawn and the garishness of its night tawdry and ashamed by daylight. The rendezvous was at Forty-fifth and Broadway, a basement athletic club. The building was fourteen or fifteen stories high, with entrances on two streets. Wentworth took the only possible course, walking straight up to the main door.

Inside the double barrier of glass, the night watchman was red-eyed but awake, waiting for his relief. At Wentworth's sharp rap on the outer door, the man ambled forward, but with a hand lifted to the neck of his vest where gunmen, but rarely watchmen, carry weapons. Wentworth saw all this with eyes that seemed utterly disinterested, his manner impatient. He guessed that, even as he had expected, the guard was one of Piltsdown's own men. Surely, the leader would not have trusted so important a post to anyone not in his employ.

Wentworth rapped again on the door, gesturing sharply to the man. The watchman's face wrinkled but he shuffled forward more rapidly, fumbled one-handed with the locks while he still peered through the glass, keeping a hand near his gun. Wentworth leaned toward the glass, gestured with his hands to hold the man's attention and got a knee against the door. As he heard the bolt of the lock slip back, he threw all his weight against the portal, slamming it inward and hurling the watchman backward off-balance. Before the man's gun was half-drawn, Wentworth had reached his side and thrust his stiffened fingers against the man's throat, dropping him unconscious to the floor.

It was the work of a moment to latch the door again, to drag the nightwatchman into the elevator and allow the gate to slide shut. He would be safe there until he recovered consciousness, which would be at least a half hour from now. No one could open the door from the outside without a special key. Wentworth smiled slightly to himself as he made his way silent-footed down the stairs. If all his victories were as simple as this one. . . . Half way down he paused. It seemed to his tautly attuned ears that he had heard a footstep in the hall above, which should contain only the unconscious watchman. His smile thinning, he drew his cape about his shoulders, palmed his two automatics. It was barely possible that his return had been anticipated.

The stairway he was descending was marble and broad. It reached to the basement in three short flights describing three sides of a square. Wentworth was in the middle of the second flight now, and from his position, he could see both the head and the foot of the stairway, plus a section of the basement hall. There were two doors with upper panels of ground glass within view. Only darkness was behind them, but the corridor itself was dimly lighted by widely spaced electric bulbs. There was no repetition of the sound above and presently, the *Spider* drifted on downward. His eyes were wary.

He did not believe it possible that he had miscalculated, that the allies of Piltsdown would not be here in this basement rendezvous. Yet nothing stirred about him, there was no light or indication of life. Wentworth's disguised face became a hard mask. His certainty of a trap increased. At the foot of the stairs he paused. One corner of the upper hallway was still in view. He weighed his guns in his hands while he watched it. He wondered if he were allowing the premonition which had chilled him before his entrance to play tricks on him. But there was no answer except the weighty silence of the building about him. Slowly

Wentworth's lips lifted from his teeth. The *Spider* had come here to kill!

Deliberately, he lifted his left hand gun and blasted out the single light bulb that was in sight. His eyes flicked to it only for a heartbeat, then they were focused again on that corner of the upper hall. Hard on the heels of the crashing shot, a man sprang into view up there in the hallway above, racing for the stairs, a gun in his hand. Wentworth's right-hand automatic blasted and the man's head jerked. His gun hand half-lifted with a queer, wooden stiffness. But it did not quite level. In the midst of deliberate movement, the man's body went abruptly limp and he pitched in a heap down the first flight of stairs, landed with a sodden thump on the second platform above Wentworth.

The *Spider* pressed close against the wall at the corner of the hall and watched the two doors he could see, glanced now and again at that corner of the hallway above. The echo of his shots could not fail to have roused someone. It was his one course of action. Barker had not known the layout of the club, so he could only launch the attack and so draw the leaders to him.

Still no sound reached his waiting ears. The corridor seemed to be empty even of the echo of his shots. Wentworth's eyes narrowed on one of the glass doors. Abruptly, he sprang forward, casting a quick glance up and down the hallway as he moved. No one was in sight. Wentworth put his shoulders against the wall between the two doors and listened again. He was almost certain he had glimpsed movement behind that ground glass panel.

Suddenly, without warning, the silence of the hallway was shattered by a blasting roar. He saw the glass panel of the door to his right smash to the floor, but its fall was soundless in the greater, overwhelming chatter of a machine gun. With a sensation of cold that crept up the flesh of his back, Wentworth saw the bullets claw the wall at the corner where, a brief moment

48

before, he had stood. They splashed white powder from the marble steps, scored black holes in the plaster.

He crouched, ready for action. When the machine gun stammered into surprised silence, Wentworth sprang past the doorway. He was visible for only a heartbeat to those inside, but in that speck of time, Wentworth had fired twice. His cape whipped backward from his shoulders and before it was clear, the machine gun roared again. The *Spider* felt the lead tug at his cape, but through its chatter came a sound that was between a gasp and a moan. The machine gun ceased its angry cackle and a man's footsteps, slapping heavily on the floor in flight, echoed from the room.

The *Spider* nodded. His bullets had sped truly once more. He sprang past the doorway once more, saw that the room was empty except for a dead man who lay hunched grotesquely over his silent machine gun. Wentworth moved quietly into the room, while his eyes quested about. He opened the base of each of his guns in turn and reloaded from a supply of cartridges he carried loose in his pocket. It was clearly a waiting room, with hard benches against the wall and, in the corner, a box of an office with a window-like cashier's cage.

Thoughtfully, Wentworth holstered his automatics and eased the machine gun out from under the dead man. The man had an extra drum of ammunition beside him and the one on the gun was only half-emptied. Wentworth nodded his satisfaction and, the machine gun cradled against his hip, went toward the door where the other fugitive gunman had disappeared. The room beyond was empty, but as the *Spider* sprang sideways through the doorway, seeking instantly the cover of the wall, an automatic banged through the letter slot of a door directly opposite it.

Wentworth drummed out a short burst in answer, heard bullets clang upon the slot and hit with a flat, dull ring upon the door. He recognized the sound. The door was steel, impregnable to his bullets. But the lead that he had fanned through the letter slot had gone true, for the automatic ceased. His face alight with eagerness for the battle, he crossed the room in long strides, set the muzzle of the machine gun against the slot and swept it in an arc across the room beyond, which he could not see. Men's screams came clearly through the steel portal, their shrillness rising even above the deafening changor of the gun.

Until the last bullet sped from the barrel, Wentworth held the gun to the slot, then he ran lightly back across the room, detaching the spent drum, snapping new ammunition into place. By the time he reached the hallway again, the machine gun was once more cradled against his hip. As he sprang from the door, he caught a fragmentary glimpse of two men crouching down the stairs with revolvers in hand. They fired first, but they fired wildly. The machine gun moved six inches, vibrating with the roll of its discharge, and both men crumpled down the last few steps to the floor.

Over their bodies, Wentworth paused for a moment, touching the base of his gleaming platinum cigarette case to their foreheads. When he straightened, a small splotch of richest vermilion glowed there, a miniature symbol of sprawling hairy legs and poised venomous fangs, the *seal of the Spider*! These were not the men he had wanted to kill tonight, but they would do to start. Certain it was that they were hirelings of the crowd which sought to rule the city and bring El Gaucho here with his murderous cruelty and his ruthless looting.

A slow fire of anger was burning within Wentworth's breast. The leaders were keeping hidden, damn them, sending their killers to battle in their stead. But the *Spider* would find them, track them down. He went along the hallway on slow, silent feet, deliberate as death, the gun cradled against his hip. He saw then, for the first time, a lighted doorway. The light had not been there before when he had sprung across the corridor. Of that he was certain. But it glowed brightly now like a trap for unwary moths.

The *Spider* went grimly toward it, the machine gun ready. To him, that light was a challenge and he was suddenly sure that it had been intended for precisely that. Indeed, as he watched, the door swung wide and a man, back turned toward him, sauntered away from it into the lighted room. He took a seat at a long table. Four other men about the table were visible, but all remained motionless. Wentworth continued his advance until he stood in that lighted doorway and saw the whole table. Its head was occupied by Yvonne Musette.

The hands of every one of the men were in sight on the table and none held a gun. Yvonne's hands were visible, too. She held a fountain pen poised over a sheet of paper that was half-covered with her writing. She smiled jauntily at the *Spider* as he came slowly over the sill. He was wary for trickery and stepped immediately clear of the doorway so that he should not be taken from behind. This was nothing that he had expected, this apparent abject surrender, but he stood, confidently smiling, with the vicious snout of the machine gun sweeping those white-faced men about the table. There was no mistaking their terror. The sweat of fear beaded their foreheads and its power was palsying their clenched hands. Only the woman seemed fearless, her red lips curved in mockery. Wentworth's eyes went beyond the table. He was covered from no doorway, nor hidden window.

Yvonne got to her feet still with that mocking smile on her lips. She toyed with the pen in her tapering small hands.

"Please, M'seur *Spider*," she said, "do you give quarter when your prisoners surrendaire?"

Wentworth's attention focused on the fountain pen in her hands and a tension gripped all his muscles. Like lightning, his machine gun's muzzle swung about toward the woman, but he knew even as he moved that he was too late. A queer, hoarse cry sprang to his lips. He saw powder flame blaze from the end of the fountain pen and that flame set fire to his brain. Great red and white lights exploded within his skull. He thought, I

knew I would curse myself for not killing her. She shot
me with a fountain pen pistol. After that,
nothingness. . . .

As Yvonne Musette was Wentworth's last conscious
thought, so the sense of her nearness was the first thing
in his mind when he began to recover. He became
aware of her voice, imploring at first, then raging. She
was shouted down by a man. Wentworth moved his
hands gently and found them bound, found, also, that
all his clothing had been stripped from his upper body.
He shifted his legs a little and they were naked, too,
and bound. He opened his eyes, then—no need to pretend further—and looked into a circle of men's hating
faces. Yvonne was outside the circle, struggling to get
in, sobbing now.

"Please, please let me keel him," she begged.
"Can't you understan'? He keel Oscaire and he keel
Tommy Barkaire, too. It ees my righ' to keel him!"

There was the sound of a blow, and a man with the
mocking voice said: "If you don't shut up, Yvonne,
I'll have to do something about it." He spoke very
gently, but with a fierce enjoyment half concealed in
his tones. Yvonne's voice broke into French, cursing
violently, then stopped suddenly. Wentworth studied
the man who had spoken. He was six feet three or four,
with a narrow head topped by smooth, black hair, his
whole body extremely thin. His face was lean, in character with the general skinniness of his body, and it
held a wolfish look when he smiled. There was something about the eyes, too, so wide open that the whites
almost showed above the iris. . . .

Wentworth said slowly, "How are you, Peterson?
I scarcely know whether to welcome or resent your
protection. . . ."

The wolfish smile drew up the thin man's lip corners
tautly. "Greetings, *Spider*! It would be much better for
you, I imagine, if you resented it." He squatted on his
heels so he could look into Wentworth's face more
closely. There was gloating in his wide open eyes. "So

that you will be better able to judge, I'll explain just what's in store for you. You will know from the fact that we have stripped you, and by my reprimand of Yvonne, that we intend to keep you prisoner for a while. You are so neat in your escapes, *Spider*, that I have devised a special prison for you—but more of that a little later.

"Meantime—" the man's face opened in his grin again—"meantime we are going to send word to El Gaucho again—through the newspapers so that there will be no slip-up. We are going to tell him that we have the *Spider* and are holding him prisoner for his disposal. What do you think El Gaucho will do to you, eh, *Spider*?"

Wentworth lay quite still, the smile on his diguised face sinister and ugly. "That's very nice of you," he said softly. "That's just what I've been waiting for— to meet El Gaucho!"

Peterson laughed and his mirth, like his speaking voice, sounded gentle. "But not the way you will meet him, *Spider*. This Gaucho is a murdering madman from all I can hear and he won't be too pleasant with you." He stared at Wentworth speculatively. "Too bad you won't be around to see the fun. Can you imagine, *Spider,* the Gaucho taking New York like he took Jackson City this afternoon? Looting every bank in town; smacking down the police; burning the houses that get in his way. By God, *Spider,* think of New York on fire! You may see that before long, when El Gaucho comes . . . Only I forgot. *Pardon* my laughter. *You* won't see it."

He straightened and, at his signal, two men lifted the *Spider*, one at this shoulders and one at his feet, and carried him, staggering, into a hall and along that to another door. Wentworth saw that he was still in the basement athletic club which he had entered to destroy these same criminals. Then, police had not heard the shooting? The gun explosions must have been muffled by more than merely being underground. Well, it did

53

not matter. Apparently the soundproofing had been adequate. . . .

Yvonne's voice broke out sharply again. "Do you know that this *Spider* killed eleven of our men?" she cried hoarsely. "Eleven men here tonight!"

"I've been told," said Peterson lazily, "that the Gaucho has ways of taking care of such men. Now shut up, Yvonne!"

Wentworth was taken through a short hall into a tiled room with a small swimming pool, really nothing more than a plunge. He was thrust painfully into a chair and straps and ropes wound about him until they cut into the flesh. Wentworth maintained a curious smile throughout the entire proceedings.

"You see," explained Peterson, "you have *quite* a reputation for escapes. Still, I don't believe that you will be able to get out of this one. The chair is heavily weighted and you will be put in water up to your chin. The water may loosen the ropes a little, but there are handcuffs and leather belts in addition to those. You get the idea?"

The *Spider* nodded pleasantly. "It should be quite effective," he murmured politely. "May I congratulate you on your arrangements?"

Peterson bowed, but there was a slightly worried look in his eyes. It was as if the *Spider's* nonchalance had given Peterson the idea of some secret resource. Roughly, he searched Wentworth's body for some hidden implement of escape, but he found nothing. There was nothing to find. Peterson stepped back finally, satisfied.

"There will be no guard," he said. "I think that will be safer."

"It really must be quite a reputation I have," Wentworth murmured.

At Peterson's signal, four of the men caught up the chair and held it over the edge of the pool, began slowly to lower it toward the surface. The water was chill and its first shock raced up through Wentworth's legs from his feet. He smiled up at Peterson.

"Come on in," he said, "the water's fine . . . after you get used to it!"

Peterson's wolfish smile lifted his mouth corners. He said nothing and the chair dipped lower into the water. It washed about Wentworth's thighs now, and something that was colder than the water was in his breast. Its name was despair. He knew how well Peterson had planned. The first move to escape from a chair was to throw the chair to the floor, so as to change the stress on the ropes. If he tried that in the water. . . .

"I hope you've calculated the depth of the water well," he called cheerfully, "I doubt if a dead *Spider* would appeal to El Gaucho."

"Tried it out on myself," Peterson assured him and lifted a hand to his throat. "Right up to here!"

Wentworth drew in a swift breath. If Peterson were telling the truth. . . . ! He felt the water wash his throat and still the chair was sinking. He stretched his chin upward. His entrance into the plunge had caused a small wave that rippled up the other end of the pool, then back again. It slapped him in the mouth. Water that came up to Peteron's larynx would be over Wentworth's chin, lapping at his mouth! He would have to stretch his neck, strain his head backward to escape drowning!

Finally, Wentworth felt the legs of the chair touch bottom. His head was tilted far back and his mouth was just clear of the water. When the small wave rippled back again, it covered his mouth and nostrils and ears. Peterson stooped at the side of the pool and splashed a handful of water into the *Spider's* face.

"Why don't you say something nonchalant now, *Spider*?" he jeered, sloshed water again.

Wentworth caught a gasped breath just before the spray hit him, held it while that wave covered his mouth. Presently it would be still and Wentworth could breathe without interruption. As long as his neck could stand the strain. . . .

Deliberately, Wentworth lowered his head. When it

was in normal position, the water came above his eyes. He kept his eyes just above the surface and looked into Peterson's face. Without malevolence, without any expression at all except mild amusement. Peterson cursed, jerked to his feet and shouted at the others about him.

"Get out of here! Go on, get out!" They moved sluggishly, glancing back in fascination at the black head that just topped the water. Wentworth lifted his head and sucked in a deep breath, lowered his chin again so that his eyes were just above water. There was a rigid calm in his face, but the chill that was all about his body was creeping into his heart—into his very soul. How long were they going to keep him, immersed like this? Until El Gaucho could come east? But that might be days! Something like panic thrust through Wentworth like a sword. He jerked his head back, straining head and nostrils above the water, breathing shallowly and fast. Better to drown himself at once than wait for the inevitable exhaustion. . . .

Bitterly, Wentworth fought for calmness. He was not, he instructed himself, concerned with personal survival. What he must do was to live to triumph over El Gaucho and prevent the diastrous raid that marauder would certainly make on New York as soon as he accepted their invitation to come and lead them. The *Spider* had no personal life, no personal rights to die. Strangely, this thought steadied him, enabled him to continue the slow rhythm of his breathing, the resting of his neck by the slow forward and backward bending, forward until his eyes were just above the surface, backward until his mouth was clear, forward . . . back . . . forward. . . .

There was a chance, he instructed himself, that Barker and Nita together might effect a rescue. Barker was going to see Nita this morning, perhaps already was with her—Wentworth had no way of telling how long he had been unconscious. When the newspapers blazed forth the news that the *Spider* was held captive for El Gaucho, Barker would know where he was.

Wentworth told himself that over and over again, but despair was in his breast and his thoughts did not raise its cold clamminess. . . .

Backward . . . forward . . . backward . . . forward. . . . Wentworth stiffened, his eyes widening. There, at the opposite end of the pool stood Yvonne Musette. She was smiling with that half-sullen lift of her red lips. She bent down, as Wentworth watched, to a brass disc in the tiling at her feet, opened it and reached inside. Instantly, Wentworth became aware of a bubbling of the water just at the surface below where she stood. Yvonne had turned on the water in the pool! Why, damn it, within minutes, it would cover his mouth, crawl toward his nostrils. . . .

Yvonne straightened, smiling more merrily now than before. Then she sauntered toward the end where his chair had been placed. "The water do not come in too fast," she explained, happily. "You will have time to t'ink of the reasons why I keel you, before you finally die. . . ."

She bent close, spat into Wentworth's face.

"Have your good time, Yvonne," the *Spider* said gently. "The reckoning is coming." He breathed deeply, submerged to his eyes again, watched her with a calm confidence he had difficulty putting into his gaze.

Yvonne laughed and sauntered from the room, hips swaying, her whole body gesturing mockery . . . Wentworth gazed at that bubble of onrushing water at the other end. At most, he could not hold out longer than an hour. After that. . . .

The *Spider's* jaw clenched until muscles bunched along the margin of his face. He closed his eyes. There was a faintness within him. He thought: *Death!* He thought: *This is the end!* He thought: *Nita. . . . !*

CHAPTER SIX

To the Rescue!

Dawn had come and gone. The sun was high. Still sleepless, Nita van Sloan lounged on the silken cushions of the long, low seat before the huge studio window that looked out over the river traffic of the Hudson. Her eyes were unseeing. Two hours now since Dick Wentworth had phoned to say that he was beginning another attack. Two hours . . . and no further word.

She looked down at the slim whiteness of her hands and her eyes were vacant, staring. During the night, those eyes had brimmed with tears, for it was in the silent, dark hours that the fears she never allowed Dick to see arose to smite down the intrepid courage that dwelt in her slim body; it was during the night that the frustration of their love harried her most. And then it was that she quivered with the fear of death . . . Dick Wentworth's death.

That was at night. With the sun something strange and fierce came into Nita van Sloan's soul. Dick had called briefly and she had bade him be careful. Nita threw back her head, so that the sweet, long line of her throat was taut, and laughed. Dear God, the *Spider* be careful! And now she was waiting, waiting. Always she must wait. She sprang to her feet and moved about the room, a slim, lovely girl in her full-cut lounging pajamas in maroon velvet. Her white hands moved restlessly, shifting a vase on the mantel above the fireplace, plumping a cushion in a chair.

Always she was anxious for Dick's safety, but this night there was a new depth to her terror. Dick had called uselessly. That meant he felt it, too; that he had wanted once more to hear her voice, perhaps for a last time. . . . Nita hurled from her the pillow she was plumping, stood tautly facing the doorway of her home. Dick had assigned her a task to perform, to take care of Tom Barker, the grandson of dear old Professor Brownlee. But, good Lord, why didn't he come? She could do anything except wait. . . .

It was half past eight when the doorbell rang. Calmness dropped upon Nita's tortured being like soothing oil. Her hand dropped to the pocket of her pajamas, touched lingeringly the stubby automatic that rested there. She thought it would be Tom Barker ringing, but the enemies of the *Spider* had struck at her before now. She went swiftly to the kitchen, and allowed a massive Great Dane to bound out. He frisked like a puppy, tongue lolling out over cruel fangs.

Nita said, "Quiet, Apollo. On guard!"

The dog came to her side, great shoulder against her thigh and she dropped her left hand to his big head. Together they moved toward the front door. She flicked aside the peephole cover.

Frank eyes under tousled hair looked into hers, a sun-tanned face, a smile that showed glistening teeth. Nita opened the door. The man—he was little more than a boy—held out a newspaper toward her, then let her see into the palm of his browned hand. A white card lay there, and on it—the seal of the *Spider*.

Nita swept open the door. "Back, Apollo," she ordered softly and took the boy into her gay studio room. The boy could not resist a wondering look about the place, the cool green linen that draped a big window; and Nita. . . . He stared at her. If the vigil had shadowed her eyes, it had only deepened their violet hue.

Her chestnut curls made a clustering frame for the perfect oval of her face. Her lips were . . . kind.

He shuffled his feet. "Morning, ma'am. I guess you know who I came from. Is Mr. Wentworth here?"

"No. Why do you ask?"

He pointed to the seal which he had given to Nita.

"*He* said Mr. Wentworth would help me, and you'd know what I was to do."

Nita studied him carefully, and for a moment the boy lost his awareness of her beauty. Something that seemed suddenly grim and tight-lipped about her made him gaze with doubt and surprise. In a flash then, that impression was gone and again it was a gracious woman who motioned him to a chair.

"Sit down, won't you?" she said. "You're Tom Barker, of course. Mr. Wentworth is out of the city just now. What can I . . . ?"

Tom Barker dropped into a chair, tossing the newspaper to a little table beside him. It spread open and black headlines shouted at Nita. Even the perfect control which the *Spider's* schooling had given her was not proof against what she saw. Those eyes widened and her words choked in her throat. She snatched the newspaper and there was a tremor in her hands that rustled the sheets.

She whispered, "Oh God! Oh, God!"

The headlines swam before her eyes, tilted crazily, but that could not change their phrasing:

GANG CAPTURES *SPIDER*!
FAMOUS KILLER HOSTAGE FOR
EL GAUCHO!
CRIMINALS' SPOKESMAN DECLARES
THAT NEW YORK UNDERWORLD
INVITES TERROR TO RULE
IN EAST!

Nita's eyes went over the story. She forced them to, though she scarcely could grasp the import with her dazed mind. She was aware of Barker saying something—

"What is it?" she asked.

"It's hell, ma'am. I was going to show it to Mr. Wentworth. That *Spider* is a fine guy. Got me out of a jam . . ."

The words faded from Nita's mind. She drove the shocked incredulity from her heart and read, her face white, her eyes wide. The text of the Underworld's invitation to El Gaucho was there. The bandit leader of the West was assured of their ability and willingness to throw New York City wide open to him; he would have all the loot he desired; the *Spider* was being held for some of his choicest tortures.

Another column told of the pursuit of El Gaucho after the last of his raids. Two automobiles loaded with police had crashed into a pit and set off a dynamite mine which had blown them to pieces. A man had been found dead, arms and legs torn from his body in some unimaginable way. . . .

Nita crushed the papers in her hands, staring over Barker's head. "Damn them!" she said huskily. "Damn them! *They shall not!*"

Barker would not have known the voice for the rippling charming one he had heard a few moments before. Nita tossed the paper to the table as if it were unclean, leaving the boy to stare after her as she strode to a telephone, snarled Dick's number into the instrument. She must not let herself think of Dick, but only of smashing through to rescue him. Barker would know where to go.

"Ram Singh!" her voice was sharp and imperative. "You and Jackson come here at once. Buy a paper on the way. Yes, at once! Yes, Ram Singh, the *sahib!*"

Her face was set as she came back to confront Barker. "I'm going to the *Spider's* rescue," she said, her voice flat, incisive. "Mr. Wentworth, your grandfather's friend, is a close associate of the *Spider,* although the fact is not known. I am trusting you with that information so you will understand the necessity of telling

61

me everything you know. You see if . . . Mr. Wentworth . . . were here, he would go to the rescue of the *Spider* at once." Nita's voice faltered. It was as if the lie she told wrung her heart. *If Mr. Wentworth were here.* . . . She made herself go on. "I have called two of Mr. Wentworth's men. You see? You understand? I want to know everything about where you left the *Spider,* all that he said and why and what, quickly . . . quickly . . . !"

Barker stared at her, swallowed. "You'll excuse me . . . those are mighty bad men. Tough eggs. It's no job for a lady. It . . ."

Something oddly like a shadow of the *Spider's* grim face touched the features of her lovely face.

"Talk!" ordered Nita van Sloan.

Tom Barker talked, short explanations constantly interrupted by her incessant, "Yes, yes . . . and then?" Two other men entered. He noted subconsciously that they entered with their own keys. One stood on each side of the doorway, a lean, dour Hindu, his burning eyes straight before him, turbaned head held high. There was a tautness in all his powerful body and there was a curved knife at his belt.

The other was a wide-shouldered man who bore himself with military erectness. His face was square, the jaws wide and knotted with muscles. There was a grimness in both their faces. Nita's head pulled about toward the latter man.

"You read the papers, Jackson?"

"Yes, Miss Nita," Jackson's voice was clipped, had a hard ring. "I read them to Ram Singh, too. What are the orders?"

"A machine gun, Jackson, Three drums of ammunition. Two automatics around." Nita's voice was as clipped and sharp as his own. There was a lift to it now, an urgency. "Fix thirty-eights for me, I can handle them a little better."

Jackson snapped a salute. "You know anything about the major, ma'am?" Jackson had been Wentworth's sergeant during the war. He still preferred to use the service titles.

Nita said flatly, "I only know what I read in the papers. Barker, on with the story."

"That's about all, ma'am," Barker said slowly, watching the two grim-faced men through a curtained door across the room.

"The *Spider* left me. I don't think there's any doubt about where he was going. I don't know whether they kept him there or not. . . ."

Nita nodded, went out through another doorway and returned in an incredibly short time dressed in a dark, close-fitting suit, a tight hat over her eyes. Ram Singh and Jackson came back. Jackson carried over his arm a lap-robe that bulged strangely.

"Orders, Miss Nita?" Jackson's blue eyes were hard and sharp on Nita's, but it was obvious from his manner that he was devoted to her—that he would follow her orders to the death. The muscles kept working along the bulge of his wide jaws.

"I'll give them on the way," Nita said crisply. "Ram Singh, take us to Forty-fifth and Sixth Avenue."

Ram Singh flashed his white teeth in a smile, bowing, sweeping cupped hands to his forehead in a salaam.

"Han, missie sahib!" His hand dropped to the knife at his side. "We fight then?"

"We fight!"

"Say, I want to be in on this," Barker exclaimed.

Nita nodded. "You are in!"

It was a silent company that trooped to the car, a heavy low-slung sedan with a motor that throbbed with power. Once under way Nita spoke concisely, telling them what Barker had said in half the number of words.

"As soon as we enter the building, Ram Singh and Barker and I, Jackson, I want you to drive the car to a point near the entrance, wait there five minutes with the machine gun, then come in. I don't think there's much doubt we will be ambushed. You're to shoot us out of it."

Jackson's lips slitted in a grin. "Yes, Miss Nita."

Nita turned to Barker. "Can you use a revolver or automatic?" she asked quietly.

Barker nodded eagerly, "Either one, ma'am. I used to be pretty good shot."

Nita reached into a compartment of the car and drew out a thirty-eight revolver. Barker took it, handled it expertly with its muzzle pointed downward. Then, looking at her, he shoved it in his coat pocket.

"Not going to call the police?"

Nita smiled slightly. "I don't think that would be a good idea."

She sat looking straight before her then while the car was tooled expertly through traffic. It was still a little early for the automobile traffic rush, though subways would be jammed. The building she planned to attack, too, would be nearly deserted. Elevator operators would be working, of course. A few early arrivals . . . Nita's mind turned from the battle ahead to Dick. He would count on some such raid, certainly, for he knew that Barker was coming to her and that she would glean all his information. If he could, he would smash through to help. . . .

Nita's eyes felt dry and feverish. Her hand strayed to her purse, to her coat pocket. Both her light guns were ready. There was a tension throughout her body: a slight, tight smile on her lips. They would win through because they *must*. . . .

Barker's voice broke into her thoughts. "Look here, ma'am. I've got a scheme. They know me and think I'm with them. Let me go ahead. I'll find out where the *Spider* is and then. . . ."

Nita asked gently, "And then what?"

Barker looked downcast. "You don't reckon they'd let me get out again?"

Nita shook her head, but there was another thought in her mind. She was as inclined to trust this boy as Dick was. He had come to her alone, without gangster trailers apparently. But there was always a chance that he was playing some obscure game. God knew there had been enough treachery. . . . Ram Singh drew the car to a halt, sprang to the pavement and Jackson took his place behind the wheel. Nita's doubts and fears left her. Her hands went once more to her hidden guns.

"Five minutes, Jackson," she commanded softly.

Jackson grinned at her. "I'll shave that, ma'am, if I hear shooting?"

Nita nodded and walked up the street, Barker beside her, Ram Singh just behind, walking with the long, free swing of the mountain Sikhs from whom he sprang, his eyes intent, teeth just showing between his lips. His hand strayed ever and again to the knife at his girdle. There were two other knives hidden under his tunic that he used for throwing and the knife at his side he never drew except to shed human blood. It was curved and its inner edge was razor-sharp. A stroke would disembowel a man neatly. . . .

The doors of the building were wide, hooked back to the walls. Two men lounged about the foyer within, talking idly to the elevator starter. When Nita and Barker walked in, they looked about quickly, then turned back to their conversation. Nita's hand gestured behind her and Ram Singh fell back, halting just outside the outer doorway, while Nita and Barker walked straight toward the stairway that led downward.

The starter called, "Who did you want, madam? That's a men's club down there."

Nita ignored him and Barker fell in behind her as she went downward. Nita felt him hesitate when he saw the two men who had been talking with the starter move in their direction, heads lowered a little, hands rising to underarm guns.

"Ram Singh will take care of them," Nita told Barker.

The stair descended along three sides of a square, three short flights downward. When Nita reached the middle of the second flight, the two men above began to move downward, too. As soon as they were out of sight of the foyer, their guns snapped into their hands.

"Just wait there, baby!" one of them called gruffly.

Nita turned a cold, set face toward them, saw Ram Singh come softly around the corner. His knife was not in his hand. He would not draw except to kill, but that knife could leap into action as quickly as a man could squeeze a trigger. Nita waited and Ram Singh came softly, swiftly downward.

One of the men whirled about abruptly when Ram Singh was two steps above him. A startled cry burst from his throat and he threw up his gun. He would have done better to drop it and cry for mercy. As his weapon nosed up, Ram Singh's arm crossed his body. The knife flashed from its sheath, speared forward. With a gurgling, startled cry, the gunman collapsed. Ram Singh, standing high, had been forced to strike for the throat. But even as he stabbed, he sprang forward and the second gunman, whirling to face this unsuspected danger, caught the knife in his belly.

The starter was at the head of the steps now, staring down upon the white steps that were now smeared with crimson. Nita presented an automatic. "Come down here!" she called sharply.

Nita's eyes avoided the dead men on the stairs. Nausea was tugging at her stomach, and she felt a faintness sweep toward her brain. But she did not waver on her feet. The gun in her hand was steady. The elevator starter trembled. Ram Singh started toward him, the red knife in his hand and the man turned and ran, screaming. Nita did not fire. She looked down at the gun in her hand.

"He hadn't done anything," she murmured dully. "I couldn't shoot him."

Barker thrust her sharply on the shoulder and below them, from the basement, a gun barked twice thunderously. Nita dropped to her knee on the step and Barker crouched behind the marble railing. Ram Singh's right arm swept down and a streak of glinting, steely light flashed down the stairs. From behind the corner of the wall at the foot of the steps, a man staggered into view, both hands plucking at his throat from which the brass-bound hilt of a knife protruded. His knees caved and he slammed hard on his face.

Ram Singh came down the stairs softly, lifting Nita to her feet with one brawny hand. His stabbing knife was back in its scabbard. In his left hand, he held a second straight-bladed throwing knife.

"Wah! Missie sahib," his harsh, nasal voice rasped. "These are not warriors whom we fight. They are . . ."

The ripping batter of machine gun bullets, slashing down from behind choked his voice in his throat. He blundered down the steps, falling. Nita's gun spat this time and up there, where two men already had died, another slumped down, his weapon stilled. Nita's paleness now was not the pallor of faintness but of anger. She crouched beside Ram Singh who was striving valiantly to drag his wounded body up from the platform where he had fallen. There was a running red stain on his back.

"Wah! Missie sahib," he whispered, "it is nothing, nothing at all! In a moment. . . ." Ram Singh slumped down unconscious on the stairs. There were more guns above now, spatting bullets. Nita heard Barker's gun spit and she opened up with a slow, deliberate fire. For all that, lead began to whistle uncomfortably close, to snick flecks of plaster from the walls.

"You run, ma'am," whispered Barker, "I'll hold them."

Nita snapped a shot at a gun hand that showed itself over the marble railing above, saw that hand stiffen bloodily and withdraw. She whispered back. "You're forgetting Jackson."

For a dozen breaths, there was silence above, then a thunderous splash of sound washed through the hall-way, revolvers spitting and the heavier, overwhelming chatter of a machine gun.

Nita's eyes were agate hard. One hand was on Ram

Singh's shoulder; the other was clasping her automatic. She patted the Hindu's shoulder; then she sprang erect, went down the stairs swiftly.

"That's Jackson," she said. "Come on, Barker."

It would have to be swift and deadly now, or the police would crash into the battle, and all would be lost, even if they had rescued Wentworth by then. She pounded down the steps, whirled the corner of the hall where a man lay dead with Ram Singh's knife in his throat. She sprang clear of the wall and instantly her automatic began to speak. Four men were coming down the hall in a bunch, three with automatics, the fourth with a machine gun. One of them staggered and fell from the impact of Nita's lead.

A bullet burned Nita's throat and she threw herself down on her face, still firing. A second man sat down suddenly on the floor, arms doubled over his belly. But the machine gun was being lifted now, the man's face behind it was debonair, smiling beneath a smooth, black cap of hair. He was well over six feet, and there was enjoyment in his every gesture.

Barker suddenly threw down his gun and raced toward the man. "Don't shoot, Peterson! Don't shoot, I'm with you!"

He was directly in front of the machine gun now, between Nita and that deadly muzzle.

Nita lifted her automatic deliberately, her lips drawing back from her teeth. The coward, the dirty traitor! Barker's friendliness had all been trickery. In the instant she lifted her weapon to shoot him down, Barker was hurled aside by one of the gunmen. Nita sprang to her feet, firing quick shots, and before the machine gun could target on her again, she flung herself across the hall, took cover behind the corner of the steps. Jackson was on the platform above her.

"What's up, Miss Nita?" he whispered. "Ram Singh's bad hit."

"Barker turned traitor," Nita snapped, "turn your machine gun around that corner and. . . ."

A hammering hail of bullets clawed the edge off the corner, sent lead ricocheting up the marble balustrade, chipping the steps. Nita shrank back from it, reloading her automatic rapidly. There was blazing anger in her mind and despair in her soul. How could they fight their way through that leaden rain before police came? It would do no good for Jackson to attempt an attack around that corner. He would be sieved with lead . . .

Jackson caught Nita by the shoulder, dragged her up to where he stood with the machine gun braced at ready.

"Ram Singh can walk if you brace him, Miss Nita," he said sharply. "Better help him up the stairs."

Nita stood crouched behind Jackson with her gun ready. The lead continued to splat about the corner, to whine off the balustrade. She heard what Jackson said, but the words didn't register in her brain. There was only one thought in her brain, could be only one. To get down those steps and reach Dick, snatch him from this trap.

"Quickly, Miss Nita," Jackson's voice rang out. "Get Ram Singh out of this!"

Nita said, "No, no!" It was under her breath, scarcely audible. She repeated it again, "No, no. We must save Dick. *We must!*"

Jackson's gun hammered and Nita saw the muzzle of a machine gun beaten back from the corner of the wall. It spat a few bullets but they went wide.

"For God's sake, Miss Nita," Jackson said hoarsely. "You know I wouldn't desert the major if there was a chance. Retreat and we'll try again. There are only two of us now. . . ." The chatter of his gun drowned his words and even above it came the high weird whine of police sirens.

Nita staggered up the steps. Bullets sang about her, but she did not notice them. Her mind was blank. They had tried to save Dick and failed. She stooped above Ram Singh, put a hand under his arm, dragged it across her shoulders. The Hindu fought his way to his feet, leaning heavily upon Nita.

"We . . . retreat?"

"We retreat," Nita mumbled dully. She saw Jackson backing toward them swiftly, the machine gun before him. Once more that vicious snout poked around the corner of the wall and once more Jackson hammered it with bullets. Nita felt lead pluck at her skirt, but scarcely heeded. Why, good God, they were leaving Dick back there, leaving him to be murdered! She stopped on the stairway and Ram Singh reeled, braced a great hand against the wall.

"It is . . . wise, missie sahib," he gasped. "This way we live. . . . to fight again!"

Nita was dully aware of screams above her in the hallway, of the louder shrilling of the police sirens. Nita heard Jackson curse.

"Down!" he shouted. "My gun's empty!"

Nita turned stiffly to stare down the stairway, saw Jackson crouched to fit in another drum of ammunition. Down below, the tall, smiling man whom Barker had called Peterson leaped clear with the machine gun's muzzle lifted toward them. Nita snatched up her automatic and fired with the same motion. It was instinctive—a reflex of her body, for her brain was stupid with grief.

Down in the basement. Peterson reeled backward against the wall, a bloody smear across his temple. The machine gun dropped from his arms and he rolled along the wall, his hands groping, then flopped down on his face. Jackson sprang up the stairs, threw a powerful arm about Ram Singh and they went swiftly up to the foyer. Jackson fired a short burst into the ceiling and men who clustered there fearfully turned and fled. Women screamed shrilly. Jackson released his hold on Ram Singh and ran for the door.

Moments later, the giant Daimler, mighty engine humming, was at the door. Ram Singh pulled himself free, flung into the front seat while Nita sprang into the rear.

The car leaped forward. Blazed through traffic . . . vanished.

Back at the scene of battle, two men came sedately upstairs from the athletic club to meet the police. They said all they knew was that some people had started firing when they tried to come up the stairs. No, they didn't know those people. All that plaster and the holes? They really didn't know. The police sergeant looked glumly at the evidence of considerable shooting and walked through what he believed to be the entire club establishment and went out.

"Lay off," he growled to an earnest young policeman who continued to buzz the bystanders. "Lay off! Don't cha know who owns this club?"

"What of it?" indignantly demanded the rookie policeman.

The sergeant flipped a weary hand at him. "On your way." He extended the gesture to the gathering crowd. "G'wan. Nothin' happened. Just a coupla friends playing tag, see? On your way!"

In the Daimler, purring smoothly down Riverside Drive, a wild-eyed young woman stared straight before her.

"I'll kill him," she said flatly. "The next time I see him, I'll kill him. The traitor! To think that he would desert to the enemies of the *Spider*. . . ."

Jackson kept his eyes straight ahead, but there was a grim, hard set to his broad shoulders. Ram Singh leaned back weakly against the cushions. There was a doctor friend of Wentworth's who would care for his wounds. . . .

Nita's head sagged forward. She lifted her hands to her face. She had failed, failed. She was Dick's only hope and she had failed him. . . . After a while, her shoulders began to jerk in rhythm with her sobbing. . . .

CHAPTER SEVEN

The Traitor

It was very quiet in the room of the pool. There was only the soft whisper of the water to be heard. In that room, two pairs of steady, heavy-lidded eyes stared fixidly into each other. One pair of eyes belonged to a man and was just above the waterline in the pool. The man's head tilted back at regular intervals of a half minute, so that the nose and the mouth were clear for the space of two breaths. Then the face sank until water crossed the bridge of the nose. The eyes never ceased to hold the others.

The other eyes were those of a too sleek, too lithe, woman. She stood at the foot of the pool. In her hand there was a gun, held as steadily as though it rested on a support. The man in the water was so near exhaustion that only the exercise of the supernatural will, that was the *Spider's* strength, held him from sinking to his death. Flashes of red flickered before his eyes, and a wave of black oblivion rose again and again. He fought it back doggedly.

Nita! It was that one word which brought up Wentworth's head against the shrieks of tortured nerves and lungs and muscles. But at the back of his mind a giant hammer seemed to beat constantly with "*finished—finished—finished*" as its refrain. Hours of this slow lift and bowing of his head that must not cease.

Yvonne gloated at his discomfort. "You keel my Oscaire. I shoot you for that. You keel Tom Barkaire—I kill you again for that. I lofe my Oscaire and I could lofe that Tom Barkaire. Now that police come 'ere I mus' keel you wit' the gun instead of wait for the so nice water to do it for me. . . ."

She leveled the gun. The *Spider's* eyes never wavered. *Here it comes, that thing you have escaped so often, now, at last,* said that hammering in his head, and something monstrous and chill flooded all of his body. He felt it as a thing alive, as a cold breath from another world invading his vitals. As in the gaze of all men about to die, and knowing it, there came a terrible power, a ghastly, weird beauty of unblinking, fixed, enlarged eyes. Many a murderer has been at least momentarily halted by such eyes of a victim. Even the hardened woman felt an instant's shock. It stayed her hand.

At that moment, someone began tapping along the wall of the room, the wall that showed no doorway anywhere. Yvonne's eyes turned toward the sound and the *Spider,* desperately braced against the unconsciousness which would long since have struck down any lesser man, almost slipped into the blackness through sheer relief from the pressure of her cruel, mocking eyes.

Beyond the wall, a voice began calling, a voice the *Spider* could not rouse himself to answer:

"*Spider—Spider*—it's Barker! *Spider, can you hear me?* It's Tom!"

Yvonne gave a strangled cry, ran to open a secret sliding door. She met the man with uplifted arms. The *Spider* saw the gun clasped between the shoulders of Tom Barker as her arms went about his neck.

"Honey bunch," Barker half-laughed, "You sure got sudden ways. Glad to see me, huh?"

"I thought *he* keel you. W'ere you been?"

"Oh, around. What's happened here, girlie? The boys blow out and leave you holding the fort?"

73

"The poleece—but first, some othairs—very much shooting. It was better I keel this *Spider*."

"I see." Barker walked over and looked down at the *Spider*. The *Spider* tilted back his head and looked up, breathing gaspingly. He clung to the remnants of his consciousness. Friend or foe, this Tom Barker? Wentworth did not know. The water whispered softly. He realized that in a few minutes more it would be impossible, even with his steely will, to keep his nose out of it. It was already impossible to lift his mouth above its level. Barker looked down, speculatively, seemingly without a trace of interest.

"Going to shoot him, eh?" he mused. "El Gaucho will be nice and pleased, I don't think, to have it spread all over the papers that he has the redoubtable *Spider* here waiting for him and then, when he comes, find that someone bumped off his special game for him."

"I don't care. I keel him. He keel my Oscaire."

"Here, here," Barker bantered, "I thought it was *me* that you had a crush on."

Yvonne's face had hardened and she moved away from Barker to the end of the pool which faced the *Spider*. Barker said seriously: "Listen here, baby, you'll get yourself in an awful mess doing that."

He sidled cautiously toward her, and realized suddenly that a small door immediately behind her had opened. He pointed to it then sprang to throw his big arms about her. She shot but her aim was wild and she turned, spitting like a wild cat, only to have the soft-spoken Peterson, a bloody smear across his forehead, smile maddeningly at her. It was he who had slipped through the door. Barker gave Yvonne to Peterson's long, powerful arms.

"Just what do you think you are up to, my darling?" laughed Peterson. "Going to take away one of our best reasons for getting in touch with El Gaucho? You will have to be disciplined, little devil." He looked at Barker. "Thanks for coming to my aid out there in the hall. That dame of the *Spider's* had a bead on my head and she'd have dropped me cold meat if you hadn't butted in.''

The *Spider's* eyes shot open and he made another exhausted effort to keep from sinking beneath the water. *Nita*—he had not even heard the shooting. But now he knew. She had come to rescue him and been driven back. Now his last hope was gone. He felt muscles relaxing throughout his body. That dread blackness was very near. . . .

As if the *Spider* had spoken, Peterson turned to him, still holding the squirming Yvonne easily, as though she were a rag doll; ''Yes, *Spider*, that girl of yours came with two men. They made Barker show them the place, but just as soon as he could he let me know he was with us. Some piece of fire, that lady—but all nice girls are like that.'' He smiled down at the raging Yvonne, then suddenly threw her from him on the slack of his arms, so that she slammed against the wall, gasped, and slumped to the floor unconscious. Not by the flick of an eyelid did Peterson show awareness of her.

Now there were other men in the room, but The *Spider*, his ears full of water, the hammering in his ears a vast, cosmic clash of doom, was too near death to heed or care. Nita had been driven back. All hope was gone. This was . . . the end . . .

''If you want to save The *Spider* for El Gaucho,'' said Barker, coolly, ''you'd better haul him out. Unless I'm mistaken, he'll be gone in another minute or two.''

Even as Barker spoke, the blackness triumphed at last. It rushed over Wentworth with a clap like a thunderous wave. His head sagged forward beneath the water so that only a scalp lock of black hair was awash on the surface.

Barker cried, ''Hey! Wait!'' He jumped into the water and lifted the *Spider's* face above the surface. ''You want him alive, Peterson?''

Peterson was scowling. ''Hell, no, I don't *want* him. But I got to have him for the Gauch'. Hold on, feller, and . . . Get in there, Scottie, and give him a hand. . . ."

They got The *Spider* loose finally and laid him out on the tiles. Barker left him then, wringing water out of his coat tails, out of the cuffs of his trousers. Peterson came around and grinned down while the man called Scottie poured whisky down Wentworth's throat, slapped his cheeks to restore circulation.

"Listen, Peterson," Barker said, "if you don't mind my saying so, we got to do some tall moving out of here. That bunch of flatfeet that was here a while ago may get frozen dogs because they're afraid of you big noises, but there's others, higher up, that will come around."

"You are all fools," Yvonne had staggered to her feet and stood, glowering. "You will regret that you make me angree!"

"Yes, darling," Peterson agreed. His face was bland but Yvonne shrank, turned pale and said nothing more. Barker laughed, and sauntered over to put an arm caressingly about her shoulders, whispered in her ear. A reluctant, vanity-stirred smile crept over Yvonne's mouth.

The *Spider* regained consciousness with the taste of whisky on his lips. He rolled his heavy eyelids up and saw the smiling face of Peterson bending over him.

"That's good, men," Peterson purred. "Got to get you up and out, m'lad. The cops will be here—some of the higher-ups are trampling over the bodies of our friends on the Force. Come on now, shake a leg—" The hands which heaved The *Spider* to his feet were strong and cruel. They shut down like pincers on the arms. A man in less superb condition than The Spider and so recently near death would have fainted at the pain. But although Peterson looked sideways under his cruel eyelids, he could not see even a quiver on the strange face of the man who already was beginning to walk almost firmly. The miracle of that recovery was so great that even the hardened men who ringed him around looked with half-superstitious awe at the *Spider*. Some of the fear with which his name had always been associated came over them. They threw his clothes upon him, fell back and left him to walk alone. His long black cape clung to him like a shroud; he was the color of putty—but, somehow, inexpressively terrible. His hands were bound tightly and the wrists swollen, he staggered as he walked, but hope and fierce rage sprang up in him.

His escape *was* a miracle. Belief in his mission, in the power of fate, flailing a great, protective sword above his head, made him radiate a confidence, a power which could actually be felt. Men fell back before him. But when he passed through the little, secret door at the back of the room, he would have fallen down the steps if Barker had not caught him. . . .

It was as the young man caught his elbow that The Spider was galvanized by a flash of hope, for those fingers pressed in a strange series of nips, holds and repeated pressures, rhythmic as breathing. It couldn't be, but . . . it was! *Morse code!* Barker was trying to give him some message!

Stairs went down steeply into a cellar. "Go ahead of me," Barker said impatiently, to the rest of them. "This guy can't walk easy and I'm damned if I'll carry him, he might throttle me."

The men all crowded past and again the fingers started their silent talk on Wentworth's arm. *I had to play it this way; Peterson had the lady covered*—The *Spider's* preternaturally keen senses were dulled. He found it hard to follow the unaccustomed signaling, but he got it finally and the hope that had burgeoned within him grew stronger. If one were on his side, he could achieve miracles. He used his elbow to press out a laborious message.

"Where are we going?"

He glanced sideways out of his eyes, saw Barker shaking his head. Well, it did not matter. With an ally in camp, he could conquer. Just now he needed rest

. . . rest . . . They left the building by way of a dark alley and entered two powerful cars. Wentworth relaxed and slept.

He awoke to find the cars rolling into Newark airport. He looked around. Peterson, seated beside him, was climbing out as an official strode to meet him. The gangster made no attempt to hide the gun in his hand; guns were in the other men's hands, too, and Wentworth peered about, saw that several more sedans had mysteriously fallen in behind them.

"Plane chartered by phone an hour ago," Peterson rasped. "Name? Does that matter? Conduct us to it and I'd like to have about two more."

The official, white as his collar, stuttered; "Th—th—there isn't—aren't—any others!"

"Oh, yes, there are," said Peterson, gently, "and if there are not, it will be extremely unfortunate for a number of people—not in my party, my dear fellow."

The frightened eyes of the airport agent, uncertainly standing beside the car, fell on the *Spider*, his hands now held in handcuffs. "You—you are officers?" the man stuttered. "Is—are you demanding these planes in the name of the law—for a prisoner?"

Peterson laughed gently. "For a prisoner, yes—for the law? Oh, no! For the outlaws!"

The *Spider* smiled bleakly. Peterson was enjoying himself and, since he had spoken, Wentworth was no longer interested in escape. Not for the present, at least. The sense of power was in his veins again. No doubt now as to the destination of Peterson and his gang. They flew to a rendezvous with El Gaucho! It was well. The *Spider* would rest and gather strength for the battle to come. . . .

A small cabin plane taxied up, the white, startled face of the pilot peering from the cockpit. One of the gang stood over him, a gun at the aviator's head. Barker and The *Spider*, Peterson and Scottie got in. The plane lumbered down the field, turned into the wind, got under way. Wentworth peered down at the field as it dropped away. The bitter, sardonic spirit of the *Spider,* which had held him until that moment, went away and Wentworth—who loved the sweetest woman in the world, and was neither sardonic nor bitter—thought strangely that it was as if he were really dead and were leaving Wentworth behind.

Barker seemed entirely indifferent toward the *Spider,* although he sat near him and whistled tonelessly. The heavy drone of the motors beat upon Wentworth's brain, numbing his exhausted sensibilities. He leaned his head back and slept. . . . He had no idea how much time had passed when a touch on his elbow awakened him. He looked about cautiously. Barker still gazed out of the window and whistled without tune. Peterson, ahead, dozed over a newspaper and, across the aisle, the man called Scottie, sandy-gray head bowed on his chest, was sleeping, too.

Barker looked toward Wentworth and, still whistling, bent as if to tie his shoelace and with a pocket knife he had palmed, sliced through the bonds about Wentworth's ankles. The *Spider* almost cried out for him to cease, that he did not wish to escape yet. They were headed for the spot where they would meet El Gaucho . . . then his eyes became crafty. It would be better to be free to act then, and he had a plan. . . .

Barker reached across the aisle then, slipped a small key into the handcuffs on Wentworth's wrists and tried to turn it. It rasped, make a snapping sound and—

"Put 'em up, boys," said Scottie, lifting the head that had seemed to sleep. Wentworth's gaze jerked that way and he looked into the black eye of a leveled gun. "Damn it, put 'em up. Didn't I tell you, Peterson? I told you this guy was a double-crosser." The gun was steady, the man's evil squinting face alight. "Shall I bump 'em?"

"By no means, my dear chap," Peterson murmured, "Have we brought them thus far to surrender live hostages to the Gauch' only to—er-a—bump them off now? Not at all, my dear Scottie. It's just. . . ."

Wentworth flashed a warning glance at Barker and sprang toward Scottie with his manacles jerked high. He saw Barker's hand dive for his gun pocket and then he had closed with Scottie. The man threw his left arm high as a shield and leveled the revolver beneath it, but he had not calculated on the violence of the *Spider's* blow. When the handcuffs slashed down against his left elbow, the arm went limp and a howl of pain tore from Scottie's lips. He dropped the gun and grabbed for his elbow. His lower arm swung limply, the bone fractured.

Wentworth heard a shot behind him, heard Barker groan. Peterson, laughing, was still in his seat with an automatic resting on his knee.

"My dear Barker, did you really think I would give you a loaded gun?" he asked gently.

Barker was sagging back into his chair, grasping his shoulder, and Peterson's gun was turned now toward Wentworth.

"I have no intention of killing you, *Spider*," said Peterson, "but I can break a leg or an arm. . . ."

The flat, mocking laughter of the *Spider* filled the cabin, cutting through the roar of the motor. Scottie had shrunk away from Wentworth's attack, moaning over his arm. Wentworth caught him by coat lapels and whipped him about, hurled him almost bodily toward where Peterson sat. He went charging in behind Scottie.

The plane slithered and jerked under Wentworth's feet and he saw the white, frightened face of the pilot show in the doorway. The *Spider* laughed again. Strength was leaping through his veins. Once more he raised his handcuffs and slashed down with them. Scottie groaned and pitched to the floor and Wentworth sprang forward with his manacles lifted. . . .

As Scottie fell, Peterson's legs came up and Wentworth fought vainly to dodge the two-footed kick that lanced straight for his chest. He staggered backward with the violence of that blow, tangled with Barker who was rising to resume the battle. The two of them tangled on the floor.

"For God's sake!" the pilot screamed. "You'll wreck us."

Peterson's fast breathing interfered with his laughter, but he laughed hoarsely anyway. He ran his left hand through his black hair to smooth it into place, held his gun ready.

"Listen," he said raspingly, "I don't want to kill you two, but I by God will if you move again."

He squeezed the trigger of his automatic and a bullet smacked into a seat within an inch of Wentworth's head. He gazed up into Peterson's face and realized that the man meant precisely what he said. The murder light was in Peterson's small, black eyes. Scottie was slouching to his knees, staggering to his feet. He turned about with his broken arm swinging, stepped close and slammed his good fist into Wentworth's face. The *Spider* had only time to set his jaw and tense his neck muscles. Long ago he had learned that trick in the prize ring to prevent a knockout. Scottie turned and hit Barker viciously, then the two gangsters went cautiously about binding their prisoners to the seats.

Wentworth felt his weariness swarm over him again, felt the cold hint of despair. He fought it down and smiled slowly, the harsh, mocking smile of the *Spider*.

"A nice little party, wasn't it?" he said softly.

Scottie slugged him again. . . .

CHAPTER EIGHT

Audience With El Gaucho!

It was not a half hour later that the drone of the plane's engine dwindled and Wentworth felt the ship sag toward earth. He leaned toward the window, as did all others. The plane was settling down on a hard-packed field without hangars or other evidence of air-ship facilities. Beyond it, among a fringe of straggling trees, a few houses were scattered among streets of tents. The pilot bumped down and sat still, peering back with frightened eyes.

A big car with a strangely steady motion rolled out from the clump of trees and raced across the rough ground with surprising speed and ease, and with a curious straddling action of the wheels. The *Spider* had time as he climbed to the earth for a quick estimate that it was specially constructed for rough country. The auto halted and a military man in spotless but unfamiliar uniform of dark red got out, escorted by two orderlies in similar, plainer garb, who stood rigidly at attention behind him.

The officer's stern eye swept over the plane. He ignored Peterson and the other three, addressed the pilot who was climbing down from the ship.

"Pilot, have you fuel enough for a return trip?"

"Yes, sir," said the pilot, his deference enthusiastic as he realized the intention behind the man's question.

"Then you have our leave to go—at once!"

"Yes, *sir*!" The pilot sprang back to his ship, but Peterson's shout stopped him.

"You will remain here until I dismiss you. As for you," he turned to the officer, "we've come here to see El Gaucho—"

The orderlies behind the officer blew, simultaneously, two small silver whistles which were surprisingly shrill and clear. Instantly, some twenty men, all clad in the same dark uniforms and armed with machine guns, started at a trot toward the field. Wentworth smiled slightly as he saw the color drain from Peterson's face. The officer was scowling darkly, but if he planned to say anything it was drowned in the roar of the plane's motor as the pilot gunned and kicked the rudder to turn into the wind. A cloud of dust swept over them. The officer, whose black mustaches curved upward in brisk militant points, threw up an arm. The whistles piped again and the machine gunners halted, returned again to the trees.

Wentworth saw that they were well disciplined, well drilled and there was a speculative frown about his eyes as he gazed again at the brisk, mustached officer. What manner of criminal was this Gaucho that he had well-trained soldiers to serve him? The *Spider* shook his head. It was no wonder that he took cities with such ease. What chance did small-town police stand against disciplined troops? Wentworth's lips tightened against his teeth. Well, he would see how the troops would function without their leaders after the *Spider* struck! . . . He became aware that Peterson was answering the officer's questions, his debonair manner blanketed by sullenness.

"There will be two other planes here in a short while," Peterson growled. "D'you realize we have come here on an *official* visit to El Gaucho—on an important official visit—and that we are representing very important interests. We've brought the *Spider*, a captive."

The officer was utterly cold. "Learn to address yourself in better terms to your superiors, my man," he said, incisively. "I am not at all sure you will be permitted to see El Gaucho. If our Commander decides against it we will return you in our own plane. I will ask for an audience for you. If it is granted, you will remember not to speak unless you are spoken to. El Gaucho is one of the few authentic kings of an ancient line and of an ancient kingdom. Time only is needed to make him practically the sole ruler of the world!"

Wentworth watched the man's face narrowly while he spoke. There was first contempt for Peterson and later when he spoke of El Gaucho, an exaltation. The *Spider* realized that the officer, at least, believed what he said. To him, El Gaucho was a king, a future world-ruler. And he had mentioned planes. Truly, the army was well equipped!

The officer turned his back, stalked away to his car alone; the orderlies remained to conduct the four new arrivals across the dusty field toward the trees. The sun beat down hotly. Wentworth, looking about at the well-armed, well-trained men, felt the slow rise of despair in his heart.

Suddenly it seemed ridiculous that he, a lone man—and a prisoner at that!—should consider the possibility of victory over El Gaucho and his organziation. They were all silent as they trudged across the sun-parched field. When automobiles bore them away, a few minutes later, the officer stayed behind, apparently waiting for the other planes.

It had not escaped the keen eyes of the *Spider* that while the land seemed flat for miles around, there really were depressions in it here and there. The cars followed a faint track in the heavy dust, the ground gradually rose, became rocky, began to run through scraggly trees into thicker timber. Abruptly it wound around a bend, and an exclamation of surprise came even from Peterson.

A sunken plateau lay below this mounting land, a mile wide, ringed about with rocky slopes, closed at the north to a narrow pass, opening out to the south. It had suffered less than most of the country in the dust storms which had ravaged the region, and there were patches of meadow and a fair-sized stream. Horses and cattle were grazing and there were some standing crops. At the widest part of the plateau, however, there were military arrangements. The wall of a fort, an immense parade ground, and streets of tents. In the rear, set in a ribbon of bright garden, formally laid out, was a small but very handsome house with a large pennant— a purple stripe above a bright scarlet one—flying on its flagstaff. Wentworth saw these things with a sense of amazement. Counting the tents, he estimated that there were enough for a thousand men!

He noticed many of them lolling about in front of the tents as the cars with the orderlies, Peterson, Barker, Scottie, and himself drew near. Wentworth and Barker were herded into a tent with the gangsters, and there they were kept under armed guard until the low sun sent golden shafts slanting through the tent flap and measured steps sounded outside. The guards stood, their guns snapping to present. The officer who had first received them at the air field stepped in and looked them over slowly with a dull, flat eye. He saw that Wentworth's wrists were still manacled and shortly demanded the key. Peterson surrendered it with a shrug.

"After all," he smiled blandly at the *Spider,* "you are now El Gaucho's prisoner, not mine. I hope that you enjoy your meeting."

The officer watched without expression as Barker was cut loose from the ropes that bound him. Wentworth stretched and massaged his wrists, eyes covertly surveying the tent. By a quick dash, he might spring behind his cot, roll out under the canvas wall . . . and then? But there would be a score of guards posted about with rifles. No, no, such a break required the sheltering kindness of night. He was in the midst of an armed camp. He crossed to Barker, threw an arm about the boy's shoulders.

85

"How you feel, Barker?"

Barker grinned up at him, white teeth flashing from his brown face. "Swelegant, *Spider*. Simply swelegant!"

Wentworth knew that the officer's eyes were upon him, but he ignored that, chatting lightly with the boy who had risked his life to help him. Still Wentworth managed to see Peterson's mocking grin, his wink toward the officer.

"Guess you know what you're doing, Chief," Peterson drawled, "but this *Spider* has the keenest reputation in the world for getting himself out of tight scrapes."

The officer ignored Peterson, but when the gangsters filed out of the tent, the two rifle-armed guards took a position on either side of Wentworth. An amused gleam touched the *Spider's* eyes. Rifles were splendid if a man were running from you, but when he was close . . . Still nothing was to be gained by downing these two men and overpowering the officer. He could glimpse the uniformed legs of guards outside, forming a square about the gangsters. He looked directly into the officer's eyes.

The man nodded, "I am quite aware that you could make a break for it," he said, his manner much more courteous than that he used toward Peterson. "Your reputation has reached even to my country. But it would not be wise. There are too many rifles outside. It is possible the King will be . . . amiably . . . inclined toward you."

Wentworth bowed wordlessly, his gesture graceful despite the false hunch of his shoulders. Barker was looking at him admiringly, and there was no mistaking the respect in the officer's glance. He snapped a command at the two guards and, between them, Wentworth and Barker marched out through the tent flap, pivoted left. There were eight more soldiers waiting there and, at an order, they fell in before and in back of the two prisoners.

The *Spider's* eyes took in the entire scene, even the

circling airplanes overhead which obviously kept watch over the field. Along the left side of the parade grounds, fronted by the tents, two companies of the red-clad soldiers were drawn up in faultless array. On the ends of the field, behind the troops, were a motley assembly of others who numbered fully a thousand. Mexicans in silver-slashed velvet and broad-brimmed sombreros; hard-bitten men of the plains with six-shooters strapped low on thighs; city-clothed men who obviously were gangsters as vicious as any Peterson might command.

These things were taken in at a glance, then Wentworth's eyes swung to the side of the grounds opposite the soldiers. Enthroned on a raised dais sat a man in the maroon garb of the soldiers, splendidly piped in gold, medals catching the glint of the setting sun. El Gaucho! Wentworth gazed at him curiously, but he was still too far away to see clearly. There was a plumed honor-guard of soldiers in shining cuirass and helmets about El Gaucho—a girl in flowing ceremonial robes on his left; on his right an arrogant man in a high, black shako like a Death's-Head Hussar. . . . But he would inspect those when he was closer to them. There were other things now to absorb his attention. Before the dais of El Gaucho, four huge draught horses were held motionless by eight grooms, one to each side of the bit. They had scarlet harnesses—a cross-tree lay at the heels of each.

A sense of uneasiness rippled over Wentworth and he frowned slightly. His eyes slanted to right and left, taking in two thick, stubby posts with a cross bar near the top which had been set deeply in the ground within thirty feet of the dais, on each side of the place where the horses stood. The posts were like crude crosses, like . . . the *Spider's* grim jaw set harshly. Suddenly he knew the reason for the brooding silence that hung over the field, the stiff waiting of the crowds. Those were flogging posts, and the horses . . . *Good God!* It couldn't be what he thought it was. Such barbarity as that had died in the sixteenth century!

He felt Barker's hand on his arm. "What's up, *Spider*?" he asked with worry in his tones. "I don't like the looks of things."

Wentworth shook his head. "I hope it's not what I think it is," he said flatly, "but whatever happens, keep that upper lip stiff."

"What do you mean?"

"Torture, Barker."

Wentworth heard the boy's breath suck in shudderingly. He said hoarsely, "The damned . . . fiends! Well, they won't get a squeak out of me."

"Of course not," said the *Spider,* making his voice light with an effort. "I'm probably all wrong, but it's as well to be prepared." He knew suddenly that he wasn't wrong and his throat closed dryly. Not for himself—torture had been tried on him before this, torture of the soul that is harder to bear than torture of the body. But this splendid boy! Tommy Barker was in this peril solely because he had risked his life to help the *Spider*. He must not suffer for that. He must not . . . Wentworth turned quietly to the guard on his right.

"Fall out and give my compliments to the officer. The prisoner wishes to speak to him," he said it quietly, but in the accent of command that comes only to those who have commanded. "Fall out!"

The soldier saluted mechanically, hesitated as he realized what he had done, then went at double-time, gun on shoulder, to the side of the officer. Wentworth saw the hesitation of the officer, then he dropped back and fell into step beside him.

"Be quick," he said. "What is it?"

"If it is to be torture," Wentworth said quietly, "I wish to appeal to El Gaucho for this boy with me. Let him inflict double penalties on me."

The officer looked down at the dusty ground beneath their feet as they marched along, stirring a slow gray mist from the earth; then he glanced at Wentworth.

"It is a man's request," he said somberly, "I'll do what I can."

Wentworth said, "Thank you."

Barker cried sharply, "No, no. I didn't understand. You can't do that, *Spider*."

The officer said harshly, "Quiet, prisoner." He rapidly overtook the leading platoon again and fell in position. The soldier who had dropped out to obey the *Spider's* order looked narrowly at him from the corner of his eyes. Strange that he had obeyed a prisoner, strange when it might have brought rebuke and sharp punishment upon his head. But he need not have felt disconcerted. Stronger men than he had obeyed the *Spider* and felt it honor to hear his commands.

Barker's hand came to Wentworth's arm again. "I won't permit that."

Wentworth said, "Quiet."

There was a brooding pain in his heart. He had small hope that El Gauncho would permit what he requested, but at least it might achieve the end of all this fearfulness that was intrinsic in this armed force El Gaucho had gathered about him. The *Spider* might succeed in snatching a gun and killing El Gaucho! Forlorn hope!

For Wentworth could see no escape for himself. It was likely that this man who called himself King and arrogated to himself regal powers, would have the flogging continued until Wentworth and Barker died. The *Spider's* mind harked back to the cruelty of ancient days at sea when the cat-o'-nine-tails had been the instrument of harsh discipline. A short-shafted whip with nine lashes of rawhide stemming from it—the last two inches of each lash wound in brass wire and tipped with a leaden knout. A man had once survived a hundred lashes. . . .

Yes, it would be better to make the effort to kill El Gaucho. In the anger afterward, soldiers might cut down both him and Barker. . . .

In response to a sharp command, the soldiers about Wentworth and Barker took a stand to the left of the dais. The squad surrounding the ten gangsters who had flown west were flanking the dais on the opposite side. They stood like that, waiting, and the officer who commanded the squad braced himself and marched stalwartly to a position directly in front of the throne, dropped to one knee and bowed his bared head.

Wentworth watched the man and suddenly realized that he had asked a tremendous thing of this officer, that the man had gone with fear and trembling to carry his petition to El Gaucho. The *Spider* saw that the man spoke without lifting his head and he saw El Gaucho lean forward slightly, frowning. For the first time, then, he had a close sight of this man who was terrorizing the west, who now threatened to carry his pillaging, slaughtering host to destroy the East. His carriage was arrogant, the head shapely and proudly held. And the face was strong, intelligent, the profile like something on a coin. A full beard covered his mouth. The nose was acquiline, finely chiseled, and the eyes beneath smoothly arched brows were deep and wide—the eyes, Wentworth realized with a start, of a dreamer! Good God! A dreamer who slaughtered scores and could torture men with the ancient horror of the four horses!

El Gaucho lifted his hand and the officer rose, backed away for five paces before he arose, replaced his hat and right-faced to march to where Wentworth stood. He spoke sharply to the guard, and four soldiers removed their hats and handed them to comrades with their rifles, seized Wentworth's arms and marched him down the line of men. A feeling of sharp disappointment turned the *Spider's* heart to lead. There would be no weapon within his reach that he could grab, even if he could break the holds of these four men gripping his arms. He felt his hat snatched off, then the four men dropped to their knees, dragging him down also.

Wentworth did not bow his head and shoulders. He kneeled there as erectly as he could, facing El Gaucho. The eyes of the two met and held. What the *Spider* saw confirmed his distant judgment of the man. His eyes were those of a dreamer, but his gaze held command. There was something magnetic, too, about his personality. Neither man spoke for a long moment, then El Gaucho nodded shortly.

"If you hoped to have a chance to kill me by this audience," he said. "It's a hopeless attempt."

Irresistibly, the *Spider* smiled, but the expression was not amiable. His disguised face twisted into sinister, mocking lines.

"You reason soundly, Gaucho," he said pleasantly, "but my plea is sincere. The boy had no idea with what he was embroiling himself. He merely likes me personally as I admire him. He sought to do what he could to defend me, and had no intent of an assault upon your majesty."

A loud shout pulled Gaucho's eyes to the left. It was Barker. "He lies! He lies!" Barker cried. "Don't listen to him, Gau . . ." A soldier's fist smashing against his lips stopped Barker's voice and El Gaucho turned his face steadily back to Wentworth.

"The lad has courage," he said quietly, his voice firm, resonant. "You, too, have courage, *Spider,* but no man has ever needed to think twice about that." He hesitated, looking piercingly into Wentworth's face, then shook his head slowly. "That isn't your true face. It doesn't match your eyes. I could use men like you two in my company. There would be high places in my court, but the proffer would be useless, I know. You will be true to yourself though it means death."

A slow smile moved El Gaucho's bearded lips. "It is a pity you must die, *Spider,* without a sword in your hand."

The *Spider's* eyes held his. "I accept my fate," he said shortly. "I did not come before you to ask mercy for myself. But I did not think El Gaucho stooped to murder children."

El Gaucho jerked to his feet, red rage flashing from his eyes. "You dare!"

"Dare, hell," Wentworth returned laconically. "You're a cheap four-flusher, killing children like Barker to inflate your self-esteem!"

Two guards sprang forward with swords ripping from their sheaths, bright points glittering toward Wentworth's throat. Rage distorted their faces. It was the chance for which the *Spider* had angled. With a violent wrench, he freed his right arm from the hands of the soldiers on that side. He crossed his right fist against the jaw of one of those on his left and slammed him against his companion.

Free then for the moment, he sprang to meet the two guards with their glittering swords drawn back to thrust. Behind them, he had a glimpse of El Gaucho, towering on the dais in his anger, of other guards jostling forward, while the insolent man in the black shako held an automatic ready in his right hand. The girl, whose face he had not seen until now, was leaning forward with her white hands clenched against her throat. It was impossible to tell whether it was fear or anxiety for . . . Wentworth suddenly realized that the woman wanted him to conquer! The sight of her intensely white face, her starry eyes, was a draught of courage to his lips.

Laughter leaped from his mouth and he sprang to meet the two guardsmen with their swords. They held them not in a fencing position but clenched at their sides for a stabbing thrust that would eliminate this mocker once and for all. As he sprang forward, Wentworth whipped his cape from his shoulders, hurled it in the face of the foremost guard. Instinctively, he flung up hands and sword to tear the blinding thing away and in that instant, Wentworth had his sword wrist. With a wrench he tore the weapon from the swordman's grasp. His right arm had gone about the soldier's armored body and with the same movement, he hurled the fellow against his charging comrade.

A muffled scream tore from the man's cloak-covered face and his fellow guard's sword point protruded bloodily from his thigh. It had taken no more than seconds, this struggle, then Wentworth was vaulting the ten feet to the dais with his sword ready in his right hand. He saw the gun of the man in the shako rise, saw the raised swords of guardsmen thrusting toward him and knew joyously that none of them could reach him in time to stop a death thrust. Nothing could stop him save . . . Even as he sprang to the first step of the dais with his saber licking out, El Gaucho's own sword whipped from its scabbard. . . .

Here was one thing, Wentworth knew, that could defeat him, and he realized in the first movement of El Gaucho's saber that this man, too, was a master swordsman. It was not that the *Spider* doubted his own ability to pierce that guard and kill, given a few moments, but he knew that before their blades had clashed a second time, death would be upon the *Spider* from behind. Useless to press his attack. A smile thinned his lips, death sat in his eyes.

"Dare you to fight me, man to man, El Gaucho!" he cried.

He drew back a pace, grounding the point of his saber and El Gaucho lowered his point, too, lifted his left hand to stop the assault upon Wentworth by the guards about him, by his right.

"Surrender the saber, *Spider*," he said calmly, "or you will be wounded, not killed, so that you will live for the whipping post. It would give me great pleasure, *Spider*, to meet you with swords, but it cannot be. My cause is greater than I. There must be. . . ." He cut his words short with a lift of his left hand. "Surrender your sword, *Spider*."

What, had he lost then? Wentworth's proud, disdainful eyes swept the faces about him, saw their wrath, met the pity and the admiration in the eyes of the woman, and saw there was no chance. El Gaucho, with that blade in his hand, was invulnerable since there were so many others to strike Wentworth down from behind. The *Spider* shrugged, disguising his despair with a smile. He lifted the blade above his head with both hands and brought its flat side down across his knee, snapping the steel off sheer.

"It was a good try, *Spider*," said El Gaucho smiling.

Wentworth laughed bitterly, felt soldier's hands seize his arms violently again and drag him backward. He had failed, and with his effort he had doomed Barker, too. His laughter died on his lips. The sacrifice was necessary. If it meant Barker's death now, there at least had been a chance that he might save hundreds—thousands—of others from sharing the fate of so many who had perished in El Gaucho's bloody raids.

He held his head proudly, defiantly as he was marched back to Barker. Ropes were wound about his arms now, locking them behind him and the officer stared angrily at him. He said nothing, but there was hatred in his eyes, hatred and a touch, too, of fear. The glance made the *Spider's* lips curve in self-mockery. No man need fear him now. Death was near, ignoble death, and yonder sat a man who would be too strong, too mighty for all the forces of law and order. Triumph sat upon his head like an accolade.

Wentworth lifted his eyes to the sunset fires of the skies. There must, *there must* be some power greater than this El Gaucho. . . .

CHAPTER NINE

Gaucho Justice

The uproar occasioned by the *Spider's* attack upon El Gaucho faded swiftly. Once more the brooding silence of those who wait for death settled over the parade grounds. The sun was a baleful red eye upon the horizon which seemed strangely appropriate to the horror that was to come. Wentworth stood erect, with set face and grimly gazing eyes, beside Barker, who, he had seen, was bound also.

"You shouldn't have done that, *Spider*—tried to save me," Barker whispered softly. "You might have known it was no dice."

Wentworth nodded slightly. "It was the only chance. I had to," he said shortly. "Is that the girl?"

Barker's voice sank to a whisper. "Isn't she glorious?"

The *Spider* nodded again. She was lovely enough with her truly regal bearing and her starry eyes beneath the black crown of her hair. But that was not what he was thinking. If he could survive or escape the torture that impended, would she be willing to help? If not for the sake of aiding doomed men, then for the sake of this fine boy at his side? The woman beside El Gaucho was no older than Tommy Barker, for all her stern, straight-backed poise. Possibly she was a year or two younger. . . .

Wentworth's course of thought broke as he caught the muffled tap of drums. He lifted his eyes to behold a new squad of soldiers approaching from a small, white house which had barred windows. Amid them, one marched who was not in uniform, whose bare shoulders rose above those of the others. He was uttering a thin, despairing, wailing sound. It was scarcely human, the whine that rose from that poor wretch. It was the cry a suffering animal might make. . . .

Barker said, "Good God, what is that?"

Wentworth did not answer. Why tell Barker that this was the sound that is made by tortured men, suffering pain beyond the ability of man to endure?

Barker's breath was noisy in his mouth. "They're taking him to the horses! What are they going to do to him with horses?"

Three men walked in front of the squad, a man in a black robe with a scarlet cap that covered his entire head and face. Behind him walked two men stripped to the waist, their arms folded across thick-muscled chests. Each bore in his right hand the short haft of a cat-o'-nine-tails, its leaded lashes slapping gently against their thighs. And as they came nearer, the four horses were being maneuvered by the eight grooms, backed together so that each great gray Percheron formed with its body the corner of a square. They were led slightly apart, the cross-trees dragging at their heels.

The marching squad was very near now and the man they led began to strain and lurch against the grasp of his captors. He was weak—too weak to escape. Already, Wentworth surmised, he had felt the cunning work of the torturers. For him, this would only be a final, insupportable agony before the blessed release of death. The soldiers halted beside the horses and the two torturers thrust whips into their belts, seized the luckless victim. The soldiers were white-faced, a little uncertain in their step as they marched away. Wentworth glanced cautiously at the men to either side and they were sick-faced, too. A chance to escape? The *Spider* shook his head. Not with bound arms, not with all these hundreds surrounding him.

Barker was moaning. "Oh lord! Look at that man's chest! Why—why . . . they've *burned* him! It's burned black!"

"Quiet, Barker," Wentworth snapped. "Quiet!"

The boy moved closer for a moment, but soldiers yanked him away again. "Stand still, you!" Their fear and their nausea was reflected in the savagery of their voices. Their quaking made them cruel. The torturers held the man there beside the horses and a soldier stepped forward, sword swaying against his side, began to read in a drone that nevertheless carried emphatically over the hushed parade grounds.

". . . A traitor to the cause," rang his voice. "He deserted his post in Jackson City. . . ."

Wentworth's lips curved in a hard thin smile. The *Spider* was leaning forward as if to go to the man's rescue, but what purpose could it serve? He knew it was useless, but he gazed at the wretched victim of El Gaucho and his eyes were cold. He would watch—and someday, somehow, he would wreak his vengeance upon this Gaucho! A while ago, Wentworth had felt a nascent admiration for the man's conduct and courage. This torture, too, had a purpose, of course. It was discipline, designed to hold the men in line against all danger and temptation with the certainty that, if they wavered, this same death awaited them. He knew its reason, but he was sure that there must be a deep-seated cruelty in the soul of a man who would permit such things.

The wretch tried to drop on his knees, to beg for mercy, but the torturers held him erect. Abruptly they slammed him to the ground and bound thongs about his wrists and ankles. While he screamed horribly, they fastened one limb in turn to the harness of each of the four horses. The grooms who held the horses faced away from where the man lay, stroking the Percherons, calming them with caresses. The torturers stepped away and the scarlet-masked executioner moved forward. . . .

Barker sobbed, the sounds strangled in his throat. He gasped out words. "Oh, God! Oh God! They're going . . . going to *pull him to pieces!*"

Wentworth's bound fists were aching knots behind him as the shrill toneless shrieking of that man, helpless on the ground among the four horses, pierced his ears. Barker had named it. When the weight of those mighty horses was put upon the harness, the man's limbs would be slowly, slowly torn from his body while he still lived. In spite of himself, the *Spider* took a slow step forward, but soldiers' hands jerked him backward. Barker was shouting meaningless sounds, too, until a soldier mercifully slapped his head with the butt of his gun. It was not hard enough to knock the boy out, but it stunned him so that he swayed, dazed, on his feet in the grip of the soldiers. He was silenced.

The executioner lifted the hand and the four men who held the horses attached to the victim's arms made the Percherons lean gently into their harness. The straps straightened, taunted. If the screams before had been heart-rending, those that rose now were enough to tear the soul of God. Wentworth, steeling himself, his jaw set, the tendons of his neck rigid, saw blood spurt from the man's wrists and shoulders, from his ankles. The executioner lifted his hand again and the horses eased in their harness. It was not then that he was merely to be pulled to pieces. That was not sufficient torture. He was to be allowed, too, the agony of dislocated arms and legs.

Wentworth's soul squeezed out a curse between his set teeth. He pulled his eyes away from the scene. To either side of him, men stood rigidly, some with their eyes closed, some shaken with fear and agony. A soldier reeled out of line and fell, his body wracked with nausea. Wentworth's gaze sought out El Gaucho. Impassively, unmoving, leaning slightly forward in an attitude of interest, El Gaucho sat upon his throne watching the torture which was enacted before him.

A new, shrill cry came from the tortured man. It was weaker, hoarser, without meaning except for its inarticulate agony. The girl on the left side of the throne was leaning against the chair, her hand covering her eyes. But she could not stop her ears. El Gaucho turned toward her and his lips moved. The girl stood rigidly, her hand dropping from before her eyes and . . . the man screamed again.

So piercing, so wracking, was the cry that Wentworth's eyes were pulled involuntarily toward the torture. The gray horses were startled, half-frightened by the cries that seemed to issue from the earth at their very heels. They tried to turn their great heads to look at this gibbering thing behind them, but the grooms gentled them, patted their necks with hands that trembled in spite of themselves. At a gesture from the executioner, they once more eased the strain for a moment while the screams died to a bubbling moan. Then they began again a slow, forward pull, all four horses straining together, horses that weighed a ton apiece, straining their powerful muscles. The rays of the setting sun seemed to gild them with the blood of their victim, great gentle beasts goaded into a fearful killing by kind, patting hands. But the red of the sun could not match the hot crimson that was spurting now from the lump of flesh that had been human. . . .

Barker had recovered full consciousness now and, shuddering from head to foot, clung to one of the soldiers for support, though that man, too, was trembling. Many of the spectators were like that and the *Spider* knew that nothing save fear of a similar fate held them subject to El Gaucho. Even among the guards and officers who surrounded the throne faces were deathly pale. . . .

At last there was such a cry that even the *Spider's* iron control slipped for a moment and his body bounded against the ropes, against the restraining hands of soldiers. But it was already too late, irreparably too late.

The straining horses trembled and reared against the drag of that screaming thing behind them. No groom's hand could gentle them now. One of them broke free of the men who held him, galloped headlong away across the parade ground, dragging a crimson something in the swirling dust behind him. No one tried to stop the horse. One of the men who had been in charge of him dropped where he stood, a limp, unconscious figure. Little rills and streams of blood from that other still thing puddled the dust about him.

There was still a twitching, still some ghost of sound issuing from that mangled flesh, but the horses, standing, trembling now beneath the caresses of their grooms, had done their work. The man was dismembered. . . .

There was a great aching silence following the last shrieks of a man horribly dying. El Gaucho stepped down slowly, deliberately, from his throne, walked close to where at last that twitching human thing was silent. His deep voice matched his great frame. It boomed forth gigantically:

"You have seen a traitor die, my people," he roared. *"Remember!"*

Just that followed by awed silence. Then one of the officers lifted a hand, and from the stricken hundreds there came a broken, hoarse salute:

"Hail! El Gaucho! Hail!"

CHAPTER TEN

Promise of Death

After the last shout had died, people began to slip away. There was none of the confused sounds, none of the talking which usually attends the break-up of a crowd. Each one stole away as if he sought to avoid observation—as if some fearful, vengeful god watched gloatingly.

The little group of officers remained with El Gaucho and the soldiers stood fast while the torturers tossed what was left of their victim into a bag for a servant to drag away. In the silence that followed, El Gaucho's voice, addressing the girl beside him, was clearly audible to Wentworth.

"I did not think you would have so weak a heart, Carollotta," he said, "when justice was being done."

The girl laid a flower-like hand on the arm of the throne and swayed a little on her feet. "Justice!" she whispered. The sound hissed out into the gathering dusk.

"A useful lesson in justice, my niece," El Gaucho's voice was deep, grave. "You must remember that you have a high destiny. You will be the mother of the Line, the new royalty founded by my blood. It is for this reason I require you to meet more than ordinary women can stand. Your beauty is a glorious thing to pass on to the blood; but a soldier's heart must go with it!''

Wentworth felt the anger of the boy beside him. He glared at El Gaucho and the wish rose overwhelmingly in his heart that he had succeeded in that reckless dash with the sword. Even if he had afterward died by the torture of the horses, it would have been worth it to strike down the author of so much infamy. The muffled tap of drums came again and, despite himself, Wentworth's head pulled toward the sound to see what new torture portended. The executioner with his scarlet cowl marched as before ahead of the two men with the many-shaped whips. Wentworth's shoulder muscles corded. This time they came—*for him*!

Carollotta's voice rang out behind him in a frightened cry. ''Oh, Uncle,'' she implored. ''No more today! In heaven's name, no more today!''

Wentworth's eyes were fixed in a fascination he could not break on the two broad-shouldered torturers with their lead-tipped whips.

''No, no, Uncle!'' cried the girl. ''These men have done nothing to you. They are the enemies of the gangsters. Why should you exact vengeance. They have done nothing, nothing . . . !''

''Nothing,'' drawled El Gaucho amusedly, ''except make an attempt on our lives!''

Wentworth felt the quivering of Barker, close against his shoulder now. ''Why does she do that?'' he whispered. ''She won't accomplish anything. Only make it tough for herself. . . .''

Wentworth forced his eyes away from the torturers to gaze on the girl. She had drawn herself up scornfully, her head with its plaited coronet of smooth black hair defiantly lifted.

''You call yourself king!'' she said contemptuously, ''yet you quibble with the truth! Why not admit that you like to see men tortured?''

''Silence, woman!'' thundered El Gaucho. ''The man is an assassin!''

Carollotta laughed musically. ''Yes, my uncle,'' she

agreed, "but you had determined on his torture *before you ever saw him.* Why then equivocate? Why pretend that the torture is because of what happened here? Is this the vaunted justice of King Carlos of Bethania?"

She was silent, gazing scornfully at the man before the throne. There was not even the movement of a foot among the guard of officers about the throne. There were white, fearful faces there, startled eyes gazing straight ahead. Across the parade grounds the squad of soldiers marched on with muffled drums and the dull thudding of the drums was like the beating of a great cosmic heart, slow, heavy, portentous.

El Gaucho's eyes remained locked with those of the girl who had defied him and it was he who first turned swaying, bowing his head as if in thought. One foot was placed forward a little; his right hand was thrust in the breast of his coat. He made a brooding somber picture. Wentworth tried to appraise him coldly, but hatred prodded his brain with sharp hot points.

This Gaucho, this Carlos, who called himself King of Bethania, believed himself far above the average man; a super-being, almost god-like, Wentworth decided. And because he had the will and the strength, because he was gifted with the personality that commands, he was dangerously near what he believed. No ordinary man could have assembled this force of men and held them strongly in leash to do his bidding.

Abruptly, El Gaucho's head came up. He spun toward the man who had stood throughout the scene at his right hand, the man with the black shako of the Death's-Head Hussars.

"Von Hapszollern," he asked dryly, "will you have those two men brought before me again?"

Wentworth gazed at the man called Von Hapszollern and a start of surprise jerked at his muscles. He knew that protruding lower lip; that prominent nose and black eyes. By the Gods! It was Prince Wilhelm of Ruthia! Wentworth had been presented at a reception in the Prince's honor in New York four years ago. The *Spider*

103

prodded his memory, recalling the man's country, Ruthia, a tiny key state in the Balkans—and he remembered, too, the whereabouts of Bethania. Bethania was a republic neighboring on the other state . . . Wentworth's eyes flashed back to Prince Wilhelm.

"Pardon, your majesty," said Wilhelm, swaggering forward a little, "Do you think this is wise? These two men are extremely dangerous. You have seen already how this—er-a—vermin behaves. The whip would be good for them and—" he leaned closer, whispering. Wentworth read his lips easily—"It would be a salutary lesson for these others of whom we know little."

Carollota's face turned even paler. "My uncle, consider your justice!"

"Why should two soldiers," growled Wilhelm, "listen to a girl? Come, let us decide this as it should be."

Wentworth turned his head slightly toward Barker, and a smile touched his lips. "That does it," he whispered. "We will be spared."

Barker frowned in bewilderment, but El Gaucho's deep booming voice thick with anger confirmed the *Spider's* keen estimate of his character.

" 'Let us,' did you say, Wilhelm?" El Gaucho thundered. "Prince, you forget yourself!"

Wilhelm drew himself up, but it was obvious that El Gaucho's manner intimidated him. He stammered and retreated before the glare of the man. El Gaucho turned deliberately to Carollotta, bowed over her white hand.

"My niece, I thank you," he said gravely, "my justice is more imperative than the need to chastise dogs."

He turned back to Wilhelm, speaking more pleasantly, "I give my niece into the hands of her affianced," he said. "Will you see her to the ladies' quarters?"

Prince Wilhelm took his dismissal with ill grace, but he could not object. Wentworth stared in amazement, heard the sharp low cursing of Barker at the information that it was to this stripling of Ruthia's royalty that the girl, Carollotta, had been pledged in marriage.

Abruptly, Wentworth saw the whole set-up. It was fairly clear now that El Gaucho sought in his American crimes the money to restore himself to his Bethanian throne. The girl was to be used to bind him in peace to his neighboring state. Good God, what a colossal egoist the man was! So that he might place himself on his throne again, he organized criminals to ravage an entire country-side, killed hundreds of fellow men ruthlessly! And the heady wine of power had gone to his head. He dreamed now of world dominion!

If only Washington knew what portended. A few companies of United States Marines could wipe out this camp of bandits in quick time. But no one yet realized the immensity of El Gaucho's activities. Troops had not even been called out by the governors. And if they were, what would it accomplish? Many of the national guard would be green to actual warfare and though officered by men of war experience, they would still be civilians, unused to discipline. And El Gaucho's army had been recruited from border badmen. . . .

El Gaucho mounted his throne deliberately and sent for the gangsters under Peterson's leadership. Peterson swaggered up to the throne, tossed a hand in jaunty salute.

"How're yah, Gauch?" He started to step up on the dais to shake hands. A short, stocky man in the armor of the guards stepped forward violently, hurled him backward so that Peterson almost fell. The gangster snarled, his hand flashed to his coat lapel. Then, remembering he was without arms, he turned white.

The stocky man in cuirass and helmet stood furiously before him, broad German face twisted in anger.

"Do not shpeak, *Schwein*," he growled, "until you are shpoken to!"

Peterson was not without courage, whatever his faults. He stepped up close to the officer and tapped the cuirass with a stiff forefinger.

"Listen, punk," he said flatly, his veneer of suave speech gone. "Don't try any funny business with me or you'll run into the dirty end of a chopper. . . ."

Peterson's voice cut short, for another guardsmen stepped up behind him and clapped a large, competent hand over his mouth. Four more guardsmen confronted the other disarmed gangsters with naked swords and the criminals wilted.

The officer's thick voice instructed Peterson unemotionally. "Do not shpeak unless you are first addressed, *Schwein*."

He lifted a hand and the guard who had seized Peterson from behind stepped back a pace, drew his sword and presented its point to the gangster's back.

"If he shpeaks out of turn again . . . remind him," said the officer, and stepped back to his former position beside the throne.

"This is well, De Moltkez," said El Gaucho, eyeing Peterson.

The officer, De Moltkez, saluted with a wide sweep of his hand and automaton precision. Wentworth's lips lifted at the corners in spite of himself at Peterson's rebuke but the smile quickly faded as Peterson presented the proposal of the gangsters.

He used a remarkably humble voice, battling against the anger that shook him. He told of the fortunes to be had in the East, of the ease with which police could be evaded. Then he itemized the loosely coupled groups of criminals whom, in making this plea, he represented. They were all "big shots," he declared. They had the political powers "sewed up."

"Why, when some of the *Spider's* pals," he went on, "busted into one of our minor headquarters in New York to rescue him, we just had to tell the police to skip out and they did."

He paused a moment, apparently trying to estimate what impression he had made upon El Gaucho. Obviously, disconcerted by his treatment, he tried to build himself large with words. When he paused, El Gaucho's face was as inscrutable as ever.

"What we need, your majesty," Peterson rushed on, "is a man like you, who can lead. A king. The big shots out East saw what you did here and it was great stuff. No kidding. You make us all look like pikers. Now, if you'll come East and run the works, there won't be anybody can stop us. We'll own the country! And don't think you can do it without us. We know the ropes, and we know . . . other things."

El Gaucho said gently, "What other things, for instance?"

Peterson sucked in a deep breath. "We big shots don't like competition," he said slowly. "Maybe you've heard of being taken for a ride?"

There was a breathless silence then, while guards and officers watched El Gaucho. Wentworth's own eyes narrowed with attention. Peterson had shown more courage than he had expected. How would El Gaucho take this quite definite threat? It would show to a large extent just how great he was, or how great he thought himself. And Wentworth saw. El Gaucho merely moved his bearded lips in a smile.

"We are too occupied just now," he said gravely, "to give your proposition due deliberation. In the morning we are taking Grand Junction, a town just south of here. Tomorrow night, we will give you our decision."

El Gaucho's answer was entirely adequate. He merely smiled at the threat, made a courteous, but utterly confident reply. It was as if the matter were too trivial for notice. Wentworth caught that, realized anew the man's power. But his thoughts were swept away to the slaughter and pillage that impended and which El Gaucho had mentioned so casually. *In the morning we are taking Grand Junction* . . . And Wentworth saw something else. He saw that the officer of the guards, who was called De Moltkez, had stepped back from the throne and was in close conversation with Prince Wilhelm. The two men's eyes were on Wentworth and it needed no lip-reading to tell what they planned.

". . . kill them quietly," Wilhelm was saying. "After the battle, Carlos will have forgotten. . . ."

A sharp determination shot through Wentworth, battling with the hopelessness of his and Barker's position.

He must escape and race to the rescue of Grand Junction. With a warning, the citizens could barricade their streets and fight off the regiment of bandits. But to accomplish that, he would have to evade not only the soldiers, but also the assassins whom De Moltkez and Wilhelm would send to destroy them. . . . Even while Wentworth considered plans, he was thrust forward by a soldier. He realized that El Gaucho had ordered them away. He and Barker were thrown alone into the tiny, white-washed jail with its barred windows.

The jail's walls were of thick, squared logs and the chinks were filled with cement. The windows . . . They were impossible. Wentworth's jaw set stubbornly, he would, he *must* escape. He spun toward Barker. The boy was seated on one of the two iron cots that were the room's sole furniture. His face was alight, his smile wide. His mind was elsewhere. Wentworth wavered. Should he tell him about what threatened, the grim future that lay before them? Slowly, he shook his head.

"You saw her, *Spider,*" Barker said, "Did you ever see any one to compare with her, did you? Gee, she's wonderful! And she smiled at me. She smiled at me! You noticed that?"

"I noticed," said Wentworth dryly, "that she is to be married to Prince Wilhelm of Ruthia. What chance do you suppose you have? A fine chance to get pulled to pieces by horses, that's all. You heard El Gaucho? He'll marry her to the sour Teutonic sausage who's the simon-pure crown prince of Ruthia . . . Better think of some of the girls you went to school with."

Barker waved a hand airily. "Nuts to that. I tell you she smiled at me." He stretched out on the cot, and put his hands behind his head, grinning at the ceiling. Wentworth smiled at him gently. His heart was heavy with foreboding. He felt sure that El Gaucho would throw in with Peterson, even if it were only to gain control of the gangs the gangster nominally headed. What happened to Peterson after that union did not matter. The gangs were only loosely affiliated now, could easily be smashed by the right attack, but once they were bound together under the iron hand of El Gaucho . . . !

Orderlies brought two tin buckets of simple fare with bread and water in crocks to complete it. The last rays of the sun had faded from the bare wall opposite their one barred window, when they finished eating and presently Wentworth heard the soft, regular breathing of his companion. When, Wentworth wondered, would the assassins come? He climbed up to test the bars of the windows. They were firm and had been recently erected. Probably they were tool steel. Impossible to attack them with any but the best of instruments and the *Spider* had been stripped of all the devices with which usually he could force his way out. It must rest with strategy then.

He crossed to the barred grating of the cell, looked through the narrow antechamber to the outside door of this log hut. A sentry paced back and forth at regular, short intervals. There was another guard beneath the cell window. Wentworth timed the passing of the sentries and worked silently, swiftly, when they were not in sight. He filled the tin pails in which their dinner had come with water and drinking jugs. Then he balanced them to hang on spoons which were thrust into the frame just above the cell door. He ripped strips from his shirt to make a cord which he attached to them. He laid his blanket on the floor just inside the door and tied a stronger cord, made of a strip of the blanket itself, to that. Then he lay down to wait. Feeble artifices, but they would have to serve. He was quite sure that the assassins would not risk the noise of shooting and it would be next to impossible to throw a knife between the bars of either door or window. That meant that Prince Wilhelm's killers would have to enter the cell through the door. When they did. . . .

Wentworth lay down upon his cot, holding the ends of the two improvised cords and pretended to sleep. He had not apprized Barker of his plans for it was doubtful if the boy would be able to fake sleep, to remain quiet and wait for the killers. . . .

The long watches of the night dragged on. The sergeant of the guard made his rounds, and the challenges rang out clearly on the thin, chill air of the plains. It was a half hour after the sergeant passed that the sentry in front of the cell house challenged sharply. There was a muttered colloquy, then three men slipped in through the outer door. Despite his preparedness, Wentworth felt his body stiffening and he had to force himself to resume the deep regular breathing of sleep. His hand was alert on the cords attached to his feeble traps. In the dimness of the outer room, he caught the gleam of steel. Two of the men carried swords in their hands. The third hung back as they advanced. Wentworth's face became set and grim. They knew their work, these three. That one who hung back would carry a revolver and in extremity, he would use it on "escaping" prisoners.

As silently as shadows, the two assasins drifted to the door and peered for long seconds between the bars. Wentworth blessed the deep, noisy sleep of Barker for its naturalness. It covered up any discrepancies in his own imitation. There was a tautness in his nerves. Everything depended on his own swift action at the right moment. Barker could be counted on to spring to the attack when he was aroused. . . .

The lock rasped faintly in its socket, the door pivoted on oiled hinges. For a breath, the two men hung back, as if some fear stayed them from immediate entrance; then they came in together. The man in front took a long stride into the room, then checked, staring down at the softness of the blanket which he felt beneath his feet. It was the moment for which Wentworth had waited. He snapped erect and, putting his whole weight into a single heave, yanked at the cords fastened to blanket and to the dinner pails, loaded with water, the scraps of the dinner and the water crocks!

The tin pails struck upon the head and shoulders of

the second man. The one in front was thrown to his back by the sudden yank upon the blanket on which he stood. His sword hand flew high, a choked cry in his throat.

"Barker!" Wentworth cried. "We're attacked!"

While he shouted, he was leaping forward. It was no trick to take the sword from the man who sprawled upon the floor, but the second assassin was already recovering from the blow of pails upon his head and shoulders. His sword licked out to meet the saber Wentworth had captured. Twice the steel rang, then the *Spider* lunged savagely and sliced through the other's guard.

Even as his thrust went home, he felt the arms of the man he had upset close about his legs. The *Spider* dropped to his knees and the sword, wedged between his victim's ribs, broke off short in his hand.

"Don't let him lock the door, Barker!" Wentworth cried. "Hold the door."

He had a glimpse of Barker springing for the steel door, then he was locked in a life-and-death struggle with the man who had tripped him. The man had a dagger. Wentworth had two inches of blade on the hilt of the saber, blunt ended, nearly useless. He dodged a stab and his left hand darted to the man's throat. With a cry of pain, the assassin reeled to his feet. For a moment then, the two stood face to face in the darkness. Wentworth could see the gleam of the man's teeth and his own lips curved in a savage smile. Barker was tussling there in the antechamber with the third assassin and the alarm of the sentries—two rifle shots crashing into the sky—sounded like thunder. It would have to be fast now, or all would be lost. And that, to the *Spider,* meant not only his own life but also the scores who would die in Grand Junction tomorrow if he did not escape; the hundreds who would die throughout the United States if he failed to smash this conspiracy.

With a shout, he sprang toward his enemy, saw the knife slice upward for his belly, a blow almost impossible to parry. He could take a chance at striking it aside with his left fist . . . Instead, Wentworth sprang to the right, hitting for the face with the abbreviated stub of his saber. The man flinched back and they were squared off again. Despite the masking darkness, the movements of steel caught glints of light and betrayed the whereabouts of each. The *Spider* pressed in. There could be no delay. Delay would mean victory for his assailant. And the man seemed to realize that. Feinted about in the darkness. He snatched up a blanket from Barker's cot and flapped it toward Wentworth to blind him.

The *Spider* laughed. He caught the blanket in the air and yanked violently, springing forward and to the left of the assassin. The man realized his mistake too late. He cried out despairingly, stumbled, threw his arms wide . . . and the *Spider* struck with the saber hilt. The broken blade, with all his weight and strength behind it, slipped behind the man's upthrown arm and caught him just back of the jaw in the soft, fatal spot beneath the ear.

Wentworth did not wait to see the result of that blow. He did not need to, for the man's life blood was spurting out from his jugular. Through the open door of the cell, the *Spider* sprang, pausing a moment to snatch up the sword of the first man he had killed. Barker reeled to his feet from the body of the officer.

"Good work, Barker," Wentworth said crisply. He stood and ran his hand over the floor, searching vainly for the man's revolver. No time to hunt though the weapon would have increased their chances a hundredfold. Sword ready in his hand, Wentworth leaped to the outer door. A rifle blazed at him at almost contact range, but his hand had jolted up its barrel just in time. The sword slid in under it and they were out of the jail house. The sentry died in his tracks.

Over by the tents, a bugle was blaring: "To arms!" Wentworth tossed the sword to Barker, snatched up the sentry's bayoneted rifle. He led a sprint toward the parade grounds and the house of El Gaucho. That was

112

still his first goal, the death of that evil genius. As he and Barker sallied from the shadow of the jail, a running squad of men, rifles at port, smashed into them.

Wentworth pivoted and the rifle blasted from his hip, blew a soldier back upon his comrades. The bayonet licked out, and another fell. Barker's sword in his inexperienced hand, smashed down on another man's shoulder. Then a bayonet parried the saber, brushed it aside.

"Take them alive!" an officer shouted from somewhere behind. "Take them alive!"

It was just in time to stop a bayonet thrust which had Barker cold. The tip raked up the side of the boy's face, but he only growled in his throat and went in with the sword before him like a lance. The soldier who had spared him died. Wentworth fired once more and with his next shot, the hammer clicked on the empty chamber. He had snatched the rifle from the guard who had fired the alarm!

He was viciously engaged with two men who wielded the bayonet like experts. If they had heard the order to take the prisoners alive, it apparently meant nothing whatsoever to them. They were thrusting savagely for throat and belly. The *Spider* sprang to his right, so that one antagonist blocked the other. His first lunge stretched one soldier on the earth. The second man retreated and was finished with a point in his throat. Wentworth saw that Barker was down on his face, and a burning rage seethed up within him. He sprang to the rescue. Three men with bayonets pivoted to meet him. The officer stood to one side with sword in hand—and around a corner of the jail came a platoon of men at double quick march!

For a moment, Wentworth hesitated. All his heart dictated that he fight over the fallen body of this brave lad, though he knew it to be futile. Probably Barker was still alive. His sword would not have been too formidable against men with bayonets. The butt end of a rifle would have put him out. And rifle butts do not always kill . . . His desire was to stand by the unconscious lad on the ground. . . .

But the *Spider* could not tarry.

Bitterness like the taste of ashes was in his soul. A town and a nation would lie at the mercy of murderers if he were slain or captured tonight, if he remained to help this brave boy . . . With a curse, Wentworth spun and ran into the dark gloom that lay upon the parade grounds.

"Halt!" cried the officer. "Halt, or we fire!"

Wentworth ran on, zigzagging. There were only three riflemen in a position to fire. They were panting from their exertions and it was doubtful if they could hold a bead on a moving figure in the darkness. The platoon coming at the double would have to swing out of the column, the front rank drop to their knees, before they could fire. It would take a couple of seconds and those seconds counted with Wentworth. He detached the bayonet from the gun as he raced and dropped the useless rifle behind him. He quickened his stride directly toward the mansion of El Gaucho!

No lights there, no lights anywhere to guide the bullets. Fifty yards away from the rifleman, whose lead was beginning to sing through the night, Wentworth turned at right angles to his course and plunged for the tents of the soldiers bivouacked to southward. The dark cloak of the night was his salvation. He heard the rifle fire cease, heard the beat of soldier's feet moving double quick across the parade grounds toward El Gaucho's home.

It had been deliberate, the rush toward the mansion. Soldiers would search the place, and fail to find him. When he finally went there, as he intended presently to do, he would not be expected. He ceased his running, crept up to the tents and lay at full length in the shadows between two of them. His breathing quieted slowly, but his mind raced on. It would be useless to attempt tonight to free Barker. There would be an overwhelming guard and in seeking to help his friend, he probably would find only death for himself. And the *Spider's* life was incalculably precious now. He knew damaging things about El Gaucho. If he could only kill the man, get clear of the camp. . . .

Wentworth dug the point of his bayonet deep into the earth until it was clean and bright, fondled it in his hands. A slim weapon against a regiment of killers! The whole thing suddenly seemed fantastic to him. On the plains of the middle west, what state he did not know, he lay in the midst of a camp that the government did not guess existed, with a commander they thought merely a common bandit. The G-men would be after him, without a doubt, and they were efficient, but they were often slow in action. And they would have no force competent to cope with this terror. It was work for an army—or for a single man!

Wentworth got cautiously to his feet. The search of the Gaucho's house had ended. There would be double sentries now—ceaseless patrolling.

The *Spider's* eyes were narrow and hard as he stole toward the house of El Gaucho with the bayonet covered in his cloak lest its gleam betray him. One thing they would not expect, that any fugitive would further endanger himself by a deliberate attack upon the generalissimo of their forces! Well, it would be death for one of them when they met and the *Spider* had trained himself to kill. . . .

CHAPTER ELEVEN

When Foes Meet

The mansion, when the *Spider* peered at it from the middle of its fragrant flower garden, was only lightly guarded and unlighted. Two sentries made a slow circuit. That, apparently, was all. Wentworth waited until the two men had met and started back on their rounds away from him. Then he raced swiftly forward, hid close to the building.

When the two guards returned, they stood a moment talking idly.

"Damned shame we couldn't be in on this raid," one of them said.

"Yeah," the other grunted. "Gaucho must be a quarter of the way there by now. He'll wait, to have his men in place before it gets light."

"Sure, but that's what I hate, that waiting for the banks to open."

The two shouldered their rifles, and went back to their rounds again. Wentworth crouched unmoving. With El Gaucho gone, there was no hope of a quick, all-conquering blow. There remained then only to dash for Grand Junction, to warn the town . . . The opening of a window above where he crouched against the foundations of the building startled him. He shrank close against the wall, peered upward, saw a woman's hands clasped upon the sill. He held his breath, waiting, and the sentries paced back slowly.

"Sentry!" the woman called. It was Carollotta!

The sentry brought his gun to present. "Yes, Princess?"

"Sentry, the escaped prisoner is directly under my window!"

Her cry was stultifying, but Wentworth caught its import the moment the word "escaped" passed her lips. He was in action before the stiffly standing sentry could grasp her meaning. The sentry glimpsed a black cloaked figure springing from the shadows. He tried to bring his bayonet into position, but it was already too late. Wentworth's own bayonet whistled through the air and its dull edge caught the sentry behind the ear, hurled him unconscious to the ground. The other soldier was running forward with his bayonet leveled and the *Spider* awaited his coming. Then, sharply, his arm jerked upward from his side and the bayonet, butt-first, caught the man between the eyes and spilled him, also, senseless to the earth.

Wentworth snatched up a rifle and, in a long stride, was beneath the window with the needle point of the bayonet lifted to touch the white throat of the princess!

"Don't make a sound, Carollotta," he said quietly.

The woman looked down on him contemptuously. "You are a coward and a traitor," she said scornfully. "You deserted Tom Barker."

The words hurt Wentworth.

"I feel the same way about it," he said heavily, "but it was a matter of leaving him or getting warning to Grand Junction before your uncle strikes there. It was one life against many."

Carollotta said, "You deserted your friend!"

The *Spider's* voice was bitter, "Yes, I deserted my friend! I have deserted many friends so that I might fulfill my duty. I have deserted the woman I love, too, on occasion to fates more horrible than mere death by torture. I have done all those things."

"You sound . . . bitter," said Carollotta.

The *Spider* laughed shortly. "Tell me, Carollotta, where I may find guns and a horse."

Carollota took the bayonet between her fingers and moved it aside. Wentworth let it waver and she leaned down toward him with her forearms on the sill.

"Stay," she whispered. "Stay and I will hide you. We will find means to free Tom Barker and. . . ."

". . . . And," Wentworth interrupted flatly, "let a dozen—a score of people be killed in Grand Junction!"

Carollotta's breath caught between her bitten lips. She started to speak, then stood stiffly at the window. Her hair was about her shoulders in two long, soft braids and fell across the silken weight of her negligee. She was very lovely, very young with the soft dusk of night about her. How could she realize the bitter philosophy of the *Spider*?

Carollotta said, "Oh it is hard, hard! I know you are right. . . ." She bent forward. "Hurry before I change my mind. There are guns here in the house. My horse is stabled behind—a bay mare called . . . Wilhemina. See, *Spider*, I trust you. You are my only hope. In God's name—in the name of whatever you hold sacred—come back and save . . . *my love!*"

Wentworth tossed the rifle to the ground, sprang to the sill and drew himself inside. He stood gazing at Carollotta, then he lifted her white hand to his lips.

"I will come back," he said simply. *"The Spider swears it!"*

He felt her small, soft fingers cling to his hand. . . .

Wentworth strapped on two shoulder holsters with forty-five automatics in them, dropped spare clips into his pockets. He put two thirty-eight revolvers in the waist band of his trousers, girded on a keen-edged saber whose balance delighted his heart. He had to kill a sentry to take Carollotta's mare. Then he disappeared into the night, soft-footing toward the South where lay Grand Junction and where the marauding army of El Gaucho soon would spring its trap. He rode to his duty, but his heart was heavy within him. The *Spider* must succeed tonight and the *Spider* must not die. Too many hopes, too many hearts hung upon the success of his ventures.

But Wentworth was not one to contemplate failure. Once out of hearing of the camp, he gave the mare her head. There was so little time to reach Grand Junction, fifteen miles away, and prepare the town to resist an armed invasion. So little time—for already there was in the East the hint of gray which is the false dawn. The *Spider* leaned far forward on the horse's withers to ease his weight, guiding her in the darkness with a firm hand on the bridle. He knew again the sensation, like nothing else in the world, of being one with great sinews, of terrific power for speed, which comes to the man who rides a great horse and loves that horse.

The plains flew backward under the mare's heels in a steady canter that needed no stops for breathing, but the sun was red above the horizon before the smudge of smoke above Grand Junction brushed the hilltop ahead. As if she knew her duty, the horse bounded up the incline with new vigor. The rough trace of a road which he followed became a concrete highway and he set the mare to a gallop along its margin. Abruptly, he hauled her up on her haunches and she shied about while the *Spider* leaned from the saddle to confront the three men who had sprung from ambush. They held shotguns with their gaping black muzzles of death leveled on Wentworth. . . .

"Now where might you be going, stranger?" drawled the leader, a weary-looking man in faded overalls. "Your hawss is downright lathered."

The *Spider* eyed the man suspiciously through a tense moment, saw honesty in the steady, blue eyes. "El Gaucho is going to raid Grand Junction as soon as the banks open," he said sharply, patting his restive mare's neck. "There was need to lather her."

The mare nickered and somehow the men drew nearer and looked at this dark-cloaked figure with more confidence. They knew and loved horses in this country. A man who loved his horse, and whose horse loved him. . . .

"Who are you, stranger, and how come you know about the Gaucho?" the weary one asked. His whole appearance was dejected, even to the drooping of his sandy mustache, but the brightness of his eyes belied his manner.

Wentworth leaned on his saddle bow. "Where I come from, it isn't considered real bright to ask questions like that," he drawled. "Who are you?"

For a moment there was a sharpening of those steady, blue eyes, then the man laughed. "Reckon you're right. My monicker's Hart."

The *Spider* nodded. "I am Gaucho's enemy," he said grimly. "I just escaped from his camp. Will one of you gentlemen go with me to warn the town?"

Hart gazed at him, then disappeared into the bushes and returned with a buckskin horse that looked tough. He swung up easily. "You boys," he told his companions, "keep on watching here for this here Gaucho and dash back anyway if you hear shooting."

The mare and the buckskin leveled out for the city, hoofs flying. Wentworth shouted a question above the whip of the wind, but the answer disappointed him. He had hoped the men in the shrubbery were outposts on guard against El Gaucho, but they were merely a posse hunting a thief. The *Spider's* mouth shut more grimly at the news. That meant no preparations had been made for the battle to come . . . Hart was sheriff, Wentworth gathered. That would help some in speeding the assembly of a defense force.

Finally the first scattered houses of the town began to flash past, their horses hoofs were beating on pavement. Hart raised a voice that had shrill carrying power.

"El Gaucho is coming! To the town hall! Bring your guns!"

Over and over, he shouted that warning as he raced. Before the two on horseback had passed from sight, men and women were running into the streets, carrying rifles, strapping revolvers to their thighs. It had not been a full generation since these people had harked to other cries of alarm that were almost as terrible. Wentworth and Hart might have been men in doeskins with long rifles across their saddles. "To the blockhouse! The Indians are coming!"

Wentworth's eyes shot all about him, surveying the town in the early morning light. To the west flowed a shallow stream whose banks were cut steep by erosion. A bridge . . . That would be easily guarded. The Gaucho would hardly attack from that direction. To the South, where the main highway led out, was broken terrain, but to reach that, El Gaucho's raiders would have to circle the entire town. Still it must be either from that direction or East. The *Spider* had come from the north without sighting the killer's cohorts.

The town was narrow, strung out along the river bank and it seemed certain El Gaucho would seek to enter from the side so as to travel through as little hostile territory as possible. A smoldering anger had possession of Wentworth now as he glanced over the fleeing people. So many of these neat white-painted homes would be destroyed in the battle to come. Too many of them were frame. They would scarcely resist rifle bullets, and flames would play havoc.

In the small, grassy plot before the old town hall, which was built of red brick and topped with a belled cupola, Hart flung himself from his horse and dashed inside the building. Seconds later, the bell began an excited, bellowing clangor. People stopped in the streets to stare, automobiles spun to the curb. Wentworth sat his horse before the old steps of the building and threw his arms high above his head gesturing to everyone in sight. When Hart came out again, his gun in plain evidence on his thigh and a rifle in the crook of his elbow, there was a growing crowd and, moment by moment, other men came. The ranks bristled with the barrels of rifles.

Hart glanced at Wentworth, sitting calmly erect on

his lathered horse, his head thrown back, the cape draped in almost military style from his shoulders.

"Tell them about it, stranger," he ordered calmly.

Wentworth nodded. The sheriff was a shrewd man. He knew that the startling words that were to be pronounced would gain more credence, swifter action from the *Spider* because of his dramatic appearance—since Hart supported what he said. The *Spider's* calculating gray-blue eyes swept the crowd. Men were here who had fought before, grim-faced, eyes narrowed from the hot sun of the plains. Wentworth felt a growing sense of satisfaction. He was glad that the first organized stand against El Gaucho was to be made by men like these.

He lifted a slow hand toward the sun and there was an instant, waiting silence among the thousand men who had gathered before him.

"El Gaucho is coming to destroy Grand Junction," Wentworth said, his voice deep and strong. He paused then, saw the faces before him grow hard and determined. It pleased him. "I was their prisoner and escaped to bring you the warning. Do I need to tell you what El Gaucho's men will do if they are allowed to enter?"

A rumbling voice of anger answered him, the cry of bitter men. Wentworth turned to Hart. "I have some plans for defense," he said. "Shall I. . . .?"

"Go ahead," Hart nodded. "I'll check."

Wentworth smiled grimly. Hart thought he was all right, but he was giving notice that he'd keep an eye on the proceedings. The *Spider* turned to the crowd again, studied faces. He knew men. His life had often depended on the faculty for reading men's character at a glance. He had been a soldier . . . He leveled a hand pointing to a middle-aged man with a square, heavy face.

"Pick out ten men and ambush the south entrance of the highway," he said. "If you lack arms, commandeer them from stores. If El Gaucho's men come by automo-

122

bile, remember a wrecked car will disable more men than a dead occupant of the car.''

Hart cut in: ''Go to it, Johnson.''

Johnson pivoted and began picking men from the crowd about him. Wentworth sent another similar squad to the northern entry, to the bridge; sent fifty men to cover the eastern fringe of the town where there was no road. Twenty were sent to barricade each of the town's three banks. Autos were to blackade every street that led to a bank.

''As much as possible,'' Wentworth said sharply, ''get all women and children into the town hall and other stone or brick buildings. El Gaucho will use fire and his men are beasts.''

At the town hall, which was pretty much the center of the place, a force of three hundred men was assembled, roughly divided into six companies. There were ranks of automobiles parked before the building for quick action. Those who could not pile into the cars would go on foot. When these arrangements had been made, Wentworth and Hart stood quietly together on the steps of the town hall with the men who would head the companies. Hart had a machine gun in his hands. Wentworth would depend upon his automatics and revolvers for which he got a supply of extra ammunition. He felt a hard readiness in all his body for the battle. If it were well fought, they might be able to turn back El Gaucho and damage the morale of his men. It would take a good many tortures to stiffen their backbone for a new assault. The difficulty of the defense lay in the shortage of rifles and of ammunition. The supplies of the stores had soon been exhausted. They provided enough for about two hours of hard fighting if men conserved their shots. But El Gaucho would have machine guns. He had entire squads armed with portable rapid-fire weapons stolen from police arsenals in some of his raids. He would have grenades and tear-gas bombs. . . .

Wentworth glanced at his watch. A quarter past nine. The assault would begin any moment. The men about

123

him moved restlessly, peering off toward the streets and the ranks of automobiles. A steady procession of women and children hurried, many weeping, into the town hall which already was jammed to overflowing. Ten minutes ticked past and nothing happened. The *Spider's* eyes quested over the city, stopped abruptly as they caught a smudge of greenish smoke. His gaze narrowed, and he turned toward Hart.

"I don't think there's any doubt El Gaucho has been warned that we are ready for him," he said quietly, "but that won't turn him back. Do you know of any reason, Hart, why that man's chimney over there would be sending out *green* smoke?"

Hart gazed where Wentworth indicated and a harsh curse rasped from his throat. He took a quick step forward, then checked. He said, "Why, damn it, stranger, that's *my* house . . . But there ain't any fire in my furnace. Or there wasn't when I left. I. . . .!"

His voice choked off as a ragged burst of firing ripped out to the south and, almost simultaneously, at the north end of town. The group of men on the steps of the town hall stiffened. A few started toward their companies.

"Wait," Wentworth rasped shortly. "Wait for motorcycle couriers."

The firing continued. Machine guns took up their sharp, throaty chattering. There was the thudding rumble of a grenade. Hart stood, stony-faced, eyes hot with rage.

"Look, Hart," a man said to him. "Johnson is going to be wiped out if we don't. . . ."

A motorcycle roared up the street, bumped the curb and chattered straight up to the steps. The rider flung off and ran up to Hart.

"Five cars tried to crash through at the south end," he panted. "Johnson stopped three, but the other two got past. He's got three men left."

"Ten more men ought to take care of those two cars," Wentworth said. Hart nodded, though his face was pale with the knowledge that seven defenders had fallen. He jerked out an order to the head of one of the companies. The man raced forward and his voice reached ahead of him. Ten men detached themselves from one of the huddled groups and went toward cars. The other men were dead quiet, waiting. Off to the North, the shooting had stopped entirely and no courier appeared. A full company was sent in that direction, scattered over four different streets, keeping close to buildings, hunting cover.

Hart turned, thin-lipped, to Wentworth. "It's the East all right," he said flatly. "Two companies ought to back up the fifty men we sent over there."

Wentworth nodded agreement. "If you'll stay here with the other three companies in reserve," he said, "I'll go to the East. But, Hart, I'm after just one thing . . . I'm going to kill El Gaucho!"

Hart held out his hand. "Good luck, stranger. None of us will ever forget this."

Wentworth's lips were tight against his teeth, but his grip of Hart's hand was firm and solid. "Good luck!"

Hart nodded. "Good luck . . . *Spider!*"

His last word was no more than a movement of lips, an almost soundless whisper. Wentworth's hand tightened upon his a bit more. Then he was gone, springing to the saddle of Carollotta's mare. He paused for a brief moment before the two companies nearest the eastern end of the town hall yard, looking at them slowly.

"The attack is on the East," he said, making his voice carry to them all easily. "These two companies are going there before it begins. You will be outnumbered and outarmed, but you will fight from cover . . . and you are fighting for your homes and your wives and sweethearts!"

A rumble of anger ran over the men. Their hands upon their guns were white with tension.

"You are brave," Wentworth said flatly, "but don't be foolish. Hide as well as you can; keep to cover. *Don't* be brave. Be stubborn. Don't give way, but don't

125

show yourselves. Machine gunners are not brave, just deadly. And, one last word—'' He paused, and held them with his silence, every eye centered on him— "Don't let one of your women fall into their hands. It would be kinder to—kill the women! These men of El Gaucho are the renegades of the border, the wolves of the cities. That's all!''

He saluted the two captains. "Carry on," he said shortly, then he spun his horse in a *demi-volte* and sent her thudding across the grass. She took the chain railing in an easy spring and was racing down the street. Before he had gone a block, he heard ahead of him to the eastward a ragged burst of firing that was heavier and more vicious than any that had broken out before. A half-dozen machine guns began to splutter. Bombs sent their rumbling thunder across the town. Then came a sound that brought a cry to Wentworth's lips, drew him far forward on the neck of his horse with the urgency for greater speed.

Field artillery had opened fire!

CHAPTER TWELVE

El Gaucho Strikes

Even as he dashed to bolster the courage of the defenders, Wentworth saw the roof and the wall of a house lift before the blast of a screaming shell and collapse in débris. Three men were huddled in the ruins, dead. Down the length of the street, he could see a ragged line of soldiers in red advancing with the motley mob of El Gaucho's killers behind them. Some of the red men were falling, but the others came on unwavering.

Lead began to sing viciously past Wentworth's ears. He swung into a side street, picketed his horse and rushed forward on foot, keeping close to the walls until he was within a block of the outer rim of houses. Three shells in quick succession landed among the buildings ahead. One house lifted, fell in upon itself. Another had a gaping hole torn in its side and over the ruins, smoke . . . then red tongues of fire, began to creep.

He saw a dozen of the defenders flee backward from the front line and he called to them.

"More troops are coming," he shouted, "rally here!"

He got the twelve together in a side street, sent one back as a courier, with orders for the two companies that were coming to line both sides of three parallel streets to take cover inside of buildings, especially in cellars. The eleven men who remained he posted at opposite corners of the side streets. They caught up débris from a shell-wrecked house, hurriedly erected barricades, threw mattresses and pieces of furniture down as shields.

The soldiers of El Gaucho were still yards away and Wentworth left the men at work, preparing to enfilade the attackers while he rushed on to build a similar defense at the next corner, leaving orders to fire three rounds, then retreat through the trap that was being laid by the two supporting companies.

At each corner, parallel to the line of attack, he set up barricades in side streets. Two of them were weakly manned by four men and it was with these that Wentworth stayed, waiting for the attack. The field pieces, of which Wentworth figured there were three, had ceased firing with the breaking of resistance along the outer edge of the town. Now the soldiers of El Gaucho were advancing double-quick time.

Wentworth looked at the grim faces of the men about him. They would die rather than retreat, Wentworth knew. He ordered them to hold their fire when the first of the attackers came in sight, advancing cautiously with bayonets on their rifles. With them sauntered El Gaucho's lieutenant, De Moltkez, without a weapon in his hand, although there was a sword at his side, and an automatic in its holster. The *Spider's* automatic came into his palm without conscious thought, but he, too, held his fire, waiting.

A feeble, feeble force, these four men with him! Two behind the barricade across the street, two here with him. But they were well protected. Wentworth lifted his automatic as the soliders came warily forward. Scarcely thirty feet away now. Aiming at De Moltkez's stomach, Wentworth squeezed the trigger, signaling a volley at the same time.

Four rifles crashed with his automatic and four men went down with De Moltkez. The four soldiers lay where they had fallen, but De Moltkez stumbled to his feet. His sword rasped from its scabbard and he hailed those in the rear.

"Forward!" he shouted. "Forward!"

Wentworth's lips felt cold and hard. His eyes burned. He knew the meaning of that failure to kill. The man wore armor beneath his uniform. And now, as he stood facing the rear, his spiked helmet protected his head and the back of his neck. Wentworth aimed deliberately at the hand that held the sword, shattered it with a swift shot.

The sword fell; De Moltkez's arm flung down with the impact of the lead. He continued to order his men on, and the *Spider* felt a momentary glow of admiration. Courage was a rare and priceless thing and, though this man's cause was an evil, a murderous one, it was impossible not to respect, a brave enemy. Wentworth put a bullet through De Moltkez's leg, saw him fall, saw soldiers cluster about him.

The four rifles were taking heavy toll among the thick press of red men who continued to crowd forward, but the answering hail of lead was a hot breath of death. One of the riflemen with Wentworth surged to his feet with a slug through his head and pitched forward over the barricade. With the second, Wentworth sprang into the house beside them, raced through it to the back yard and climbed fences along the block to safety. On the next corner, they took a new stand. He caught a low cry, whirled to see a man signal from a window. The captain of one of the supporting companies was in the basement of a house directly opposite!

Wentworth raced to him. "Hold fire until they fill the entire distance you have men posted, then mow them down," he ordered rapidly. "We'll lead him. . . .!"

The thud of a bullet, the sigh of the rifleman with him interrupted Wentworth, the man collapsed against him, dying. A curse was torn from the captain's throat.

"Jack," he said hoarsely. "Damn them to hell! They killed Jack!"

Wentworth crouched against the side of the house, his two automatics speaking in slow rhythm. His marksmanship was the product of endless hours of practice; the guns were like parts of his own body. When he shot a man fell. During that long minute, the bodies of the dead checked further advance. He turned back to the captain, saw tears streaming down his white face.

"He was my brother," the company-leader said.

Wentworth pointed down the street, his own face drawn and pale.

"There are the men who killed him," he announced flatly. "Wait until there are many in your trap!"

He retreated, dodging from doorway to doorway, reloading his automatic as he went. This defense was costing a terrific number of casualties, but El Gaucho was taking even heavier losses. This would be a costly raid for him.

Wentworth's continued escape from harm was a seeming miracle, but actually it was caution and experience. Men had gone through two and three years of the World War, through countless bitter battles, without a wound. They were those who knew how to take advantage of every bit of cover—who kept their eyes and their guns on the enemy every second. A man who was quick with his guns had an armor in his bullets.

But the *Spider* felt that he had done all he could here. The soldiers already were marching double quick time into the trap. It was useless to expose himself further. The *Spider* must live—to kill El Gaucho! Wentworth became aware, now that the pressure of close attack was fading with his retreat, that heavy firing was going on in the center of the city. From the sound, Hart's three companies must be bitterly engaged also.

Wentworth recovered his picketed horse, raced toward the town hall. His eyes flicked the sky-line. Black smoke and flames were tonguing up in a dozen places and the scream of shells shrilled overhead, echoed by the bellowing thunder of their explosions. There were other, less pleasant sounds. Now and then, the scream of a woman arose.

Curses squeezed out between Wentworth's teeth. Those renegades of El Gaucho! He suspected that the bandit king encouraged bestiality to spread the terror of his advance. As he raced past a side street, he saw a girl fleeing from a man—and losing the race. Wentworth reined his horse back on its haunches, pivoted back to the street corner. His automatic spoke once and the man twisted backward violently, rolled over twice before he lay, limp in death, in the dusty street.

The girl looked up with a startled, white face, then dodged into a house. Wentworth swore as he swung the horse about again. Of what use to save one woman when all over the city . . . ? The mare was stretched out like an arrow, head thrust forward, tail flying out straight behind. Her rhythmic gait was a song of power. Wentworth patted her neck as he raced on. A brave little beast. After her rest, she was as fresh and strong as ever. . . .

The Town Hall Square was deserted when he smashed out into the open from a side street. He pulled the mare up, rearing, to peer about. Dead men lay like abandoned bundles of clothing about the street. The bank across the street was shattered by explosions, its windows blank gaping holes, its barricades breached by grenade craters. What, was it all in vain then? Had El Gaucho swept in from some other direction while his men had fought a futile skirmish there on the east?

But the firing was still heavy up the street there. A tight group of men broke out of the opposite side of the square coming at a hard run. The square-built Johnson was in their lead, eight men behind him. At sight of Wentworth, they swerved in his direction and he sent the mare to meet them.

"We cleaned them up on the South," Johnson rasped. There was a blood stain on his shoulder, a jagged rip across his temple. His hat was gone, but his thick, brown hand was steady on the butt of his revolver.

"I think they're stopped on the East, too," Wentworth said. "I got one of their leaders and they were walking into a trap of a hundred rifles."

Johnson looked about him haggardly. "God, they're dead here, too," he said dully. "I lost thirteen men."

Wentworth looked over the squad behind the man. They were white-faced, but their anger was a hard, enduring thing. He nodded. "I'll see what's happening up the street here," he said. "You follow, but keep to cover."

He dashed forward, hearing still the battering of the three field pieces off there to the East, hearing the crashing of volley fire where the soldiers in red walked into ambush. Dropping from the horse at a run, he peered about the corner.

From the cover of surrounding buildings, fully fifty of El Gaucho's renegades were pumping lead, hurling grenades at a bank building that was being stubbornly defended. Even as he looked, a group of bandits burst from cover and went forward with bayonets fixed.

Wentworth threw up an arm in urgent signal to the nine behind him and, dropping prone on the ground, opened fire with both automatics. His guns bellowed death. Johnson's voice was breathless, but sharp in command, and Wentworth heard his men hit the ground, heard their rifles blasting about him.

Almost before their flanking fire had begun, the charge was broken, and a dozen men lay dead on the ground outside the barricade. From the bank, a cheer went up and redoubled fire blasted from its windows and fortified door. Wentworth drew his little command back to cover just in time as machine gun lead hurricaned up the street.

He led his small squad in a rapid sweep around the block. While El Gaucho's men still scoured their first position with lead, they reached a second street that opened on their flanks. A dozen bandits were in sight, behind posts and automobiles. Before they were aware of their new peril, the rifles of Johnson's men opened again and death was among them.

The firing to eastward was dwindling now and Wentworth detached a man to summon reinforcements from the ambushing companies. Once more, he executed a circling movement, but this time the enemy was prepared and two of Wentworth's little command went down. The squad kept moving anyway. There was no danger of a frontal attack because of covering fire from the bank's barricades, but they were open to a flanking assault.

Wentworth turned over his command to the competent, grim-faced Johnson, and galloped on through the streets of the town. He had failed to sight El Gaucho here and that was his chief concern. Whirling to the left, to intercept the northern highway which stretched toward the plains encampment of El Gaucho, Wentworth met sentry lines. He dropped two men whose rifles were too slow and whirled back. In an alleyway, he left the mare again and went through backyards toward the highway again. There, if anywhere, El Gaucho would pass.

The *Spider,* creeping along fences toward a position that would command the highway, felt a new respect for El Gaucho. The man was a skillful strategist. If he failed, it was because of the inefficiency of his lieutenants. He had posted men to protect his line of retreat through a city that would be full of his enemies. But not all were enemies, Wentworth recalled. Some one had signaled that the town was prepared for defense— the green smoke from the sheriff's house.

Also there had been, along the streets he had covered, certain homes which apparently were immune to attack, their windows were whole, their doors unshattered by marauding men. Possibly they were allies of El Gaucho! Wentworth felt the tension of anger creeping into his muscles. It was damnable to think that anyone should ally himself with such a criminal, but it gave new proof of the man's power.

The house toward which Wentworth worked his way was darkly shuttered and apparently deserted. It had the look of those other places that he had seen, which he suspected of being those of El Gaucho sympathizers. There was a certain grim set to his lips as he stole forward, an implacable coldness in his eyes. An abrupt thought struck him that this house must be near where the green smoke had arisen. . . .

A cellar window yielded silently to his shrewd manipulations and he slipped across the dark basement toward stairs which he could dimly discern on its opposite side. Nothing hindered him as he went through the kitchen toward the front hall. . . . He froze in the shadow of the stairs that led upward. Soft footsteps creaked across the floor over his head.

Cautiously, the *Spider* slid up the stairs. The footsteps were still now. With their ceasing, a throbbing silence filled the house, as if the building itself were waiting. For what?

Wentworth frowned at the whisper of his nerves; his mind which was recalling what had happened when before he ignored that warning of his subconscious mind. He knew suddenly that danger was here! The certainty stopped him half-way up the stair. He drew out his sword, clamping the blade between his fingers to prevent sound.

Out in the street, a woman screamed and a gale of ribald laughter followed. A volley of rifle fire crackled in the distance. On the floor below the *Spider,* a mouse squeaked and scampered across bare wood with a faint scratching noise. Presently, Wentworth became aware of movement above him again, dim creaking of boards beneath unwary feet. Some one was shifting his weight. Wentworth looked upward along his sword blade and saw a man's hair edge over the bannister, followed by two inches of forehead, then the eyes. . . .

Wentworth jabbed with his sword, held its point within a half-inch of the eyes.

"Stand up!" he ordered softly.

The eyes widened and, as the sword advanced, a man raised his body.

"I have an automatic in my left hand," Wentworth cautioned. "If you should try to shoot, you would be

134

dead before you could wink. Now, walk to the head of the steps with me.''

The man had not opened his lips. He walked along the railing as Wentworth climbed the stairs. The gun in his right hand hung limply, and he made no resistance when it was taken.

''What kind of mercuric compound did you use to make the green smoke?'' asked the *Spider* softly.

A quiver ran over the man's face, a flaccid, weakening of his jaw, a quiver of his eyelids. Wentworth cursed. He dropped guns and sword, caught the man's shirt with his left hand and hit him twice with his fist, let the man slump to the floor. He stooped and bound him rapidly with his own belt, tied his shoe laces together, then wrote rapidly on a card, using his left hand, sealed what he had written with the emblem of the *Spider*. When he left, he would deposit this gentleman where he could be found. Sheriff Hart would do the rest to the man who had signaled to the enemy with the green smoke. His guilt was unquestionable.

The *Spider* slipped to the front of the house and peered out between the slats of the closed blinds. The laughter and the screams still sounded there and now he saw the reason. Soldiers and gangsters of El Gaucho lined the street. About ten of them were in sight and Wentworth knew from their spacing that the guard extended that way from the center of the town to its outskirts. Between the lines of men were three girls, hysterical with fear, trying frantically to escape their tormentors. Each time they dashed toward the lines, a soldier would seize them and rip off another bit of their clothing. One girl was already entirely nude. Whenever a girl crouched to the earth, seeking to escape further torment, a bullet would scorch the ground near her. Once more the *Spider's* guns leaped to his hands, but he stayed the shot, looked rapidly about. The room was a sleeping chamber and he crossed to the bed in a long bound, snatched up a pillow, then darted back to the window.

When next a soldier caught a girl, Wentworth pressed the muzzle of his automatic deep into the pillow and fired. His aim was instinctive, never-failing, like the aim of a baseball pitcher. The soldier reeled backward and the girl broke through the line and escaped into an alleyway. The muffled cough of the automatic was not noticed, but the soldier lay on his back with a bullet through his forehead. No man left his post, but there was a panic stiffness among them that betrayed their sudden terror. Their eyes desperately searched the houses about them. A grim smile touched the *Spider's* lips as the other two girls stole away unnoticed. If only El Gaucho would betray himself to his guns in the same way. . . .

Wentworth settled down to wait. The soldiers took no action, but they indulged in no more ribaldry. Death hovered over their heads. The minutes dragged past. One automobile roared up the street, but Wentworth was confident it did not contain El Gaucho, for the soldiers made no move to salute. El Gaucho would not have permitted such a laxness even in the midst of battle. Sounds of the fight, still drifted down wind from the center of the town and a great restlessness seized Wentworth. Had he been too confident of victory?

He took short turns up and down before the window, went back to inspect his prisoner, who had recovered consciousness. Wentworth gazed down into his fear-stricken face. This man was responsible for many deaths this day. If El Gaucho had not been warned, he might have attempted the raid without strategy and been wiped out by an unexpected ambush. The supine man quailed beneath the *Spider's* blazing glare.

Abruptly, Wentworth jerked him to his feet. Deliberately, he removed his own belt and made a noose which he fitted about the man's throat. He then fastened its end over a hook so that the man was pulled upon his tiptoes. In that position, he could manage to keep himself from strangling, but if he sagged to his heels. . . . Wentworth stalked back to the window.

"For God's sake," the man begged, "don't leave me like this! I'll . . . I'll choke to death!" His voice came pitifully to Wentworth. Once his words were strangled in his throat when he sagged with the noose. When that had happened three times, Wentworth returned to confront him.

"For God's sake," the man pleaded hoarsely. "Let me go. I'll . . . I'll do anything you say, but please . . ."

Wentworth appeared to consider while the man dropped once more into the noose. His face turned blue with congested blood and his eyes bulged before he could balance himself again on his toes.

"You couldn't do anything that would be worth saving your life," said the *Spider* sceptically, but there was a hard, swift eagerness in his heart. It was barely possible the prisoner had information of importance. That was the hope behind his torture.

"I have information about El Gaucho," the man whispered hoarsely.

The *Spider* looked dubious. "If it's good enough. . . ."

"I know the next town he's going to raid," the man panted. "It's Jamesville, Indiana."

"When?"

"Day after tomorrow."

"Is that all?"

The man tried to get his shoulders against the wall to help support himself, but the belt was too short. He gagged. "I'm supposed to go ahead and warn him if they know about it, as I did here, I . . . I could give him the wrong signal."

Wentworth learned that the favorable signal was red smoke, then he released the man from his strangling belt, locked him in the closet and went back to the window. The soldiers stood at present arms, a salute! The *Spider's* teeth showed between tight lips and he weighed his automatic in his hand. But even as his hopes of killing El Gaucho rose, the soldiers grounded

137

their arms again and began hopping to the running board of automobiles that stopped to take them on.

A jagged curse ripped from Wentworth's lips. He knew what that meant. El Gaucho already had passed! While the *Spider* had been busy with his prisoner, the leader himself had gone by within reach of his guns! Deliberately, savagely, Wentworth opened fire on the autos that were speeding the soldiers away. His shots ticked off as regularly as a clock's balance wheel. And each bullet pierced a gasoline tank. Pursuers would overtake many bandits this day. . . .

When the last of the automobiles had sped past, Wentworth caught up his prisoner and, with the man on his shoulder, ran from the house. He deposited the man in the middle of the highway, then hastened to his picketed horse. Moments later, he was sending the valiant mare out into the plains, racing, racing back to the encampment of El Gaucho. He had a two-fold purpose: Death and life; justice against El Gaucho, rescue of Tom Barker!

CHAPTER THIRTEEN

Threat of Disaster

It was a weary ride back to the encampment of El Gaucho, horse and rider jaded from hours of violent activity. Wentworth had had no sleep since his few hours on the plane flying westward and before that. . . . His mind felt numbed, but there could be no rest. The *Spider* was confident that, after the costly partial defeat at Grand Junction, El Gaucho would not dare to continue his encampment. If he left there, Wentworth would have no clue to his whereabouts prior to the promised attack upon Jamesville, Indiana. Even that might have been a lie told by the prisoner to save his life. And by that time, Barker might be slain.

Wentworth thus spurred himself as the horse drummed out the long miles, stirred his wearied body to new efforts. His thoughts turned inward. A smile that was strange to the harsh face of the *Spider* touched his lips. At least, Nita's fears would have been relieved by now. The telegraph wires must be humming with the news of the battle at Grand Junction and, if Sheriff Hart did not reveal his guess of Wentworth's identity as the *Spider*, at least there would be accounts of a stranger in a black cape who brought the warning. Yes, Nita would know he was safe.

Safe! The word mocked him. Safe for a while, yes, escaped from the immediate threat of El Gaucho's torture, but speeding back as rapidly as possible to new encounters. El Gaucho was a graver menace than he had believed possible. Already the tentacles of criminal organization were reaching out beyond the man's immediate following. World dominion was his crazy dream. He would never attain that, but in the process of his efforts, he could destroy thousands of lives and lay a hundred cities to waste. . . .

Dusk was crawling up the slope of the rounded hill when at last Wentworth reached the brink of the sunken plateau where El Gaucho had his encampment. He stopped the weary mare short of the crest and crawled the last fifteen feet on his belly. When, at last, he could look down into the valley, a great shout of anger rose in his throat. He sprang to his feet, ran back to the mare, raced her headlong down the slope. There was not a tent in the valley, not a trace of its former occupation except the refuge of an encampment. But there was a single light burning in a room of the mansion El Gaucho had used as headquarters. Could it be possible that the man was still there? Wentworth weighed hope against hope.

He knew when he was fifty yards away from the building that his hope was vain. There was no automobile in front and even the garden had a stripped and deserted aspect. Wentworth pulled down the nearly exhausted mare to a walk, finally halted within twenty feet of the window from which the light came. It was the room where, the night before, he had talked with Carollotta, and made her a promise that he would return.

With the thought, he threw himself from the horse's back and strode toward the window. He was suddenly strong with hope again. He had promised he would return and the girl had been forced to leave before that time. She had left a light burning, unnoticeable in daytime, but a guiding star at night. There would be a note inside, a message from Carollotta. Wentworth was abruptly positive of that. He heard the mare nicker, then her feet clopped rapidly away. He spun about, but

140

she was only going toward the stable from which he had taken her at dawn. He smiled after the hungry mare, then caught the sill and muscled himself upward. . . .

A sudden gust of irresistible wind pinned him against the side of the house. His hat was blown through the window and smashed glass rained down upon his head. His eardrums felt bursted. Half dazed, he dropped to the ground and turned toward the stable. The building was gone, blown to bits and of the mare there was nothing at all to be seen. Wentworth leaned his shoulders against the wall, breathing heavily, almost sobbing. His concussion-numbed mind groped its way to the answer. A bomb planted in the stable—a trap! For himself? He shook his head. It must be it was intended, then, for the pursuers. By the heavens, El Gaucho planned well!

There could be no doubt that the camp had been evacuated before El Gaucho attacked Grand Junction. These mines—there would be others—had been planted in the hope of destroying those who came here at the bidding of his escaped prisoner.

Wentworth turned back to the window, climbed in. There was grief in his heart for the mare as at the loss of a personal friend. She had been faithful and great-hearted, willing even in exhaustion. . . . He stooped slowly and picked up his hat, pulled it down over his head. The light—it was a lamp burning beside the bed. He lifted it and under the base lay a folded piece of paper. Simple, that light signal, but effective. Carollotta had brains.

The note read:

"I believe you will come back for Tommy. El Gaucho is taking him with us and I think he will surely die by the horses when there is time and a place for that. They all believe he is your servant and that you have left him behind to observe and in some way communicate with you. I don't know where we are going, except that it is toward the East. I heard them talking about

New York but I do not know if that is where we go. I will do what I can for Tommy, but my only weapon is that I know El Gaucho . . . too well!''

There was no greeting, no signature. Wentworth pulled his cigarette lighter from his pocket and touched flame to the paper, watched it burn to ashes which crushed to powder beneath his foot. He was frowning heavily, wishing that there had been something more definite that Carollotta might tell him . . . Suddenly he threw himself face down on the floor and rolled. When his shoulders hit the floor, his guns leaped to his hands and he fired. The man whose stealthy step he had heard in the hallway, was hammered against the door-jamb and pivoted there, slowly, painfully, with both hands clutching the wood. His gun dropped where he fell, straight backward to the floor. His head bounced.

Wentworth got to his feet slowly, guns ready for further enemies. He fired twice through the doorway, skimming each doorpost at the height of a man's peeping head. But there was no indication of a hit. Nevertheless, as he walked forward, he kept his eyes on the shadows. For a moment, he had known poignant fear. It had flashed through his mind that the forces of Grand Junction might have arrived, and in the surprise, he had killed a man of the law. And the *Spider* would take a wound himself, even a mortal injury, rather than fire on the police or any of their allies. But a glance at the victim of his lead dispelled his apprehension. His was the face of the criminal, vicious and cruel.

Wentworth bent slowly over him, frowning at an armband insignia on his arm, the colors of El Gaucho's pennant, a purple and a scarlet stripe. As he bowed, he heard stealthy movement in the hallway, but even as he pulled up his head it was too late. He saw a little body springing through the air, the gleam of a drawn knife. . . . Wentworth threw himself aside to avoid the violent downstroke of the blade. He dodged that, but impact hurled him to the floor.

There was a moment of desperate scramble. The knife nicked the *Spider's* ear, crunched into the floor.

The moment's delay while his assailant dislodged it was all that Wentworth needed. His hands shot up and closed crushingly about the man's throat. He wrenched, rolled and threw his body straight forward in a somersault, while his hands kept close hold on the neck of the other. His thumbs were locked beneath the chin, his fingers biting into the vertebrae at the back. When he came down, all the weight of his body would be in the wrench upon the spine. A broken neck. . . .

Then, in the midst of the movement, Wentworth got a glimpse of the face of his attacker. Touseled, brown hair straggled over his forehead and the eyes were deep blue, bulging now with the throttling fingers at his throat, the teeth were bared by drawn-back lips. Wentworth had a flashing thought that the boy beneath him was Tommy Barker. He was no more than a kid, eighteen or nineteen. . . . The glimpse was enough to loosen Wentworth's fingers. He somersaulted, came to his feet and spun about to face his antagonist.

The boy lay flat on his back, his right hand drawn up against his body. As Wentworth stared, the hand came limply loose and revealed the hilt of the knife driven deep into his side. The wrench of the throw Wentworth had contrived had turned the knife on its wielder. The *Spider* came slowly close to him, frowning, his eyes dark. The lad had a wild, willful face, but there was no viciousness here, none of the criminal taint.

"You got me . . . *Spider*," the boy gasped. "You're . . . pretty good."

Wentworth went down on one knee beside him, but he did not look at the wound. He already knew there was nothing he could do to save him. He brushed the hair back from the boy's forehead and a bitter inward grief twisted him, a grief strangely mixed with rage. This boy might have made a splendid man. There was strength and courage in his face. And, because of El Gaucho, he lay here dying.

"I thought I'd play smart," the boy panted. "Said

143

Joe couldn't take you . . . with guns. Said I'd get you when . . . he was dead. It's other way 'round, *Spider*, . . . ain't it?''

Wentworth's lips were twisted. ''No use kidding you, son,'' he said. ''You're right.''

Dark fear sprang into the boy's blue eyes, his lips quivered, then set. ''I don't feel no pain yet,'' he whispered. ''Gee, this is going to be . . . tough on Ma. There's seven younger than me. And Dad. . . . got himself killed . . . just like I did. Playing fool.''

Wentworth was shaken. Death he had seen a thousand times, but this boy was so young! His youth cried up from the softness of his relaxed mouth, from the gangling long body of him. Wentworth drew out his handkerchief and wiped off the cold perspiration that stood out suddenly on the boy's forehead. He swallowed twice before he could speak.

''Listen, son,'' he said slowly, his compassion in his voice. ''I'm damned sorry this had to happen.'' It was not Wentworth speaking, though he sometimes hated his dual nature. It was his other self, the *Spider*, telling him that perhaps something valuable could be learned from this dying member of El Gaucho's band. . . . The kid was whispering . . .

''Gaucho paid me a hundred a month . . . and a bonus when he fought . . . Gee-whli-whilikins, I'd a gone to hell for that . . .!'' The boy laughed and a bloody froth came to his lips for the *Spider* to sponge away. ''Reckon I'm going there . . . fast. But Mom has the farm paid for now.''

The *Spider* it was who bent above the boy now. ''Son,'' he said, ''if you will tell me all you know, I'll see that your mother gets a hundred dollars a month for the rest of her life. I'll set up a trust fund.''

The eyes of man and boy met and those of the younger seemed very old. Pain was in them, pain and fear and now suspicion joined those, too. A spasm quivered over his gangling body, the eyes closed and his breath came, sharp and quick, through his mouth.

With his eyes closed, he whispered, "Swear it, *Spider*? They say . . . you always . . . keep your word."

Wentworth said heavily, "I swear."

The whispering went on for a long time, longer than Wentworth would have believed life could remain in that thin, battered body. When it was all done, the boy's eyes seemed luminous and large and his breathing was a heavy labor.

"Take care of Ma," he breathed, "or I'll . . . h'ant you shore!"

Wentworth smiled and it was not the smile of the *Spider,* but of the human, sympathetic man whose altruism had brought that dread killer of the night into being. He held out his hand.

"Shake, son," he said, "you're a real man. I'm . . . I'm sorry as hell about this."

The boy's lips moved faintly. It might have been a smile. His hand lay limp and cold within Wentworth's. He said, "Nuts to you."

A shudder swept him and the labor of his breathing no longer tortured him. Wentworth touched the eyelids and pressed them shut. He stood through a long minute staring down at the boy's still form. Then he straightened with a wide movement of his shoulders as if he adjusted them to an odd and heavy burden. He strode across the room to the window and was gone.

He went across-country to the spot the boy had indicated, found two horses tethered there. Then he rode down the valley toward the highway that led from Grand Junction. The sky was black as his cape, but spangled with stars. The moon pushed an orange rim above the valley's rim. He had fought off the depression that had held him there beside the dying boy, thrust such thoughts from his mind. What he had learned would send him as swiftly as planes could carry him to New York, but first he must wait to warn the troops which would presently come here that the buildings in the valley were all mined.

Leading the second horse, the *Spider* reached presently a point at the valley's end where he could mount a ridge above the dusty track that trailed beside the creek. There he dismounted and squatted on his heels to wait. The boy had said that New York, not Jamesville, was the next objective of El Gaucho. That meant that he had joined forces with Peterson, that all the nation's Underworld would be with him. Only loosely affiliated at first, of course, but El Gaucho, if he were allowed to continue, would soon tighten and strengthen the alliance.

After the disaster of Grand Junction, El Gaucho had separated his forces. Hereafter, they would never be assembled in one unit except at the scene of his crimes. Scattered into small bands, not wearing uniforms, they would travel as gypsies, as hoboes, as people touring in good cars, traveling in old cars and seeming to look for work; as work gangs going to seemingly authenticated places where factories awaited them.

The looting of the banks at the Junction had been part of a plan for financing these movements and preparing for greater victories to come. But that was not all. The *Spider's* discovery of sympathizers in Grand Junction had pointed to widespread affiliations and these were confirmed by the boy. These persons, highly paid, secretly opened banks, betrayed towns, gave information—some even contributed funds! There were thousands of dollars pouring in from such sources all the time, in addition to the tremendous loot.

El Gaucho had made, tentatively, a deal with Peterson, which had been confirmed from ten other cities beside New York, through the gang leaders, agreeing that the Underworld and political affiliations of those criminals should be thrown into the balance behind El Gaucho the moment that El Gaucho captured New York City!

The boy whispered that El Gaucho no longer had his eyes turned toward Bethania. Drunk with power, he proposed to take over the United States as his private kingdom! He had said, in a speech before his assembled myrmidons that, when the Underworld threw in with him, he would be proclaimed President! He intimated that members of Congress, high army and navy officials had been bought over. Ten days after that, the dying boy had whispered, El Gaucho promised that Washington would be in his power, and he would be installed in the White House itself!

To Wentworth it sounded like the dream of an opium eater, but, before this, fanatics who believed in themselves had seized control of a nation. There was no reason to believe that the United States could not be similarly conquered. There were enough self-seekers in the high places to make bribery possible. Yes, it was fantastic, but not as impossible as it sounded. The *Spider* could look with equanimity upon the boy's death now. No martyr's death had ever contributed more to a cause than this boy's mortal wound. . . .

Only one other thing had the boy told Wentworth. El Gaucho had offered to pay its weight in gold to the man who obtained—*the Spider's head*!

It was bloodthirstily like El Gaucho to make such a proposition as that. He stipulated that the head itself must be brought to him to be weighed upon his scales and redeemed. Wentworth's face set grimly. He had had prices on his head before this. Fifty thousand dollars was standing against his name in a half dozen different rewards. But never before had so barbaric a proposal been made. He thought whimsically that his head was worth considerably more than its weight in gold to him—so long as it remained on his shoulders.

A whisper of hoofs on the sandy earth brought him to his feet and he arose from where he had picketed the two horses below the crest of the ridge and climbed until he stood plainly in the moonlight—fifty yards from the long black line of horses that moved on toward El Gaucho's former encampment.

Wentworth sent a shrill cry toward the troops, then flaunted his cape against the night sky. "El Gaucho is gone!" he shouted. "But beware, there are bombs planted there. Beware! The *Spider* warns you!"

147

He repeated the message to make sure he was understood, but as he spoke, he stepped slowly backward and with the last word, he leaped below the crest of the ridge. Seconds later, he vaulted to the saddle, ignoring the guns that had blasted up the slope toward him. The hoof beats of pursuers racketed up the slope, but it was slow work against sliding sand. When they reached the top, the *Spider* was a black figure speeding into the moon, with his cape flying backward from his shoulders.

Then, abruptly, the rider vanished, dipping into one of those numerous depressions which are scattered over the plains. But to those who watched from the ridge, it was as if he had leaped into the moon and disappeared, like a black-caped witch riding a broomstick. They looked at each other and one man's hand rose surreptitiously to cross himself.

"The *Spider*!" he whispered.

CHAPTER FOURTEEN

Citadel of Crime

When the *Spider* reached Grand Junction again by a circuitous route, no one would have recognized him for the sinister being who, eight hours before, had led the people of the town into battle. The *Spider's* disguise had been destroyed, one of the many dead had supplied him with clothing and his face was now that of Richard Wentworth.

It was a weary face, but it had a virility and a magnetism that drew the eyes of women and men, too. His entire body radiated strength, and despite his fatigue, there was a jaunty self-confidence about his shoulders, an arrogance in the poise of his head that would have marked him in any crowd.

Wentworth avoided any place where Sheriff Hart might be met, for Hart had heard the *Spider* use Wentworth's voice and his sudden memory of it might be fresh so soon after the happening. Wentworth visited a telegraph office first and sent two messages—one to Nita to say he was bound for New York; one to Jackson to bid him bring the Daimler to Newark airport. He made one more stop for clothing; then motored to the air field and chartered a plane to carry him East.

For a few minutes after the ship had lifted toward the sky, Wentworth sat watching the earth flow backward to the West, but his eyelids were weighted and presently, gratefully, he leaned his head back against the crash pad and slept, while the slip stream roared past his ears and the bellow of the engine beat on his brain. Nor did he awake until the slight jounce of landing the plane bounced his head against the pad. He opened his eyes then, saw Newark airport's hangars rushing toward him through the dusk. His sleep had rested him and he looked eagerly about for the Daimler, spotted its powerful bulk finally as the ship came to a stop and the pilot cut the engine.

It was Jackson, his stalwart shoulders set soldier-fashion, who came marching forward to greet him. He said only, "Good evening, major," but there was joy in his blue eyes. Jackson paid off the pilot while Wentworth hurried toward the car, his eyes peering vainly to penetrate its dark interior. He had not formulated any hope in his thoughts, but . . .

He opened the door and the dome light glowed softly in the tonneau. He stood gazing into the car. He did not speak, nor did Nita van Sloan, who smiled gaily at him from the rear seat.

"You're an old meanie," said Nita. "You didn't tell me where you'd be landing and I had to phone Jackson. Most humiliating, Mr. Wentworth. Most humiliating."

Wentworth got in slowly and closed the door. "You seem to bear up under the humiliation very well, Miss van Sloan," he whispered as he gathered her into his arms in the darkness that dropped as the door shut. Nita's hand clutched at his coat and she relaxed on his shoulder with a long shuddering sigh.

"Oh, Dick!" she whispered. "Oh, Dick!"

It was one of those precious moments snatched from eternity when these two who loved so greatly might surrender themselves to their love; when the anxieties of long days during which Death stalked them could be forgotten for a while. But it was over too soon. The gravity of the peril that hung over the nation could not be put aside and Wentworth began to talk rapidly, telling all that he knew about El Gaucho's plans.

Nita told him then of her own stint, of the battle to

150

rescue him, of Ram Singh's wounds, from which he was rapidly recovering.

"We've kept track of everyone we could," she said. "Peterson left town with you, but Yvonne is here." She gave Wentworth the address. "I'm sorry I misjudged Tommy Barker that way, but his actions were scarcely conducive to trust. Oh, let all that wait a little while, Dick. I have dinner prepared at home, a bottle of that excellent Chambertin from your own cellar. . . ."

Wentworth squeezed Nita's hand, weakening for the moment. Food? He had eaten hastily in Grand Junction before the take-off. Rest? He had slept in the plane. The laughter that came from his lips was not all pleasant.

"There is no time for it," he said shortly. "I haven't the slightest idea when the attack upon New York will be made. Any hour. . . . There's work for you, too, darling. See Commissioner Flynn. If Governor Kirkpatrick is in town, see him and tell them what I have told you tonight. Tell them I'll see them in the morning . . . with proof."

Nita made her voice cheerful. "You have this proof?"

"That's what I'm going for now," Wentworth said grimly. "I'll have to take this car, darling, for my disguise. . . ."

Nita's hand touched his arm. "I knew it would be this way," she said without expression. "That's why I came to the field. Would you even have telephoned me, Dick?"

Wentworth's hand closed over hers. "No, darling," he said. "You give me strength, dearest, but tonight I could be weak . . . Forget it, sweetheart. Not many more days and we'll have El Gaucho out of the running."

"And then there'll be another and another . . . and another," Nita's voice was muffled, but the words came out with vehemence, as if each one were alive

151

and driving itself individually from between her teeth. "Oh, Dick, will there never be an end?"

Wentworth sat rigidly beside her, hearing Nita voice the cry that had risen in his own soul. They had thought the end was near before El Gaucho had arisen. . . . His hand, patting hers, moved mechanically.

"Not tonight, sweetheart," he said huskily. "I . . ." He leaned forward and rapped on the glass. "Get that taxi, Jackson."

Wentworth turned to Nita in the darkness and her arms tightened about his shoulders. "Hurry, Dick," she whispered against his mouth, "I'll be waiting. And forgive me. It's just that sometimes . . ."

"I know! I know!" Wentworth pulled sharply away, descended from the car to help Nita into the taxi, then sprang back into his own car, threw Yvonne Musette's address at Jackson, and sank back on the cushions. But the relaxation that usually he could force upon himself—the one thing that enabled him to carry on through months and years of ceaseless battle—had deserted him. Black despair, an utter dejection had him by the throat. His dauntless spirit quailed before the task before him, the power of El Gaucho and his thousands.

Was he never, his traitor heart cried to him, to have the ordinary joys of life that other men knew? Was he always to duel with death, to hear the vicious whine of bullets that just miss . . . until some day one flew straight? For the moment, he hated the thing he was, the *Spider*. It rebelled against the rigid discipline of mind which could make him ruthless and nearly super-human. Of what good were all these things beside the sweets of a great love that could never be? His human heart almost failed him, his great will shaken by a burden almost too great for a mortal to bear.

No one had ever seen Wentworth in one of these attacks of black despair and he intended that no one ever should. That was why he had thrust Nita brusquely from the car. The sweat beaded his forehead and his hands, clenched and clenched again, were cold and clammy. He was fighting a greater battle than even the

Spider's reckless dueling. He commanded his inner soul, the core of indomitable strength that bore him through all trials, and somewhere, somehow, that spirit answered. He dragged out of his heart the superb fighting power—that unbreakable will—which had carried him through many crises.

There was a moment when his hands shook, a moment when his mouth was dry with the longing and the terror that gripped him, then it was gone. As quickly as it had seized on him, the depression vanished. Slowly, stiffly he turned his head and saw that the car was near his goal. He gripped the speaking tube:

"Circle the park!"

He leaned out of the open window, breathed deep of the aromatic odors of trees and banks of shrubs as the Daimler purred along. Then he sank back into the car. His face slowly became molded to a new sternness, a bitter power. He was . . . the *Spider!*

His hands had never been surer nor swifter, the impersonation never more sinister. Wentworth's lips twisted a little as he saw the face of the *Spider* take form over his own in the brilliant light of the make-up table which was concealed with a wardrobe in the back of the Daimler's rear seat. The impersonation was good, but the pangs of its birth had been great.

It would be well, he considered, to carry his sword-cane tonight. . . . When the car stopped in the shadows of the trees and Jackson sprang to the pavement to throw open the door, Wentworth saw in his man's eyes the reflection of his own opinion. By the heavens! Jackson, used as he was to this make-up, was startled and a little frightened at his appearance!

"Wait," Wentworth said simply. Then he slipped into the shadows and moved toward Yvonne's living quarters. This was, Wentworth knew, the most secret meeting place of the gangs whose loose confederation had practically ruled New York for ten years. Wentworth had nearly lost his life there once, when he had entered in disguise, and he knew something of its layout.

He entered through an iron grating opening beneath the front steps of the ancient brownstone house which were preferred by many of the criminals since they were practically sound-proof. From a tiny tool kit which the *Spider* always wore strapped beneath his left arm, Wentworth extracted a slender probe of surgical steel and the locks yielded swiftly to his lockpick. It was a satisfaction to have his tools again.

The basement of the building was a large dining room and behind it was a kitchen, both deserted now. He made his way rapidly upward through halls that were dimly lighted. Shreds of faint illumination slitted out from under some of the doors. Behind one, a man was humming in a light, throaty voice. In another, a woman quarreled monotonously in a high, tedious tone. How was he to find Yvonne? He smiled slightly, mockingly.

It shouldn't be too difficult. She used a musky perfume which, for some unknown reason, underworld women seemed to prefer. That scent should penetrate half a dozen wooden doors. There was no trace of it here, and the *Spider* climbed to the next floor. The hall was chiefly redolent of stale cigarette smoke and he made the rounds of the doors, listening at each in turn, sniffing. It struck Wentworth as grimly humorous that he should be sniffing for a trail like a bloodhound. Queer that he felt so buoyant after his spell of depression. Even the fact that there were gangsters in the building who would rush to kill him at the slightest alarm did not bother him.

Well, the musk trail had failed him. He would have to try another method, simply walk into one of these rooms and force its occupant to tell where Yvonne was. Afterwards, a few knots would keep that person from broadcasting an alarm . . . Wentworth's hand, thinly gloved now, went to a doorknob. He twisted it gently, thrust, and sprang into the room with gun drawn. Then he smiled, heeled the door shut. He was in a luxuriously sensuous bedroom, all pink taffeta drapes and over-cushioned divans. Luck had been with him. . . .

Wentworth said, "Pff! What a stench, my dear Yvonne. Really, you should retain a better perfumer."

Yvonne Musette crouched like a cat in the middle of her over-draped bedroom. Her negligée was black and diaphanous, but her manner was the reverse of alluring.

"I can't understand," the *Spider* went on gently, "why the stench didn't penetrate to the hall. . . . Say, Yvonne, why did El Gaucho pull Tommy Barker to pieces with the horses?"

The suddenness of his questions seemed to stun her. She straightened out of the crouch, her face white beneath the scarlet of her lips. A tremor raced over her.

"No, no!" she cried out. "He didn't do that! He wouldn't dare. I send word by Peterson that Barkaire is to be safe. I lofe him. If that Gaunch' 'ave—" Her words closed her throat. Her eyes widened, staring into the *Spider's* harshly sinister face. "*Les chevaux! The 'orses! O Mon Dieu*, no!"

The *Spider* nodded his head slowly. "If it was not Barker, then whom did El Gaucho put to the horses?"

Yvonne shook her head. She lifted her hands to the side of her face and pushed them up into her hair, rocked her head between them. "No, no!" she whispered. "He could not do that to my Barkaire. . . . Why, Why . . . *le canaille! fils d'une cochone!* I keel him!"

Wentworth studied the woman with his cold gray-blue eyes and he judged that, as much as she could, she loved Tommy Barker.

But how far would she be willing to go to save him? These French women of *les Apaches* knew no limit.

"Listen," he said. "When we were in the plane flying west, Barker tried to turn me loose and El Gaucho held him prisoner. He has promised to tear him apart with the horses. I've got to find El Gaucho so I can turn Barker loose, see?"

Yvonne's eyes were blank with terror, but as Wentworth spoke, she grew calmer and moved toward him. Suspicion was in her glance now.

"Why you do that?" she asked swiftly. "Barkaire and you not friends. Barkaire is wit' Peterson's gang. For why?"

Wentworth looked steadily into the woman's eyes. "Barker means a great deal to me," he said.

She came even closer, her black eyes flicking back and forth as she searched his face. "What is the truth?" she asked swiftly. "You are hiding somethin'. He mean' a great deal to you. Why?"

"Why does a son mean a lot to his father?" he asked quietly.

Yvonne's eyes widened on his face, then abruptly she threw her arms about his neck. "You are his *father*! You!" She danced back from him, her black eyes sparkling. "He is . . . your son, but not your wife's son, eh? Oh, I know, I know! Oh, my Barkaire's father. That is nize. Soo nize!"

Wentworth cut her short with a sharp gesture. He had allowed her to infer precisely that because he could see no other way, short of torture, of forcing her to tell what she knew.

"You see," he said swiftly, "why I must find El Gaucho and Tommy. I've *got* to. Tell me now. Where is El Gaucho? What is he planning to do?"

Yvonne shrugged, searching Wentworth's face with her eyes. "He come to New Yor' sometime tonight. He send 'is plan' to theese 'ouse and many men downstair' get them ready to mail to all othaire men. What they 'ave to do and w'en? Theese Gauch' one, he do many funny things!"

The *Spider's* eyes brightened with triumph, but he looked down at the platinum cigarette-case he had slipped from his vest pocket lest the expression show. He offered Yvonne a cigarette, holding the case so that she must take one of three at the left hand side of the container. Then he took one from the other section and lighted both.

"El Gaucho comes to this building?"

Yvonne shruggedd "I do not know w'ere 'e come," she said. "Listen you do not objec' to Barkaire and me? He is so nize boy. I teach 'im much. Please?"

Wentworth shrugged. "I have very little control over Tommy," he said truthfully. "He will probably do just what he chooses." He was watching her secretly and saw her drag the back of her hand upward across her forehead, pushing up her black hair. He crushed out his own cigarette and stepped toward her, caught her under the arms and carried her to the bed. She protested weakly, but the fumes of the cigarette which Wentworth had given her were fuddling her brain. A moment after the *Spider* laid her down, she had fallen into a deep narcotic sleep.

Wentworth locked the door, pocketed the key. Then he slipped down the steps, bearing the blade of his sword cane as he went. The heavy, thorn-wood of the stick clenched like a club in his left hand, the abbreviated rapier ready in his right. These buildings were nearly sound-proof, but a forty-five caliber bullet made a terrific racket between walls. . . .

Swiftly, he made his way to the room that Yvonne had indicated, stooped to peer through the keyhole. There were only two men there, leaning back smoking cigarettes beside a great pile of sealed envelopes. It was apparent that their work was done, for a gray-striped mail bag lay beside them. The *Spider* turned the knob carelessly and strode in. One man stared wide-mouthed and startled into the grim *Spider's* face. The other fumbled as he snatched for his gun. He opened his mouth to shout a warning and, almost instinctively, the *Spider's* rapier speared into the opening. The man's cry was instantly dead as the blade slipped through his tongue and death came a moment later.

The second man was recovering now from his fright, but his gun accomplished no more. He tried to drop behind the table, but the sword blade found his throat and dropped him there a moment, with his chin against the steel, until Wentworth withdrew it. There was a fierce scowl upon the *Spider's* face and he stooped once beside each man, pressing to their foreheads the base of his cigarette lighter. When he had risen again, his seal glowed like a vermillion threat upon each brow.

With swift hands, Wentworth thrust the sealed envelopes into the gray mail bag and, three minutes after his entrance, Wentworth was creeping downward to the basement exit. He had to thrust his rapier through another man in the darkness of the basement hallway, but there was no further interruption to his retreat. The Daimler glided from the shadows and, a half hour later, he was back in his own penthouse, fifteen stories above the street. On the way home, he had skimmed through a dozen of the letters.

They were not, as he had expected, exclusively directions for New York. They envisaged, too, the *destruction by bombs of eleven major cities of the United States*!

CHAPTER FIFTEEN

Battle Lines

With horror dawning in his eyes as Wentworth realized the incredible scope of El Gaucho's intended assault upon America, he turned toward Nita, who had come to his penthouse to await his return after she had performed the errand he had assigned her. Nita came swiftly toward him.

"You must rest, beloved," she said warmly. "You are weary. When did you sleep?"

Wentworth swept aside her words with a sharp gesture of his arm. "No, no," he cried. "There is no time to be lost. It's gigantic, this thing. We have never had anything like this. Never in all my battles with the Underworld has such a fiend arisen. Why, damn it, Nita, he's going to destroy a dozen cities! Think of the thousands who will die. . . ."

Nita's arms went about Wentworth's shoulders. "Dick, in justice to your cause, you must rest. Commissioner Flynn isn't convinced. He says he'll come around in the morning and see your proofs."

Wentworth tossed the gray mail bag to the table and stood looking at it. No one believed in danger until the criminals were at their very doors, until they had swept the forces of law and order from the field and were marauding among the innocent sheep. . . . Even the Commissioner of Police doubted. Wentworth's wide, confident shoulders sagged a little. He realized, suddenly, that his sleep had been a broken nap in a plane and that his food had been not of the best. . . . and that there were many hours of strenuous battle ahead. Damn it, they could not wait until morning. The attack was four days from now, but four days was a pitifully short time for preparation when there were traitors in all strongholds. . . .

"Flynn must come here tonight," Wentworth said savagely. "There is no time to wait! Isn't Kirkpatrick in town? I glimpsed a headline in a paper. . . ."

Nita's violet eyes held him. Her voice was low, warm. "Steady, dear," she said. "I doubt that you will have much rest from now on, Dick. And . . . you are strained. Everything depends on you. Give me an hour, Dick, to rest you. I will call Flynn and Kirkpatrick and ask them to come in an hour."

Wentworth hesitated, aware of the exhaustion of all his faculties. He knew the wisdom of what Nita said. It was not his habit to drive himself too far, for he knew exactly how long he could continue to force weary mind and body along. After all it was only an hour. He said, "You are right, Nita. By all means, call Flynn and Kirk."

Jenkyns brought them food after Nita had made her call and they sat together on a deep divan and drank strong coffee laced with cognac, ate delicate pigeon's eggs, beaten up with sugar and hot sherry. Then Nita bade the *Spider* rest. She slid her soft arm beneath his head, pressed her lips to his forehead and cheeks, to his tired eyes. Her white hand smoothed away the ache from his forehead.

Supine, relaxing from the inner muscles outward and breathing more and more deeply, as the *yogis* had taught him in ancient Lahore, the *Spider* rested, absorbing love, purity, unselfishness and faith from the radiant girl who poured it out to him. So he prepared himself for battle. Strength seemed actually to flow from Nita to Wentworth. Finally, she relaxed there by him on the divan and the two slept.

160

*   *   *

It was there Jenkyns' wise old eyes found them later when Flynn and Kirkpatrick came together to the aerie of the *Spider,* far above Fifth Avenue. For a full minute, the butler who had served Wentworth's father before him stood there looking, sadness on his ruddy, wrinkled face. His eyes misted. He would not have known how to say what he felt: that it was a pity for such bright beauty and such virile, superb youth, to be always dancing in a duel with death.

Jenkyns cleared his throat politely and they were both instantly awake, sat smiling up at him.

"Ask them if they will wait ten minutes," Nita said when he spoke. "Master Dick is resting."

She led Wentworth to the terrace where they stood together in the moonlight and looked down on the city. The sight braced them, sent every trace of languor from them. Wentworth knew, as he looked, that he never had loved this city more, the bright jewel of the Western world, and he had never loved the vast reaches of the country as well; this fair land that El Gaucho sought to destroy. Commissioner Flynn and Governor Kirkpatrick felt almost an electric shock of vitality when they came into the presence of the two.

Commissioner Patrick O. Flynn had been a brigadier general in the army and the military imprint was strong upon his lean, angular body. Even the iron-gray hair on his narrow head seemed still to bear the imprint of his officer's cap.

"The proof?" he asked, laconic as always. It was his greeting.

Wentworth gestured toward the mail bag. "There's the tangible evidence," he said, his voice crisp and full. "I'll tell you about it presently."

He turned toward Governor Kirkpatrick who was waiting to one side with a deep smile on his saturnine face. While Flynn turned to the evidence, Wentworth strode toward Kirkpatrick and their hands clasped strongly, the keen gray-blue eyes of the *Spider* looked into blue eyes that could be as frosty as his own.

"It's been a long time since I saw you," Kirkpatrick said gravely. "Damn your eyes, where have you been keeping yourself? I believe you got me elected to the governorship just so you could get me out of the way."

Wentworth laughed, saying nothing, throwing an arm about the hard shoulders of the Governor. They were not demonstrative, these two men, but they were old friends, dating from the days when Kirkpatrick had been Commissioner of Police and Wentworth had been his hated enemy, the *Spider*. Not that Wentworth ever admitted in so many words to Kirkpatrick that he was the *Spider*. . . . There was no need. Kirkpatrick had been sure and had directly told Wentworth so, but he had added that he admired this stern wolf of justice who called himself the *Spider;* that so long as no positive evidence fell into his hands, he would assist Wentworth; but if that proof ever came to his attention, he would prosecute to the best of his ability.

The understanding remained between them that way. Kirkpatrick had refused once to pardon Wentworth when he was sentenced to die on what was proved afterward to be a framed murder charge. And Wentworth had not appealed to him to help. These two understood each other and each respected the other for the man that he was.

Even this after-midnight call had not caught Kirkpatrick carelessly attired. He was faultless in evening dress, a gardenia gracing his lapel, his black hair smooth and ordered on his scalp. The points of his militant, black mustache were carefully waxed. Wentworth took in these outward aspects of his friend's well-being in a glance and was glad, for travail lay ahead for him, too.

Flynn looked up at the two from where he stood beside the letter-littered table. "Monstrous!" he said sharply. "Monstrous! All details of plot, Kirkpatrick. Every damned one. Eleven cities."

"I can tell you more briefly than you can dig it from

that mass of detail," Wentworth said, his voice harshening. "Here's a summary:

"Number one. Instructions to the Garling gang in Boston. All harbor shipping and piers except those containing very valuable cargo to be blown up at midnight. All police stations and headquarters ditto. Bridge over the Charles, same. El Gaucho is sending armed forces to supplement the gangsters and they are to be placed with an incredibly keen eye for strategy.

"Number two, San Francisco. First of all, a break on Alcatraz Island, releasing all prisoners . . ."

"Can't be done," snapped Flynn. "Good God! Powerful prison. One of the strongest. . . ."

"Not even with keepers in the plot?" Wentworth asked softly.

"Good God!" gasped Flynn.

"This thing has been going on for years," Wentworth explained. "Ever since this Gaucho and Von Hapszollern and De Moltkez got together and aggravated one another's egos until they became monsters. I tell you, this is an octopus which will strangle us with a thousand arms unless we understand what we are fighting.

"Well, San Francisco. All police stations and headquarters, all officers *and* homes of officials of law and order, and all shipping which can be a means of defense, are to go up at the same moment that the same is happening in Boston.

"Every large city in this country *and* in Canada is to receive the same treatment, simultaneously. They are going to prevent our neighbor and friend from coming to our aid by destroying Canada; I tell you El Gaucho already regards the United States, Canada, Mexico and Central and South America as his kingdom!

"Mark that the police headquarters and stations and shipping of New York are to be spared 'if possible.' And why? Because this is to be Gaucho's capital. He regards its building and shipping with a fond eye. He intends to reduce all other cities to much less than their present size and importance. He plans to extend New

163

York clear down to the end of Long Island and there to have the gigantic harbor that we, ourselves, ought to have started twenty years ago.

"As for our soldiers, the third who are already El Gaucho's men—oh, yes, Flynn, it's true—will by various pretexts draw away from the main body on the appointed night and touch off the mines, long since laid, which will blow every soul to bits. West Point is to be gassed along with Annapolis." Wentworth paused, looking at the two men before him. His own breathing had quickened.

Kirkpatrick said gravely, "It's the worst yet, Dick."

Wentworth nodded. "The worst ever fought. It's damnable. Even in Washington there's treachery, especially among many of the foreign legations. You must remember that Bethania and Ruthia are regarded with almost superstitious awe by Europe. They have unbroken lines of kings, running back to Roman days. This Gaucho and Von Hapszollern are the real thing, so far as that goes—rotten, if a plain American's opinion holds—with about one thousand too many years of believing themselves God's anointed rulers over the rest of the world.

"Here are the plans that were to go to every chief city tonight. I don't know that it was tonight, but I am sure that their duplicates with some details changed, must go, if the great night is to come off. We have *just four days* in which to meet this catastrophe—just four days to organize a decent democratic existence, not only for ourselves, Flynn, Kirk, not only for our country, but for the entire world!

"This man, with his ability to half-hypnotize men . . . the same thing that made Napoleon a menace, that made Hilter a menace—this man has in even greater degree, and, what is more, he has the terrible fascination which utter cruelty has. If you had seen—"

Wentworth stopped abruptly. He could not admit his identity as the *Spider*. "If you had seen something which he did recently, how he enjoyed the sight of the most dreadful human suffering and how steadily and calmly he contemplated what drove the most hardened men almost mad to witness—and if you had seen how that very ability of his hypnotized those hard men—you'd know what I mean.''

The Commissioner and Governor Kirkpatrick, faces very white, looked at Wentworth for a long moment.

"You are right," Kirkpatrick said tightly. "By God! What it would have meant if you had not discovered all this!" The Governor strode forward, clasped his hand. "Dick, boy, you're a wonder. But what in heaven's name are we going to do?"

Wentworth said gravely, "We can take every possible precaution against him. We can guard the points he has listed to destroy. Regardless of the fact that we have his plans, any attack he makes must envisage destruction of the same places."

Nita had listened gravely. Now she stepped forward. She had never been more beautiful, Wentworth thought, her whole body radiating her woman's indomitable spirit.

"Listen," she said, "make this a headquarters for the battle. For it will be a battle, you know, from the first. There are traitors and treachery everywhere. Police headquarters, any place you used, would be full of spies. But this place, we can protect and defend. Let me have a dozen women stenographers and typists. Women are less apt to have been bought in by El Gaucho, since his every action indicates his contempt of the sex, his oversight of our possibilities. Put in radio equipment, a half-dozen trunklines and a telephone switchboard. . . ."

Kirkpatrick frowned down at the floor, his hand going slowly to his mustache as always when he was puzzled or worried. Gravely, he nodded.

"It's a good plan, Flynn."

Flynn looked about the room sharply and Wentworth's lifted hand brought Jenkyns with a telephone which he plugged in near the Commissioner. He got police headquarters and Flynn's brisk, military voice began to bark orders. Wentworth turned to Nita, pressed his lips to her cheek, then his hand clasped hers in a firm, steady, comrade's grip. That, they both knew, was the last time that either could think of the other except as a human pawn in the battle for the life of the country, neither to be considered again in the face of the world's safety.

As he turned toward the door, a tall figure in spotless white entered the room and bowed smoothly, touching cupped hands to his brow.

"Salaam, sahib!" he murmured.

Wentworth caught Ram Singh by the shoulders, gripping hard. "My heart is made glad," he said in swift Hindustani, "to find you strong and well again. It has come to my ears how you fought for me and for the *missie sahib* and I give you honor, Ram Singh. Verily, thou art a great warrior!"

Ram Singh's white teeth flashed in a smile. *"Wah! Sahib!* It was nothing. Those were not men, but mice who scampered at the sight of a warrior's knife!"

Wentworth smiled. "Ram Singh," he said, growing grave, "I have a task for thee."

"Han, sahib!"

"A great battle is ahead. This, my home, will be the heart of that battle," he said, "and my heart, too, will be here."

Ram Singh's eyes flashed to Nita, standing just behind his master's shoulder.

"Yes," said Wentworth, "thou art my strong warrior. With you here, my heart will be safe. My courage will be strong. Guard, Ram Singh."

"Han, sahib!" Ram Singh's assent rang like a trumpet. He stepped back, shoulders against the wall, arms folded across his deep chest and Wentworth knew that he would die with many wounds before he would permit harm to come to Nita.

Governor Kirkpatrick looked on with keen, intelligent eyes. "I take it you won't be with us, Dick?" he commented quietly.

Wentworth turned toward him. "I'm going to seek out El Gaucho himself," he said. "He will be destroyed in battle and as long as he lives, with the magic of his personality, he can continue to generate new armies against humanity. As for staying here, there is no need of me. You can do what must be done as well—better than I!"

"Not better, Dick," Kirkpatrick said, "but we will do our best. Do you know where to go for this El Gaucho?"

"Only a clue," Wentworth said grimly. "A weak clue, but it must lead to success. I have also a plan which is based on the fact that El Gaucho has offered to pay its weight in gold to the man who brings him the *Spider's* head. You can see how serious it is.

"It is not Europe against America. It is an archfiend—a madman—against all the rest of the world. We cannot, we *shall* not fail!"

CHAPTER SIXTEEN

A Grim Task

Wentworth did not at once leave the apartment. He retired to his bedroom and went swiftly to work with make-up kit. He altered his mouth so that it had a one-sided sneer and his eyes, too, participated in the leer, drooping at their outer corners. Cleverly placed bits of wax in his nostrils flattened out the bridge and gave him a heavy, noisy habit of breathing. He parted his hair in the middle and let strands straggle on his forehead. He was not a prepossessing creature and the clothing he donned did not help.

Afterward, he worked for an hour in his laboratory and when he came out, he carried a black satchel which bulged about some rounded object. He slipped back then to the drawing room and showed himself suddenly in a doorway. Kirkpatrick started to his feet, hand flipping to a gun beneath his armpit and Ram Singh's knife flashed to his hand. Wentworth lifted his arms.

"Gosh sake, guv'nor," he whined, "give a guy a chanct!"

Nita laughed. "For heaven's sake, Kirk," she said, "haven't you got used to Dick's tricks yet?"

"Dick!" Kirkpatrick holstered his gun. "Damn your soul, Dick, you had me scared for a minute!"

Flynn regarded him grimly. "You're good at that

stuff,'' he grunted. ''Wish I had a few of you in the department.''

Nita's laughter was soft, ''There's only one Dick Wentworth, Commissioner!''

Wentworth bowed with his customary suavity. ''I am more than flattered,'' he said. ''Well, I'm off. Look for me . . . when you see me.''

Kirkpatrick smiled wryly, ''And we probably won't know when we do!''

They were all laughing when he left, but Wentworth's own face was grim beneath its disguise and there was a hard bitterness in his soul. It was necessary that they should have confidence, these friends and allies of his, but only Wentworth knew how titanic was the struggle ahead. Even before he had left, Kirkpatrick had been having trouble getting telephonic messages through to warn distant cities of El Gaucho's plot. Telegraph companies reported ''indefinite delays.''

On the second floor of the apartment building, Wentworth left the elevator and went to a front window in spite of the protest of the operator who did not like his looks. At the window Wentworth drew a monocle from his vest pocket and squinted through it at the top of a new Ford coupé parked at the curb. He nodded in satisfaction, returned to the elevator and its glowering operator.

Once in the Ford he had inspected, Wentworth sped northward along Fifth Avenue. His Hispano-Suiza roadster would have been more to his liking but this car was fast enough for all practical purposes and it was inconspicuous—more suited to the character he had assumed.

The *Spider* made good time through the almost deserted streets. It was nearly three o'clock in the morning and there was nothing moving except a few nighthawk taxis and skylarking private cars. All of which was perfectly suited to Wentworth's purposes. He was speeding to the home of a high police official whose name had been on the payrolls of El Gaucho, a man whose record was studded with brutal actions, but who had retained

169

his position because of political influence which transcended even that of Commissioner Flynn.

He had been one of those the *Spider* had marked down for his vengeance before the uprising of El Gaucho had swept all minor criminalities from consideration. . . .

Deliberately, Wentworth had secreted the letter addressed to that man. He was for private vengeance—and it was possible that his death might yet serve the people he had betrayed. Wentworth's hand, as he thought of this, went to a stout walking cane beside him, a cane which covered a straight, two-edged sword. The rest of his features, made more sinister by the disguise he had assumed, was a fearful thing. It was a fearful thing that he planned to do, but the end—which would be the death of El Gaucho—was full justification to his *Spider's* mind, however much Richard Wentworth might shrink from the deed ahead.

Forty minutes after leaving his apartment, Wentworth parked his car beside a rather elaborate estate in Pelham Manor, an exclusive suburb on Long Island Sound. He caught up the cane, the black handbag and a rubberized blanket from beside him and stole toward the place. A husky dog rushed toward him, bellowing an alarm, and the stick swung once. Thereafter, deep silence lay upon the place. Wentworth crouched motionless in the shadow of a shrub for ten minutes before he was confident no one had been awakened. Then he stole forward again.

Wentworth, creeping upon the home of Lieutenant Schwartz, was as silent as the death he came to bring. A basement window yielded to a glass cutter, Wentworth removing the excised segment with a suction cup that he attached to its surface. Five dragging minutes later, he was on the second floor of the house.

There were three men in the house, no women. Wentworth pricked the throat of two of these men with a narcotic needle that deepened their sleep, then he stole to the master-bedroom where Lieutenant Schwartz

170

slept between silken sheets. Wentworth's lips drew back from his teeth at sight of the sensually luxurious room. Where would an honest lieutenant of police obtain the money for such quarters?

Wentworth flicked on the lights of the room, drew his sword from its wooden case with a thin whisper of fine steel and walked toward the bed. The man who slept there was brawnily built, but lines of dissipation marked his face. Well, those could easily be changed. . . .

Lieutenant Schwartz awoke with a jerk of muscles, a leap that carried him three feet from the side of his bed, revolver in hand. He leveled it at the *Spider,* staring in amazement at the man before him with the short, heavy-bladed sword in his hand. But his surprise passed and a slow, thick-lipped smile crossed his face.

"Well, well," he drawled, "What the hell do you think you're doing here?"

Wentworth smiled, hard-eyed. "I have come to kill you, Lieutenant Schwartz. In fact, I have come to cut off your head!"

Schwartz's revolver trembled a little in his hand. The sleep flush faded from his cheeks and he retreated a quick, frightened step. Something in the supremely confident manner of the *Spider*—his conversational statement of a terrifying fact—utterly disconcerted the man. He knew as he retreated that here was no ordinary criminal invading a rich house to rob. His bulging eyes shifted before the steady gaze of Wentworth.

"Who . . . *Who are you?*" he whispered.

Wentworth laughed and the sound was flat and mocking, sinister as night. It was a sound that many a criminal had heard before his death, this laughter of the *Spider*. And others had heard it, too, and trembled at its mere memory.

"You asked," Wentworth purred softly, "who I am. Well, I'll tell you. . . . I am . . . *the Spider*!"

A terrified shriek rose from Schwartz's throat, for as Wentworth pronounced *the Spider* he sprang forward

171

with his sword sweeping upward, then forward in a resistless slash. He did not spring blindly onto the muzzle of the gun. He saw Schwartz thrust the weapon forward in his terror, jerking at the trigger. It was no trick for a man with the split-second reflexes of the *Spider* to knock that weapon's muzzle aside with a swift blow of the scabbard cane. His sword swung true, its thin steel edge hissing a little song of death. . . . There was no second shot.

Afterward, the rubberized blanket a heavy burden on his shoulder, Wentworth made his swift, silent way to his car and deposited what he carried in the rumble seat. His black bag he set upon the seat beside him. His face was down and there was a haggard darkness about his eyes. An hour and twenty minutes after he left his apartment, Wentworth tooled the car again into the northernmost end of Fifth Avenue. He slowed then, drifted southward, watching the thin scattering of traffic. Finally, in the Twenties, he swerved to the curb. Only one taxi was in sight and that turned a corner and vanished as he parked. He flipped open the rumble seat and dragged out the rubberized blanket.

The headless body which he laid upon the sidewalk bore no resemblance to that of the pajamaed man he had killed. There was a long black cape from it shoulders and on the pavement beside it, Wentworth tossed a broad brimmed black hat such as the *Spider* wore.

Wentworth sprang to the car again and raced to a nearby all-night drug store, sidled into a booth and called police headquarters excitedly.

"Geez!" he gasped into the mouthpiece. "I just saw the *Spider* and another guy fighting up on Fifth Avenue—Twenty-seventh, I t'ink it was. Sure! Yeah! Listen, if you catch him do I get the reward, huh?"

He heard the cop's voice grow excited, too, and then he hung up and slipped from the booth, got his car away fast. He was in the crowd that assembled a few minutes later when police radio-cars raced to the spot and found the headless body on the sidewalk.

Wentworth nudged the man next to him in the crowd,

"Geez!" he whispered. "It's the *Spider*! See that there cape? See the hat? It's the *Spider*!" His whisper raced through the crowd, such a group of men as will assemble any hour of the day or night in New York, seemingly appearing almost from the sidewalks when there is something to excite their morbid curiosity. The police growled out the words, too, the magical words that could strike terror to a thousand hearts: "*The Spider!*"

Wentworth's work was accomplished for the night, but he did not return to the penthouse where the forces of the law were mobilizing their strength. He went to a hotel, he insisted on carrying the black bag which bulged so oddly in the middle of his room. Once there, he threw himself down for the sleep he had been needing. The *Spider* could sleep for awhile now. Kirkpatrick would do everything that was possible and the campaign of the *Spider* must wait for a few hours, wait until the newspapers screamed aloud that the *Spider* was dead, his head hacked from his shoulders and his body left on the pavements of Fifth Avenue.

CHAPTER SEVENTEEN

Cell for the *Spider*

Five hours' sleep sufficed Wentworth and he awoke greatly refreshed, spent a luxurious twenty minutes bathing, then resumed his shoddy identity and sent out for the morning newspapers. The discovery of the false *Spider's* body had been late for even the final edition, but all of the dailies had made over the front page with heavy eight-column headlines screaming that the *Spider* was dead. Even the cautious *Times* seemed reasonably certain of the dead man's identity. From somewhere, too, had come information that El Gaucho had offered to redeem the head of the *Spider* with its weight in gold. . . .

His restless necessity for action drove Wentworth from his hotel room though he had intended to remain idle most of the day, gathering his resources, husbanding his strength for the crucial battle—more critical than ever—which loomed for him. With the black handbag, over whose contents he worked before he left, he spent the day in the usual criminal haunts of the city. Police patrols of four kept watch in the district, but did nothing to prevent the harsh whispers that were heard everywhere.

"El Gaucho is coming! He'll be king!"

But no one seemed to know where El Gaucho was, or when he would come, or what he would do next.

Wentworth had a few addresses of Gaucho's allies which he had taken from the gang orders, but he did not wish to approach any one of the men named openly, lest suspicions be aroused. Finally, he was forced to that expedient.

He went to a hotel where one Arthur Morrow was supposed to be registered and bribed a bellhop to point the man out to him in the lobby. Afterward, he took a seat beside the man and hugged the black bag to his chest. Arthur Morrow was fat, with a face that seemed the genial wrinkled countenance of most fat men until the shifty, small greenish eyes were studied. After that, there could be no question of his true nature. In Wentworth's disguised face, his subtly furtive manner, Morrow recognized a kindred being. He wheezily offered Wentworth a cigarette. Wentworth curtly refused, moved a little away from Morrow. It was exactly the move calculated to arouse the criminal's interest. Morrow watched silently for awhile, then bent forward.

"Listen pal," he whispered, "you don't need to be scared of me. I ain't no dick."

Wentworth eyed him suspiciously. There was shrewdness in this fat man, and danger, too.

"I don't give a damn what you are," Wentworth said roughly, and slid the black bag around on the opposite side of his body.

Morrow wheezed with laughter. "Cripes, you're a lousy crook," he said. "Anybody would know you had swag in that bag of yours."

"That's what you think!" Wentworth jeered.

Arthur Morrow heaved to his feet and towered over Wentworth's cringing body. There was greed in his beady little eyes, and he was bold with the expected glory to come, with the confidence the Underworld felt in El Gaucho.

"Listen, rat," snarled Morrow, "you're coming up to my room, see, and we're going to talk."

Wentworth slid out past his big body. He was defiant and cringing at once, in the manner of petty crooks. "Geez, I ain't done nothin'," he whined. "I was just sittin' here and you have to pull this stuff. There ain't nothin' in the bag except some clothes. . . ."

"Upstairs," Morrow grunted. He leaned forward, pushing his fat face close to Wentworth's. "Listen, crook. Did you ever hear of El Gaucho?"

Wentworth's face lighted with eagerness. "Say, do you know him? Say, where's your room?"

In the elevator going upward, Wentworth leaned close to the fat man. "Listen," he said. "You get me to the Gaucho and I'll split with you. This here bag is worth its weight in gold to Gaucho."

Arthur Morrow's little eyes squeezed almost shut. *"It's weight in gold!"* he said softly. He looked furtively at Wentworth and when they went along the hallway toward his room, they walked side by side, each watching the other. They went into the room with locked gaze.

Morrow locked the door, came close to Wentworth. "Listen," he said. "What you said has got me interested as all hell. There ain't but one thing worth its weight in gold to El Gaucho. Just one, and you. . . ." He stared deeply into Wentworth's eyes and stepped back a quick step, hand fluttering toward his coat pocket. He didn't draw a gun, but he kept his fat hand close to his pocket while he studied the leering face of Wentworth's disguise.

Wentworth laughed, set the bag down on the bed with a little swagger.

"What's in the bag?" Morrow whispered.

Wentworth laughed. "You wouldn't want to see," he jeered. Seemingly, he had gained confidence from the other's manner. He chuckled when Morrow licked his over-red lips. "No, you wouldn't want to see what I got in that little black bag." He patted the hard bulge.

Morrow's eyes were wide now. "If you've got . . . what I think you've got," he wheezed, "I'll . . . By God, I'll take you to El Gaucho himself!" He took a step nearer, licking his lips. "Let's see!"

Wentworth appeared to consider for a moment, then

he opened the bag, stepped back with a wave of his hand. He slid a hand to his coat lapel then, with Morrow's eyes upon him.

"Go ahead and look," he said.

Morrow gingerly pulled open the sides of the bag, peered in and staggered back with his fat hands trembling. He swallowed with enormous effort.

"Cripes!" he whispered. "Cripes! How did you do it?"

Wentworth pulled his lips back from discolored teeth. "That's my business," he said thinly. "Gaucho promised to pay and I'm going to collect."

Morrow's eyes had turned crafty and the sneer on Wentworth's disguised face widened. His gun slipped smoothly into his palm.

"Listen, fat boy," he said, "I've promised you a cut if you'll take me to El Gaucho. But don't think you're going to get more than a cut. I killed the *Spider* and I guess I can take care of a fat skunk. . . ."

"Don't call me fat!" Morrow spluttered, but he looked cowed. "Come on, get your bag and I'll take you. . . ."

"We'll wait until dark," Wentworth snapped. "Cops can see too well now. I got a car and when it's night, we'll get in that and go for a ride, see? And if there's any funny business, you ain't comin' back from that ride."

Morrow snarled at him. "Listen, just because you killed the *Spider*. . . ."

Wentworth pushed Morrow suddenly, tripped him on the bed and held him with a gun while he put cords he took from his pocket about the gangster's arms and legs.

Morrow lay breathing hard, hatred and cupidity quarreling in his eyes. "Listen, pal," he whined, "you hadn't ought to treat me this way. And listen, we can't wait till dark. It's a long trip up to where El Gaucho is and he's going to take this town at midnight. Hell, he'd . . . he'd kill me if I wasn't on the job then."

*　　*　　*

Wentworth's heart sprang painfully into his throat at the news. El Gaucho must have performed miracles to have his men ready to strike three days before the date set in the orders he was sending out. He would catch New York absolutely unprepared. The nation would be practically at his mercy, unless . . . unless the *Spider* could get through!

He paced up and down the floor with bowed head, thinking frantically. He had counted on a night trip. The top of the Ford he was driving had been painted with a preparation that threw off infra-red rays which were invisible to the human eye. Jackson was cruising over the city in a small semi-rigid dirigible they had chartered from the Goodyear people and, by means of specially treated lenses, Jackson could spot the car with its infra-red paint among a stream of other automobiles. Jackson was to follow him when he started for the headquarters of El Gaucho, then summon help by radio from the dirigible.

The infra-red rays would be easily detected at night, but what would be the result by daylight? Wentworth could not know—yet he did not feel that he could afford to wait until darkness to make the attempt upon El Gaucho. Too much depended upon his success and there would be no margin of safety. . . .

From the bed, Morrow pleaded, "Cripes, pal, you're puttin' me on the spot doin' this. Come on, let's go now."

Wentworth came to an abrupt decision.

"Okay, fats," the *Spider* snarled. "We'll go now, but if you try any double-cross on me, you fat louse, I'll shoot you to pieces, see?"

Morrow wheezed, "I see, pal. I wouldn't do nothin' like that."

"Of course not! Pal!" Wentworth freed Morrow from the bed after relieving him of two light guns he carried in his pockets. Then they went from the hotel, striding close together, Wentworth with the black bag in one hand, his gun in the other, though hidden in his pocket.

178

Morrow climbed into his car without protest and Wentworth, circling the coupé, had time to give a boy a telegram to Nita which he had secretly written to warn her of El Gaucho's changed plans. He had time to glance upward and see that a dirigible was passing low and sluggishly over the street. He felt a thrill of hope.

Perhaps Jackson could actually detect infra-red rays by daylight! His hope died almost as soon as it was born, for the dirigible passed on out of sight. Just cruising, apparently. With some forlorn idea of helping Jackson identify the car, he threw his cap upside down into the rumble seat. The cap had a red lining.

Wentworth climbed in and began to drive by Morrow's directions. The black bag was beneath Wentworth's knees and he caught the fat man staring at it time after time, half in fascination, half in greed. The course lay northward toward Albany and when Wentworth learned that he had a hundred and fifty miles to drive he began to bear down upon the accelerator. The light car lifted and bucked against the steering wheel. He longed for the smooth power of his Hispano or his Daimler, but neither could have served him in this day's crisis. . . .

The sun was near the horizon when Morrow directed Wentworth to turn off the main road into a narrow dirt lane that zigzagged between the thick trunks of trees, dived sharply to ford a stream or surged upward over rocky slopes. When they had gone a mile along that road, a sentry challenged, his bayoneted rifle leveled at Wentworth's chest.

Morrow spoke eagerly to him. "This guy has got the *Spider's* head. We want to take it to his Majesty."

The sentry stepped back behind a tree and Wentworth perceived with narrowed eyes that there was a telephone there. The man talked for a swift minute, then waited for what seemed interminable hours while the car's engine chugged quietly and nothing moved about them at all. Finally the sentry came back.

179

"Morrow is to wait here. You go ahead," he told Wentworth.

Wentworth nodded, smiling thinly at Morrow. The fat man protested, but climbed out promptly. It was clear that El Gaucho obtained instantaneous obedience even among the least of his servitors. Wentworth heard the sentry tell Morrow, "A car will take you back to the city. You will be fined half your bonus for leaving your post."

Wentworth's lips were twisted wryly. He remembered another man who had been treated less kindly for leaving his post. Evidently, El Gaucho was anxious to receive the proof of his enemy's death.

Three sentries passed him without challenge and it became apparent that word had gone ahead. El Gaucho had his camp superbly protected. Undoubtedly these telephone equipped guards surrounded the place in all directions. The first evidence of an invading force would instantly alarm El Gaucho's entire army of killers. . . .

Past five more sentries, Wentworth drove before his car was stopped at a high, barbed-wire fence. He left it then, was stripped of his two forty-five caliber automatics, but allowed to retain the black bag at which men stared curiously. Here, once more, was the orderly array of earth-colored tents. Houses, too, were painted so as to make them inconspicuous. Wentworth recalled the other encampment in that sunken plateau far to the West and surmised that here El Gaucho had fewer allies among the air pilots who would be supposed to watch out for his headquarters.

There were three barbed-wire fences and each was backed by entanglements of long-spined wire and by trenches. Wentworth's heart sank with each new indication of power. Even if authorities did locate this place, it would take them days to move up the troops and equipment to destroy it and the encampment was strategically placed atop a hill, the highest promontory anywhere about. Damn it, no one would have believed that such a thing as this was possible; an armed and en-

180

trenched force in the heart of America, ready to sweep the authorities of law and order from power.

Wentworth realized abruptly that he was not being taken toward the main, large building, but toward a smaller structure with barred windows. He halted in his tracks and the bayonets of four soldiers ringed him in.

"Listen," he said, "I want to see El Gaucho! I can go to jail any day." He lifted the black bag. "El Gaucho wants to see this!"

The sentries' bayonets pressed closer. "You will await word from His Majesty," one announced flatly, and there could be no more argument against those bare, steel blades. Wentworth was thrust into a cell and the door clanged sullenly behind him.

CHAPTER EIGHTEEN

The *Spider's* Head

Long hours dragged past while Wentworth paced slowly back and forth in his cell. Beyond the wall of solid metal that separated him from the next cubicle, he could hear some other man pacing too. It occurred to him fleetingly that it might be Tommy Barker. But there could be no communication between them, no help one for the other. He was in disguise, probably watched. . . .

As the black night wheeled on, Wentworth's anxiety mounted. He could not fail, now that he was this near his goal. He could not! He had come prepared for possible imprisonment. Inside of his strong, white teeth, fastened to his lower molars and curved against the inner surfaces of his teeth was a saw blade of such temper hardness that it would slice through the toughest steel. Within an hour, if unobserved, he could hack through the bars of his window.

But that was only a last extremity. It was an expedient to save his life. And what he wanted now was the death of El Gaucho. If he escaped from his cell, he would have to force his way through armed sentries to the throne. If El Gaucho finally relented and permitted him to bring his black bag into his presence there would be no difficulty at all. Wentworth was convinced there would be no help from Jackson. He had watched the evening skies in vain for any trace of the dirigible in which his man was to have followed him. No, it must all come from within himself.

The *Spider* stood motionless at the window of his cell, staring into the blackness. He closed his eyes, breathing strength into his body with deep inhalations. He was watching the time with sharp eyes. If he were not released and taken to El Gaucho, by quarter of twelve, he would have to burst from his cell, and take chances with death to reach El Gaucho.

The hands of his watch dragged to eleven-thirty, to twenty-five minutes of twelve. In a dozen cities throughout the United States, Wentworth knew that gangsters were preparing to strike. They would destroy buildings and leaders of American life. They would, in one titanic blow, smash American institutions to the earth, bring back the reign of tyranny and selfish greed to the world.

"It shall not happen," Wentworth whispered to himself. "It shall not!"

Twenty minutes of twelve now. Wentworth crossed to his black bag, picked it up with deliberate hands. His mouth was tight, his lips cold and hard against his teeth. It was a desperate chance, but he must take it in five minutes more. . . .

Minutes limped by. The *Spider* stood on braced feet before the door. There was a stirring now out there beyond the jail door, the clop of horses' hoofs. . . . Wentworth's blood turned cold. Horses' hoofs in this enclosed camp could mean but one thing. Some one had been doomed to death by the torture of the horses! Had a sentry penetrated his disguise? Had he been sentenced to that death? Or was it for Tommy Barker, prisoner somewhere in camp, perhaps in the cell next to his?

Wentworth jerked his head angrily. He could not think of such things when the fate of Christian civilization hung in the balance. Tom Barker, the *Spider*. . . . they were nothing in the scales of justice. Wentworth crossed deliberately to the iron cot against the wall,

183

picked up the black bag and returned to the door. It lacked only one minute of quarter to twelve. . . .

Even as Wentworth prepared to take his last desperate measure, he heard rhythmic footsteps and knew that soldiers were marching toward the tiny, barred prison. The detail halted outside the building and four men entered, unlocked Wentworth's door and escorted him outside. After him, came the man from the other cubicle. Wentworth dared a glance in his direction and his heart gave a leap at glimpse of a browned face, brave despite the haggard hint of what was to come in his blue eyes. The boy carried his head high, his shoulders thrown back.

"I hope you've been feeding the horses well," he joked at one of the soldiers. "They're going to lose their dinner over what happens to me."

Wentworth longed to clap the boy on the back, shake his hand for that brave display, but he must act out his character. He carried himself with cringing insolence, hugging the black bag against his chest as if that were his protection against all evils, and his guarantee of heaven. Tommy Barker looked at him contemptuously.

The *Spider's* mind raced on ahead of the slow march of the soldiers toward the main building, which they circled deliberately. There was a white blaze of lights behind it and Wentworth knew that it was there the torture was to take place. Tommy Barker and those great kind horses driven to murder by El Gaucho. . . . His eyes quested ahead. Files of soldiers as before, but few of the motley mob of killers that had witnessed the last execution. They would be in the cities, leading the gangsters who, within minutes, would destroy thousands.

There on the opposite side of this square of soldiers, drowned in blazing white light, stood the throne of El Gaucho and upon it the author of the hell that brewed above America tonight. He stood there upon the raised dais, arrogance in the lift of his head, utter confidence in his bearing.

When Wentworth, carrying out his part, had dropped to his knees before the throne; when Tommy Barker had been forced down into the dirt, El Gaucho turned his smile upon the assembled soldiers. Wentworth looked up into his bearded face and hugged the black bag. Such a slim chance. . . . His eyes flicked to the faces about the throne. De Moltkez with his right hand in a sling, Von Hapszollern in his Death's-Head Hussar's shako. Two women were by the throne, Carollotta—pale and straight-mouthed with some emotion that he could not discern—and Yvonne Musette!

Wentworth perceived that El Gaucho was about to make a speech.

"My people!" his deep voice boomed across the square of soldiers. "Tonight is the night of our glory. Tonight we triumph over all enemies. Here before us, we have one who will pay tonight for his opposition, and the head of one who already has paid. The *Spider* and the *Spider's* slave. . . . !"

He paused and an obedient cheer rose from the assembled men. Carollotta swayed on her feet. Yvonne's red lips parted in that slow, cruel smile that Wentworth had seen once before when she had planned his murder.

"Here behind our throne," El Gaucho went on, in an expansive mood, "are telegraph instruments connecting us with all America. We will send to our allies the news of our triumph here and they will bring us the news of our triumphs over a dozen cities, over all America."

El Gaucho flung out his arm. "Bring the horses!"

A quiver raced over Wentworth. Carollotta, despite her obvious effort at control, lifted a hand to her mouth and sank teeth into her wrist. Tom Barker turned toward Wentworth.

"If there's any justice on earth," he said vehemently, "you'll die by the vilest torture known. I'll bet you stabbed the *Spider* in the back!"

Barker was wrenched to his feet and pulled backward toward where the four great horses stood. Wentworth's heart beat high and in his throat. There was a dryness in his mouth.

Wentworth looked up toward the throne. "Hey, Gauch'," he called, "how about making the slave kiss the *Spider's* head?"

El Gaucho stared sternly, but there was a gleam in his eyes that showed the proposal met with his approval.

"Bring me the head," he said.

Wentworth got to his feet and held the black bag in his two hands as he went forward, a soldier on either side of him. El Gaucho lifted his hand and a soldier whispered in Wentworth's ear.

"Hold up the head!"

The *Spider's* lips set grimly as he reached into the black bag. The time was not yet. These two soldiers. . . . He grasped coarse hair, pulled the black bag clear and lifted a human head high into the air before him. Carollotta's sobs burst through the gag of her wrist and Wentworth saw her sag against the throne, weeping. Yvonne laughed and laughed. And El Gaucho. . . .

El Gaucho leaned forward with his elbow on his knee and stared into the features of the *Spider* which Wentworth had built over the German features of Lieutenant Schwartz. El Gaucho nodded.

"It should be a heavy head," he said crisply. "You will earn high reward in our kingdom."

Then El Gaucho's eyes lifted above Wentworth's head and an eager light sprang into his eyes. He stood up.

"Wait!" he called. "I myself will fasten the last rope to the traitor."

The soldiers thrust Wentworth aside and El Gaucho stepped down from his throne, stalked toward where Tommy Barker lay prone upon the ground among the four horses. It was, Wentworth saw suddenly, the moment for which he had waited. It was now or never!

Wentworth jerked the head back over his shoulders and hurled it violently at El Gaucho! Skull struck skull

186

and El Gaucho pitched forward in the dust. For a full dozen heartbeats there was absolute silence, absolute quiet over the entire assembly of soldiers. A deep curse groaned from Wentworth's throat. There was a bomb inside that skull, placed there while nausea wretched at his stomach at the thing he did, while the *Spider* goaded himself with thoughts of his duty to humanity that could be performed in no other way. And *the bomb had failed to explode*! Even while he cursed at his failure, Wentworth sprang upon De Moltkez. He ripped the man's sword from its sheath, dragged its flying point across the officer's throat as he whirled toward the body of El Gaucho.

He lifted the sword high over his head and in that same moment, Carollotta screamed a warning. Wentworth whirled, was barely in time to dash aside the sword of Von Hapszollern, stabbing at his back. A half dozen soldiers rushed forward to strike him down but Von Hapszollern's snarling voice rang out.

"Hold!" he cried, "I claim the right to kill. this dog!"

Wentworth found that he held in his hand only a nickel-plated dress sword. It had a sharp point which had done for De Moltkez, but it was very short and light and the greater war saber of Von Hapszollern beat upon its feeble strength violently. The two men circled, Wentworth guarding against the attack of the other, looking for his chance to stab through the other's defense.

In a quick, side-glance, he saw that El Gaucho had staggered to his feet and was looking stupidly about. He saw the duel, saw Wentworth's apparent help-lessness and laughed aloud.

"Don't kill him, my friend," El Gaucho called to Von Hapszollern. "Just run him through the belly. Af-terward, the horses may have their pleasure with him."

Von Hapszollern shouted a deep assent and El Gau-cho turned toward Tommy Barker, supine among the horses. He laughed again and there was a thin, wild note to his laughter. Wentworth was allowing himself to be forced backward toward the throne now. Behind that were the telegraph instruments. Even in the midst of his desperate battle for life, Wentworth was thinking more of his country, of the people he loved, than of his own life. There was an indomitable strength in his arm tonight, for he fought not alone for himself, but for all those countless thousands over the nation who would die if he did not conquer.

Now he had achieved what he wanted. One foot was on the steps of the throne, the other braced before him and his light sword moved like a flicker of light in and out of the slashing attack of Von Hapszollern.

"Carollotta," he whispered, "Carollotta!"

He heard her gasped response beside him and a smile touched his lips. He might yet win. It was a desperate venture. . . .

"Carollotta," he whispered. "If you love Tommy, get a revolver and *shoot the head of the Spider!*"

He heard her sobs crowding against her teeth. Then the sound faded away from him. He hoped she would obey. Von Hapszollern was raging at his inability to break through the guard of this man who had cringed before the throne. He slashed wildly, recklessly and Wentworth's defense grew more cautious, tighter. His wrist did not move more than four inches against the most dangerous of the Prince's cuts.

But time grew short. There were only seconds now between him and midnight. Two minutes perhaps, maybe three. Certainly no more than that. Glancing beyond Von Hapszollern, Wentworth saw El Gaucho belaboring the great Percherons with a cat of nine tails that he had caught from one of the torturers. The horse stood, shivering in every muscle, but did not move. Wentworth gritted his teeth together. Why didn't Carollotta hurry? El Gaucho must have gone completely mad. No man could control a Percheron with a whip. Only kindness would move the great horses, and this fool. . . .

Carollotta's voice whispered in his ear. "I have the

revolver," she murmured, "but I have never fired one in my life."

Wentworth thrust back his left hand, caught the gun and at the same instant lunged furiously through Von Hapszollern's anger-opened guard. The light dress sword struck the golden buckle that held the baldrick of Von Hapszollern's sword, glanced off, ripped cloth and flesh, then found its sheath in the Prince's body. The blade snapped off short.

Wentworth sprang to El Gaucho's throne, the revolver held at his hip.

"If any man moves," he shouted, "El Gaucho dies. Carollotta—" a whisper now—"go cut Tommy loose with Von Hapszollern's sword."

He saw the swift movement of the girl while his eyes quested over the amphitheater. No one of the soldiers moved to lift his gun, but there were men near him who held their bayonets ready. If he lost control for a moment. . . . Wentworth's thoughts were desperate. If only Carollotta would hurry. He didn't want to kill Tommy Barker if he could help it, but if he must. . . . He glanced at his watch. One minute of twelve. For God's sake, Carollottta, hurry, hurry!

El Gaucho was still slashing at the Percherons with the heavy whip, failing to stir them from their tracks. Carollotta circled to get at Barker from the opposite side. Wentworth cursed. In *heaven's name, Carollotta. Don't you know that thousands of lives depend on your speed. I cannot wait any longer. I dare not. Thousands of lives against that of one man whom we both love. Our love is nothing.* . . .

Wentworth lifted the revolver, a hand on the back of the throne. He must fire and leap from the dais in the same split second of time, find the telegraph imstruments . . . He could hear their tinny clicking there and subconsciously he listened. They were asking for the signal!

Merciful God, they would not strike until they had the signal from El Gaucho! But an officer was slipping behind the throne. There were only seconds between the *Spider* and death; between thousands and their doom; between civilization and its destruction. . . . !

The bright blade of the saber Carollotta held flashed high in the air and slashed down, once, twice and Tommy Barker was scrambling to his feet. The whip of El Gaucho swept down and Barker cried aloud and fell back, hands rising to his face. Carollotta had been struck also by one of those lead-ended lashes and reeled backward, unconscious.

El Gaucho dropped his whip, sprang to the ropes to lash them once more to the man he would destroy. Wentworth caught a glimpse of his face as he bent and there was utter madness there—the insanity of an egotist thwarted in his moment of triumph. A cry rose in Wentworth's throat. He lifted the revolver and fired— at the "head of the *Spider*" that lay on the ground. In the same moment, he hurled himself violently backward from the dias. He had a final glance as he leaped, of Yvonne Musette running to help El Gaucho, of her feet flying past the head of the *Spider*. . . .

Then everything was blacked out in a cataclysm of wind and sound. The bullet had exploded the bomb within the skull. Wentworth, safe behind the throne, peered out and saw a great crater in the earth, saw that Yvonne had vanished and saw something else that pulled him erect with a shout pouring from his lungs. El Gaucho was struggling between two of the horses who were rearing with fright after the blast. His arms were stretched out rigidly to each side of him toward the horses, as if . . . as if he himself were caught in the torture he had planned for Tommy Barker. . . . !

And suddenly Wentworth understood. In his final, furious effort to destroy Barker, he had himself become entangled in the ropes of the horses! Shrill cries rosed from El Gaucho's lips, shrill screams of extreme agony. One great, ton-heavy Percheron reared into the air, its entire weight thrown against the tortured joints of El Gaucho's arms. And at once, the Percheron was racing across the field toward the bomb-scattered ranks of soldiers and El Gaucho was being dragged in the opposite direction by a second horse, dragged through the dust, screaming and screaming. Then he was free of that horse, too, and ran shrieking in circles. But he did not throw his arms to heaven. He did not have any arms. . . .

Behind the throne, feverish eyes on the dying man who had so nearly become king of America, Wentworth was pounding out messages on the telegraph keys.

"El Gaucho is dead," he sent. "El Gaucho is dead. Disband your gangs or you will die, too. The *Spider* swears it! El Gaucho is dead. . . ."

And even as he sent that message, El Gaucho was collapsing out there among the men he had befuddled with his talk of glory, was dying in the dust where he had dragged so many others. Carollotta, in the dust, too, cradled Tommy Barker's head in her lap. . . .

The roar of an explosion blasted over the armed camp. It was followed instantly by another and another and between the rumble of bombs, Wentworth caught the swooping, diving roar of airplanes. He sprang to his feet, flinging his hands in the air. Jackson! Jackson had followed after all, followed the car and had brought the bombing planes of the government to destroy this hell-hole of El Gaucho.

Slowly, Wentworth calmed, seeing the soldiers flee. He smiled gently, looking at Carollotta and Tommy Barker, their arms tight about each other, and he stole through the shadows that fell with the extinction of the lights, while the bombs still fell out there on the barbed-wire entanglements—to the car that had brought destruction to the power of El Gaucho.

When the soldiers of freedom came, they found Tommy and Carollotta. They found dead men . . . but the *Spider* had vanished!

Green Globes of
Death

Richard Wentworth—who, as the swift-killing *Spider*, is the scourge of the Underworld—thought the Fly was dead. But once more that most formidable enemy had arisen, pillaging, slaying wantonly, armed with a ghastly new weapon, the Green Globes of Death! Ruthless and astute, heading a gigantic criminal syndicate, the Fly was butchering innocent persons only, it seemed, to see their red blood flow. It was with flagging hope and heavy heart that the *Spider* took up his newest battle with the preying jackals of crime!

CHAPTER ONE

Danse Macabre

Wentworth watched the girl in scarlet saunter toward him and, when she glided to a halt, he swept her a bow that made his black cape swirl . . . but he did not lose sight of the two men in costume who watched him with hostile furtiveness from across the ballroom. A masquerade dance might not seem a place for murder, but Wentworth thought that he could read the will to kill in those two men—to kill Wentworth, who had worn to the masquerade the costume of—the *Spider*! The girl's blue eyes were intent from behind a silken mask. . . .

"Does the *Spider* dance?" she asked mockingly, half-lifting her warm bare arms in invitation. A black patch beside her faintly smiling mouth was shaped like a heart.

Wentworth laughed lightly. He could appreciate beauty, even when it came to him in treachery as this girl undoubtedly did. There was another reason for laughter: he had come tonight in the costume of the *Spider* as a deliberate challenge to a new and rising criminal power, and, beyond question, this charming girl in scarlet and powdered wig brought him the enemy's answer!

"The *Spider* dances, yes," he told her gravely, "but not to measures that you would enjoy. I understand

195

there are benches in the conservatory. . . ." He offered his arm, letting his thin, hard lips curve upward. It was not a pleasant thing, that smile, but Wentworth knew there were reasons other than his facial expression for the faint shudder which abruptly shook the girl's slim shoulders. The girl might not know that he was actually the *Spider*; but even a man disguised as the *Spider* became a sinister and ominous creature. Throughout the world, he was known as a merciless avenger. More than a hundred criminals had died with the mocking red seal of the *Spider* upon their foreheads—and some had died horribly. . . . Small wonder then, that the girl shuddered when the *Spider* offered his arm! She covered her fright with a trilling laugh, put a white hand almost caressingly upon his arm. . . .

"Is it . . . *safe* to have a rendezvous with the *Spider*?" she whispered.

"Treachery is never safe," Wentworth informed her flatly, and his eyes went deliberately to the two men who kept watch—one costumed as a cavalier with his palm upon the pommel of a long sword, the other in fool's motley, his bell stick like a battle mace. They were moving deftly across the crowded dance floor toward the darkened conservatory to which Wentworth was leading the girl. . . .

"Treachery?" the girl gasped.

Wentworth bowed his head. His eyes were mocking. "I am certain that the escort of such a charming lady as you will consider your desertion . . . *treachery*!"

The girl's answering laughter, as they entered the conservatory was off-key. That of the *Spider* was strangely flat and mocking, a challenge to whomsoever might be lurking in the shadows. Enemies were behind him and at his side. There well might be others in hiding. . . . He felt his blood quicken. He had come ready to fight. How else could the *Spider* enter the home of Charles Holland, whose brother the *Spider* had killed?

Wentworth had not been invited to the masquerade—

men do not soon forget the slaying of their brothers, even though that brother had been a criminal—but it had seemed the best way to attack the new uprising of the Underworld which Wentworth feared. His life was dedicated to the defense of the people against the wolves of injustice, and it seemed that the shrewdest foe he had ever fought was come to life again!

When Jack Holland, brother of Wentworth's involuntary host, had turned criminal, he had taken for himself the name of the Fly, as a deliberate taunt to the *Spider*. His genius for successful slaughter and robbery had united the entire Underworld behind the leadership of his gold-hilted knife—which was crested, mockingly, with the image of a fly.

Almost he had smashed the powers of law and order; almost he had defeated and slain the *Spider*. In the end, Wentworth had triumphed. But now, amazingly, the Fly had struck again!

Openly, and with the unrivaled daring which only the Fly had ever shown before, this new Fly had murdered the Mayor of New York City! And he had left his fly-crested knife buried in the Mayor's heart as a token and a challenge!

Suspicion of Jack Holland's younger brother, Charles, had seemed ridiculously obvious, yet it was a line of investigation Wentworth could not ignore. He had chosen the direct, frontal attack of crashing Charles Holland's masquerade in the costume of the *Spider*. His host, seeing him as he entered, had stiffened, his frosty blue eyes going cold. But he had not challenged . . . until now. In the twilight of the conservatory, Wentworth seated the girl upon a marble bench, stood before her with both hands upon the head of his cane.

"I'm afraid," he said gently, "that we will shortly be interrupted. Won't you first unmask?"

Through the easy banter of his voice, his ears were acutely attuned. It was one of the *Spider's* favorite tricks, to be on guard while seeming totally unaware of approaching danger. He twisted the head of his cane slightly to the left. He did not grip it in his fist, but held it across his palm between thumb and fingers as a man grasps the hilt of a sword. . . . There could be no doubt that Holland, or certainly some of his guests, had understood the nature of his challenge, knew that no one without the right would dare to wear the costume of the *Spider*.

The girl sat with a rigidity that betrayed her tension, her hands folded in her lap upon the looped and flounced silk of her period gown. Her elaborate, powdered coiffeur seemed too heavy for the slender column of her throat and Wentworth read fright in her eyes. She was new to this game of treachery and death. . . . She came abruptly to her feet, took a step forward, hands reaching out.

"Leave here before it is too late," she said quickly. "Please, don't wait for explanations. I . . . *Oh!*"

If this was new treachery, it was cleverly executed. Her voice, the fervor of her pleading face, would have prevented any man less alert than Wentworth from hearing the approach of his enemies. As it was, he had to thrust her sharply away lest she interfere with his defense. The girl fell, rather than sat, upon the bench and Wentworth spun about with a litheness which his assumed limp and hunched shoulders would seem to make impossible. He was instantly on guard, the cane in his right hand with its ferrule forward and just touching the floor. The two men who had watched him were within three paces of the *Spider*! The cavalier's sword was a gleam of deadly steel in his right hand and the man in motley gripped his bell stick like a club. Through the holes in their masks, their eyes were glittering beads.

"Leave us, Lou," the cavalier ordered the girl, and with the words, Wentworth recognized him. He had changed his evening dress, which he had worn in the reception line, for the silks of a period costume, but the voice was unmistakable. It was Charles Holland. The girl got to her feet and moved toward him. . . . He thrust out his left hand in a stiff gesture.

"Leave us, Lou," he repeated.

Lou hesitated, her head swinging as she looked first at Holland, then at Wentworth. Her slim shoulders slumped and she stumbled toward the door that gave on the gaiety of the ballroom.

"Close the doors, Shock, and guard them," Holland said then, and the man in motley backed away. The closing of the doors turned the orchestra and the laugher into a faint, distant music. Holland lifted his sword in salute. "You have a sword in your cane," he said bitterly to Wentworth. "You have challenged me, and I would not decline if I could."

Wentworth laughed sharply. He flicked his wrist and the wooden sheath slithered musically from his cane sword, left the steel glittering in his hand.

"Why did you kill the Mayor, Holland?" he asked. "And especially, why have you taken your brother's *nom de crime*?"

Holland replied raspingly, "On guard, *Spider*!" His rapier sang against Wentworth's steel. "I'm going to kill you!"

Wentworth's thinned lips smiled slightly. He feinted for the left breast, tapped Holland's blade hard, circled—and lunged like lightning for the right breast. But his adversary's parry was swift and sure, and a *riposte* missed Wentworth's throat only because his recovery was of a speed that had never been surpassed on the mat of any *salle d'armes* of the world. Wentworth smiled and nodded. Holland's dead brother had been superb with the saber. Holland was master of the rapier. This would be no easy task. . . .

The blades rang harshly as Holland began a fiery attack. Wentworth stood firm, steely wrist turning thrust and lunge in bewildering sequence. He perceived abruptly what Holland was trying to do. Behind Wentworth was a narrow passageway between high waving fronds of palm and fern. There might be other men hidden there! If Holland could only drive him back into that corridor. . . . A lunge so swift and savage that it was impossible to turn forced Wentworth to leap backward a full yard. His *riposte* kept Holland from pressing

199

the advantage, but Wentworth was dangerously close to the shrubs.

There was a smile on Holland's lips to match Wentworth's own. Even when death hovered over their heads, these two could joy in the fight for its own sake. Their swords glinted in the twilight of the conservatory, found each other as much by instinct as by vision. Each thrust found its parry; every *riposte* was warded. Wentworth's right forearm had been scratched, Holland had felt the sting of the point upon his cheek. He could not force Wentworth back another foot, but neither could Wentworth fight his way out into clear floor space again. And there was always the consciousness that there might be more men hidden there behind the flowers. . . . !

It was the *Spider* who broke the deadlock. He had never been a conventional swordsman. He knew the French and Italian schools of fence, the tricks of a score of masters. It was apparent that Holland was equally familiar with the rapier. It was obvious to Wentworth that, if he were to triumph, he must go outside all he had learned, ignore precedent and danger. . . . Without a preliminary flourish, he broke the half-instinctive rhythm of thrust and parry, lunge and *riposte*. He did a thing many expert swordsmen would have feared to attempt because of its overwhelming peril. An inch of miscalculation, a moment's misreading of his opponent's intentions . . . !

He sensed that Holland planned a lunge, the most savage and violent attack which can be made with the rapier. Even as the thought flicked through Wentworth's mind, Holland struck. His arm shot out and behind the leveled blade, he hurled the entire weight of his body. He bounded clear of the floor, left leg trailing behind him for balance, right knee cushioned upward against his body to catch his weight and hurl him backward on guard should his attack fail. But he did not intend to fail. All the pent-up hatred of the years that had passed since his brother's death went into it. And Wentworth did not attempt a parry!

He should have caught the tip of his opponent's sword close against the hilt of his own, turned it aside and attempted to *riposte* with a swift thrust before Holland could recover. He knew that *riposte* was impossible. However swiftly he thrust after a parry, he was too slow to catch Holland before the man returned to his original position, blade on guard.

Wentworth shut his lips grimly and threw his life into the balance. If he miscalculated by an inch, he would be run entirely through by that fiercely darting sword, but he took that chance as he had taken a thousand before. Instead of parrying, he swayed his body aside at the hips and his rapier licked out for the breast of Charles Holland!

The maneuver was perfectly executed. Holland's point ripped through Wentworth's coat, but missed flesh. Wentworth's sword pierced—and then Wentworth did a queer thing—a mad thing! Instead of driving his point home with stiffened arm and shoulder, he threw his hand up, as if he had driven a harmless foil button against an opponent's plastron in a friendly assault!

Holland's grin had twisted into a surprised grimace in that last instant. He had failed, had felt the point of the man he strove to kill prick the skin above his heart—and he still lived! Holland recovered from his lunge, faltered backward and dropped the point of his sword. His left hand went slowly to his breast, where Wentworth's sword had pricked and the warmth of his own blood wet his fingers. He knew it was no serious wound. His eyes met Wentworth's. . . .

"Why?" he whispered. "You could have killed me, yet you spared my life. Why?"

Wentworth himself was frowning. He had come here this night for the express purpose of determining whether Charles Holland was the Fly, and killing him if he were guilty. Holland had attacked him, had not denied the charges and yet, when the moment came to strike, the *Spider's* hand, which never before had faltered, had swerved from its task!

"Why?" Holland repeated.

Wentworth shook his head and the man in motley sprang from the shadows to Holland's side. "Master Charles!" he cried. "In the ballroom. Robbers! *The Fly!*"

Holland and Wentworth both whirled toward the man costumed so garishly in the green and red dress of a fool. A bell on his cap jingled softly as he nodded.

"The Fly," he cried urgently, "is robbing your guests, Master Charles!"

CHAPTER TWO

Masque of Death

Wentworth was instantly in motion, charging toward the doors with long, smooth bounds, his black cape whipping backward from his shoulders. He thrust the puzzle of his failure to kill Charles Holland completely out of his brain. That was something which leisure must resolve, and here was a problem that demanded immediate cyphering. In the ball room, the Fly, who had been his enemy through one of the gravest battles of his career, was robbing the wealthy guests of Charles Holland!

He was wrong in one thing, Wentworth corrected himself as he ran. This could not be the same Fly whom he had fought previously. He and that first Fly had dueled with swords on a narrow bridge a half dozen stories above the street. In the end, the *Spider's* saber had slipped through and the Fly had fallen nearly a hundred feet to the pavement below. . . . No, this must be some other killer trading in on the Fly's prestige. . . .

Just outside the closed doors of the ball room, Wentworth checked his plunge and found that Charles Holland was close beside him, rapier still in hand. Together, these two who had sought to kill each other, peered through the curtained glass. A muffled oath squeezed out through Holland's teeth and he ripped open the door, darted through. Wentworth reached out to snatch him back and a savage blow from behind drove him to his knees. First numbness, then pain lanced across Wentworth's shoulder, through his nape, and his sword cane skittered across the polished floor. He braced his body on stiffened arms, was dimly aware that Holland, sword lifted high above his head, was rushing forward.

"After me, Shock!" he cried and his voice reached Wentworth as from a great distance.

Something struck the floor beside the *Spider* with savage violence and he realized that it had been the man Shock who slugged him and that a second blow had been averted only by Holland's shout. . . . The ball room was in tableau before the dazed *Spider*. Along one wall stood all the women, hands raised, their pale faces at stark contrast with their gay costumes, facing them stood the men—two bandits with sub-machine guns, whose muzzles roved with ceaseless hunger, held them motionless. A third robber, seeming no more than a boy in a gay scarlet raiment of a court page, was gathering the jewels and money surrendered by the prisoners. And ranged before the leader who stood, weaponless, to supervise the work, were Charles Holland with his challenging sword and the man in motley who served him.

Wentworth was aware of all these things without conscious inspection, for his eyes went inevitably to the leader, to the Fly! He stood between the two machine gunners at the end of the long hall and the mere sight of him jerked Wentworth to his feet as if his nerves had been shocked by galvanic batteries. He could not mistake that dapper, smiling man with the lazy, savage eyes of black and the suavely cruel face. It was . . . *the Fly!*

Once more Wentworth scoffed at himself, at his involuntary mental recognition of this man as the one he had slain. The *Spider's* piercing eyes narrowed to the inspection. He reminded himself deliberately that the

entire identity of that other Fly had been assumed—
that the face, even the color of the eyes had been a
manufactured thing. There was no reason why another
crook could not do as Holland's dead brother had, build
the face of the fly over his own. No, no, the Fly was
dead, and this man . . . a mere imposter.

Wentworth's brain, with the facility of long training,
had snapped back to normal. He knew that the man
called Shock had struck him with the bell stick and he
did not understand why; nor did he understand why
Charles Holland, alone before that deadly killer and
his machine gunners, had been allowed to approach
unscathed, unless . . . unless he and the Fly were allies!

Wentworth's gaze returned to the Fly. The killer was
garbed from head to foot in a monk's black robe. The
hood was dropped back from his smooth blond head
and, at the waist instead of a rope girdle, he wore twin
gun holsters from whose open tops thrust the butts of
heavy revolvers. So far, no one had been injured among
the guests, but Wentworth remembered the Fly's work
of old. Always, the killer had covered his tracks with
a brutal massacre!

The Fly bowed to Wentworth. "An unexpected pleasure," he murmured. He turned to a machine gunner.
"Wilson, give the gentleman in black your entire attention. If he so much as blinks an eyelid, empty your
entire drum of bullets into his carcass. He is the
Spider!"

The man called Wilson turned a paling face and a
menacing gun muzzle upon Wentworth. His eyes
burned. He crouched in his eagerness. Wentworth
smiled slightly. That order was very typical of the Fly's
alertness, but he would have been much wiser had he
ordered the man to shoot immediately.

Charles Holland was speaking angrily. . . .

"I demand that you leave this house immediately,"
he cried. "You are an impostor, attempting to dishonor my brother's memory. He has made his atone-
ment and . . ." Holland stook a short, furious step
forward, his rapier coming up. The Fly did not move,

205

but his hands, hanging loosely at his sides, were very close to his revolvers. The men were ten feet apart. A fierce lunge. . . .

The Fly said drily, "Don't try it, my dear brother, though I appreciate your defense of my name. I'd hate to soil my hands with fratricidal blood. . . ."

Holland reeled and a hoarse cry pushed from his throat. The Fly smiled slightly, looked beyond him at the boy who was collecting jewels. "Hurry there, Gary. We haven't much time. . . ."

Wentworth pulled his eyes from the stricken horror on Charles Holland's face and looked toward the boy who was collecting the loot. A woman had echoed the name uttered by the Fly, and her voice was a gasp. "Gary, *Gary* . . . !" It was the girl in scarlet, the one who had led him into Holland's trap. Her hands were reaching out in appeal to the man in page's scarlet. She started from the line of women, and the machine gunner on guard rasped a curse and jerked the snout of his weapon toward her. She ignored that, caught the man she called Gary by the arm.

"You can't do this, Gary," she cried. "In heaven's name, what are you doing here with that . . . that *beast*!"

Gary looked shamed. He peered over his shoulder toward the Fly, who was smiling, though not pleasantly. "Well, Gary," he drawled. "The lady is charming, but we have no time now for dalliance. . . ."

Gary jerked his arm from the girl's hand, slapped her heavily across the face with the back of his hand and sent her reeling against the wall. "Tend to your own business," he said roughly. The girl—Wentworth remembered her name was Lou—sagged against the wall, her eyes large and frightened above the hand she pressed to her cheek. Holland shouted out hoarsely and took a quick stride toward Gary, but a drawled word from the Fly stopped him. The machine gunners were jittery. It would take very little to make them release their thunderous death. . . .

Wentworth watched the whole scene with hard, narrowed eyes. He did not quite understand what had happened there. He did not think that Gary was the girl's lover. Holland might more accurately be thought to hold that position. But it was all of a piece with the usual cruelty of the Fly. It was not unlikely that the Fly had planned just this scene, knowing of a relationship between his minion and a guest at Holland's masquerade. . . . Swift anger, and doubt, raced over Wentworth. Already in his own mind, he was classing this killer before him with that other Fly whom he had fought—and slain, he swore—months ago. He claimed to be the same man. . . . But all that did not matter. What was of importance was the man's assertion that he was the Fly, for it undoubtedly portended another such crime as those which had shocked a world when the Fly was in his heyday. It meant that he would conclude this polite looting with slaughter!

Wentworth's hands ached for his guns. Somehow, and it must be quickly! The *Spider* must evade the menace of that machine gun and kill the Fly. He was certain that the Fly did not mean that the *Spider* should survive this night. He was delaying assassination only because he did not wish shots to give the alarm before he had completed his work. . . .

Wentworth, after the first look, had not glanced again toward the machine gunner. The man's attention was much more apt to wander if the *Spider* did not hold his eyes. . . . If only some one would create a diversion, the *Spider* could go into action.

It would be the work of much less than a second to bring his guns into play. But he could not count on help. The girl's cry had caused a few moment's disturbance, but she was quiet now, standing with her head very high, not even looking at the boy who was collecting the loot. There were both pride and fear on her face. . . .

Wentworth smiled in the direction of the Fly and began to whistle softly between his teeth. The tune was piercing and dwelt on minor notes, such as he used sometimes to summon his Hindu servant, Ram Singh. The doughty Sikh was not within call tonight, but the Fly, who knew the *Spider's* habits so well, would not know that. . . . The Fly whipped about savagely.

"Quiet!" he shouted. "Wilson, he's trying to call that Hindu servant of his. You'd better go to the door and then take a gander through the conservatory. I'll watch Mr. *Spider*." He drew the revolvers with a movement as swift and smooth as thought. "If you make a sound. . . ."

Wentworth shrugged at the guns, his lips derisive. "Sorry, I was merely whistling away a dull moment." There were only three bandits left to fight against now. . . .

The Fly's heavy black gaze was upon Wentworth. His face took on sharp, venomous lines. Disguised his countenance undoubtedly was, but it was suited admirably to his character. It was plain that he wavered between greed for more jewels and the mad urge to murder. Delay would bring more wealth into his pouch, but it exposed him for long minutes to this calm, black-robed killer. However calm and self-confident a criminal might be, he could not gaze with equanimity on the *Spider*. Too many such men as he had died by that deadly hand—had been found by police with that mocking red seal shaped like a spider on their foreheads. . . . The Fly's right gun came up slowly to sight on the *Spider's* breast. The Fly's mouth twitched. He had to choose between caution and greed and his fear of the *Spider* was conquering. He would kill him now!

The thing happened then for which Wentworth had been playing. He had seen concentrated hostility upon the face of Charles Holland, standing stiff and straight with his rapier in his hand. If only he could pull the Fly's attention wholly away from Holland for a brief moment, even at the cost of risking a shot at himself. . . .

Even as the Fly leveled the revolver, Holland struck with the speed that Wentworth had found so nearly fatal—a long, straight lunge in which sword and body united into a single, striking weapon. The rapier struck, and the gun fell from the Fly's right hand, blasting futilely into the floor.

Furiously, the Fly whipped his second revolver about. But Holland followed his lunge with a leap forward that brought him breast to breast with the man who had called him brother. . . .

Wentworth cursed raggedly. The instant Holland struck, his hands whipped beneath his cloak to the twin automatics that nestled beneath his arms. He crouched now with them ready in his fists—and they availed him nothing! He had seen that Holland, instead of wounding the Fly, had clicked his rapier point against the revolver itself and hurled it from the Fly's hand. That was understandable, since nothing except a blow against the weapon would have saved Wentworth. What had happened afterward was more strange. Holland had made no attempt to injure the Fly with his sword! Surely, he did not believe that claim of brotherhood! Yet, it must be so. For, breast to breast, he wrestled with the Fly and his body was a perfect shield against the *Spider's* lead.

Wentworth sprang across the floor with long, bounding strides, seeking a position from which to strike, and . . . *the room exploded*!

A concussion soundless as a vacuum burst upon the crowd. The ceiling chandeliers swung in crazy circles and crashed; a wall dissolved in a blast of red fire and the floor rose up under Wentworth's feet and struck him on the chest. He scrambled to his feet, peering through the momentary blackness.

The fall had destroyed his sense of direction. He groped for the spot where the Fly and Holland struggled, and, in the thick darkness, a shot crashed out and women screamed on a wild, tearing note.

The darkness vanished in a flickering red dance of flame which pushed up through the floor and in from three walls of the room. Outside in the night, a machine gun cackled into deadly action and, even above the cries of panic-stricken women and the mounting turmoil of the flames, Wentworth could hear the nearby thud of bullets. He could tell, too, when they found flesh from the frenzied cries which were wrung from the stricken.

Wentworth stood stockstill and tried to orient himself. His face was twisted in fierce anger. The Fly was playing his old tricks again, covering his tracks with slaughter—turning loose fire and murder in a holocaust which would blot out all thought of pursuit. The fumes of burning gasoline were stifling. Somewhere, the Fly was racing to safety with his killers, and the *Spider*. . . .

With a groan, Wentworth recognized the keenness of the Fly's strategy. Even the *Spider* could not abandon these poor helpless souls to the death the Fly had planned for them, though it meant that the murderer would escape. The Fly's plan would succeed now, but there would be a reckoning when the Fly paid for each second's misery of this night. *The Spider swore it!*

Throwing a quick glance about him, Wentworth spotted the doors of the conservatory through the thick lurid glare of the flames. "This way!" he shouted, making for the doors. "This way to safety!" He stumbled over a crumpled body, heaved the woman's limp form to his shoulder. *"This way to safety . . . !"*

CHAPTER THREE

The Fly Hunts the *Spider*!

Wentworth began the rescue work in a tearing rage. Everything in him cried out for the necessity of rescuing these people, trapped by walls of fire, but it was damnable to be so close to the Fly and then to fail. . . . Through the conservatory, with the woman's limp body across his shoulder, Wentworth raced. There were windows on the far side and he caught up a light bench and hurled it through the glass. The breakage made a draft, would suck the flames to fury, but there must be an exit and those gasoline-born flames had blocked all others.

Beside the broken window he whirled about, found a man reeling toward him. "Get out through that window," he ordered. "Carry this woman to a safe place and come back. There will be more."

The man looked at him without reason and Wentworth's right palm flicked hard and flat against his cheek. Anger flared briefly in the man's eyes, then came recognition and fear. He shrank back and when Wentworth repeated the order, he obeyed. The *Spider* raced back to the ballroom. . . . There was plenty of light cast by lurid flame. But fumes and black roiling smoke made the scene hazy. Men stumbled blindly about, racked by coughing, blinded by heat and vapor. Some already had collapsed to the floor or else had fallen prey to the hammering of the machine gun which had signaled the explosion.

"This way!" Wentworth made his voice pierce the chaos of fire roar and whimpering terror. "This way!" He attracted attention at last. A few turned toward him. He could make out Charles Holland, sword gone, carrying a woman in his arms. Another man whose face was not clear ran lithely among the trapped people, turning them toward the door where Wentworth shouted the way to safety. They got the ballroom cleared finally, though the last of the victims was snatched smoldering from the very teeth of the flames.

Wentworth stood in the smoke-filled conservatory and looked slowly about to make sure there were no more. He had counted eleven dead. . . . At his side, Holland panted and the other man who had helped stepped close and thrust out his hand.

"Heard a lot about you, *Spider*," he said hoarsely, "but I never expected to meet you. Glad now that I have. Name is Claiborne Lee. If you ever need help for this kind of work. . . ."

Wentworth studied the man's sharply eager eyes and nodded. He motioned the other two out of the window and would not leave until they had reached safety. He was afire with anger. Eleven dead and loot that would run into hundreds of thousands—and the Fly had got clean away. There were fire department men working at last, and the police out there in the street would have thrown a cordon around the block. . . .

Wentworth smiled bitterly as he drew into the shadows with the two men. Now that they could accomplish nothing, the police were here to make it hard for the *Spider*. . . . Holland turned toward him stiffly.

"I . . . I owe you an apology," he said awkwardly. "If it had not been for your help, many more of my friends might have died. And I . . . I tried to kill you. You had me at your mercy and did not run me through. I do not understand, *Spider*."

*   *   *

212

Claiborne Lee broke in eagerly, his voice deep, and vibrant. "You mean, Holland, that the *Spider* bested you at rapiers? Gad, *Spider,* you must be quite a man. Holland is easily the city champion, and in France. . . ."

"Shut up, Lee," Holland said roughly, "*Spider,* I want to apologize. I know that if . . . if you killed my brother, there was . . . just cause."

Wentworth bowed coldly. It was all very well for Holland to make pretty speeches, but he had spared the Fly when he might have driven his sword through the man's heart. That mercy had brought death to six women and five men there in the storm of flame and lead. He could not seriously believe that this Fly was his brother. . . . Wentworth's old suspicions of Holland returned sharply. It would not be the first time that a man had made a grandstand pretense of being himself a victim of the very criminal organization he directed. . . ."

"If you will excuse me," Wentworth bowed. "There is a lady here I'd like to see. . . ."

He stepped backward into the darkness of a clump of high shrubs. Claiborne Lee moved as if to stop him. Holland started a protest, but he was gone. Their eyes were dazzled by the high-licking flames that reached out heat into the chill March night and they did not see that the *Spider* had simply covered hands and face with his black cape and stepped behind a shrub. The two men moved off, hunting for him, and Wentworth left his place of concealment. He had spoken the truth. He wanted desperately to find Lou, the girl in scarlet whom he had allowed to lead him into the trap. He must make her talk. In the first place, she probably knew what part Holland played in the affairs of the Fly, and in the second, she had recognized the bandit who collected the stolen jewelry. . . .

He spotted her presently, standing weakly beside an emergency station which an ambulance interne had hurriedly established. There was a listlessness about her entire body. The slope of her young shoulders was weary. . . . Wentworth circled through the shadows, for he dared not approach openly. Several times while he advanced he was forced to halt while men in uniform raced past, but finally he achieved a place in the darkness by a high hedge.

"Lou!" he called softly. He stepped into the edge of the light. "Lou, I want to talk with you!"

Lou stiffened, then whirled, her face eager. That faded as she glimpsed the caped figure in the half-light. She clung to the side of the ambulance, her face terrified. She glanced behind her as if seeking help. . . . Wentworth stepped forward and smiled into her eyes.

"I intend you no harm, Lou," he said softly. "Won't you come and talk with me a little while?"

The girl's panic did not lessen. Her blue eyes stared oddly at Wentworth, her lips parted. She was very lovely, with the red light of the fire playing upon the soft line of her warm, young shoulders. . . .

"You didn't lead me into the trap," Wentworth told her. "I knew what was behind it and went willingly. I just wanted to ask you a few questions. Who are you? Who was the boy in red with the Fly? I'd like to help him. He can't be all bad."

Slowly, the girl's fear faded. Men and women had always trusted Wentworth instinctively. It was as if the fine, generous character of the man pierced even through his disguise to touch her. "Oh, he *isn't* bad, *Spider*," she cried softly. "His companions are bad. He's my little brother, *Spider*. God help him, now he has. . . ."

It was at that moment an automatic spoke from nearby. The girl screamed, driven forward to her knees by the impact of a bullet which Wentworth heard pluck into her soft flesh. Her hands clawed at Wentworth's arms as she pitched forward. He threw his arms about her, dragged her flat to the ground as a second shot crashed out. His lips were writhing in sudden rage. This poor child. . . . His automatic leaped to his hand. He rolled free of where Lou lay, without sound or motion, sought out the shrub from which those cowardly shots had sped. It was impossible to fire. Those shots had thrown the already terrified men and women into panic and their black silhouettes darted back and forth in front of and behind the shrub where the assassin had hidden. . . .

Wentworth delayed only a moment to lay a gentle hand on the unconscious girl. She had been so fresh and eager. . . .

His lips twisted into a harsh smile, Wentworth hurled himself back into the shadows, raced forward. So the Fly, too, had seen the danger of the girl! Woman killer! Wentworth cursed raggedly as he darted toward the assassin. It came to him with overwhelming suddenness that this shooting was a further count against Charles Holland. Holland had known that Wentworth was hunting the girl and could easily guess the reason. . . . It was possible, of course, that the Fly had left a gunman behind to account for the girl, since she had identified one of his men. . . .

The *Spider's* charge had not been a direct rush into the muzzle of the hidden gunman's weapon, but a circling movement which would bring him to the flank. It took time, but his eyes were acutely watchful. He had detected no signs of a fugitive. . . . The spot was only a score of feet away now, on his right. Wentworth crept forward, then rose slowly to his feet. It was quite apparent that no one was any longer behind the shrub. He saw that it would have been quite possible for the assassin to crawl away on hands and knees, keeping the shrub between the ambulance and himself.

Wentworth strode angrily to the spot, bent over to study the earth. There were knee-prints there, but the exploded shells were gone, giving sufficient proof of the man's coolness. Wentworth bent closer. The knee-prints retreated across the damp earth, reached the border of a patch of shrubbery and . . . Wentworth barely choked back a cry of triumph! There in the mud was the print of a man's palm! Deftly, Wentworth scooped out the cake of earth and nested it in his hat.

So intent had been Wentworth's pursuit that until now he had not noticed three policemen charging on the bush behind which the gunman had crouched, closing in on where the *Spider* now was hidden! The police would have no means of knowing that it had not been the *Spider* who had done the shooting. They would open fire on sight, and Wentworth would be helpless! For the *Spider* did not fight the police. He might violate laws, but though the police considered him a criminal, he was actually their staunchest ally. Against the men in blue, his deadly guns were quite useless. . . .

Frowning, Wentworth faded back into the dense heart of the thicket. This would offer only brief sanctuary for the policemen would certainly beat through every inch of cover in their search for the assassin. Wentworth was further handicapped by the necessity of keeping that palm print of soft earth in its original condition. This palm-print would identify the killer as readily as his fingerprints, though police experts had not yet been able to devise a method of classification which would make palm-prints useful in criminal identification systems.

Wentworth threw a searching look through the night. His hiding place was on the skirts of the lurid firelight. Smoke and fumes whipped acridly downwind. The police were drawing dangerously close! Wentworth's thinned lips tightened. He had only the slimmest chance to escape, but he must avail himself of it, or be slain! With deft movements, he stripped off cape and draped it over a shrub, placed his hat atop it as if the *Spider* knelt in the darkness to give battle. The dirt with its precious print he folded carefully into a handkerchief and placed it in the heart of a shrub, among thick stems where no one could step. . . . The police were no more than fifty feet away, approaching cautiously behind ready guns. Wentworth crept toward them, deftly unloading an automatic as he went. From a pocket he drew a half dozen fresh cartridges whose noses were colored a bright red. He put one in the chamber of the automatic, held the others in his palm. The *Spider* was ready. . . .

One of the policemen abruptly threw himself prone on the earth. "There he is!" he shouted. "There he is! *Surrender or we'll blast you to hell!*"

Wentworth muffled his mouth with his hands and laughed softly, the challenging mockery of the *Spider*. He wanted them to open fire, so that his own shots would not be conspicuous. The other two policemen went prone, inching forward on elbows and toes, guns ready. The one who had first challenged pointed his revolver high and fired a shot. . . .

"*Surrender!*" he cried again.

"Come and get me!" Wentworth challenged, still muffling his mouth. He held the muzzle of his automatic against his coat to conceal the powder flame and fired through it at the ground just ahead of the nearest policeman. The echo of his shot was drowned in a crashing fusillade that sent lead ripping through the shrubbery! The black cape of the *Spider* twitched to the pound of lead. Coolly, Wentworth worked the bolt of the automatic, ejecting the empty shell whose recoil had been too weak to throw it clear. He shoved another of the red-nosed cartridges into the gun, leveled it again. . . . Abruptly the policeman at whom he had first shot reeled to his feet with piercing cries, his hands clapped to his eyes. He danced in sharp agony. . . .

"Tear gas!" he howled. "*Tear gas!*"

Wentworth smiled in the darkness where he crouched and once more fired through the edge of his coat, thus hiding the flash. The cloth smouldered and he crushed it out between his palms, went about loading a third tear gas cartridge into the automatic. Before he was ready to fire again, the second policeman was rolling on the ground, coughing and groaning with the pain of the gas. In an hour or two, the men would be fully recovered, but for the moment the agony was intense. They could no more manipulate their guns than they could see. Wentworth fired his third shot, crept back to his cloak and hat. They must not be left behind to brand the *Spider* with the stigma of shooting that girl. . . . He drew his second automatic and sprayed singing lead high through the night, sending the men and women who had been the restless spectators of the attack fleeing into the night.

Wentworth smiled pleasantly as he regained the dirt containing the palm print and, carrying cape and hat, stole away into the night. Matters had worked out much better than he had dared to hope. He still had to pass the police cordon, a line that would be drawn even tighter when word reached the line that a criminal was within. But for a man who could move with the silent ease of a shadow—to whose skilled touch any lock would yield—the task was not too difficult. . . . Wentworth scaled a fence, entered a house whose door lock he picked, climbed upward on ghostly feet to the roof, and traveled rapidly westward.

When he descended, outside the lines, the facial disguise of the *Spider* had vanished, and a taxicab sped him homeward. He would make a *moulage* cast of that palm print in the dirt and when he tracked down a suspect, he would carry in his pocket the proof of the man's guilt. There would be a special punishment for the man who had shot that gay young girl! By the Gods, the Fly should not again acquire a foothold in the Underworld, nor trod with muderous feet upon the necks of the people! The *Spider* would find and kill him. Wentworth's modeled lips drew out thinly. His hand strayed to a gun. . . .

A truck trundled out from a side street and dragged its length across the path of Wentworth's taxi. When the van filled the roadway from curb to curb, it stopped. Wentworth jerked erect in his seat. He whirled about and saw two autos spin around the corner and come racing toward him, saw that in each car men held weapons in their hands, sawed-off automatic shotguns and sub-machine guns. Even as he looked, they opened fire on him! Wentworth laughed sharply as he flung to his knees on the floor, guns leaping to his hands. The *Spider* might evade the police, but the Fly kept to his trail. If only the Fly had come to do his murder work in person. . . .

CHAPTER FOUR

The *Spider* in a Trap!

As always in emergency, Wentworth's mind leaped swiftly to the only possible defense—though even that would afford slim chance of escape. He ripped aside the glass panel that separated him from the driver of his taxi.

"Back up!" he shouted. "Back up full speed. *For your life!*"

As deftly as an old soldier finds cover, Wentworth had snatched at the narrow opening the attackers gave. Slamming in, with guns blasting death, they had made the mistake of separating to take the *Spider* from two sides at once. He was sure, abruptly, that the Fly was not present. He would not have left the way clear for the taxi to escape by a dash in reverse. . . .

Now that Wentworth had pointed the way, the taxi driver saw what was needed and the gears snarled as he rasped into reverse and slapped his foot on the gas pedal. In the moment the cab started backward, a shot gun blasted twice from the car on the left and the driver slammed against his wheel, his hands beating against the air in a spasm of death. The back of his head . . .

Wentworth grated out a curse. The mockery that had lingered about his lips was wiped out and the glacial bleakness of his eyes, the thin harshness of his mouth were fearful things to see.

The cab continued backward, swerved slightly to the left, and the sway of the driver's limp body whipped the wheel in the opposite direction. The swerve was violent this time, and the cab slammed, back-first, into the attacking car on the right. Swaying, the killers' sedan skittered toward the curb, and Wentworth's taxi went into a slow, end-for-end spin.

The *Spider* was smiling again as he braced shoulders and knees against the seats. Brakes were shrieking as the killers tried to stop. A single sub-machine gun hammered at the spinning taxi, but all other weapons were silent. The *Spider,* an automatic pistol in either hand, took what shots the twisting cab allowed, and the unerring accuracy of years of practice sped his bullets true. He shot a back tire off the sedan the cab had rammed. He smashed a forty-five caliber slug through the brain of the machine gunner who had poked out the rear window of the other car. It took five shots to do these things, then the taxi hit the curbing broadside, teetered on two wheels and slapped over on its side on the walkway.

It was a new cab, its windows safety glass, and though they shattered into myriad fragments, they did not rain Wentworth with dagger-like shards. He was wrenched from his braced position, thrown heavily on his shoulder against the roof of the cab. His hat fell from his head. The crisp, black locks of his hair straggled across his forehead and blood welled from a cut on his eyebrow. For one instant, flashing white lights danced before his eyes. He shook his head violently, got to his feet. He was standing on one door of the cab and its bottom with its steel frame and transmission formed a bulwark before him. It was not completely bullet-proof, but for the *Spider* it was enough. . . . He peered cautiously through a smashed window, guns ready.

The sedan from which he had shot a tire was canted against the curb and three men were pouring from it. The second machine had stopped and one man, machine gun cradled against his hip, was crouched against its side. They were twenty yards away, Wentworth figured—just target range distance. His smile became an ugly twisted thing. His guns lifted calmly and fell on his targets. . . .

History tells of famous marksmen who could make their sidearms do everything but speak Spanish, and modern tests have duplicated every feat that the records have revealed. There are at least three men in the United States who can duplicate the famous performance of Billy the Kid in which he shot two guns at once from the hip at dime-size targets thirty feet away and thirty feet from each other—and hit both! A matter of practice, of experience.

Richard Wentworth's life had depended on his automatics more times than he could remember. He had drilled with them until they were like nerve ends of his own brain. He fired four times and there were four dead men in the street. To be sure, their guns blasted at him, but their targets were only two moving guns and the upper half of a man's head. Their practice consisted of machine-gun work at ranges up to fifteen feet. . . .

When he had fired the fourth shot, Wentworth stood motionless for a moment, seeing the last of his enemies squirm out his life in the street. His guns swung heavily to his sides, and he turned to the lifeless body of the taxi driver. Wentworth's keenly intelligent face was distraught. This man was innocent. He had died merely because it had been his misfortune to carry the *Spider* as a fare. His photograph grinned at Wentworth from his license card posted in the rear of the cab. Wentworth clamped his jaw shut hard. He drew out a notebook and scribbled down the man's name and address. At least, his people would not suffer want. That much the *Spider* could do. . . .

Wentworth climbed out of the upmost door of the cab, tugged jerkily at the brim of his felt, shrugged his shoulders to settle the cape smoothly. He strode with hard, slapping heels toward the dead man. . . . It would have been impossible to tell which came first, the shot from the parked car, or Wentworth's flinching dodge which threw him three feet to the side and prone in the street; impossible except for one thing. Wentworth's right hand whipped a gun into view even before his body hit, and his weapon blasted in concert with the second shot from the cab. Then he climbed stiffly to his feet, brushed off his clothing. His lips moved in soundless curses. Childish of him to let that cab driver's death upset him so that he failed to realize that there must be at least one more man in that sedan. He had slain only two in that machine and gangster cars did not go forth to do murder with only two gunmen.

There was a set frown on his face as he slipped a platinum cigarette lighter from his vest pocket and stooped over each of the men he had slain. He pressed the base of the ligher to the foreheads of the dead, then he walked swiftly away. . . . The truck that blocked the street had long since gone, heads had popped out of a hundred windows and a police siren whimpered in the near distance. Two boys ran at Wentworth's heels, pointing fingers, shouting and capering. He disguised his manner of walking, kept his head tilted forward so that the broad brim of his black hat shaded his eyes. He had violated one of the few rules he had ever set for himself; he had used the seal of the *Spider* while in his own identity of Richard Wentworth! It meant his death on any one of a score of murder charges if police should be able to prove that the *Spider* and Wentworth were the same man. These boys and many of the people peering from their windows had seen him press his lighter to the foreheads of the dead, and when police arrived they would find gleaming there the blood-red seal of the *Spider*!

It had been necessary, Wentworth assured himself, even while he quickened his pace with the nearer approach of police sirens. The Fly had struck at him. It could not be allowed to pass without sending back the challenge, a dead man with the seal on his forehead. . . .

Wentworth turned the corner not five seconds ahead of the first police car. He jumped into a taxi and the

223

driver, who had been watching his approach, turned and ran. With an oath, Wentworth got behind the wheel and sent the cab racing up the street. He saw a man race to another taxi, saw it get under way . . . The *Spider* had a lead of three blocks, and within minutes the entire radio patrol of the city would be on his trail, looking for him in the stolen taxi. . . . It took five minutes of swift maneuvering to make two turns out of sight of pursuit, then Wentworth abandoned the cab in the middle of the street at a red traffic light. Seconds later, he was lost in the early morning crowd that thronged the walks on the way to their various offices. . . .

A half hour afterward, Richard Wentworth strolled into the foyer of the fifteen-story building that was his fortress against crime. He owned the entire structure, had bought it so that he could control the personnel and the tenancy. Here, if anywhere, the *Spider* could feel safe, but today he knew no sense of sanctuary. He was restless, harassed by thoughts of peril. The doorman bowed deferentially. A private elevator whisked him to his fifteen-room duplex penthouse and, within seconds of his entry, his white-haired old butler was relieving him of cape and hat. He looked down at them with a woodenness of expression on his ruddy face that Wentworth knew betokened his distaste. Not at the cut of the garments, for that was impeccable, but for the thing they represented, his master's constant duel with death. . . .

Wentworth carefully handed Jenkyns the cake of hardening mud which contained a palm print. "Make a moulage cast," he told him, "and prepare me some prints from it. Be very careful. That print may hang a man. . . ."

Jenkyns' old eyes followed his Master Dick lovingly as Wentworth strode briskly into his drawing room and threw wide to the morning air the French doors that opened on the terrace. "Send Jackson to me," he called back.

Jenkyns' hand brushed the cape he carried with a

slow, tender movement. He shook his head, started to turn away, then remembered. . . .

"Miss Nita called, Master Dick," he said. A smile deepened the wrinkles of his mouth corners. That way lay Jenkyns' hopes. If only, now, Master Dick would marry. . . .

Wentworth sucked in a deep breath of the brash spring air, closed the doors again and spun, clasping his lean, powerful hands together. He was a proud, arrogant man, built with a compact strength that was lithe and inconspicuous, but which gave him an appearance of solidity. The carriage of his shoulders and head was a banner of self-confidence, of quiet self-assurance too dignified for jauntiness. He smiled and nodded in answer to Jenkyn's message. "It's too early to disturb her just yet. . . ."

"Oh, Master Dick," Jenkyns protested, "you know . . ." Then he realized that Wentworth was making a joke. Of course Miss Nita wasn't asleep, not while the master wore the garb of the *Spider,* not while he fought the Underworld. Jenkyns had shared some of those restless vigils which grew harder, rather than easier, as the months slid by. . . . He turned away to the telephone, his old head shaking gently. It was madness, but it was the sort of thing Master Dick would do. Afraid that, if he and the woman he loved, fulfilled their love in marriage and children, the grim hand of disgrace might touch them all. . . .

He remembered then to send Jackson to Wentworth and when he returned to the drawing room with the portable telephone, Jackson had left the building and Master Dick was in the music room, brushing the strings of his beloved Stradivarius to harmony. Wentworth was frowning, which was not his usual manner when he held his violin. The truth was that an increasing dread gripped him which even his music could not dispel. . . . He nodded to Jenkyns and the butler set the phone upon the concert grand beside which Wentworth stood, turned the transmitter toward him and went slowly from the room. Wentworth's lips curved tenderly. He nestled the violin under his chin, began to play. . . .

It was one of his greatest delights, his violin. It gave him relief and rest when his soul and heart were torn as they had been this morning. Death and pillage lay ahead and the hand of the *Spider* would be mighty in vengeance—if he lived. But now let there be a little moment of peace while his heart sang to the woman he loved. Let the fingers which tomorrow, perhaps in an hour, might squeeze the triggers of his deadly guns, draw forth sweet music. . . .

Afterward, Wentworth breakfasted, pheasant eggs whipped to a delicate froth in sherry that would have graced the table of a king, breasts of pigeons. Jenkyns had prepared them with his own hands. He had never been able to find a cook he thought worthy of his master. Then a shower, an alcohol rub and Wentworth forced his restless mind to sleep.

In a few hours he was up again. A second rub-down, fresh clothing when he arose for his luncheon with Nita, which she would share in his apartment, and he was as rested as if from hours on hours of sleep. Yet the feeling of relaxation and ease which usually attended this swift recuperative process failed to come to him. Even his Stradivarius could not beguile him and he strode restlessly from room to room while he waited for his Hindu body servant, Ram Singh, to bring Nita. He stalked back and forth upon his terrace. If he had not sent Jackson out on the *Spider's* business he could have a bout with the sabers. If it were true this Fly and that other were one, he would have need of all his skill. . . .

Wentworth slammed the French doors behind him as he went indoors again, threw coat and cap carelessly to a chair. Impatiently, he jabbed a bell button and Jenkyns came on swift, silent feet.

"How long ago did Ram Singh leave to get Miss Nita?" he asked sharply.

Jenkyns took a heavy silver watch from his pocket and studied its face. "Just twenty minutes, Master

Dick," he said gently. "In perhaps ten minutes, sir. . . ."

Wentworth had already stalked from the room. He knew what these moods of his portended. His nerves were crying aloud of danger. Not the peril that was a constant companion of his days and nights, but something imminent and heavy about him. Danger that would strike like a knife in the back. . . . He spun about, hand going to his lapel, to the guns that never left him, waking or asleep. Nothing, absolutely nothing here. He fled from the gymnasium to which he had wandered, loped again into the drawing room. There he halted himself, required of his muscles that they relax, that they keep him quiet for a full five minutes. Deliberately, he took out a cigarette and snapped flame to it from the same lighter that had a few hours before printed his signature of death upon the foreheads of six men. . . . He turned the lighter over curiously in his hand, looking at it with eyes that saw through and beyond it. How many times had that bit of gleaming metal touched the dead foreheads of his victims? A strong shudder shook him.

Wentworth was a gentle man by instinct. The arts held more appeal for him than for most other men. If he had not chosen the hard path of the *Spider,* he might have become the world's greatest virtuoso of the violin, a composer of note. Now and again, nature took this tool of the body and soul that he drove to such labors to exact the *Spider's* justice. Black despair. . . .

Damn it, nothing could happen to Nita, not in the crowded streets of noon, not in his bullet-proof Daimler with that fierce Sikh, Ram Singh, at the wheel. He was a fool to worry, but his enemies had struck so many times at him through the woman he loved. . . . Abruptly, Wentworth snatched up his topcoat, belted it tightly about his waist, but left the lapels gaping wide. He stood for another minute staring before him toward the door that opened on the hall. He snatched a cap and strode out, walked restlessly about while he waited for the elevator, continued his pacing in the foyer on the first floor, his eyes straying ever and again to the curb before the marquis where presently Nita would alight. . . . Of course she would. He was mad to think. . . . Ah, *there*!

The slim, chromium-slashed nose of the Daimler slid into sight. The chauffeur stepped to the door to open it for Nita . . . and Wentworth hurled himself toward the street in a pounding sprint. Before he had slammed through the first set of doors, he had whipped out an automatic. He fired through the glass of the outer doors. The car that had pulled up just beside his own had poured out a flood of men, five of them with guns in their hands. They swept about the Daimler. The doorman went down beneath a hard-swung blackjack. Ram Singh attempted to slam shut the bullet-proof, self-locking doors and save Nita, but he was already too late. The Fly had prepared his men for that. One of them wedged his shoulder into the crack, leveled his gun at Nita. A second fired point-blank at Ram Singh. . . .

CHAPTER FIVE

Hostage to Doom

Wentworth's first shot, flung through the outer doors, caught the last man to leave the gang car and hurled him back against the driver. The *Spider* was aware of muffled reports within the Daimler and knew that Nita's lighter automatic had gone into action, but there was no time even to look there. As he slammed out onto the pavement, he threw a second bullet at a gunman just rounding the nose of the limousine to the attack. The lead spun him about and his hands clawed at the shining chromium as he went down. Wentworth swung toward the Daimler. Only one man was left on his feet and he was fleeing frantically toward the gang car. Even as Wentworth spotted him, he had put the bullet-proof bulk of the limousine before him as a shield. . . .

Wentworth sprang to his car. With swift hands, he tugged aside the bodies of the two men who had fallen there before Nita's swift gun and the keen knife of Ram Singh. As he leaped into the tonneau, Ram Singh whipped the Daimler out into the traffic. Wentworth dropped back against the cushions and laughed sharply. He turned to Nita van Sloan. Her violet eyes were wide, her red lips pursed in anger. She still held the automatic with which she had shot her assailant and she let it sag to her knee with a slight shudder, smiled wanly into

Wentworth's eyes. It was not the first time she had killed, but it always shook her. . . . She threw it off bravely.

"It looks as if our luncheon is being postponed," she said, smiling.

Wentworth's lips curved in answer. It was like strong drink to have this gallant woman beside him. "Jenkyns will be disappointed," he agreed. "He's been busy in the kitchen for hours."

Nita's hand went to Wentworth's arm and he closed his own over it, his eyes peering ahead once more. Ram Singh was wriggling the powerful Daimler through traffic at incredible speed, but the fugitive sedan managed to keep its lead. Wentworth caught up the speaking tube.

"Let them think they've lost us," he ordered, "but keep the trail. I saw, O Ram Singh, that thy knife gained honor again!" He had lapsed into Ram Singh's native Punjabi for the last phrase and he saw the Sikh's shoulders straighten with pride. The Hindu was a tower of strength in Wentworth's many battles.

Wentworth relaxed again, confident that Ram Singh would perform the task assigned to him. He gazed into the warm depths of Nita's eyes. The smile on her full lips was wonderfully sweet.

"I shall have to feed you very soon," Nita said gravely. "You're trying to devour me with your eyes." She laughed, but with a touch of sadness, as there always must be in all their happiness. She knew why his eyes were hungry, why bitterness must always touch them. Death had been very close a few moments ago for all that they had made light of it, and death might lie in their path no further away than the next corner. She tried not to think of that, tried, too, to forget that probably she and Dick would never marry. No longer than a fortnight ago, she and Dick had stood together at the altar. Wentworth had foresworn his work—and word had came that the Fly had struck. Wentworth's mouth had gone grim as he stood there beside his brideto-be. He had forced his lips to smile, had lifted a shoulder in a shrug.

"The Fly?" he said casually. "He means nothing to me."

He had pledged Nita that never again would the *Spider* seek his prey—and he intended to keep that promise. The moment had been incomparably sweet to Nita. She had savored it to the full—and had put it from her. With a smile, she had sent the lover who might never be more than that back into the battle. Never again would she flinch from the task he had set. If the end must come at the hands of his enemies, it would find them side by side. . . . Nita drew a little closer to Wentworth. *Side by side. . . .*

Wentworth threw her a quick smile, then his eyes went back to the sedan they trailed. He drew his automatics and filled the partly emptied clips, saw that they were ready. He had hopes that this pursuit would lead him to some hideout of the Fly. What he would do then he did not know, but one thing was sure: The Fly must die before he gained still greater ascendency over the Underworld. Already, his power must be enormous. . . .

The speed of the pursuit had slackened and it seemed clear that the men ahead did not know they still were followed. What brought Wentworth rigidly erect in his seat was the abrupt realization that the direction of the chase had changed and that the killers were bound downtown—toward New York's famous financial district, where the richest banks of the world were situated! There could be no mistake. Already, they were too far southward in Manhattan to make any other destination possible. There was nothing save docks and office buildings, a few Syrian tenements. Wentworth whipped about.

"Nita, you must drop out. Phone the police that I think the Fly is about to raid a downtown bank." He rapped on the glass.

Ram Singh swerved the Daimler to the curb and

Wentworth jerked open the door. Nita did not hesitate, though her lips were pressed together tightly. She gave Dick a twisted smile as he sprang past her with no more than a hand upon her arm for farewell. The Daimler leaped forward. For a moment, Nita watched. Her vision blurred. She pulled her head down and went blindly toward a tobacco shop to find a phone. She collided with some one, muttered an apology, but when she tried to go on, a hand gripped her arm painfully. . . .

"Why, Nita," said a man's jeering voice. "This is indeed a surprise!"

Her head pulled up sharply. The man was a complete stranger to her, but his hard, leering eyes told her clearly that these were the men of the Fly! Nita's lips flew open. The man's eyes tightened. "Let me present my friend, Bull," he said. "That's short for Bullseye, because that's what he always hits."

Nita's head whipped about and she saw a dapper, small man bow jerkily. His eyes were black and mildly amused. His hands were in his coat pockets and those pockets bulged much too large for mere fists. He stepped to her side. "Let's take a walk," he said, and in his voice, too, was quiet amusement.

Nita's eyes flew about her wildly, but no one noticed this apparently friendly meeting. If she cried out, men might stare curiously, but no more. There were no police nearby. No help for it, but to submit to capture and hope that her chance would come later. . . . She was ushered smoothly to a waiting automobile which leaped instantly forward and Nita saw then how this had happened. There had been more than one of the Fly's cars on Fifth Avenue when she and Dick had been attacked. This second car had followed Wentworth while he trailed the killers. She was close to tears of vexation and despair, but she held her head high and there was even a faint smile on her lips. She could not permit these hirelings of a butcher to see that the *Spider's* mate was worried. . . .

While the gangster car, with Nita a prisoner, sped

after him, Wentworth's attention was wholly centered on the men that he followed. He counted on Nita to phone his friend, Commissioner Kirkpatrick, of the police, the warning of what impended. He leaned tensely forward, trying to discover in advance just which bank was the target of the Fly's men. If he could do that and get fresh word to Kirkpatrick. . . .

Abruptly, the car ahead whirled from broad West Street and shot up a side lane toward Broadway. Without an order, Ram Singh sent the Daimler racing forward at mounting speed. Wentworth uttered a low cry. The Bank of New York! Of all the financial institutions in the city, the Bank of New York carried the largest cash reserve and it was two blocks farther east along the street these men traveled. The Fly picked well!

Wentworth shot open the glass panel behind Ram Singh. "Wreck them!" he ordered sharply.

The Daimler was off like a thoroughbred from the barrier. In half a block, it was crowding the tail of the gangster car. Ram Singh slammed into second gear, trod the gas pedal and rammed the sedan with a concussion like dynamite.

The gang car swerved, ploughed into a parked machine. The Fly's men did not wait to investigate. They flung to the pavement, plunged into the crowds upon the sidewalks. Wentworth let them go. He did not know what part they played in the Fly's plans, but at least this cog was stripped bare of its teeth. . . .

The powerful engine of the Daimler was driving it steadily forward. The sedan was wedged out of the way. A quick spurt backward, a wrench at the wheel and Ram Singh was racing on upgrade toward Broadway, toward the corner where the Bank of New York reared its solid mass.

Wentworth was still a half block away when the brazen alarm gong outside the bank burst into a frantic clanger. Before it had fairly started, a sedan spurted across the mouth of the street, heading up Broadway. A sub-machine gun cackled from its window. A woman who stood talking to a man on the corner had frozen at the sound of the gong. As the gun blasted she leaped up on tiptoes, grasping the man's arms, then both of them crumpled to the pavement. The woman's back was embroidered with red-rimmed holes. The man's face had been blown away. Five other persons fell before Wentworth's Daimler roared around the corner.

He was just in time to see the fleeing auto whirl a corner. Half way to that corner, the Daimler yawed wildly as a small coupé started sharply out from the curb. There was a ripping crash. The coupé was hurled back into its slot in the parking line, but Ram Singh could not recover control quickly enough to follow behind the fugitives. Wentworth, peering back, saw the driver of the coupé leap from his seat and sprint away down Broadway. He lifted his gun, squeezed. The man fell. One trick of the Fly had failed!

His elation was short-lived. As the Daimler took the next corner eastward, he saw a second sedan with bellowing guns come racing up Broadway. From a side street, another lunged; off to westward, Wentworth could make out the chatter of still more guns. Damnation! The district was full of the men of the Fly! And where were the police? Surely, there had been time since Nita's warning. Police plans were laid so that within three minutes of an alarm, the financial section could be flooded with men, with armored motorcycles mounting machine guns, with squad cars loaded with men bearing riot guns and rifles. A small worry began to gnaw at the back of his brain. Why hadn't that alarm been given?

Broadway was left behind and the Daimler was sprinting eastward, crashing through stalled lanes of traffic. Ram Singh swung once to the sidewalk where machine gun bullets had spilled dead men, rounded a block in the street, and raced on. They had almost reached South Street before Wentworth heard the first police siren. He saw a car with spitting guns flash past the cross-street's end, and a moment later a police coupé shot into sight in its wake. One officer's revolver was speaking in slow, spaced rhythm. Wentworth had a glimpse of the bold lettering on the coupé's side, then the whole moving picture vanished northward. . . .

"Cut back to Broadway!" Wentworth snapped. That car was trailed. There was no use in his joining the chase when there were so many other loads of killers racing amok through the district. As always, the Fly had been devastatingly clever in his conspiracy. In this multiplicity of scattered attacks, a half-dozen murder cars racing with blazing guns through the streets, police could not concentrate their efforts, and the chances that they would close with the car which carried the loot were remote. Probably, that car would not even carry gunmen, but would cruise quietly away from the district, or else park in a side street nearby until the excitement had ended. The Fly might easily escape by subway with a grip full of loot. . . .

"Faster!" Wentworth snapped. "Back to the bank!" Kirkpatrick would be there and from him must come the orders which would close the gaps that Wentworth's keen brain found. The Daimler flashed across William Street and a leaden hail hammered on the windows of the left side. They frosted over, but stopped the bullets. Ram Singh spun the steering wheel and the tires howled as they gripped the pavement in a sharp turn to the right. Wentworth had had no chance to speak, but he had reached forward to tap Ram Singh's right shoulder. No words had been necessary. While the car still rocked as it straightened out, the drum-roll of fire switched to the Daimler's right hand side. Wentworth cranked open a small gun port. He was deadly calm, but it was the quietness of rage. At last he was to have a chance to strike at the men who slew so wantonly. . . .

Only one gun from the Fly's murder car was directed on Wentworth. Others swept the sidewalks to right and left. A newsboy cowered behind a lifted armful of papers and lead chewed through the pulp, hurled him kicking to the pavement. The litter of papers covered him, but from beneath their edges there crept thickening threads of red. A man dressing a store window stood staring, his mouth agape, a woman's brilliant frock in his hand. The window dissolved into silver powder. The dress whipped in the air like a flag. It was the man's death convulsion. These things Wentworth saw kaleidescopically as the two cars raced side by side up narrow William Street.

Wentworth's first shot smashed the machine gun against the chest of the man who fired it, drove him backward to the floor. His second tore through the eyes of the driver, slashing in from the side, obliterating the bridge of his nose. He screamed horribly, jerking his hands to his face, and the gang car swung in a wide circle to the left. The Daimler's brakes took hold barely in time. Another killer tried to snatch at the wheel of his car, but he was too late. The sedan hit a fireplug, twisted sideways and snapped off a light post, jounced there with the three hundred pound pressure of the bursted water main hammering upward through its bottom.

"To the bank," Wentworth told Ram Singh. His voice rasped harshly in his throat. The car rolled forward.

The *Spider's* face was drained of all blood. Coolly, he reloaded his automatics, and his hands did not tremble, but there was a surging turmoil within him. That poor newsboy with his pitiful shroud of papers, that gay young couple whose nuptial bed was the cold, blood-washed pavement of Broadway. . . . The air was shivering with a furious crescendo of sirens and through a thickening stream of police cars, Wentworth made his way toward the Bank of New York. Everywhere the streets told a tale of wanton murder. Once more, a tragic massacre had covered the steps of the Fly.

Somberly, Wentworth counted more than twenty dead in the few short blocks he traversed. When he sprang from the Daimler a quarter block from the bank, age seemed suddenly to sit upon his face. Harsh lines bit into his cheeks beside his mouth and there were smudges of shadow beneath his eyes. Within these few moments, he seemed to have taken on years. . . . A policeman on guard at the bank door saluted him by name.

"Commissioner's inside, sir," he said respectfully.

They knew Richard Wentworth in the police force, knew him for a trusted friend of the Commissioner. If they had suspected that he was the *Spider*, there might have been a different sort of salute, thundering guns whose bullets would pierce his flesh! He passed two more guards before he strode into the presence of Commissioner Kirkpatrick.

Kirkpatrick stood in the middle of the lobby of the rifled bank and on the floor about him were five still figures covered in the merciful white shroud that the emergency wagons always carried. At Wentworth's crisp step, the Commissioner's head came up sharply, frosty blue eyes alert. A stiff smile stirred his lips. These two had met on the scenes of a hundred tragedies, but rarely had death conjured up such pictures as this.

"The Fly has surpassed himself," Kirkpatrick's voice came forth clipped and strained. "Already there have been reported forty-seven dead in the streets. That fiend out of hell! I'll . . ." His hoarse anger choked him. He trembled with it, then fought himself to calmness. "Know anything that will help, Dick?"

Wentworth's lips twisted as he told swiftly what he had seen and done. In times like these, he and Kirkpatrick could work side by side. In peaceful days, they were warmest friends, but Kirkpatrick was very sure that Wentworth was the *Spider*. There had been days when the entire police force of the city hounded him with orders to bring him in, dead or alive—and always Wentworth had proved that he could not possibly be the *Spider* . . . But now they must work together.

". . . And block the subways," he finished his suggestions, which were transmuted into orders even as he talked. "Have you had a report from a twenty-fourth

237

precinct police coupé which trailed a gangster car up South Street?''

Kirkpatrick's long-fingered hand rose to his pointed black moustache, brushed first one side, then the other. He was frowning. He snapped a query at an officer nearby and received a negative answer. No car had been reported trailing a gangster sedan. . . .

Wentworth stared at Kirkpatrick with his blue-gray eyes sharply excited. ''Where is the twenty-fourth precinct?'' he demanded. ''In the west Nineties, isn't it?''

Kirkpatrick nodded slowly. ''That's exactly it,'' he said. ''Why should a car from that far uptown be down here on the trail of that gangster car before any of the other police had time. . . .?'' He broke off, slapped a fist into his palm. ''By God, that was . . .''

Wentworth nodded grimly. ''That was the Fly, beyond a doubt, in a stolen or faked police coupé. And, also beyond a doubt, one of those two cars carried the loot of this bank!''

Kirkpatrick whirled from him. His orders crackled with the speed of high frequency electric sparks, but Wentworth was silent. All this was useless now. It had been fully fifteen, probably twenty, minutes since he had seen that police car. The Fly had made good his escape, abandoned the coupé. . . . It was damnably clever. He had had the benefits of a police siren in clearing the way for his flight, and the blazing guns of the car which he apparently pursued, actually his convoy, would protect him in case of discovery. . . .

Kirkpatrick was back again. ''A pity we didn't have more warning,'' he said, ''but I doubt that even then we would have penetrated that trick in time to stop the Fly.''

Wentworth's head had jerked up at the words. The small worry that had popped into his brain at the slowness of police response came back to him again and gripped his heart with icy fingers. He stepped close and seized Kirkpatrick's arm. He had to squeeze out words and they had a strained, harsh sound.

"Kirk, how . . . did you get the alarm?" He thought: Nita! Good God, *Nita!*

Kirkpatrick stared at him curiously. "The alarm system," he said. "When the gong went off outside. . . ."

Wentworth's fingers bit deeply into the arm. He strained forward, eyes questioning Kirkpatrick's, then his hand dropped. He straightened and drew in a slow, hissing breath.

"The Fly has Nita," he whispered.

Kirkpatrick cried. "What, Dick? What about Nita?"

Wentworth explained heavily how Nita had left the car to phone a warning. "There can't be any other explanation," he said slowly. "If Nita did not telephone you, it was because she was prevented. Only the Fly could have . . . stopped her."

Kirkpatrick did not attempt to deny it. He whipped about to shout an order, stopped as a man in the uniform of a Western Union messenger came limping across the lobby. Wentworth watched him come and a pain throbbed in his heart. Somehow he knew, even before Kirkpatrick ripped open the envelope, what it would contain.

"For you!" Kirkpatrick said, his voice shaky.

Wentworth read the yellow slip that quivered in Kirkpatrick's fingers. It was signed "the Fly." It read:

"Nita came into my parlor, Spider!"

CHAPTER SIX

A Dangerous Game

Wentworth gazed fixedly at the taunting message of the Fly. His lips twitched once, he moved his shoulders heavily. He was aware of Kirkpatrick shouting orders that the telegram be traced, but neither of them expected any success from that line of inquiry.

"The Fly never dared do such a thing as this before," Kirkpatrick said harshly. "We'll break him. We'll destroy his every man. . . ."

Wentworth smiled slightly. "How—?" he demanded, quietly. "If you don't mind, I'm going home." He turned away. His thoughts swung in crazy circles. The premonitions which had harassed him were fulfilled to the utmost. To be sure, it was not the first time that Nita had been kidnaped by his enemies, but repetition never dulled the edge of his despair. Too often he had snatched his loved one back from the very brink of death. Ultimately, he must fail, and the Fly was the most clever criminal he had ever engaged. He could not lift the black veil from his thoughts. . . .

Wentworth brought up short as he saw two uniformed men dragging a prisoner toward Kirkpatrick. The man seemed more infuriated at their touch than reluctant to confront the Commissioner, but at any rate he was resisting violently. Abruptly, Wentworth recognized the prisoner. *Charles Holland!* The policemen held him rigidly before Kirkpatrick. Holland lifted his head in proud defiance. He gripped the upper half of a broken cane. . . . Wentworth made his way after Holland. He had no inkling as to the reason for the arrest, but the mere sight of that man on the scene of this atrocious crime was enough to arouse suspicion. His brother, that earlier Fly, had frequently used the trick of wearing a disguise during a crime, then reverting to his own identity and showing himself to the police. Was it possible that Charles Holland was following the same tactics?

Wentworth drew near enough to hear the policeman tell of finding Holland. "He was up on the fifteenth floor, looking through offices. A girl got scared and phoned up headquarters, so we took him."

Kirkpatrick nodded, "All right. Go back to your post."

The cop's heavy face worked. "Shall I iron him, Commissioner?"

Kirkpatrick shook his head, his frosty blue eyes holding Holland's. The Commissioner was easily fifteen years older than the other, as the gray at his temples attested. There were grim lines about his mouth corners and his eyes were tired. They could be very kindly; just now they were grimly quizzical.

The cop said, "Commissioner, you better let me iron him. He took a poke at me and, cheez, did I see stars!"

"Back to your post," Kirkpatrick ordered quietly and the policeman curved his mouth corners down, lifted his brows, resigning all responsibility. He walked away with his partner and Holland only shrugged his shoulders, pulled down his coat sleeves. Anger had flushed the fresh color of his cheeks. Kirkpatrick smiled slightly.

"You shouldn't have hit Morgan," he reproved. "It's a wonder he didn't use his stick on you. He'd have been justified, you know."

Holland laughed shortly, and lifted the broken cane. "He tried to, but I had my stick. I agreed to go with

241

them and then they grabbed me and roughed me along. You should teach your men manners, Kirkpatrick."

"Where they work," Kirkpatrick said quietly, "manners are considered a weakness. Do you want to explain your presence here or at headquarters—later?"

Holland stiffened under the crisp lash of the words. "I was not aware that explanation was called for. I had business in the building. . . ."

"Business of what sort?"

Wentworth laid a hand on Kirkpatrick's arm. The Commissioner was distraught. He would not, under ordinary circumstances, handle Holland in this way.

"Kirk," he said, "I'll be responsible for Holland, if you like."

Kirkpatrick eyed Wentworth, fingered his mustache, then nodded abruptly. If Dick wanted the man, there was a reason behind it, and a sound one. He nodded.

Wentworth motioned to the man. "Holland," he said quietly, "the Fly has kidnapped by fiancée, and I thought you might give me a little help in tracing her."

"I know nothing of the Fly," Holland retorted testily.

"I'm willing to believe that," Wentworth conceded. "Would you come with me, please? I'm going to my apartment."

"I have no choice, and you know it. I won't run from the police and for the present you're my custodian."

Wentworth made no answer to that. Holland was fiery and young and his behavior seemed sincere. It was true that he had a chip on his shoulder, but that was an outgrowth from the fact that his brother had gone outside the law. Wentworth bowed Holland into the Daimler, told Ram Singh to drive home slowly. He sank back in his corner of the seat and sat staring straight ahead of him. He felt like a fighter who has taken too many heavy blows below the heart, tired, with the spring gone out of his legs. Yes, below the heart . . . *Nita.* He closed his eyes and presently began to talk that way, his voice muffled with fatigue.

"I'm told, Holland, that last night, during the raid on your masquerade party, you didn't kill the Fly when you had an opportunity. . . ."

Holland's voice exploded out of him. "He called me his brother! It sounded like . . . Jack."

"Didn't you bury Jack?"

"I don't . . . know," Holland was clearly worried. "The body was pretty badly mangled and had landed on its head. I'll tell you now that we found no saber wound on the body."

Wentworth whipped erect, his eyes narrowed on Holland's face. "This is painful to you, I know," he said, "but my thrust touched here." He tapped his finger above the collar bone on the left side. "An eight-inch thrust there would have pierced the heart. Four inches would have severed the aorta. I could not swear to the depth of penetration, but you know the feel of steel in flesh. . . ."

Holland's face was white. This was his brother that they talked about, this was the man who had slain him, or at least run a sword into his body. Wentworth had been in his own identity when he had sabered Jack Holland, though there were *Spider* seals upon many of the Fly's companions. A tremor shook Wentworth's prisoner, but he held on to himself. It was moments before he could speak. . . .

"There was no such wound on the body," he said shakily. "I inspected it closely, trying to make sure of identification. Naturally, I did not reveal my doubts. If Jack had escaped . . . Well, my investigations proved that another man had fallen from a window in the building. He was executed in that way at Jack's order, I was told. But, Mr. Wentworth, are you sure . . . the saber penetrated?"

Wentworth closed his eyes, leaned back to think. It was clear that Charles Holland wanted to believe his brother dead. He tried to remember that windy moment when, on a ladder bridging a gulf between two apartment building roofs, the Fly had hurled himself forward, close to the ladder, in a violent lunge; Wentworth had parried the lunge with a stop-thrust, driven at the base of the throat. The Fly had instantly plunged from the ladder, but he might have been overbalanced by his lunge . . . Wentworth opened his eyes.

"I used to be sure, Holland," he said, "but now, when I think of it, I can't be."

The men were silent through minutes while the Daimler wove its way northward. They were on Fifth Avenue. In a half-dozen blocks, they would be at Wentworth's apartment. He stirred himself. A resolution was forming within him. If he succeeded in freeing Nita from this dilemma, he would make sure that she was never involved again. How he would arrange that . . . ? He smiled sardonically. How many times had he made that same oath—and broken it! . . . Through years of constant, secret warfare, he had put the people he thanklessly served before everything, even before Nita, and she had rarely complained. And, once more, now, he must do that. The Fly would communicate with him with a demand that he drop out of the fight, on pain of Nita's death. He would refuse, even though it doomed Nita. He couldn't do anything else, and Nita. . . . Would he be able to snatch her once more from destruction? He must, he must. . . .

"Holland, the girl called Lou, who was shot last night," Wentworth said. "Would you mind telling me her name?"

"I would!" Holland said sharply. "She wasn't badly hurt, a flesh wound under the arm, and I won't permit her to be prosecuted."

Wentworth nodded, as if it did not matter. "I see, and who is Gary?"

Holland's hands gripped Wentworth's arm. "In heaven's name, Mr. Wentworth, what prompts these questions?" he cried. "I tell you that Lou and her brother are entirely innocent. It's just that the Fly has got hold of the kid. . . . You must believe me. They're innocent.''

Wentworth lifted his shoulders slightly, but beneath his lowered lids, his blue-gray eyes were speculative. A girl named Lou and her brother, Gary, in the Fly's power. And Charles Holland was in love with the girl. . . . The Daimler drew to a halt and Ram Singh sprang to the pavement, flung wide the door.

"I'd be pleased to have you come up, Holland," he said, "but if you wish, you may go. I gave my word that you would be available when ready. I know that you will respect that promise and hold yourself ready for Mr. Kirkpatrick."

Holland had alighted. He turned to Wentworth with a smile. "You're an all right guy," he said eagerly. "I'm beginning to understand why Kirkpatrick trusts you . . . and why other people hate you." He hesitated. "I'm going to call on Lou. I can't object now to telling you her name because I know you won't misuse the knowledge. She's Lou Cox. Gary is her brother. They're quite well-to-do, even wealthy, in their own right, and they live with their uncle and guardian. . . ."

Wentworth's face cleared. "Of course," he said. "They're Foster Sherwood's wards. I knew that those names were familiar. You're right, Holland, I won't misuse the information, but I'm going to find that young man and have a talk with him. Gary Cox."

Holland said fervently, "I wish to God you would!"

He stepped back, bowed and lifted his hat, as men do on the Continent as a mark of extreme respect. He pivoted and was about to march off along the street. Wentworth stopped him with a hail, smiling slightly as he pointed to the stub of a broken cane which Holland still carried.

"Don't you want me to dispose of that for you?" he said. "It looks rather ridiculous."

Holland laughed, handed it over to Wentworth with hurried thanks, and strode on. He did not notice that Wentworth gripped the cane very carefully by its broken end, so as not to disturb any palm prints that might be upon its head. Ram Singh closed the door and stood beside Wentworth, waiting for orders.

"Missie sahib has been kidnaped by the Fly," Wentworth told him flatly. His acquisition of the broken cane had been almost instinctive. His mind bore heavily on the misfortune of Nita. . . . He saw fierceness leap into the Sikh's eyes. Devotion to women did not come traditionally to this Hindu, but he had fought under Nita's orders and had found her braver even than the women of his own Punjab hills. As his master's mate, she would deserve his most devoted service, even if she were not so strong in her own right. Ram Singh's hand went to the knife hilt at his sash.

"Park the car and come after me," Wentworth told him. "I'm waiting for word, either from the Fly or from Jackson."

He went heavily to his penthouse, shed coat and hat and handed the broken cane carefully to Jenkyns with instructions to develop the prints on it. He had not looked at Jenkyns while he spoke, but abruptly seeing his face, Wentworth felt hope spring up within him. Jenkyns smiled like that for only one person in the world. . . .

"Miss Nita . . . ?" Wentworth whispered.

"Yes, Master Dick," said Jenkyns, "Miss Nita and a Mr. Claiborne Lee are waiting for you, sir."

His heart singing, Wentworth strode through the hall. Nita van Sloan was seated on the low, long davenport that faced the brick fireplace. Before her, Claiborne Lee stood easily, a wine glass lifted in salute. Their smiles held comradeship, a mutural respect. They had not heard his entrance. . . .

"To the bravest, and the most beautiful woman I have ever met," said Claiborne Lee, bowing. Nita laughed, her contralto a sweet bell note.

"You have your own share of bravery, Mr. Lee," she answered him.

Wentworth stood looking at them, his eyes burning. He guessed what had happened. This talk of bravery could mean only that Lee had rescued her from the Fly. His lips pressed thinly together. How had Lee managed to be on the scene, why had he undertaken the rescue? So far as Wentworth was aware, Lee did not know Nita and it was improbable that the kidnaping had been spectacular or even obvious. Foolish to suspect Claiborne Lee on such little evidence, if he could call it that, but Wentworth had realized that "hunches" were frequently the functioning of the subconscious mind. . . . What he determined on was inspirational. For this one time, at least, he could protect Nita and, if Lee were guilty, plant a spy in the heart of the enemy camp. . . . Nita would understand, her quick mind would grasp what he wanted.

From his position just inside the door, Wentworth spoke: "I see you returned safely from your little affair with the Fly." There was a sneer and harshness in its syllables. Claiborne Lee's head whipped about. Nita started, then turned toward him. She came slowly to her feet as Wentworth strode across the room. She smiled, held out her hands to him. . . .

"Dick," she said, "I want you to know Mr. Claiborne Lee." She hurriedly told the story of her seizure by the men of the Fly. "When their car was stopped by the next traffic light, Mr. Lee pulled up beside us, shot the driver and came straight at the other two men with his gun out. He used the side of the car for protection, killed another of them, and the third one tried to get away. But he shot him dead, too. He's almost as good a shot as you are, Dick."

Wentworth bowed coldly. "And a much braver man, I am sure. Would you mind, Lee, telling me just how you happened to be in the downtown district and why you killed your own men?"

Lee frowned. "I don't know what you're talking about, or why you are being so unmannerly," he said coldly. "But I shall certainly demand explanations when you are a little less distraught." He bowed.

"Miss van Sloan, are you staying, or may I see you home?"

Wentworth's hand reached out, caught the man's arm. He jerked him about so that their eyes met each other's with an almost solid impact. "I'll tell you what I mean, Lee," he said with metallic sharpness. "I mean that you are the man who directed the bandits at Holland's home last night and planned the looting of the Bank of New York today. You are the man who shot Lou Cox. In short, Mr. Lee, you are the Fly!"

Lee wrenched his arm free, stared coldly at Wentworth, turned to Nita. "I'm afraid Mr. Wentworth has gone completely mad. I think it would be much better if you went with me."

"She will not!" Wentworth rasped. He made a deliberately awkward punch at Lee's face which the man easily evaded. He kept his face twisted into a furious frown, and would not look at Nita. Lee must not become suspicious of their simulated quarrel. . . . Nita's hand touched Wentworth's arm.

"Dick, boy," she said gently, "what's the matter? You surely don't mean what you said to Mr. Lee. I know. . . ."

Wentworth wrenched his arm free of her hand. "Were you really kidnaped by the Fly?" he sneered, "or is this just some story of yours to trick me?"

Nita flinched back, the pure oval of her face very pale, her eyes startled and hurt.

Claiborne Lee said, "I really must insist that you go with me, Miss van Sloan."

"By all means," Wentworth sneered. "By all means. Perhaps his bravery will protect you!"

He strode from the room. Jenkyns stood in the hallway, his face strained and amazed. Wentworth stopped before him, shouting, "Get them out of here, you doddering old fool! Get them out of here before I kill them both!"

He stormed along the hall, reached his own suite and rushed inside. He closed and locked the door, stood with his legs braced apart, his breath coming sharply. He was frowning. Damn it, Nita had seemed so startled and hurt! Surely, she understood his purpose, that the quarrel was simulated. He had had to make it forceful, even to bellowing at poor old Jenkyns. He smiled briefly at the memory of Jenkyns' amazed face, but his amusement quickly died. Nita *had* to understand. He could not communicate with her, for if Lee were the Fly he would suspect a false quarrel, would be on the lookout for secret conversations. . . . Oh, damn it, this was. . . .

The tapping at the door was very gentle, "Dick, boy," Nita called. "Come here and talk with me."

Wentworth whirled toward the door, his jaw tightly clenched, his hands knotted at his sides. This was harder than that other, but Lee would be watching. He must force himself still to simulate anger. If only he could be sure that Nita understood! He swallowed twice before he could force out words.

"Get the hell out of here!" he shouted. "Leave my house and don't come back."

Silence then. Wentworth stood, straining his ears, leaning forward, his eyes peering as if he would see through that barrier which separated him from the woman he loved. The silence kept on and on. Dimly, Wentworth thought he heard a door slam. With a gasp that was dry and hard in his throat, he started toward the door of his room. He forced himself to remain inside. Of course, Nita understood. It was foolish of him to think even for a moment that she could take him seriously. She knew how deeply he loved her, and. . . . The startled, hurt face of Nita arose before his eyes to mock him. He walked slowly back across the room, glimpsed himself in the mirror and moved closer, staring at his reflection, the creases that each month etched more deeply about his lips, the stipple of premature silver there above his temples. He had always driven himself to the right course regardless of what it cost and the iron of his will was there in the lines that marked the frequent compression of his mouth. He smiled at himself with a quizzical lift of his brows. Agonizing, eh? Playing at melodramatics. But, damn it, life was made up of melodramatics. . . . It was going to be hard to fight this battle without the strong support of Nita at his side, still harder to keep up the pretense of bitterness and anger. A dry, hard sound forced itself up out of his throat. He changed that sound to a laugh, kept on laughing, laughing. . . .

CHAPTER SEVEN

Is Nita a Traitor?

It was two hours before Wentworth left his room, and his face was so sternly forbidding that old Jenkyns, who had served Wentworth's father before him, thought better of speaking to him. Ram Singh stood with his shoulders close to the wall, arms folded across his white tunic. His eyes followed Wentworth ceaselessly, but he did not speak. The ways of western men with western women were past his understanding. . . .

Wentworth moved restlessly about the drawing room. He had a driving urge for decisive, slashing action. As yet, there was no opportunity for that, but when it came . . .

"Has Jackson called?" The harshness of his voice surprised Wentworth's own ear. His eyes burned on Jenkyns'.

"No, Master Dick," Jenkyns said quietly. "Master, I saw tears in Miss Nita's eyes when she left."

Wentworth reached Jenkyns with three long strides. "Jenkyns," he said harshly. "You've been with me a long time, and you should know—"

Old Jenkyns looked at his young master with miserable eyes. There could be no question of his devotion, but this was terribly wrong, this anger against Miss Nita. His bowed shoulders straightened, his silvery head came up. He would have defied Wentworth then, but the telephone bell rang. . . . Jenkyns hesitated, then his shoulders drooped and he turned away. He came back slowly.

"Jackson on the phone, Master Dick."

Wentworth did not wait for the portable to be brought to him, but strode rapidly along the hall to the butler's pantry. "Yes, Jackson?" He listened to the rapid words of the man who was as much his friend as his servant. They had served together in the World War, Sergeant Jackson and Major Wentworth . . . "I'll join you in ten minutes."

He hung up, sent his shout to Ram Singh ringing ahead of him, caught hat and coat from Jenkyns' hands. There was a smile hard on his lips, his eyes were narrowed and bitter. The *Spider* was on the warpath. God help whatever men interposed between him and the Fly.

The Daimler surged with power as Wentworth gave swift instructions. "I told Jackson we'd be there in ten minutes," Wentworth said quietly. This rush of reckless speed, this evasion of traffic lights was his answer. He was well served. . . . In his quandary over Nita, Wentworth thought briefly that it would be better were the *Spider* to fight his battles alone. Gallant men he had had beyond a doubt, but their attachment to him could never bring them other than death in the end. Both Jackson and Ram Singh had been wounded a half-dozen times in his service.

Such thoughts would not do. He forced himself to consider the information that Jackson had given him. Gary Cox lived with his guardian, Foster Sherwood, who was a young man for the responsibility of handling the millions of the Cox heirs, younger than Wentworth. They occupied an ancient house near Long Island Sound in Pelham. The house had a history; it had been built on the site of an old-time tavern known as the Smuglers' Rest. . . .

Wentworth's mind would not concentrate on the possibilities of the situation. He was considering falteringly the chance that Foster Sherwood might be stealing from the estate of the two Cox heirs, that he had driven his ward and nephew into crime with a view to being rid of him. . . . Hell, could Sherwood be the Fly? He was able with a rapier, Wentworth knew. He ridiculed his thoughts. Damnable that every person he knew must fall under suspicion. . . . Wearily, he took up his duties. . . .

Wentworth caught up the speaking tube that communicated with Ram Singh. Always, when he went into danger, he left a record of his progress in the case that, in event of disaster, would be turned over to Kirkpatrick. Formerly, Nita had served him in that capacity, but he dared not communicate with her. . . . His lips were awry as he began talking to Ram Singh. . . .

"In the safe that you know of in my room," he said, "is a moulage cast of a man's palm print. I am reasonably sure that this is the palm print of the Fly—" he explained his reasons for thinking so, the adventures at Holland's masquerade. "On my return from the masquerade, I sent Jackson to determine the name of the girl who was shot, to learn what person connected with her was named Gary and to find and trail that person. He has followed her brother, named Gary Cox, to a doctor's office on the East Side. We are going there now. Gary Cox went into the doctor's office a half hour ago and, when Jackson went into the waiting room, he was not in sight. Keep this carefully in mind. It shall be your duty to preserve your life and to carry this message to Kirkpatrick if misfortune should befall me. Understand?"

Ram Singh's usually prompt "Han, sahib!" was delayed. In Punjabi, he asked slowly, "Does this mean, my master, that thy servant may not fight beside thee?"

Wentworth rasped out a repetition of his order and Ram Singh was silent. This was not his master's manner, to order him harshly and without explanation to become a coward! Wentworth bowed his head, inspected his automatics with dry eyes as he checked the clips, the chamber and the cock, threw on the safety before restoring them to their holsters. Even Ram Singh's bravery did not stir him as formerly. "If misfortune should befall me. . . ."

His lips set thinly. He opened a compartment in the back of the front seat and took out a notebook, unscrewed a fountain pen cap and wrote slow and painful words across the white paper. This car, along with everything else he possessed, would go to Nita in the event of his death. She would find this notebook. . . .

It was not like the *Spider* to go into battle with such despair in his heart, but even that fact did not make him falter. It had been many years since the thought of death had disturbed him. . . . The car slowed to the curb and a man with a wide stocky body stepped from a dark doorway to meet it. At Wentworth's curt invitation, he entered the back seat.

"You beat your time by two minutes, Major," he said. "The lad hasn't come out yet."

Wentworth nodded. "Go into the office and wait for the doctor. Ram Singh will watch at the window. I'll come in later in disguise. If you don't see Gary Cox by that time, we'll take the doctor and ask some questions."

Jackson's wide jaws ceased with a grin. "Yes, Major!"

Ram Singh glided from the front seat of the car and strode away beside Jackson. Wentworth drew the curtains of the car and pressed a button beneath the edge of the left half of the seat. The seat slid slowly forward, revolved and revealed a closely hung wardrobe, a mirror brilliantly lighted by a ring of neon tubes beneath which was a make-up tray. With skillful fingers then, Wentworth set to work to disguise his face. Under his deft fingers, his nose became beaked and predatory; the skin over his cheekbones tautened in sallowness, the mouth became lipless. . . . In short, the face of the *Spider* grew over his own. It was swiftly done. Long practice had done that for him. His hat was a light brown fedora and he wore a threadbare overcoat rather than the black cape and hat of the *Spider*. It was not yet his purpose to terrify. That might come later. . . He hoped it would.

Wentworth's lips had a thinness that was not all due to disguise as he limped across the street toward where the doctor's lighted sign glowed against the dusk. His shoulders were twisted awkwardly and it gave his carriage a singularly sinister aspect. As he entered the outer door, the four patients in the room glanced up toward him and Wentworth was struck immediately with the faces of two of them. They had the wary, shallow eyes of killers and their hands had the nervous habit of gunmen. They never strayed far from weapons. Jackson was in the seat nearest the door. He shook his head slightly to indicate that Gary Cox had not yet shown himself and Wentworth limped directly to the doctor, whose name, the sign had said, was Leaming.

"Dr. Leaming," Wentworth's voice was high and disagreeable. "Would you mind taking me next? I'm suffering awful pain in my back and I need relief. I must have relief! Do you hear? I must have relief." Wentworth lifted his hands, shaking them violently. His artificially pinched face was thrust forward. He was studying this Dr. Leaming closely. The man's face was smooth and round, the eyes might have been kindly behind horn-rimmed spectacles except for a cold light in their depths. . . .

"I'm sorry, I can't do that," said Dr. Leaming. "If you'll just have a seat."

"Aw, let him in first, doc," Jackson broke in. "Can't you see the guy's in pain?"

"I must have relief!" Wentworth cried. Out of the corner of his eyes, he was watching the two men he had spotted as gunmen. They were sitting at rigid attention, hands in their gun pockets. What was their purpose here? Were they guards for this Leaming, or were they prospective patients as they pretended to be? Wentworth faced them, whining, "You don't mind if a man what's suffering goes in ahead of you? I know you don't. You're kind men. I can see it in your faces. See, Doctor, they don't object. . . ."

Jackson was on his feet beside the doctor and, though Jackson's lips did not move, Wentworth saw abruptly that he had spoken, that his right hand was out of direct sight behind the doctor's back and that perspiration was standing out on the man's forehead.

"A-all right," he stuttered. "Come right in. . . ."

He backed into his office. Wentworth followed him, and Jackson sat down again to keep watch on the two men whom Wentworth suspected. Wentworth followed the doctor and took his gun out at the same instant.

"Pardon the haste," he murmured, "but I must take every precaution, as you will understand when you learn my identity."

The doctor reeled into the seat behind his desk and lifted a wavering hand to his forehead. "I—I have no narcotics," he whispered, "and very little money."

"I'm inclined to doubt both statements," Wentworth replied suavely, "but I did not come here in quest of either article you mention. I came to . . ."

The doctor's round face lifted, a puzzled frown on the smooth forehead. The eyes were slowly widening. His shoulders cringed in the chair. "What, oh what do you want?" he cried.

Wentworth bent forward. "Where," he whispered, "is Gary Cox?"

There was no answering flair in the doctor's eyes and Wentworth saw that the name meant absolutely nothing to Leaming. Yet it wasn't possible that Jackson was mistaken and there were those two men on guard in the ante-room. What this meant was that Dr. Leaming had acted without knowing the man's name. It all had some definite criminal significance. . . .

"He's quite young and very handsome. What message did you give him?" Wentworth asked next.

Dr. Leaming had got back a modicum of courage when the first question had shown that Wentworth was ignorant of his work. Wentworth saw that and smiled somberly. He reached out his right hand and something that gleamed in it touched fleetingly the prescription pad that rested before the man. When his hand had returned to his side, something crimson glowed there against the white paper and Dr. Leaming rose to his feet with a muffled scream, backing frantically away from the *seal of the Spider* which stared up at him with its mocking threat of death.

"Don't kill me, *Spider*," babbled Dr. Leaming. "Don't kill me . . . !"

Wentworth's lipless mouth twisted in a smile of mockery. "Where is Gary Cox?" he demanded again.

"I don't know, *Spider*. For God's sake, I don't know the names of any of the men who come here. Any time one of them mentions the Fly and his own number, I give him a little prescription that's already written out, one for each number, and he goes out the back entrance of the apartment building. That's all I know. . . ."

Wentworth held out his left hand. "Let me have all the prescriptions that are written out, Dr. Leaming. If the Fly asks you about it, tell him that the *Spider* paid you a call. . . ."

Leaming surrendered the prescriptions, and Wentworth glanced hastily at them. At first glance, they told him nothing. He said, "Good, now call in the man who held a gun at your back. After which we'll both go out through the back entrance. Remember, though, if you make a single hostile move . . ." Wentworth lifted the muzzle of his gun and Dr. Leaming cringed toward the door, called Jackson in with a strained voice. As Wentworth's man moved in, Wentworth whistled a few bars of a weird minor strain. It told Ram Singh that everything was all right, to go back to the car. . . . Two minutes later, the doctor having been strapped competently in his chair and gagged with his own adhesive tape, Wentworth and Jackson made their way out of the back entrance. They kept sharp lookout, but could find no trace of a hidden headquarters of the Fly. Wentworth did not seriously expect to find any,

257

for it was pretty clear that the Fly used the doctor's office as a clearing place for orders to his men.

Wentworth posted Jackson to keep watch on the rear entrance and to follow either of the two men who left, or if they remained, to trail Dr. Leaming when next he went out. Ram Singh would keep similar lookout in front. And the *Spider* . . . ? Wentworth smiled slightly. This was not the action he wished, but at least it would keep him busy. . . .

"These prescriptions carry some sort of coded message," Wentworth announced briefly. "I shall wait in the Daimler around the corner and try to decipher them. Communicate there."

In the Daimler, Wentworth drew a desk tray from the back of the seat ahead of him and spread the prescriptions under its hooded light. At first glance they were innocent enough, one for a sedative, another apparently some compound for a sick stomach, the third a liniment. Yet Wentworth was sure that somewhere in these scribbled formulas were messages to members of the Fly's band dealing with some new atrocity which he planned.

The Fly had proved that he could strike rapidly and with force. Here was none of the slow preparation that had characterized the previous visitation of the criminal who used that name. Last night, it had been the raid on Holland's masquerade, then two swift attacks upon the *Spider* and as close on the heels of the second as possible, the looting of the Bank of New York. Wentworth had every reason then to think that still another atrocity was being planned, that these slips of paper. . . .

All three prescriptions had been signed by Leaming, and the names of the patients were there, too, with addresses. Wentworth's eyes narrowed abruptly. That address for one Oscar Schmidt, 765 East Fortieth street, was an impossibility. There was no such address. Could the code be hidden in those few brief numbers? Hurriedly, Wentworth examined the other prescriptions, inspecting names and addresses. He was desperate with the need for haste. Even while he puzzled over these anonymous slips, the Fly might be preparing to strike. The *Spider* knew the Fly well enough to be sure that the mere absence of three of his criminal aides would not interrupt his plans. He would arrange duplicate and even triplicate coverage. . . .

Wentworth's attention was drawn sharply to the pepsin prescription, made out in a woman's name, a Riverside Drive address. Good God, it was Nita's address! This was madness. Could they be planning to strike again at the woman he loved! His lips shut grimly. Why shouldn't they? There was a way to make sure. He would seize the three who came for these prescriptions, force them to talk. . . .

Wentworth slid from the car, stole through the thickened night to where he knew Ram Singh kept watch. He stood beside him in a darkened doorway. "Has anyone entered?" he asked softly.

"None yet, *sahib*," Ram Singh replied, "but a woman and a man come there at the corner. . . ."

Wentworth's eyes shot where the Sikh indicated and his breath caught in his throat as he saw the woman. It wasn't possible, and yet, God knew, he should recognize that proud carriage of the head, that easy grace of movement.

"Sahib!" whispered Ram Singh, "it is . . ." His breath choked off as Wentworth closed his hand upon the Hindu's arm. He could no longer doubt, but perhaps she was not going to the doctor's office? He told himself that, but there was no belief in him. The woman and man came rapidly nearer, the sharp taps of her heels making staccato echoes along the street, the man's much slower and deliberate. They paused for a moment before the entrance of the doctor's office, looked at the gleaming sign, then ran up the steps and entered. . . . Wentworth's hand dropped from Ram Singh's arm. He did not know the man, but he understood the address on the woman's prescription now, for the woman who had just entered the office of the Fly's go-between was . . . *Nita van Sloan*!

CHAPTER EIGHT

The *Spider* Finds Despair

For once, surprise held Wentworth inactive. He stood in the shadowed doorway with Ram Singh and stared sightlessly at the door across the street into which Nita van Sloan had disappeared. What in the world did her presence here at this place mean? Who was this man? It was plain they had come to receive coded orders from the Fly. . . .

Wentworth gnawed at his lip, gazed and gazed until his eyes were dazzled by the lighted doctor's sign. He could sense the impatience of Ram Singh and he thought with a twisted smile that even the Sikh must be wondering at his behavior toward the *missie sahib* whose orders he had been taught to accept as implicitly as the *Spider's* own. But he must do something.

"Wait here," he ordered Ram Singh harshly. "If the *missie sahib* comes out, follow her and phone back your report to Jenkyns. I'll call there. . . ."

In the darkness, Wentworth caught the movement of the Sikh's abrupt salaam, cupped hands lifted to his turbaned head. Wentworth then strode toward the alleyway where Jackson kept watch. His feet hit the ground violently. Anger had him by the throat, anger at himself, at the thing he had possibly done to Nita. . . . Damn it, she should understand. . . .

In the mouth of the alley, Wentworth paused, peering

into the shadows that clustered thick against the fences, the walls of buildings. Somewhere here, Jackson should be keeping watch. He had been posted close to this end. Softly, Wentworth whistled the minor notes of their signal. He waited and there was no answer. Alarm stabbed sharply into the *Spider's* vitals. Where the devil was Jackson? Swiftly, Wentworth crept into the black, narrow defile of the alley, found the gate that was the back door of the doctor's office. He entered . . . and stumbled over a soft and yielding object.

With a curse, Wentworth dropped to his knees. He did not need his eyes to know that this was Jackson. His swift fingers detected the uniform, found his throat pulse. . . . A breath of relief forced itself out of Wentworth's set lips. He was only unconscious. How had any one managed to get close enough to that doughty warrior to overpower him? No way of telling until he regained consciousness, but his presence here meant one sure thing: the birds had flown. Nita . . . ?

Wentworth sprang to his feet, dragging Jackson's weight across his shoulders in a fireman's lift. He moved rapidly toward the office of the doctor. Leaming was gone, so were the two gunmen. The other legitimate patient was just stirring to consciousness. Bitter laughter shook Wentworth. He crossed to the window, signaled Ram Singh. It was his own weakness that had done this, his delay in deciding on action against Nita.

In a few minutes, Wentworth had the story. The patient, having recovered, said that a good-looking woman had come in with a man and told the other two men in the office that the place was watched. "She went to the office, found the doctor tied up—" The man swallowed hard—"She spun about, pointed to me and said 'Conk him!' One of them did, with a blackjack."

Jackson's face was puzzled and ashamed. He kept glancing at Wentworth, then looking down at the floor. "Out with it," Wentworth told him grimly. "I know it was Miss Nita."

"You could of knocked me down with a feather,"

Jackson said humbly. "Miss Nita comes out into the alley and whistles the way you do. 'Jackson?' she whispers. Hell, I walked up to her and she let me have it. Blackjack, I think, sir."

"I rather imagine it wasn't a feather," Wentworth said drily. There was no real humor in him. His men were puzzled, their morale shaken as well it might be. How Nita had discovered that the house was watched, he had no idea, but she knew the Spider's methods very thoroughly. She would have known that it was Jackson he would place at the secret entrance where he would have to use discretion in his action. Ram Singh was equally brave, but he knew only one form of action, to obey or to kill. When in doubt, he killed. . . .

Wentworth said heavily, "We'll have to change our signals. Both of you disregard any further orders from Miss Nita. She is not . . . our ally any longer. By the way, Jackson, did you know the third man with Miss Nita?"

Jackson started. "Yes, by God! I knew there was something I was trying to remember. That blackjack. . . . It was Foster Sherwood, Major."

Wentworth uttered a sharp exclamation. What was Foster Sherwood doing with Nita at a meeting place of the Fly's men? It was strange—strange! His suspicions of the Cox heirs' guardian flashed back again. He shook his head. That must all come later. For the present. . . . He moved on leaden feet toward the doctor's inner office, began to go methodically through the files. His heart was not in it, and the thought of Nita came between him and his work. An unrest fermented within him. Since this point was known to the Spider, it was of no further use to the Fly. He might well send the police here to trap the *Spider*. "Jackson, Ram Singh. Lookout, rear and front. Whistle if you sight police!" Jackson moved sluggishly through the office, opened the rear door, then crashed it shut!

"They're already here, sir," he whispered.

Wentworth's hand flashed to the lamp on the desk and extinguished it. He was instantly out of his seat, but it wasn't necessary to order Ram Singh to lock the front door. He had already done it. Their position was totally untenable. This was a first floor office, the windows were only about six feet from the ground and there were too many openings to guard. Besides, the *Spider* did not fight the police. . . . His usually swift brain was clogged with bewilderment. Nita must have done this. Not so soon could she have communicated with the Fly and received his orders. But why, why . . . ? He laughed sharply, harshly. . . .

A fist hammered hard on the door, shook it in its frame. "Open in the name of the law, *Spider*!" a man growled. "If we have to come after you, we'll come shooting."

"You'll have to," Wentworth called back suavely. "Just a minute before you begin hostilities!" As he talked, his hands were swiftly at work. He stripped off his wig and thrust it into his pocket, left his bushy eyebrows. He mashed the beaked nose of the *Spider* in a pugilist's flattened feature. "There's an innocent man in here!" Wentworth continued. "He was a patient of the doctor and got caught in the fight. Before you begin your attack, you ought to let him out. He might get hurt."

"For God's sake," cried the man in frightened tones. "Let me out. The *Spider* . . . God, I'll be killed." He ran to the door and beat on it with frenzied hands. "Let me out. . . ."

"Wait a minute," Wentworth said, drawing the screaming man back from the door. "We'll put him out the window, then you can't use him to get in. Is that all right, gentlemen? Surely, you wouldn't want to hurt him?"

"Oh, don't hurt me," the man whimpered.

Outside the door, voices rumbled. Wentworth turned to Ram Singh and spoke swiftly in the Sikh's native Punjabi, keeping his tones low. "Tell Jackson what I say afterward. I am going to knock out this man and go out the window in his place. You will lower me.

Once I am behind the policemen, I'll create a diversion so that you can escape. Understood?''

Ram Singh's smile was in his voice. *"Han, sahib!"*

"How about it?" Wentworth shouted impatiently to the policemen in his own voice. "I won't surrender. You should know that by now."

"All right," growled a policeman, "lower the other guy out the window, but we'll pump you full of lead if anybody tries funny stuff."

"I don't even feel humorous," Wentworth agreed. His spirits had risen with the peril. Danger was to him the stimulant that most men find in drink. It put an edge to his wits, limbered his tongue, gave him a new courage.

"Oh thank you," cried the patient. "Thank you. . . ."

Wentworth's fingers thrust sharply against his throat, hit important nerve centers which rendered him instantly unconscious. He smiled gently down at the man as he lowered him to the floor. He would be quite safe here and he would be well repaid for his inconvenience. Wentworth slipped two hundred-dollar bills into his limp palm, then he snatched a sheet from the doctor's examining table, tied it under his own arms and signaled to Ram Singh who was rapidly whispering the plan to Jackson. Jackson's wide, muscular jaws creased in a grin.

"I'll put him out the front window," Wentworth called to the police. He changed his voice to the whimpering of the patient. "Oh, thank you, gentlemen. This is kind of you, *Spider*. I won't forget it. . . ."

Jackson took Wentworth's coat and hat, draped them over his shoulders which he hunched as best he could in an imitation of the *Spider's* twisted form.

"Don't show yourself recklessly," Wentworth urged. "They're likely to shoot, in spite of the truce."

Jackson nodded and Wentworth, whimpering pleas and thanksgiving was lowered out the window. The instant his feet hit the ground, a sub-machine gun stammered and the window fell in fragments. Inside the office, there was a hoarse cry, but Wentworth could not tell whether one of his men was hit, or whether they were shamming to gain time. . . . Enacting his role to its utmost, he cowered to the ground for a moment, then when a policeman yelled to him he scuttled across the pavement at a swift run.

"Watch that man," a sharp voice ordered. "It would be just like the *Spider* to let himself out the window, and . . ." The voice choked off. Wentworth had reached the man, and his fingers had struck the throat nerves again. He whipped out both of his automatics, leaped to the driving seat of a parked squad car and kicked it into motion. He emptied an automatic straight up into the air. Behind him, pandemonium broke out. The machine gunner turned toward him and lead hammered over the body of the squad car. Revolvers blazed from roofs, from doorways. . . .

Wentworth crouched to the floor. He had the squad car rolling and accurate steering was much less important than cover. For two blocks, he steered erratically, then he reared high enough to see a corner which he whirled on two wheels. Immediately he had turned out of sight of the police, he stopped the squad car and ran to the shadows, ran back toward the house where Ram Singh and Jackson were trapped!

The police were too well disciplined, he knew, to abandon the siege because one man had made an escape. They would bear down harder than ever, but their strength would be weakened. Some undoubtedly were pursuing, and he would have liked to lead them further astray, but it made return too slow and difficult. They would scarcely expect him to come back to the scene of the fight, though they might send some man to check on that possibility. . . . Over a fence, Wentworth swarmed, a bare second ahead of the first pursuing car that rounded the corner. The radio roadster tried to check its speed, but was skittering at the moment brakes were clapped on. It collided violently with the rear of the squad car. Before the men could disentangle themselves, Wentworth had taken a second fence. . . .

The single cross-street he had passed was only dimly lighted, but Wentworth saw policemen at fixed posts at each end of the block. He was certain to be seen if he made an open crossing and the only alternative was to sneak up on one of them and knock him out. That would take too much time. Wentworth stepped out on the pavement and walked openly, with ringing heels, toward the street where machine guns hammered and the siege of the doctor's office was in full swing. The two policemen whipped about, guns gleaming in their hands, but as Wentworth continued openly to approach one of them, they made no move. They were waiting, suspicious, but partly calmed by the directness of the *Spider's* behavior. . . .

Fortunately, one of them was on the side of the street to which Wentworth wished to cross and he angled toward the man—and toward a fence which divided a backyard from the walk. If he made a single slip—if he gave any slightest intention of his purpose before he vaulted that fence—lead would whistle at him from two directions. At any event, the moment he made his leap, the alarm would be given. Police would know that he had doubled on his trail to release his men. His actions must be lightning-swift.

Wentworth did not make the mistake of sliding toward the fence. He walked along the curbing, sizing up the barrier he must overlap from the corners of his eyes. The policeman ahead of him was off-guard, but he still held the revolver in his hand. It would be a close thing there. What the officer behind him was doing, Wentworth could only guess. To turn his head would betray him. . . . He picked the point at which he would take the fence, but kept his body relaxed and easy. Abruptly, he took a long, leaping stride, bounced into the air and grasped the top of the fence with both hands. Wentworth was an experienced athlete. Tumbling and acrobatics had been part of his training and he kept his muscles alive and ready by constant practice. His sudden bound sent him upward, his arms stiffened and served as a pivot and he swung his legs sideways horizontally over the fence.

He had his hands on the top of the boards before the policeman realized what was happening. The man's gun flew up then, but instead of taking careful aim, he banged away wildly. That defeated him. Had he delayed for a heart-beat to take even fleeting aim. . . . The lead whimpered past inches high and Wentworth dropped out of sight behind the boards.

Wentworth guessed what the policeman had done, but he had not glanced at the man once he had gone into action. Nothing he could do, once the leap was started, could avert a true-sped bullet and he must depend on his speed and the unexpectedness of the thing he did. So his eyes, as he vaulted the fence, were on the ground toward which he plunged and, seeing that was clear, he shot his gaze ahead to the space between him and the next fence. Thirty feet. Wentworth landed on his feet, but made no effort to check his momentum. He used it to somersault and came up springing. One stride, two, and he sprang for the second fence. Not until he topped that one would he be even temporarily safe from lead. If one of the policemen was an athlete and could take the fence. . . .

There was no more shooting behind him and Wentworth took two more fences in the same swift manner and was in the yard through which the doctor's office had its exit. Men would be in hiding here, he knew, but there could be no stalking now that the enemy had sighted him. It would take time for the two policemen who had seen him to carry word to the man in charge of the raid. They were piping already, but it would take words to explain. Before that time . . .

Wentworth took the last fence as he had the other two and, sailing through the air, hands still on the top of the boards, he caught the white gleam as a man turned up a startled face where he crouched behind a large dog-house. A quick glance about the yard showed one other man, nearer the building than the dog-house, but he had not yet detected this new source of danger.

The man who had spotted Wentworth's approach whipped about his gun, his mouth opened in a cry of warning. That cry had just started, the gun only half-lifted to shoot, when Wentworth hit on his feet a bare half-dozen feet away. With the impetus of his vault behind him, Wentworth arched through the air in a head-first dive. The policeman was starting to his feet and Wentworth took him, shoulder to stomach, drove him backward against the dog-house and spilled him unconscious to the ground.

It had all happened too quickly for the policeman's companion over there to know what had occurred. He caught the half cry, the sound of a fall and jerked to his feet.

"Bill?" he cried. "What the hell . . . ?"

Wentworth crouched behind the dog-house, groping for the man's hat and his own. "Damn it," he muttered hoarsely. "I twisted my ankle. . . ." He found the unconscious man's hat, slipped it on his head and showed himself just above the dog-house. "More damned stones . . ." He had one from the gravelly earth in his hand and his arm shot forward like the beam of a catapult. The second officer grunted as the rock took him in the stomach and before he could recover from the surprise and shock of the blow, Wentworth had stepped in with two swift blows that began at his toes and exploded against the man's jaw.

Wentworth stood silent for a half minute, breathing lightly through his nostrils. His blood raced thrillingly through his veins. This was the sort of thing for which alone he lived now. . . . He puckered his lips and whistled softly, on a piercing, minor note, then he ran lightly forward to the door.

"Ram Singh! Jackson!" he called softly. "The way is clear here!"

The night echoed with the shrillness of police whistles and hoarse shouting. The rasp of men's running feet sounded on pavement. Wentworth rapped urgently on the door. "Jackson! Ram Singh!" Damn it, they would have to hurry. He had opened a way, but it would close again within brief seconds. The door jerked open under his hand and Jackson came striding out. His face was set in harsh lines and he carried a gun in one fist. Over his shoulders was drooped the unconscious form of Ram Singh.

"Got him through the chest, sir," he said harshly. "Damn them! I'd like to cut loose on them. . . ."

Wentworth's mouth shut rigidly, but he said nothing, led the way swiftly through the yard toward the alley-way. There were sure to be more guards there. He could hear footsteps racing toward the spot. Luckily the alley ran only half way through the block, did not connect with the street where Wentworth had dodged the two cops. . . .

His thoughts were lightning flashes in his brain. He crowded down the pain and regret of Ram Singh's fall, a glittering point of anger. Nita, Nita has caused this. . . . All his plans for escape must be changed. He pulled open the gate, stuck out his head with the uniform cap he had snatched. . . .

"Hey," he yelled hoarsely. "They got Bill. Come on, and we'll rush them."

There were two men in the alley and they came, head down, guns fists pumping. Both of them were cursing in their anger. Apparently, Bill was well liked. Wentworth shouted again. "Hurry!"

He ducked back inside, peered through the shadows toward Jackson. He had leaned Ram Singh against the fence and he had his right arm lifted. Wentworth nodded. They had worked together too long to have to explain a piece of action as simple as this. . . . The men lunged through, one on the other's heels and the two fell in a crumpled heap to the double blows. "Across the alley," Wentworth snapped. "Through the house. I'll get the car, pick you up on the next street."

"Right, Major," Jackson whispered. He shouldered his burden. When he reached the opposite fence, Wentworth was already at the street junction with the alley. He darted out, head down, zigzagging. If only those men in the car didn't have a machine gun. Thank God. Only revolvers spoke. He made them a bad target, but the fence ahead would be difficult. He would have to straighten and, for men whose guns were ready, his soaring vault would be slow and evenly timed—an excellent target. He'd have to chance it. He loosened his topcoat, let it flap behind him to confuse his body line, pulled his head well down. He checked at the curb, then lunged. He strained his muscles until they creaked to gain a tenth of a second of speed. Lead chunked into the fence by his hand. His coat jerked across his shoulders. His left arm crumpled to the hammer of a bullet.

It dropped him awkwardly into the yard beyond the fence. His leg struck the boards and sent an agony of pain throbbing up his thigh, but he was up and running instantly. His lips were motionless and cold against his teeth. He felt his left arm as he sprang for the next fence, grated his molars at the pain of fingers on the open wound. Through the muscles of the forearm, but the bone seemed undamaged, thank God! He forced the arm to operate on the next fence, and pain jabbed into his pectoral muscles. Behind him, there was an exultant yelping. They knew they had scored a hit, probably expected to find him flopping helplessly on the earth back there. . . .

He couldn't keep on taking fences with that wounded arm. The pain of it would weaken him even if he could drive his damaged muscles to the task. He swerved sharply toward the houses on his left, ducked for the basement door, thrust his elbow through the glass.

From the darkness of the corridor that stretched ahead, a revolver blasted and Wentworth flinched backward, sped toward the next fence. His breath was whistling between clenched teeth. There was desperation in his heart. It came to him like a blow to the stomach that Nita was behind all this, had sent the police to trap him. Good God, Nita!

He drove his flagging body over another fence and

the revolver cracked behind him again. He felt a blow on his right side and fell heavily on his face to the ground. He was up as if he had bounced and once more ran for a house. Oh, God, that last wound couldn't be serious. It must not be, or he and Ram Singh and Jackson. . . . But they did not matter. It was the fact that the Fly would triumph. Who was there who could meet his evil genius if the *Spider* were slain? Slain? Hell, he was as foolish as a woman. He wasn't dead yet. He elbowed out another door and, with a sob of breath caught in his throat, leaned forward into the darkeness. If there was a man here with a gun. . . . No one shot at him and he raced along the basement corridor, found a door that stuck, and then rasped, as he yanked it open, couldn't find the catch on an iron grating that closed the area under high steps where the door opened. He found that, too, after moments of groping with almost unfeeling fingers. He heard the door in the next house burst open, heard a man's hysterical yelping. . . .

"I shot him! I shot him! I shot the *Spider*!"

Rage was brassy now in Wentworth's throat. Damn it, he gave his life to the service of these people and they bayed him like hounds at the kill. He slipped from the areaway, kept close to the fence as he stole along the street. If only there were no police within sound of the man's voice.

He was still screeching, but abruptly the sound became muffled and Wentworth realized the man had darted back indoors. Wentworth swerved out from the fence, lifted his knees high in a sprint. In the next cross-street, he had parked the Daimler. If only the police had not yet found it there. . . .

Wentworth's head felt light and the pain surged through his arm. His side burned. He hoped that was a good sign, that the lead had only skimmed his side, perhaps glanced off a rib. The revolver had been of low caliber. The blast of it had told him that. . . . Another fifty yards and he would round the corner. He could better ten seconds on a hundred yards—but not in this clothing, of course. He counted feverishly as he strode, strode, strode. That damned revolver banged behind him again, once, twice . . . and he was around the corner. The Daimler! There it was. Another fifty yards. Oh, God, let the police not be on guard there! Let them not be . . . Wentworth's arm crossing his heaving chest, dragged out an automatic. If the police were there . . . A bullet through the leg, perhaps. Surely, to save his life, and that of Ram Singh and Jackson, to preserve the *Spider* for more battlings with the Fly. . . .

The Daimler was unguarded. Wentworth flung into the driver's seat, had it rolling in seconds before the man with the revolver rounded the corner. Wentworth slowed, cranked down his window and stuck out his head. The uniform cap had stayed with him. . . . "Where'd he go?" he demanded excitedly. "Where'd the *Spider* go?"

The man waved excited arms in the air, bony wrists thrusting far out of the sleeves of his dressing gown. "I shot him, and he kept on running!" he cried. "He came around this corner. Maybe he jumped the fence. He can go over a fence like a bird. He spreads his cape and flies like a bird. But I shot him, I tell you."

"Good," Wentworth shouted. "Hold him here while I get help." He sent the Daimler roaring for the corner, took it on two wheels. His lips were twisted against his teeth. His chest still heaved. He had at least planted a false lead there if the police came. They wouldn't get much sense out of the thin man in the dressing gown.

Around the corner ahead whirled a police coupé, siren ripping out. Wentworth ducked from its path, slapping on brakes. For an instant the coupé slowed, then, seeing that he had stopped, the police raced on. They didn't figure that the *Spider* would stop at the mere sounding of a siren. Wentworth sent the Daimler rolling slowly on, pulled up at the curb before dark houses. Instantly, from the shadows, Jackson sprang forward with Ram Singh still across his shoulders. He staggered a little, made the back seat and Wentworth floor-boarded the throttle. Attention made no difference to him now. The Daimler was bullet-proof. Even its tires could scarcely be affected by lead. And if they could catch him, then the *Spider* had lost all his skill.

Jackson slid back the glass slide between the front and rear. "Ram Singh got it in the lung, Major," he said heavily. "Got him on the side so he won't strangle."

"Think you can fix him up at home, Jackson?"

"Oh, sure," Jackson agreed. "You can't kill anybody as tough as Ram Singh by putting a thirty-two caliber hole in his lung. Sure, I can pull him through. But won't you be needing me?"

"Always need you," Wentworth admitted, "but this time we can't stop to get the doctor. I'm going to pay a call on Lou Cox's guardian. Something is brewing in the Fly's particular line tonight. I know that. Both the girl and her brother are in it to some degree. His presence at the doctor's office is extremely suspicious. Yes, I'll have a chat with Foster Sherwood. . . ."

"Say, Major, begging your pardon, but I know what's up tonight." Jackson's voice was as swift as a bullet. "Phone rang while we were fighting. Thought you might be calling. Answered. Gary Cox, I think. Wanted to know why other fellows hadn't come along. Said he would be damned if he could rob the Haldorf single-handed."

"The Haldorf!" It was an oath as Wentworth said it. The richest, most lavish hotel in the city, where thousands—tens of thousands—of dollars poured into the coffers nightly. And the Fly, with his murderous escape methods, was striking there!

Wentworth laughed and the sound was edged with hysteria. Wounded, Ram Singh out of the fight, Nita helping the enemy, and the Fly pressed on to his greatest villainy! Wentworth lifted his face to the damp spring sky. By God, the Fly should not win! There was still life in the *Spider* . . . !

CHAPTER NINE

Green Globes of Death!

Wentworth shut his mind to fury and despair, began to map his plans. He would have to warn the police, of course. The wholesale attacks by the Fly were not to be met single-handed, even by the *Spider*. He himself must get there as quickly as possible. He threw swift words over his shoulder. . . .

"Come up front, Jackson," he called. Jackson must drive Ram Singh to the apartment, then follow him to the Haldorf when he had taken care of Ram Singh's wounds.

"Just for luck, bring me whatever prints Jenkyns has developed and one from the *moulage* in the safe," he ordered. He would depend on Jackson to phone the warning to Kirkpatrick. . . .

A half-dozen blocks farther on, the Daimler drew to a halt beside a taxi and Wentworth flung out.

"Hurry, Jackson," he called, but his voice was drowned in the mounting roar of the engine as the Daimler spurted away. He sprang to the taxi. "The Haldorf! There's a twenty in it for you if you make it in ten minutes!"

As well as he could he dressed the wound and remedied the damage done to his facial make-up. He had the hat and cape of the *Spider*, taken from the supply in his car, but he did not don them just yet. The Fly must not know that the *Spider* was on the scene until. . . .

The taxi rocketed around a corner, scooted in ahead of a long limousine and whirled into the tunnel entrance of the Haldorf. The driver stood on his brakes, batted up the meter flag and twisted about.

"How'm I doin', buddy?" he demanded.

Wentworth smiled as he handed the man his fare and promised reward. "I hope that I do as well," he said quietly. The driver's grin left his face.

The taxi man was not the only one to mark Wentworth's entrance. In the shadows, a man in a bellboy's uniform slipped swiftly toward a door and, once inside, he almost ran. The *Spider* saw him and his eyes narrowed a trifle. He doubted that he had been recognized unless the Fly was forewarned that he might come and had set a watcher. That was possible, of course. Wentworth knew that his senses should have their usual brilliant keenness for the struggle ahead, but the zest was gone out of him. He was an actor who had gone once too often on the boards in the same role. His heart was not in it—yet he would still give a creditable performance. . . .

Where would the Fly strike first? He could loot the manager's office, where most of the money would be concentrated, without any great flourish, but that was not the custom of the Fly. He would prefer something more spectacular. Wentworth suspected that he would prefer something in which he could slaughter people wholesale. There was a perverted cruelty in the man, Wentworth was sure. Why else would he delight in such massacres as he achieved? Of course, he invariably used courage to cover his escapes.

Wentworth glanced quietly about the well-known lobby, his eyes questing over the pillars of variegated marble, the balcony with its rich hangings of tapestries and velvets. Nothing had been spared of luxury in the building of the Haldorf, nothing of beauty. The bellboy who had sped at sight of Wentworth entered an elevator and Wentworth watched the cage indicator as it swiveled over a semicircle of figures. Nineteenth floor. Good God, *the roof garden!*

The significance of the bellboy's flight gripped Wentworth with painful dread. At this hour of the night the roof garden would be thronged with the most brilliant assemblage of guests in the city.

Yes, yes, that was where the Fly would choose to strike. There was less money there than in the manager's office, but nothing would prevent his sweeping clean every till in the entire hotel. He would undoubtedly choose the fabulous, glassed-in roof garden for his first blow. What form would his murder take tonight?

Even while these thoughts coursed through Wentworth's mind he was moving swiftly across the lobby toward another elevator. His eyes, which appeared never to be raised from the floor, took in everything about him.

Strolling carelessly across the lobby came Nita van Sloan, her laughing eyes turned upward to the face of her escort: Claiborne Lee! Wentworth could not fight down a stab of swift jealousy, but he mocked himself with a bitter twist of his lips. This thing was of his own doing.

He fought down the emotion, surveyed the situation as he stood aside to let them enter the elevator ahead of him. His eyes went involuntarily to Nita's face and read in its stiffened features that she had recognized him.

He kept his eyes covertly upon her as he went with an appearance of great humbleness into the car with them. . . . He saw Nita's lovely eyes sweep him once, saw Claiborne Lee glance carelessly in his direction. There was no recognition in Lee's gaze. Wentworth had uncovered the long-haired wig that was part of the *Spider's* disguise. It gave him the aspect of a middle-aged musician of the old school. If he had had a violin case in his left hand instead of the heavy cane which it cost him so much effort merely to hold because of his wound. . . .

A suspicion Wentworth could no longer resist entered his mind about Lee. He told himself that it was born of the sudden jealousy which racked him, but the idea would not be downed. After all, Lee was going to the scene of tonight's raid by the Fly, and he was with a woman—Wentworth winced at the thought—a woman who had helped two of the Fly's men to escape from a trap the *Spider* had set, who had been with Foster Sherwood, who must certainly be classed as a suspect.

Wentworth studied the man as the cage moved swiftly upward. He had the build of the Fly, but that in itself meant nothing. Any man a little above average height, with good shoulders and a lithe carriage would resemble the Fly. The details of face and hair, even the color of the eyes, meant nothing. A man clever in disguise could change them all.

No decision was possible at this time, of course, but when the Fly struck on the roof garden. . . . Wentworth considered that it would have been possible for Claiborne Lee, supposing him to be the Fly, to wear that black monk's robe in which he had appeared at the masquerade, over the costume in which Wentworth had found him. Lee also had known that Wentworth was going to interview the girl, Lou Cox, and could have followed and shot her. There was the fact that he had appeared so opportunely at Nita's kidnaping. Might the Fly not have planned that with the intention of becoming friendly with Wentworth, through Nita, and learning his plans so as to thwart them? If only he had a palm-print of this man, such as he had obtained from Charles Holland, he might verify that once and for all. . . .

At the entrance to the roof garden, Wentworth was turned back. The headwaiter was very courteous. "I'm sorry, sir, but our rules require evening dress. . . ."

Wentworth smiled in an embarrassed way, spoke with a thick Teutonic accent. "Ach, so," he agreed. "It iss that I wish to speak mit der *meister,* Rigau. He a countryman of mine iss. His vader mine

Freund. . . .'' He smiled kindly, blinking the eyes that could be so bitter and cold. The headwaiter was disconcerted. Even in this mild role the *Spider's* personality impressed itself. The man hesitated.

"Your name, sir?" he murmured.

Wentworth whispered a famous name.

The headwaiter's hands flew high. He bowed, led Wentworth along the side aisles of the roof garden. Curious eyes turned to this blinking twisted old man before whom the headwaiter bowed so humbly. He did not even have on evening dress. . . . Wentworth's eyes shot keenly about him under the mask of his diffident smile. A magician, in the middle of the dance floor, was doing fantastic things with green glass globes. He was juggling the fragile spheres with breathtaking deftness. It was a master performance. Wentworth saw that the man's eyes returned to him again and again as he kept up a running fire of talk in connection with his juggling. . . . It was perhaps foolish, but at sight of the man, the *Spider's* feeling of danger mounted swiftly. Though what harm the magician could do with his delicate glass balls was hard to imagine. The spotlight which was focused on the man winked once and Wentworth saw his body stiffen with tension. He whirled clean about, his eyes flew to Wentworth and he snatched one of the arcking spheres from the air and scaled it directly at Wentworth's face!

There was no reasoning in the thing Wentworth did, but the *Spider* rarely had time to reason out his actions. His muscles obeyed the swift orders of his subconscious and this told him that any untoward action in this atmosphere of tension was to be viewed with suspicion. Wentworth flung himself backward, twisted and landed on his knees behind a temporarily vacant table. The headwaiter took a half-step after him and the sailing green globe caught him in the face. There was a puff of flame, a low, muffled report and the waiter screamed and reeled backward, clutching at his throat. His eyes stared blindly from their sockets, his face was mottled with scarlet splotches and about his head there swirled a small cloud of greenish gas!

Even as Wentworth glimpsed these things from the tail of his eye, the headwaiter stiffened and pitched heavily forward to the floor. His face bounced and the greenish gas settled heavily downward. . . . Before the man had fairly fallen, the magician had hurled a half-dozen more balls. They flew with a swift accuracy toward the table where Wentworth now crouched. The cloth caught fire from a puff of flame. A woman behind him screamed and beat at her shoulder which fire had dotted with crimson, then the cloud of gas found her face and she tried to flee . . . and fell dying.

Men and women were whipping to their feet in panic. Their shouts and screams made a cacophony of terror. Wentworth pulled out an automatic and shot the glass sphere in the magician's left hand. The man's scream rose high and terrible. The burst of flame, the detonation, was dazzling and it flung the magician a dozen feet across the dance floor. He landed sliding on his chest, leaped to his feet and tried to flee. Flame was billowing from a dozen patches of his clothing and each one foamed with the greenish gas. . . . His agony was quickly ended.

Wentworth whirled about and every light in the room blinked out. From everywhere came those dull, awful explosions as from somewhere—everywhere—hidden men hurled bombs of the deadly gas. The *Spider* knew that he must change his position swiftly. Undoubtedly many men had been assigned the task of killing him. He darted to the dance floor and the spot he had quitted burst into flame as several of the deadly bombs burst there. . . .

Rage twisted Wentworth's heart. What could he do against this inhuman attack? If the men had been using guns, he could have spotted them by their flashes and shot them down, but these bombs might be tossed from anywhere. The entire crowd was fleeing in wild panic from the roof garden. He could hear the brittle crash as some frenzied guests burst through the glass walls, dwindling screams as they plunged nineteen stories to their death. One thing Wentworth could do. He made all possible speed toward the manager's office where the money was kept. He could not stem the tide of panic. Indeed, flight was the safest thing for these trapped mortals. But he could strike at the leaders of this massacre and make sure that they perpetrated no more horrors. . . .

Men and women bumped against him. A hand closed on his wounded arm and caused him torture before he could rip free and charge on to his task. He knew his way perfectly in the dark. In the pleasanter days and nights when the duties of the *Spider* did not harass him, he had frequented this spot of superlative entertainment with Nita at his side. In the midst of furious action, that memory could still bring him pain.

He whipped about the screen that shielded the door of the manager's office, swung into the room and his gun flew up. On the point of firing, he hesitated, a cry rising in his throat. The manager was dead, shot through the forehead. And over him, gun and flashlight in hand, stood . . . *Charles Holland!*

CHAPTER TEN

In the Power of the Fly!

Wentworth ridiculed himself for his previous skepticism about Holland's guilt, for his failure to kill the man when his swordpoint was at his breast. Holland had whirled at the cry and his gun swept out, but even as he leveled the weapon, the beam of his flash brushed over Wentworth. Holland shouted.

"Wait, *Spider*. Wait!" He opened his fingers and his gun thudded to the floor. Wentworth's hand had already squeezed on the butt of his automatic and he could not avoid shooting. He did manage to jerk the muzzle aside so that the bullet hissed by within inches of Holland's head.

"Pick up your gun," Wentworth ordered harshly. "I do not make a rule of shooting unarmed men, but if you do not. . . ."

"For heaven's sake, *Spider*!" Holland pleaded. He took a hesitant step forward, his empty hand reaching out. "I didn't do this. I came here to guard Planter. He's a friend of mine. When I got here, he was . . . like that."

"The money is gone?" Wentworth demanded.

"Yes, *Spider*. See, the safe. . . ."

The safe door hung open and papers from its interior were scattered over the thick carpeting. Wentworth hissed an oath. "I'll call on you for explanations later," he asserted and sprang out of the office again. He was not convinced, but he felt a strange reluctance to kill Holland. In those few swift minutes of sword play, he had conceived an admiration for the man's courage, for his sense of fair play. Holland had not been compelled to fight with swords. He might simply have ambushed Wentworth with the man called Shock. . . . Still Wentworth berated himself as he sped in the wake of the fleeing crowd. God knew the evidence against Holland was not conclusive, though Wentworth had slain men on less. It was a matter of conscientious conviction that a man was guilty which governed the *Spider* in his swift forays for justice. In this case, despite repeated evidence, he could not convince himself. . . .

At the elevator doors, Wentworth halted. All of them stood open, but empty space yawned there. He peered down the shaft, throwing the feeble beam of his pocket light into the darkness. What he saw sent him reeling back, feeling nausea strike his stomach viciously. Those shafts were choked with the broken bodies of men and women!

Wentworth leaned his shoulders against the wall, sucking in deep, noisy breaths. God knew he had seen death in many forms, but this slaughter was so cruel, so utterly wanton! They had been fleeing in panic, offering no obstacle at all to the Fly's escape with his loot, and he had deliberately tricked them into a death which they thought was the avenue to escape. Heavily, Wentworth moved from door to door, closing them on the carnage below lest someone later take that fatal plunge. He whirled about, seeking Holland. If he could have seen him then, he would have killed. But the man had taken advantage of his momentary mercy to flee. That in itself was suspicious. . . .

Hell, he was wasting time. Even if Holland were the Fly and lay dead there on the floor of the office, his men would carry on with their mad massacre. Wentworth whirled to the steps, went down them with bounding, though silent, leaps. The Fly had triumphed

282

terribly on these upper floors, but he would not stop there. It would be in the main lobby, off which the manager's office opened that the big looting—and probably the big slaughter!—would be consummated.

A flight above the mezzanine balcony, Wentworth checked his mad race. For a breath, he paused there, listening. The sounds that met his ears were fearful in the message they carried. Lips shrinking from his teeth in fury, Wentworth hurled himself down that last flight. Gun poised in hand, he looked out upon a scene of horror which dimmed into insignificance even the massacre of the elevator shaft!

The floor of the lobby was strewn with the bodies of men and women in gala evening attire. Sprinkled among them were dead police, in uniforms and in plain clothes, fallen across weapons that Wentworth saw had exploded crazily in their hands. A few of them still were alive, huddled against the main doors of the lobby. Their faces were twisted with fear and rage. And over the whole scene crept and crawled in rolling waves . . . *the green gas of the Fly!*

There on the farthest edge of the tidal wave, a woman crawled with sagging head, clutching her throat with one hand while she struggled. A policeman stepped gallantly forward to help her, and pitched down beside her, writhing. The puff of flame that marked the bursting of a bomb set fire to his blue coat, but he was already dead with the strangling gas, as was the woman. One of the man's companions jerked up a riot gun in fury and leveled it at the balcony at a spot opposite from Wentworth. One of his comrades tried to knock the gun from his hand, but he must have pulled the trigger for there was a gush of flame from its muzzle and a detonation that hurled the two struggling policemen limply back against the door. Instantly, Wentworth identified the cause. It was the gas! Tremendously inflammable, it gathered and blasted when the stab of gun flame touched it off. Wentworth whipped up his own automatic, hesitated, then thrust it back into its holster. He could see now where the green transparent globes that were gas bombs were hurled. On two sides of the balcony, men in bellhops' uniforms crouched behind the marble balustrade and hurled the death dealing missiles to the lobby below. They wore gas masks, but the green vapor did not rise even to the floor of the balcony.

Creeping cautiously closer to the railing, searching for some method of attack, Wentworth saw the broad steps which curved up to the balcony. Across it, four men in gas masks fought viciously with swords while a lone man in evening dress slashed and hacked against them.

Instantly, Wentworth recognized him. He would have known that jaunty carriage of the head, the strong shoulders even if the woman who stood back to back with him had not been Nita! It was Claiborne Lee! Nita clutched a useless automatic and a slender knife. Lee made a lunge, pierced a man through the body and was instantly back on guard position again. The rapier he wielded glinted as he swept it viciously from side to side. Quick as was his recovery, he would have died then, had not Nita used her dagger. She brushed aside a point that would have pierced Claiborne Lee's side. Even above the fury of death Wentworth could hear the man's laughter ring out.

"Well played, Nita!" he cried.

He was being crowded hard by the three remaining men. At least one of them was a superior swordsman, and he kept Lee engaged while the two others tried to work past his flanks and get him from the side. . . . Unwillingly, admiration arose in Wentworth's breast. The man had courage, Nita had said, and he couldn't be the Fly, fighting thus the men of the Fly. Yet jealousy stabbed Wentworth. Nita fought beside Lee as valiantly as she had beside the *Spider*. . . .

Wentworth laughed, the sound harsh and rasping in his throat. He took his cane in his two hands and whipped steel from the wood, balanced the blade with a whipping whirl that made the rapier hiss dreadfully.

He laughed again, flung the wooden case from him and raced around the balcony. Guns might not be able to harm these killers, but a sword could not explode in a man's hand. He rounded a column. A masked man whirled to face him, eyes goggling behind the eyelets of the mask. He jerked back his hand with a small bomb on its palm and Wentworth's body straightened in a lunge that had all his fury, all his hatred and pain of heart behind it. The sword plunged into the man's chest.

Wentworth whipped it out, threw back his head and sent the flat, mocking laughter of the *Spider* over the scene.

"Death!" he shouted. "Death to the murderers! The *Spider* comes for vengeance!"

Nita heard and looked toward where he held bloody sword high above his head. The three men facing Claiborne Lee looked up and one of them died with Lee's point in his heart, for Lee did not glance around. With a fresh vigor, he smashed against the swords of his foes. . . . For the moment, all save him were held in rigid tableau, fear and hope equally striking the enemies. Before that pause was ended, Wentworth went leaping to the attack. A second and a third of the men in gas masks died before they could recover from their terror. Down the line there, a half dozen tried to flee, but a swordsman slew one and drove the others back to their bombs.

"He is only one man!" the leader cried, lifting his mask. "Throw your bombs. He will die!"

Anger twisted Wentworth's face. A leader perhaps. . . . The man was awkward and twisted, a hideously malformed hunchback! Fiercely, Wentworth whipped his wounded hand to his automatic. Death stared him in the face, whether by his weapon exploding, or under a rain of bombs. There was a chance that, before the green globes burst, other gas from below would not have risen high enough to cause an explosion.

Each twitch of the trigger was agony, but Wentworth

joyed in the pain. He fired, and the gun did not explode. The leader ducked into a doorway and a man leaped to guard him. Bullets hammered against the wall. His sword fell, ringing, from his hand, and he tried to brace himself. Two others of the men had fallen before his resistance died, as his body had before, and he slid sideways along the wall, rolled and hit on his face. Wentworth was emptying his gun in a swift drumroll of death. Not one of the six who attempted to flee survived. One of them sprang over the balustrade to the deadly gas of the lobby. . . .

Wentworth stowed away his automatic, held his sword under his arm while he drew the other gun and transferred it to his left hand. Then he raced on. Bombs were being hurled at him now across the angle where the balcony curved, but they were thrown in terror by men who feared to expose themselves to the deadly accuracy of the *Spider's* gun. Many of them missed and dropped to the floor of the lobby; the others fell short and burst their greenish flame upon the floor. They did not kill Wentworth, but one thing they accomplished. He knew that it would be fatal to attempt to use his automatic again. . . .

A huge glass window across the front of the building crashed to the floor under a hammer of machine gun bullets and the lead crept along the balcony railing where the men of the Fly crouched. Wentworth smiled grimly as he took cover behind one of the graceful marble columns that sustained the gallery. That would be Kirkpatrick's keen mind at work. Guns would not work inside? Very well, then try them outside. The rain of bullets was having its effect. Men pitched erect to fall again in death or dive over the railing to a double slaughter below. Others turned and tried to run, but there was no retreat. At one end of their passageway was the swift sword of the *Spider,* and at the other they met the vengeance of Claiborne Lee's rapier. It was slaughter, but Wentworth's heart sang as he worked. There was a queer acrid odor in the air that caught at

his throat and made his breathing difficult, and he recalled sharply that the gas of the bombs strangled men
to death. He stopped over a corpse and ripped off a
mask. A bomb almost caught him on the chest as he
rose again. His sword lifted swiftly and flame ran down
its steel length as it bit into the bomb. A whip of the
blade and the gaseous flame was in the face of him
who had hurled it. . . .

That was the end of the Fly's attack, but no more
than a score of his men had died and fully three times
that many victims lay scattered on the floor of the lobby
and there were those pitiful dead in the elevator shafts
and on the floor of the roof garden. Money? From
where Wentworth stood, he could see the open door of
the manager's office and through it the looted safe.
Certainly the Fly had flown and taken with him the
entire wealth of the hotel's many money sources. The
Fly had flown . . . Holland? Wentworth frowned as he
turned his back on the scene of victory and fled swiftly
up the stairs he had descended. There was small hope
that he would find Holland still delaying in the hotel,
but if he were . . . Even now Wentworth was doubtful
whether he would slay the man. Nevertheless, he
pushed stubbornly on, found as he expected, that the
top floor was empty of living men. . . .

Well, the *Spider's* job was done here. He had helped
to inflict a telling blow upon the Fly, though the man
had succeeded in escaping with the loot. Wentworth
had a plan. He hoped that Gary Cox had not been slain
in the night's foray, doubted somehow that he had. It
was more than likely that after his expected allies failed
to arrive, due to the *Spider's* blow at the doctor's office,
he had left the vicinity. That suited Wentworth
excellently. . . . He rapidly took off cape and hat,
stripped the disguise of the *Spider* from his face. His
sleeve, he found, was bloody, but there would be no
way for police to tell that he had not suffered the wound
during the battle at the hotel.

Gripping his wrist, then, Wentworth descended
through deserted halls to the main floor. The dead were

287

everywhere and there were signs of brutal looting upon the bodies of the women. The men of the Fly, then, had not contented themselves with the money in the safes. . . . On the floor above the mezzanine, Wentworth opened the elevator door with a lockpick, one of the tools he always carried in a kit strapped about his waist, and, mouth grimly set, climbed down among the bodies of the dead. Some here—some few—were only injured. One woman seemed unhurt, but she held her face in her hands and sobbed softly. She did not see Wentworth as he threw himself down, in simulation of unconsciousness, among the dead. . . .

It was a half hour before the gas cleared from the lobby and the elevator door was opened. Wentworth was hauled out of the shaft with the rest. He stirred himself then, staggered to his feet. He saw Commissioner Kirkpatrick grasping the hand of Claiborne Lee, congratulating him. Kirkpatrick looked queerly at Nita, then strode off toward his men. He saw Wentworth, sprang to his side . . .

"You're wounded!" he cried. "By God, Dick, this is a fearful thing . . ."

Wentworth cursed harshly. "I was caught in the stampede. God knows how I survived that fall. I suppose bodies cushioned . . ." A shudder shook him. "I'm not squeamish, Kirk, but this slaughter is incredible. There must be fully five hundred dead."

A familiar figure came striding across the lobby, Jackson, with his broad, good-humored face, tortured by fear. When he saw Wentworth, his lips parted in a grin.

"Thank God you escaped, sir," he said.

Wentworth smiled slightly. "Yes, Jackson. I'm glad, too. Did you get those articles from Jenkyns?"

Jackson nodded. "You want them, sir?"

At Wentworth's assent, he reached into his pocket and took out two sheets of paper, on each of which appeared the print of a man's palm. Wentworth glanced at them and his lips closed harshly. He looked into Kirkpatrick's eyes, held out the papers. . . .

"On the night the masquerade party was raided, Kirk," he said, "I went in the masquerade of the *Spider*."

Kirkpatrick interrupted, his voice grave. "That was very dangerous, Dick. Some one might have seen you and not suspected that it was merely a masquerade."

In spite of the gravity of their surroundings, of the discovery he had just made, Wentworth smiled. "Yes, some one might have. In fact, the Fly did."

The fact that Wentworth was the *Spider* was an open secret with the Commissioner of Police. Not that Wentworth had ever admitted it, or that the Commissioner's knowledge was generally known. But Kirkpatrick was not remiss in his duty. He had never got the conclusive proof that Wentworth was the *Spider*. If ever he did, he would prosecute to the full power of his office. Wentworth knew that, nor would he have it otherwise. He could respect such devotion to duty, even if it meant his own life. . . .

"That's unimportant," Wentworth hurried on, told Kirkpatrick about the shot at Lou Cox and his finding of the palm print in the mud. "Now, compare these, Kirk," he said, offering the two sheets again.

Kirkpatrick studied them attentively. "By God, Dick, they're the same! You're saying that this is the palm print of the Fly?"

Wentworth shrugged slowly. He was frowning at the prints. "It's hard to say. You can read the circumstances as well as I. Of course, it wouldn't stand in a court of law. There is no proof save my word that the original print came from a moulage made from a mud print in Holland's garden."

"It's good enough for me," Kirkpatrick said harshly. "Whose palm print is it?"

Wentworth bit his lip. Ridiculous of him to hold back now when it seemed so sure that the evidence was sound. Kirkpatrick repeated his demand before Wentworth made up his mind. He made a broad gesture with both hands, palms upward.

"Charles Holland," he said, "but I'll have to admit there's nothing surprising about his palm print being in his own garden, even supposing it was at the exact spot that the assassin was hidden. You could find out whether he works in his garden himself. . . ."

Kirkpatrick uttered a sharp exclamation of impatience. "You let him go, Wentworth," he said sternly. "I left him in your hands and you let him go scot-free."

Wentworth nodded slowly. "He was upstairs in the roof garden tonight. I saw him, with a gun in his hand, and could have killed him, but didn't. I wasn't sure, you see, Kirk. He swore to me he would surrender at any time you asked, and, damn it, Kirk, I believe him!"

"You don't believe your own evidence, Dick?" Kirkpatrick was angry. "Damn it, he's the logical suspect. It was his brother who became the Fly at first. What more natural or logical than that his brother should follow in his footsteps?"

"That's just it," Wentworth said slowly, "it's too damned logical."

Kirkpatrick's lips were grim beneath the pointed black mustache. "Somehow, Dick, that doesn't convince me." He whirled, shouted to a policeman. "I want Charles Holland picked up at once and taken to headquarters! The charge is suspicion of murder!"

Wentworth shrugged. "I think you'll be sorry about that, Kirk," he said somberly. "There are some other possibilities as suspects. Foster Sherwood, and—" His lips tightened—"Claiborne Lee."

Kirkpatrick eyed him steadily, as he outlined the case against Sherwood. "I'll admit," Wentworth concluded, "that none of this is as conclusive as the evidence against Holland. Lee, for instance, killed several of the Fly's men tonight, but I might point out to you that the Fly cares nothing for human life and, provided his men did not know his true identity, which is very likely, Claiborne Lee could provide himself an excellent alibi by himself killing his own men—if he were the Fly. Furthermore, there is always the interesting possibility, that this Fly is the Fly we thought dead. . . ."

Kirkpatrick smiled slightly, shaking his head at that last. "I notice that you and Nita are at outs, Dick," he said quietly, "and that she is here with Lee tonight. I might tell you, Dick, that Claiborne Lee is a very clever detective of a special sort. He takes only cases which interest him and he has never, as the *Spider* does, gone outside the law. He is, I believe, independently wealthy. . . . Recently, he devoted some thousands of dollars to helping the Mayor with that graft inquiry. You recall? They were very close together. . . ."

Wentworth said drily, "Thanks. It's not jealousy that prompts my suspicions, I assure you. I concede that there is but a slight case against him. I'm merely trying to prevent serious trouble resulting from your arresting Holland." He smiled, bowed stiffly. "I think I'll be going now."

He turned away with a gesture to Jackson to follow and strode across the lobby with its crumpled dead. Nita and Claiborne Lee were leaving by the main door and Wentworth stood back to wait until they had gone. Even so, he passed them on the pavement and he was aware of Nita's eyes on his back as he moved away. They hurt, those eyes. Heaven help him, he loved her so! This damnable misunderstanding! He stumbled as he walked, his eyes blurred, and Jackson's steady hand caught his elbow. He shook his head angrily. Damn it, he was acting like a school boy! And he couldn't help it!

He climbed blindly into the back of the Daimler. Jackson sprang to the box, sat stiffly waiting for orders. Deliberately, Wentworth dug his fingers into his wound. The pain hit like a hammer. He half-swooned against the cushions, but when it was gone, all emotion

291

had drained from him. He could think clearly again. . . .

"The home of Foster Sherwood," he told Jackson, and the Daimler rolled swiftly forward, turned up Park Avenue and began to race the traffic lights. Wentworth sat very straight in the rear of the car. Somehow, the physical and mental pain had left his brain very lucid. He saw the way to find the Fly. . . . He picked up the speaking tube.

"Jackson," he said clearly. "I want you to kidnap Gary Cox, hold him prisoner somewhere until two o'clock tomorrow afternoon. Then turn him loose within the city limits."

"Do I follow him, Major?" Jackson asked quickly.

Wentworth smiled into the darkness. "No, that won't be at all necessary. When you have released him, you will go directly to the home of Foster Sherwood and stand guard over him."

"Is Foster Sherwood . . . the Fly, Major? Why don't we just kill him tonight?"

Wentworth was still smiling. "The time is not ripe, Jackson. Keep very good guard, both over young Cox and over Sherwood."

He leaned back against the cushions and closed his eyes. His head still felt light and his brain lucid, but his body was very tired. Well, after tomorrow night, he could rest. . . . The hard, sharp squeal of brakes jerked Wentworth's eyes wide. His hand whipped to the gun beneath his left arm, but before he could fire it, the door of the tonneau was wrenched open and a bare-headed man in a monk's robe thrust a revolver muzzle against his side.

"Don't move, Wentworth," the man cautioned pleasantly. "I would like to chat with you awhile before I kill you."

It was the Fly . . . !

CHAPTER ELEVEN

Appointment With Death

Wentworth looked with a curious detachment up into the face of his enemy while the Fly flung orders at Jackson, telling him that if he did not obey, Wentworth would die. There was a small coupé just ahead of the Daimler. It had pinned Jackson to the curb and, as they passed it, Wentworth could see that it was empty. He smiled into the Fly's face. . . .

"Very clumsy of you, Holland," he said mildly. "You don't know anything about a gun. In fact. . . ."

Wentworth's right arm lifted in a movement too fast for eye to follow. His left hand closed over the revolver and twisted. A whimper of pain came from the Fly. He collapsed on the seat beside Wentworth, leaving the revolver in his enemy's hand. It had been a simple trick, one a man experienced in gun work never would have permitted. The muzzle had been placed against Wentworth's side—*above his forearm*. A mere lifting of the arm dislodged it. With his left hand, he had clamped the chamber of the revolver immovably, which prevented the weapon from being fired, then he had twisted the gun about so that the trigger finger was caught between the leverge of the trigger and the guard. If he had wished, he could have broken that finger. . . .

"Stop the car, Jackson," Wentworth called softly. "Now, Holland, get out. I'd advise you to strip off that disguise as quickly as possible. It's pretty good for an amateur, and it just possibly might convince the police that you're guilty. By the way, Kirkpatrick has ordered you picked up. I'll remind you of your promise to surrender when I gave the word.''

Holland's shoulders were slumped far forward. "Why didn't you kill me?" he whispered miserably. "You could have so easily."

Wentworth laughed. "So you saw Gary Cox at the Haldorf!"

Holland stiffened, whirled about. "You know! For God's sake, Wentworth, spare the kid. He doesn't know any better. He's smart, but he has moral sense. All these killings mean nothing at all to him except. . . . Don't kill him, Wentworth.''

The Daimler had stopped. Wentworth handed his revolver back to Holland. "Get out and surrender yourself to Kirkpatrick," he ordered. Holland started to plead again, looked into Wentworth's eyes and marveled at the thing he saw there. Tenderness and sympathy in the eyes of the *Spider!* Holland got out and stood staring after the Daimler as it rolled down the Avenue. He looked down at the revolver in his hand, laughed at it and flung it across the street. He turned and strode toward the car he had been driving. . . .

In the Daimler, Jackson said, "Good God, Major. You let him go. You must be awful sure. . . ."

Wentworth spoke wearily. "We must kill the Fly, but Charles Holland is not the Fly. We must kill also the man who invented and makes that death gas. If I live through tomorrow, we will win, but within an hour the Fly will know that the game is up. It will be very strange if he lets me live . . . after that.''

The Sherwood mansion was set well back from the street, an ancient brick building almost castle-like in structure. It was one of the first of the large Victorian houses, of atrocious architecture, but containing scores of rooms. Wentworth knew its history intimately, as he made it his business to know all such matters as might some day be needed by the *Spider*.

It was supposed once upon a time to have been used as a base for smugglers who brought goods up across the wide lawn from Long Island Sound. The huge gate that formerly had swung between the stone posts of the entrance had long since been unhung and the Daimler purred throatily as it swept up the gentle rise to the house.

Wentworth walked with deliberate dignity up to steps from the porte-cochère—he had disguised himself a little—and the door opened without a signal. The butler who stepped back deferentially was a man of studied inconspicuousness. He gained that effect partly by keeping his eyes continually lowered, partly by an eager clinging to the shadows. However, there was a strength in his face that belied the meekness of his manner. Wentworth noted these things without seeming to as he fingered a card from his case.

"Mr. Sherwood," he said.

The butler showed him into a reception room, turned his back to leave the room and Wentworth sprang like an arrow from the bowstring. The blackjack he had palmed thudded gently upon the base of the man's skull and he caught the butler as he collapsed. Instantly, he had his back to the wall, eyes sweeping the walls, the windows and draperies of the room. If he was right in his suppositions, death might strike at him without warning any minute during his stay in this house. His mere presence here would warn the Fly that his secret was at least guessed. . . .

The dark silence of the house brooded and Wentworth edged to the door, peered along the dim hall. Gas was still used for illumination and a red-globed lamp near the ceiling threw a pale, lurid light. Wentworth skirted its pool and went soundlessly up the steps toward the second floor. For all his caution, he moved with surprising speed. The blackjack still dangled from his wrist. He did not draw a gun.

On the second floor, he paused for a moment, listening, then he went directly to a door that showed a thread of light. No sound there, except the occasional rustle of paper. He crouched to the keyhole, could just see the foot of the bed, whose head was against the wall of the hall. There was a negligée of pale blue draped over it. Wentworth straightened, tapped gently on the door with his knuckles. At the girl's gay "Come in?" he thrust open and, in a single bound was beside the bed with his hand over Lou Cox's mouth.

Her eyes flew wide in tortured fright. Her body wrenched violently. Wentworth smiled gently. "Please," he whispered low. "I want to talk with you, and I was afraid you'd give the alarm. Will you promise to remain quiet for a few minutes?"

Lou's eyes rolled upward and her weight slumped against his hands. Wentworth released her and instantly she screamed, piercingly, on a terrified note. Wentworth laughed. It had been a neat trick. His finger tips prodded the side of her throat and the girl slumped unconscious on the pillow. It was a painless method. . . . Swiftly, he hurried into the hall. He could hear swift, heavy footsteps below.

"Lou!" a man's voice called anxiously. "What is it, Lou?"

Wentworth made his voice deep and somber in imitation of the butler who had received him. "Begging your pardon, sir, Miss Lou saw the curtain move and it startled her. She says she's sorry, sir."

The man at the foot of the steps hesitated, peering at the shadowy upper hall. His face was heavy beyond his years, his hand upon the bannister below was lean and strong. It was Foster Sherwood.

"Ask Miss Lou if she wishes me to come up," he said finally.

Wentworth responded, "Yes, sir." He moved soundlessly away from the head of the steps, opened the door of the girl's room, after a knock, closed it again. Then he returned to the shadows at the head of the stairs.

"She says no thank you, sir. She's sorry for the disturbance."

Foster Sherwood shook his head, turned and moved heavily away down the hall. He walked as though a great weight rested upon his shoulders. Wentworth's eyes were hard and speculative. . . . When the footsteps had died away, he went quietly to the girl's room. Before he wrapped her in bedding and carried her soundlessly to the car, he thrust the knife he had taken from the Fly's victim and dug its point into the door. . . .

Jackson set the Daimler into instant motion, and Wentworth smiled at the startled stiff line of his back. Obviously, Jackson had not expected a kidnaping. . . .

"It is necessary, Jackson," Wentworth said kindly, "to save her life."

Jackson said, "Yes, Major." Some of the stiffness went out of his poise. "Where to, Major?"

"Home," Wentworth said quietly. He was busy with a small hypodermic set he had taken from the compartment behind the left-hand seat. He mixed morphine and, after listening to the girl's heart, nodded his head and made an injection in her left arm. . . .

They carried the girl in through the service entrance. The superintendent of Wentworth's building knew better than to inquire into anything that transpired on that elevator. . . .

It was noon the next day that Wentworth arose from a deeply refreshing sleep. He showered, submitted himself to a rub-down at the expert hands of Jenkyns, then went to inspect his prisoner. Lou Cox still slept deeply. He listened to her heart again, counted her pulse and breathing, nodded in satisfaction. She would begin to rouse from the drug shortly and within an hour should be fully recovered. Jenkyns would have his story prepared for her. Wentworth had surprised her kidnapers, brought her here because he was ignorant of her identity. Naturally, she was free to leave at any time. . . .
It was one o'clock. In an hour, Jackson would release

Gary Cox, her brother, from captivity. The newspapers already had headlined the story of Lou's kidnaping by the Fly. . . .

Wentworth's lips were smiling grimly as he moved toward the front door of the apartment, accepted topcoat, hat, gloves and cane from Jenkyns. By tonight, the Fly would be dead, or else the *Spider*. He reached for the doorknob. . . .

"Pardon me, Master Dick," Jenkyns murmured, "but will you be home for dinner, sir?"

Wentworth laughed sharply, "That's in the hands of the gods, Jenkyns."

"But, Master Dick," Jenkyns hesitated. "Miss Nita was to come here for dinner tonight, you recall, and . . ."

"That will do, Jenkyns!" Wentworth's voice rasped in his throat. He whipped open the door, started out, and checked, his eyes tightening. He stepped back and bowed. Nita van Sloan stood there. An eager smile had lighted her lips, but that faded now and left her mouth bitter and tight.

"I'm going to talk to you," she said quietly. "I came to warn you that the Fly knows your plans, and is expecting you. Claiborne Lee asked me to come and tell you, or. . . ." There was a quiver of emotion in her tones. She was obviously holding herself in check with extreme difficulty. "I was well aware you wouldn't talk with me on the phone."

Wentworth had his hands behind him, clasping his stick. The knuckles were white. He bowed formally. "Very kind of Mr. Lee, I'm sure. Would it be impertinent to ask why he thinks the Fly knows? He wouldn't be the Fly himself, would he, and you his ally?"

Nita laughed shortly, and it was very like the bitterness of Wentworth's own voice. "How ridiculous, Dick. As to the warning. It is plain the Fly would have no reason for kidnaping Lou . . . and I know your methods. If you refer to the little affair at Dr. Leaming's office, I'll explain. Claiborne has been employed by Foster Sherwood to attempt to save his nephew, Gary, from being utterly ruined by the life of crime he seems to prefer. Naturally, that involves destroying the Fly, so I have been helping him at his work. He knew about that post at Dr. Leaming's office and I went there in an attempt to worm my way into the Fly's organization. I saw a chance to curry favor with the Fly by helping his men, so. . . ." Nita shrugged. "I received his thanks and a thousand dollars by mail, but he refused to use me in the future."

Wentworth would have given much to be able to drop this stiff and hostile role, as his heart cried to him to do. But he couldn't. "Allow me to congratulate you on your speed in cementing friendships," he said acidly, "and on your cleverness at Dr. Leaming's office. And on sending the police so promptly. They wounded Ram Singh severely."

Nita's violet eyes had fires in their depths. Her voice was dulcet. "I learned from you, sir." She ducked him a courtesy. Wentworth had rarely seen her angry. There was a dimple there at her mouth corner—it came from the compression of her lips—that was enchanting. The music of her voice swept him as it always had, struck a vibration deep within his breast. He pulled his eyes away from her lest they betray him, then looked back lest he show his weakness. God, why must she be so lovely, so infinitely desirable. What were they quarreling about?

Wentworth was surprised at the lightness of his voice. "Thank you for your warning. I rather thought I would be expected by the Fly. If you'll pardon me now, I wouldn't like to keep the Fly waiting. . . ."

Nita nodded her consent with perfect poise. Never had her round little head seemed so proud, nor her violet eyes so arrogant. His memory flitted back to the time they had first met, on the old Mauretania, bound back from Europe. She had been breathtakingly lovely in that cream satin gown that had set off the clear beauty of her shoulders and arms. There had been a lilt in her voice. God, the years that had passed since then. . . .

His voice said, "Well, I must be going. May I see you to your car?"

He was still looking at her, despite that dry burning in his eyeballs. He saw her sway a little before she swept past him toward the outer door. Jenkyns' eyes were pitiful as he bowed to her, and for a moment she paused, smiling. . . .

Wentworth said harshly, "Remember your instructions, Jenkyns!" The door closed gently behind him and they walked to the elevator.

Nita's head bowed, her hands were knotted before her. She went from the elevator without looking at him and got into her car. But when she had turned the first corner, she parked beside the curb. And she beat her small, white fists on the steering wheel; she shook her head, eyes closed, teeth set on lip. And the sobs came anyway. . . .

She whispered, "Oh, Dick . . . Oh, Dick . . . !"

Wentworth turned blindly down Fifth Avenue. He had gone two blocks before he recalled that he wanted his roadster and that the car was parked in front of the apartment house. He went back and the doorman opened the car for him and stood watching as he sent the Hispano-Suiza sharply out into the traffic stream. A taxi stopped with screaming brakes. A Fifth Avenue bus swerved wildly. Wentworth sent the Hispano up the street at forty miles an hour. . . . Gradually, he calmed himself. After today, he swore, he would go away . . . if he survived. There was a good chance that he wouldn't, if the Fly awaited him. He smiled thinly. Well, Nita had said he would be waiting. . . . The street blurred before his eyes. He blinked steadily until he could see again. He was glad abruptly that the Fly knew. Death could solve so many problems. . . .

CHAPTER TWELVE

Stop the Gas!

It was three o'clock when Wentworth turned into the driveway to the Sherwood mansion. The place looked even drearier by day than at night. The whole, bleak pile was a dusty gray and the black shine of the windows added to a mournfulness that was singularly oppressive. Very appropriate, Wentworth jeered at himself as the Hispano whispered up the driveway.

The same dour butler who had opened the door for him the night before was waiting. If he recognized his assailant, he gave no sign. Wentworth's disguise had been the scantiest. That had been deliberate. He watched the butler narrowly, waited in the reception room while his card was carried to Foster Sherwood. Wentworth kept a keen watch about him. If the Fly was ready for his arrival. . . . The butler came back soundlessly, announced in his deep voice that Mr. Sherwood would see Mr. Wentworth. . . . The way led along the dim hall, to the door of a book-lined study. Sherwood arose from behind his desk. . . .

"What can I do for you, Mr. Wentworth?" he asked pleasantly, but still he carried about him that sense of overpowering weight. He was haggard, his eyes sunken. . . .

Wentworth said quietly, "I have been trying to get a line on this man who calls himself the Fly, and I thought that there might be some clue here. Do you have any idea why he should have kidnaped your ward?''

Sherwood shook his head heavily. "None at all," he said, but he did not look at Wentworth as he spoke.

"Surely, you must have some," Wentworth urged. "Or if you haven't, perhaps her brother, Gary. . . ."

Sherwood's face seemed to become more haggard while Wentworth looked at him. He said hoarsely, "Gary has disappeared, too."

It was at that moment that the thing Wentworth had expected happened. Footsteps beat swiftly along the hall, the door flung open and Gary Cox flung himself into the room.

"Have you heard anything from Lou?" he demanded savagely.

Sherwood looked at the youth without a word, then came sharply to his feet. "Where have you been, sir?" he demanded harshly. "These disappearances of yours must stop!"

Gary sliced the air with the edge of his hand. "Nuts! How about Lou?"

Wentworth got to his feet deliberately. "I have a very poor opinion," he said sharply, "of a man who will consort with the kidnapers of his sister. Where were you when your sister was kidnaped?"

Gary whirled toward Wentworth, his right arm crooked, hand at his coat pocket. "Who the hell are you?" he demanded.

Wentworth smiled slightly, but made no other answer. Sherwood came around his desk. "Gary, this is serious," he said heavily, but even in his reprimand there seemed a lack of sincerity, of force. It was as if he were afraid of this young man before him. Gary Cox swung about to face him again.

"Where were you when she was kidnaped?" he demanded in turn. "Here in your study, so they could get up here without. . . ." He choked the words and both he and Sherwood looked toward Wentworth. Wentworth nodded his head slowly.

"That's exactly what I think," he said, "that the old smugglers' tunnel was used to carry away your sister, Gary."

Both of the men started violently and Sherwood began a quiet movement to get closer to Wentworth. Gary Cox openly put his hand into his coat pocket.

"The game is up, gentlemen," Wentworth said quietly. "Are you going to lead me to the tunnel, or shall I call in the police to find it?"

Sherwood and Gary Cox both leveled guns. Sherwood was much the more frightened of the two. "What in God's name are we going to do now?" he asked hoarsely.

"Conk him," said Gary savagely, "and then I'm going and . . ."

"Shut up!" Sherwood said roughly.

Wentworth smiled. "All right, Jackson," he said quietly, looking behind them.

The two men whirled about and Wentworth's left fist shot out, caught Sherwood on the jaw and throat, hurled him unconscious to the floor. Gary Cox whirled, his gun blasting. Wentworth had made no attempt to block that shot. He was half behind the desk and he went down with the flash, threshed his legs and clapped a quick hand to his forehead, then let it fall away. Gary Cox sprang to the end of the desk, gun ready, saw the red smear that Wentworth had made on his forehead and whirled away. When he darted through the door of the study, Wentworth was already on his feet. He followed swiftly as Gary Cox ran for a door that opened near the end of the hall. A gun stabbed flame at him from the door and he fired twice, three times in hammering succession. The butler reeled out of the doorway and plunged to his knees. He had his gun in both hands and tried to lift it upward. Gary kicked him in the throat and went past him to the door. . . .

Wentworth waited until he had ducked through the opening, then he darted after him. He could hear Gary's feet beating hollowly on steps that led downward and moments later, Wentworth dodged through a door that gave on the cellar. He crouched and peered between the railings, saw Gary squeeze in behind a huge furnace set against the wall. He seized a metal hook that protruded from the stone, twisted it violently and pushed. The stones swung inward. Instantly, there was the muffled chatter of a rapid-fire gun. Gary was driven back against the furnace. He tried to lift his revolver and the sub-machine gun kept cracking. For moments, the bullets held him against the furnace. Then they stopped and Gary wilted to the floor.

While the gun still spoke, Wentworth had flung himself to the basement and darted across to the furnace. He waited until the sub-machine gun ceased and, a split-second afterward, he thrust arm and head around the edge of the hidden door and fired a single shot. The killer was seated behind a breast-high shield of steel on which he rested the Thompson gun. But he had counted on no second enemy. The bullet smashed through his head, hurled him backward. The Tommy gun balanced for an instant atop the shield, then crashed to the floor.

When it hit the ground, Wentworth was already inside the opened door, automatic in one hand, cane in the other. He twitched the cane several times and let the wooden sheath slide from the steel rapier it covered while his eyes quested over the dim stretch of corridor that reached away in both directions from this spot. Electric lights burned at regular intervals, making little yellow pools in the darkness. Queer how criminals always preferred dimness to light, underground warrens to ordinary strongholds. Bad about Gary's death, but he had died more splendidly than he lived—killed on the way to defend his sister. In the moment before his death, he had triumphed over the evil influences that had held him so long. It was time for him to die. Living, he would have lapsed again into the old ways. A man who had glutted on slaughter by the side of the Fly . . .

An annunciator squawked abruptly from somewhere

nearby: "What's keeping you, Hank? Report what happened."

Wentworth reached Hank's body in a single long leap. "Aw, I just bumped that Cox punk," he growled. "He come at me shootin'." He kept his voice low and hoarse. The annunciator would disguise it sufficiently, if there was a connection near him. It might be that he was supposed to report in person. . . .

"Well, Hank," repeated the annunciator. "What's keeping you? Report!"

Wentworth shrugged slightly, his lips smiling calmly. He had made that play and lost. He was supposed to report in person and he had no idea how to do it. The corridor led in two directions. He would chance going to his right.

He walked with heavy, confident strides along the corridor to the right, keeping a sharp eye on the shadow patches for trace of the opening which must be somewhere near. It was plain that there was some room hollowed out of the earth. The annunciator was silent, whether because he had made the right move, or because the speaker had become suspicious, Wentworth did not know. Either way, they must make the first move, and make it soon, or else. . . .

The collapse of the floor beneath his feet was without any warning at all. Wentworth plummeted downward with no chance to do more than cross the sword over his breast so that it would not harm him, then hit violently on his feet, allowed his knees to bend under him and sprang instantly erect. The room in which he stood was white-walled and illuminated by a single overhead light. On all sides, there were the black openings of loopholes for gun muzzles and all of them were filled. Twelve guns were centered on Wentworth's body. . . .

"Ah, my dear Wentworth," purred a voice that Wentworth instantly recognized. "You have, I see, come into my parlor."

Wentworth tossed his automatic to the floor, took his

rapier in his right hand and made it sing through the air; then he stood with the point resting on his toe.

"Yes, Fly, I am ready," he said quietly.

He felt the utter hopelessness of his position. There was no need to look for mercy from the Fly, nor for compunction in such wanton murder as had been planned when this room was built. He had the slim chance of an appeal to the man's love of swords, which he well knew. Even if the Fly entered the arena, there would be no fair fight. Wentworth was doomed. . . .

There remained, though, the chance that he might kill the Fly before he was slain. That was Wentworth's only hope. To death, he was indifferent. Tonight, he might even welcome it. A weak thought, unworthy of the *Spider*. Was he a woman to pine away over a lost love? So Wentworth mocked himself while he waited, superbly ignoring the hungry gun muzzles. It made no difference. He knew that, without Nita, life held nothing desirable for him, and though he reviled the selfishness of that realization, it did not alter the fact.

"Afraid of my sting, Fly?" he called gaily, shaking the rapier over his head. "Afraid of your skill?"

The Fly spoke slowly, meditatively. "It would be madness for me to duel with you, but it is madness toward which I am inclined. I have never crossed blades with you and you defeated Holland. Yes, I am inclined to meet you. Holland was an able man. . . ."

Wentworth heard other voices in colloquy with the Fly, but presently a door opened and the Fly stepped into the white-walled room. Wentworth saw that the man had expected the duel, for he wore the knee-trouser, the white blouse of the fencer and his feet were clad in light-weight, rubber-soled shoes. Wentworth stuck the point of his rapier in the floor and stripped off coat and vest. The Fly stood watching, a mocking smile on his lips.

"Are you quite ready?" he asked when Wentworth grasped his rapier and tugged its point free of the floor.

"Quite," Wentworth agreed.

The Fly lifted his blade to a guard position and as simply as that began the most perilous duel Wentworth had ever known. Over him hovered in striking down the Fly, he would not survive him by so much as one minute! Those ominous gun muzzles assured him of that. . . . Both men fenced cautiously in those first interchanges, doing no more than feint for openings. The blades slithered in almost constant engage and there was no sound in the close room except the music of the steel and the low, constant shuffle of cautious feet.

Wentworth instantly discovered that the Fly had a powerful wrist, that his finger play was facile and accurate. They were both hesitant about making the first lunge. Wentworth saw an opening, but instead of striking into it, leaped backward a full three feet. It was the instinct of a swordsman that impelled that and he could tell by the chagrin that darkened the Fly's face that he had acted wisely. Even now, Wentworth could not decipher what trap he had avoided and the fact made him doubly cautious.

Usually impetuous in attack, Wentworth decided to outwait the Fly, to make him reveal his reach and speed. The Fly did not falter when the opportunity was offered. With the speed of a cobra, he hurled himself forward in a lunge, body in a straight line behind the rapier. It was a beautiful attack, perfectly executed, but Wentworth's parry was irreproachable, and his answering lunge was fiery and vicious. The Fly was back in position and avoided the licking tongue of steel doubly by guard and backward.

Both men had tested the mettle of the other, but Wentworth was not satisfied with what his enemy had revealed. That lunge had been swift, but it had lacked the drive of a master swordsman and there could be no doubt that the Fly was that. It seemed clear to him that the Fly was playing a waiting game, too, attempting to lull him into security by slowing his lunge. When he really struck, with his full speed, his point would be in before the timed parry so much as touched his blade. It was fine strategy and might have succeeded on a man less experienced than Wentworth. He knew, however, that no man with that splendid recovery should be so laggard in attack.

Lunge and parry, thrust and *riposte* made a regular rhythm and Wentworth realized that in spite of himself he was slowing his guard to the speed the Fly set. It was necessary, of course, to do that, but he must not allow his reflexes to become laggard. There was a cure for that. . . . Wentworth began an attack so fiery, so furious that before it the Fly gave cautious ground. He lost his smile for moments, then Wentworth played the trick for which he had planned. He pretended to let his attack grow uncertain and ill-directed, made his breath come in labored pantings. He blundered wide in answering a feint and leaped back as if in desperation as the Fly's point licked out in the flicker of an eye.

The *Spider* avoided it with seeming clumsiness, but the rapier did not get through and the swift attack that the Fly immediately began failed to find the slightest opening. Fury darkened the Fly's face as he realized that he had been tricked into displaying his real speed. He continued the attack, thrusting, lunging, inching forward to pin Wentworth against the wall. Once, twice, three times Wentworth barely avoided the point. His shirt front was ripped; there was a scratch on his throat and another on his forearm. Nor had the Fly escaped unscathed. Wentworth had scored low on his side and the point had penetrated half an inch before the Fly's backward leap had cleared him. His shirt was stuck to his body with a sprawling red stain. . . .

The increasing delay shortened the Fly's temper. It was clear to Wentworth that no man had ever stood thus before the sword of his enemy. Impatience made him reckless. He gave opening after opening and Wentworth, pretending caution, broke away. He did not cease to counter, for that might arouse suspicion. But his retreat was none the less steady. His back was within only six feet of a corner, now only five as he skittered backward. The Fly began a vicious attack. If he could squeeze his enemy into that corner. . . . Wentworth intended him to do precisely that!

Minute after slow minute dragged past as Wentworth fought with seeming desperataion against the trap into which he was being driven. Finally, he sprang back from a long, fierce lunge and his shoulders hit the wall. It was the moment for which Fly and *Spider* had both played. The Fly closed in, poised himself and lunged again! If his point broke through Wentworth's guard, there could be no further retreat. He would be pinned to the wall!

Wentworth turned the point with his sword, seized the Fly's blade with his left hand and yanked him strongly forward. At the same time, Wentworth sprang toward the Fly, dropping his own sword backward through his hand until he gripped the blade only nine inches from its point. The Fly gasped, tried to spring backward, but Wentworth's grip on his enemy's blade had become a grip on his wrist; then about his waist. With his arm locked about the Fly, he sprang backward into the corner and pressed his sword point against his enemy's side.

"Quiet!" Wentworth gasped, "or I'll kill you!"

Shoulders against the wall, the Fly held motionless against his chest under the threat of that sword point against his side, Wentworth was completely shielded from all the gunports!

"Now then, Fly," Wentworth said, more quietly. "You can order your men away from those gunports or die!"

The Fly was stubborn and before Wentworth could convince him that refusal meant death, the door opened again in the side of the room and a half-dozen swordsmen in gas masks stalked through. At the same instant, Wentworth was aware of the trap door being opened overhead. A bone-thin arm reached through, holding a huge chemical retort, from whose beak greenish vapors rose. The liquid in the retort began to stream toward the floor. It struck and greenish flames danced upward, greenish fumes roiled toward Wentworth and his prisoner!

The Fly cringed against Wentworth. "The death gas!" he gasped. "Oh, God, *stop the death gas!*"

CHAPTER THIRTEEN

Nita Understands

The terror of the Fly seemed entirely genuine. He struggled in a veritable frenzy of fear against the grip of the *Spider*. Yet it seemed strange to Wentworth that an underling of the Fly would deliberately release the death gas upon his master. The Fly wore no mask, had no chance of obtaining one while he struggled, breast to breast, with the *Spider*.

Wentworth's position was sufficiently perilous without the additional hazard of the gas. He was locked in a death embrace with the greatest terror of modern crime. The thought brought a laugh to his lips, strangely exultant laughter. He set his left hand against the chest of the Fly and hurled him back upon his fellows. He whipped up his rapier and struck swiftly. One of the masked men died. Even as he fell, Wentworth was upon him, ripping off the gas mask. Then he fell back into his corner, back to the wall, rapier weaving a swift tapestry of light and death before him.

It was awkward work, getting the mask on one-handed. For a space of seconds he would be blinded. Wentworth shouted his challenge. There were five swords against him, and one of those was the Fly, one of the most superb men with the rapier that Wentworth had ever fought. Yet, before the whirling impetuosity of Wentworth's attack, those five men retreated. Wentworth sprang far back, thrust sword-tip into the floor and, working with both hands, whipped the gas mask into place. Instantly, he had the rapier in hand again. He even had time to glance upward toward where those emaciated arms, those claw-like hands poured the green liquid of death down upon them. He could see now a face twisted horribly by hatred, a hunched back and a great cry rose in Wentworth's throat. He knew that man! Good God, it was . . . !

Wentworth's thoughts were chopped off short by a whirling attack in concert by the swordsmen. Three could face him at once across his narrow corner, and the Fly took the brunt of the attack while the two men, one on each side, crouched low and stabbed at Wentworth with their long blades. Still the swift, wild sweeping of Wentworth's sword kept their points from a vital spot. A rapier stung him in the thigh, and the man who wielded it died a moment later with the kiss of Wentworth's steel upon his throat. He was immediately hauled away and another man took his place.

The mask-covered faces were strangely blank and featureless, not even the eyes could show expression through the thick lenses of the goggles. Wentworth's own mask made his breathing difficult. The nose clamp had his nostrils raw. He attempted a foray from his corner, but a rapier darting at his heart flung him back. He managed to parry that thrust of the Fly. Another blade stabbed up at him from the floor, ripped through his coat.

Wentworth swept the swords wide with a beat of the rapier and, from behind the three men who faced him, a fourth hurled his rapier like a spear! Wentworth snatched it from the air, spun it in his hand and was doubly armed. Laughter bubbled unbidden to his panting lips, came muffled and hideous out through the mask. The man at the trapdoor had ceased to pour out the deadly liquid. He held a revolver in his hand now and it was leveled at the *Spider's* head. His time had come—but he preferred steel to that bullet from above. Steel and a chance to kill. . . .

*   *   *

He flung himself forward with such fury that his assailants retreated—two of them. The third took the point of Wentworth's second rapier in his breast. There was no time to withdraw it. The man writhed on his back and the rapier, upright in his breast, swayed like a flower in the wind. Three men left to fight. Strange that they did not use their guns, for Wentworth was sure now that the gas was a fake. A thought struck him sharply. Perhaps this gas contained only the elements which caused guns to explode in the hands of the firer. That would explain the reluctance of the Fly's men to use their automatics. . . .

Wentworth had only one defense against that revolver above, the speed of constant movement. Not for a moment could he remain still for the murderer in the trapdoor. . . . The constant exertion was telling upon the *Spider,* further handicapped by the mask. Despair ate at his heart. He was fighting not alone for himself. His own life was a small part of what must drive him on. Unless he killed the Fly and that other twisted monstrosity there in the trapdoor, the slaughter of the people would continue. Thousands of lives fought with him, the ghosts of slain hundreds powered his blade.

Abruptly, the *Spider* saw his chance. With a violence and a speed that literally defied vision, he hurled his body forward in a long, low lunge that brushed aside the Fly's parry as if it were no more than a silken strand and sent the point deep into the Fly's chest!

Instantly, Wentworth released his hold on the hilt and hurled himself aside. He was too late. The sword of the Fly's henchman licked out and caught him on the right side. It was no more than a shove against his flesh, but Wentworth knew from the instantaneous weakness that gripped him that it had bitten deep. His body was already in motion and it helped some, dragged him away from the sword. Wentworth's hand seemed leaden as it moved to his automatic. At least he could get one shot with it. The weapon would explode, but certainly that one bullet would fly true. He heard the crash of a shot, felt no blow. That monstrosity above had missed once, at least. . . . The gun was in Wentworth's hand. The swordsman had pulled his blade clear and was poised over the *Spider* for a last murderous lunge. It did not matter to him that the *Spider* was helpless, flat on his back. Now, at last, the *Spider* would die!

Wentworth ignored that swooping sword. He still must kill that fiend who had invented the green poison, who leaned through the trapdoor, gun in hand. . . . It was to him that the *Spider's* eyes went. For a space of what seemed seconds, he could not understand what he saw there, but actually his vision darting to that grim creature in the trap door, and the movement of his gun must have been simultaneous. He saw that the scrawny hand in the trapdoor no longer held either gas retort or revolver. The body sagged limply forward and from the side of the head, there came the slow drip of a dying man's blood. The *Spider's* one shot then, need not go to save humanity. It could save his own life, perhaps. . . . He squeezed the trigger of the automatic and heavy caliber lead hammered into the chest of the man with the poised sword. It lifted him inches from the floor and spun him away—and the gun did not explode!

Wentworth laughed out crazily against his mask. He pushed himself up from the floor, pressing his hand hard against his side where the sword had pierced. The blood was warm on his palm. Awkwardly, Wentworth thrust the automatic into his belt, tugged at the mask. His first guess had been right. The gas was a fake, used to disconcert him in an effort to save the Fly. He got the mask free, gripped his automatic again. The man he had shot lay on his face, not even twitching. He looked upward, toward the trapdoor and a glad cry parted his lips.

"Nita, sweetheart," he panted. "Nita!"

He reeled forward, reaching up as she swung down a light rope ladder she had dropped through the opening. He lost his footing, and on his knees crawled on until he could reach the ladder. Nita dropped on her knees beside him, began ripping at the clothing about the wound. Her face was white, lips between her teeth.

Wentworth was strangely numb to pain. His eyes joyed in Nita's alarmed face. "You should . . . smile," he whispered. "This is the end of all your troubles. You won't be kidnaped . . . any more."

"Keep quiet, Dick," Nita said. "Save your strength, until I see. . . ." She tore aside his shirt and a cry rose to her lips. She bent close, fingers moving with gentle firmness along the rip in his side. Then she leaned back, tears rolling down her dimpled cheeks. "Oh, Dick, Dick," she cried. "You gave me such a scare. I think he splintered the bone of one of your ribs a little, but it's not deep." She bent close. "Dick, boy, don't ever say cruel things to me again. I thought I knew why you did it from the first. You wanted me to spy on Claiborne Lee. But afterward . . . I didn't know."

Wentworth closed his eyes. They were stinging and it wasn't from the fake gas that had been poured into the room.

"Promise me, Dick," said Nita, her voice very close to his face. "Promise me you'll never be cruel like that again."

Wentworth laughed. "You think it has been pleasant!" he cried. "Damn it, Nita, you played your part too well. Even I thought you had thrown in with the Fly! And there was the time you sent police helter-skelter to Leaming's office. . . ."

Nita held up her hands. "But, Dick, you always get out of those jams so easily! I thought it would be no trouble to you—the back door and all. I didn't think you'd even be there, and it made my position so much stronger!"

Wentworth's eyes burned up at hers. "Yes, I see now. I should have seen then. There's a madness that gets in me when the *Spider* walks. . . . And then I found out I had thrown you to the Fly.

"Claiborne Lee," Wentworth told her briefly. "He's

315

over there, dead with my rapier in his breast. He is the Fly. You'll find that's the truth when the disguise is stripped from him.''

"But he couldn't be!" Nita cried. "He *couldn't* be. I saw him kill. . . .'' She hesitated. "Of course, that would give him a perfect alibi, killing the men of the Fly, and he did know a lot about the Fly. How in the world, Dick, did you come to think of that, and of this place under the house, these tunnels . . . ?''

"It was ridiculously simple," Wentworth said quietly. "I should have known it long ago. The clue was the murder of the Mayor. God, how long ago that was! There was absolutely no reason for the murder of the Mayor that I could discover," Wentworth said slowly. "I hadn't thought much about it until I learned that Claiborne Lee and the Mayor had been very close together. None of the other suspects had any contact with him at all, and there must be some reason other than mere spectacular crime for the murder. It reduced itself to the fact that the Mayor was killed because he knew . . . who the Fly was! It would have to be that, or revenge. And so far as I have been able to discover, the Mayor lived a pretty blameless sort of life. . . . These tunnels here? That was more obscure. Except that I couldn't see any reason for Gary Cox being an important member of the Fly's band. He was a youngster without any of the training for criminality, without any reason for going into it unless he was deliberately lured into it. That was one of the things that cleared Holland in my eyes. I couldn't see how, loving Lou Cox as he undoubtedly did, he could seduce her brother into a criminal life. Then it became clear to me that Foster Sherwood was somehow involved. I remembered the history of the house, the reports of secret tunnels. So I kidnaped Lou and her brother Gary, finally turned loose Gary after the fact that the Fly was supposed to have kidnaped his sister had been revealed. I followed him to the Fly's hideout . . . and the rest you know.''

"Most of it," Nita admitted. "Jackson was watching over Foster Sherwood when I came here. I tried to get

316

him to investigate the shooting I heard down here when I came here to . . . to meet Claiborne Lee. He wanted me to see you killed!"

Wentworth smiled. "You couldn't blame him. I think he really loved you."

Nita shuddered. "God grant that he didn't," she whispered.

Wentworth looked up into the dead face of the monster who had poured the gas. His eyes were filled with wonder. "The Fly really did come to life, Nita," he said, "and he poured out his hate against me and against the world."

"You mean . . . Jack Holland?"

Wentworth nodded. "Yes, it's plain that he was crippled terribly by that fall after our duel. If you will look up there in the trapdoor, you will see him."

Nita looked up at the man who had poured the gas into the room, who had so narrowly missed killing Wentworth.

"That man!" she cried. "Why, I . . . !"

"Yes, dear," said Wentworth softly. "You killed the real Fly."

☐ Leinster, Murray/THE FORGOTTEN PLANET $3.95
☐ Ligotti, Thomas/SONGS OF A DEAD DREAMER $3.95
☐ Lovecraft, H. P. & Derleth, A./THE LURKER ON
   THE THRESHOLD $3.50
☐ Malzberg, Barry/BEYOND APOLLO $3.50
☐ Malzberg, Barry/GALAXIES $2.95
☐ Moorcock, Michael/BEHOLD THE MAN $2.95
☐ Cawthorne and Moorcock/FANTASY: THE 100
   BEST BOOKS (Trade Paper) $8.95
☐ Pringle, David/SCIENCE FICTION: THE 100
   BEST NOVELS $8.95
☐ Sladek, John/THE MULLER-FOKKER EFFECT $3.95
☐ Sladek, John/RODERICK $3.95
☐ Sladek, John/RODERICK AT RANDOM $3.95
☐ Stableford, Brian/THE WALKING SHADOW $3.95
☐ Stoker, Bram/THE JEWEL OF SEVEN
   STARS $3.95
☐ Sturgeon, Theodore/THE DREAMING JEWELS $3.95
☐ Sturgeon, Theodore/VENUS PLUS X $3.95
☐ Sturgeon, Theodore/THE GOLDEN HELIX $3.95
☐ van Vogt, A.E./COSMIC ENCOUNTER $3.50
☐ Watson, Ian/CHEKHOV'S JOURNEY $3.95
☐ Watson, Ian/THE EMBEDDING $3.95
☐ Watson, Ian/MIRACLE VISITORS $3.95
☐ Wolfe, Bernard/LIMBO $4.95

Available from fine bookstores everywhere or use this coupon for ordering.

Carroll & Graf Publishers, Inc., 260 Fifth Avenue, N.Y., N.Y. 10001

Please send me the books I have checked above. I am enclosing $_____
(please add $1.25 per title to cover postage and handling.) Send check
or money order—no cash or C.O.D.'s please. N.Y. residents please add
8¼% sales tax.

Mr/Mrs/Ms _____
Address _____
City _____ State/Zip _____
Please allow four to six weeks for delivery.